Don't Play in the Sandpit

Enjoy!

Audrey Edwards

Don't Play in the Sandpit

Audrey Edwards

ARCHWAY
PUBLISHING

Certain characters in this work are historical figures, and certain events portrayed did take place. However, this is a work of fiction. All of the other characters, names, and events as well as all places, incidents, organizations, and dialogue in this novel are either the products of the author's imagination or are used fictitiously. Archway Publishing books may be ordered through booksellers or by contacting:

Archway Publishing
1663 Liberty Drive
Bloomington, IN 47403
www.archwaypublishing.com
1 (888) 242-5904

Because of the dynamic nature of the Internet, any web addresses or links contained in this book may have changed since publication and may no longer be valid. The views expressed in this work are solely those of the author and do not necessarily reflect the views of the publisher, and the publisher hereby disclaims any responsibility for them.

Cover Design and Author Photo by Sue Townsend

ISBN: 978-1-4808-3106-3 (sc)
ISBN: 978-1-4808-3107-0 (hc)
ISBN: 978-1-4808-3108-7 (e)

Library of Congress Control Number: 2016909495

Print information available on the last page.

Archway Publishing rev. date: 08/10/2016

To my sister Helen
1924-2013

Acknowledgments

I would like to thank everyone who contributed, whether intentionally or otherwise, to the creation of this fictionalized account of 20th Century life in America's isolated communities.

Of course, I could never name all of those who assisted me as virtually everyone I spoke with had something to offer. It seems Americans are aware of the country's ongoing battle with the growth of alcoholism.

As to Niceville? Thanks to people like those listed below, SmartTravel.Tips has placed Niceville at the top of its "10 Best Places to Live" list in Florida.

Cecil Anchors, Bill Barnhill; George Barrow, M.D., Wig Barrow, Jerald Belue, M.D., Richard Boyd, Colonel, USAF, retired: Clifford Brabham, Sherri Brabham, John Brooks, Ruby Brown, Max Bruner, Jr., James Campbell, Ben Carr, M.D., Delores Davis Celano, Eugene Celano, M.D., Roger Clary, Eugenia Culberson, William Culberson, Tasia Davis, H.A. Dobson, Steven Doheney, M.D., Finley Duncan, Robert Ellis, M.D., Rhett Enzor, Jr.; C.B. Faille, Andrew Giesen, M.D., O.Q. Hamilton, George Dana "Doodle" Harris, Jennifer Helms, Joel Astor Helms, Morris Helms, Patrick Helms, Emil Holzhauer, Marion Scofield Holzhauer, Joanne Hutchison, Wanda Jackson, A.L. Johnson, John Kobler, R.P. Maxon, M.D., John L. McKinnon, Jane Meigs, Sue Metzer, Howard Minger, Wayne Montgomery, Rosalee Neil, Jack Nichols, Maggie O'Steen, Bud Parish, Howard

Parker, M.D., Carlton Peters, Howell Phelps, Norma Phelps, Plenn Phelps, Honorable Judge Gillis Powell, Thomas Powell, William Powell, Buddy Reddick, Ted Reaves, Gilda Richardson, C. Walter Ruckel, Jean Parker Ruckel, Jim Ruckel, Honorable Robert Sikes, U.S. Congressman, John Tatum, Tut Tatum, Albert Watson, Henry White, M.D., William James Wells, Joseph Wilson, M.D., Barbara Wright, Rip Wright, Clint Wright, Jackie Wright, Rock Wright, Roger Wright.

Chapter 1

NICEVILLE WAS THE NAME OF THE PLACE, BUT THAT was clearly a misnomer. Accessible only via rough, often hazardous waters or dense, alligator-infested forests, those who survived the trip to this isolated corner of the world would find no welcome sign awaiting them. Getting there was the pits, and yet it was nothing compared with staying there.

Perched on a spit of isolated sand, the tiny settlement in the Florida Panhandle appeared at first glance to be enveloped in an atmosphere of serenity, an unexplainable field of energy imploring would-be visitors to take root there. Unfortunately, the conglomerate of inhabitants in the little fishing community didn't want them there. Most had made up their minds that anyone who dropped in was a fugitive from justice and therefore filled with wickedness and deceit.

It was a dastardly hot day in July 1918 when a stranger appeared on the settlement's main boat dock. He had maneuvered his way through the dense virgin pine forest on the north side of Niceville, a settlement created from little more than a diminutive sandpit and lots of water. Having cleared the vast wooded area, the unwanted visitor struggled to remove the skin-puncturing thorns and sharp, twisted vines he had become entangled with during his lengthy trek through the wilderness. It would have been a difficult task for two hands, and he had only one to work with. The other had a firm grasp on a loaded shotgun.

Satisfied he had done the best he could with virtually nothing to work with, he ambled to the edge of a mile-wide bayou, its sun-sparkled waves moving rhythmically toward their destiny. He stared in disbelief and forgot for a moment the gruesome murders and other heinous crimes that inhabitants in this remote area were said to have committed.

The glittering body of water was alive with boating, fishing, and swimming activities, all the things he loved and yearned to take part in. As a boy growing up in nearby Alabama, the horrific tales told to him by his parents and other adults about Niceville were terrifying, but over the years, he had become skeptical. Now, as he took in the view of what appeared to be paradise, he came to the conclusion that no such horrendous crimes could possibly have been committed in this tiny waterfront haven.

Small fishing craft and large schooners loaded with timber and barreled turpentine demanded his attention, and he gladly obliged as he ached to join them. He quickly buried what he believed were exaggerated tales of crime and punishment and allowed an unusual peacefulness to take over his mind and body.

Suddenly, a crude little craft a few hundred yards away caught his eye. Two men had abandoned the tiny vessel—an odd-looking man-made apparatus—and were actively engaged in ferociously beating at the water with their boat paddles. Who was their victim? he wanted to know. Had he discounted those tales of woe, of disagreements among lawless citizens being settled with dangerous weapons, too soon? It had never occurred to him as a youngster that one of the weapons might be a simple boat paddle.

When the fishermen finally tossed their paddles onto the piteous craft and began floating downstream, the uninvited visitor crouched down in the tall weeds and watched nervously for any sign of a human body floating along the water. When none appeared, he chastised himself for allowing his imagination to swerve out of control and focused on escaping the tall, thick canes and marshy water's edge he had wandered into.

All manner of weathered boat docks jutted past snow-white sand to reach the lively, flowing waters of this miraculous creation in the realm of nowhere. He ached to rest his weary body on one of them and soon settled atop the first one he came to, a massive, rough-hewn device obviously built for heavy traffic. It occurred to him that it was where most of the area's activities took place and that by settling there, it would be obvious to everyone that he had nothing to hide and was therefore on a peaceful mission.

His preoccupation with the waterfront activities had completely prevented his noticing anything on the opposite side of the sparse settlement. Suddenly, voices, taut and anxious, began sifting through the atmosphere. Turning away from the water, he noticed an old store building partially hidden by crooked live oak trees, their limbs heavily laden with shiny gray moss moving softly with the light wind. The shaded wooden structure was apparently Niceville's entire business center and, judging from the old shack's front porch, a favorite gathering place for old-timers.

Unfortunately for the stranger, Niceville quickly lost its charm. Even from a distance, the uninvited visitor determined that every man on the porch held a rifle or a shotgun in his hand, and most of them were pointed in his direction. He couldn't know that most were weak-sighted old men who regularly kept the sagging cane-bottomed chairs and wooden benches occupied while they entertained themselves with tales of narrow escapes from the law as well as from wild animals and rattlesnakes. Most of their tales were enhanced, but everyone knew which ones were. The thought of a stranger daring to sprawl across the little settlement's private dock raised the hair on the backs of their necks like that of a watchdog threatened by an intruder. And they had no intention of allowing him to pass unharmed.

"Where's Odell?" one of the old-timers screeched, his high-pitched voice a mix of joy for the chance to take aim at a human being again and outright fear. Others stiffened for the same reason. Where indeed was Odell?

Odell was the constable, the only officer of the law the little settlement had. The comment captured the attention of Clough Martin, a giant of a man, as he stomped his way out of the general store, shaking the porch timbers with his clumsy gait. Clough always walked with a stomp, especially on noisy surfaces like the store's creaky wooden porch. The noise he made turned heads in his direction, a big plus for a man who worshipped attention of any kind.

"Hey, Clough, where's Odell? Look out there on the dock!" one of the men shouted. Every man on the porch was out of his seat by now, his rifle pointing in the stranger's direction. Clough, meanwhile, had no interest in Odell's whereabouts. "What the hell's going on?" he bellowed. "Why didn't you call me? That's a damn fed lookin' to smash our moonshine stills, or else he's running from the law. He may even be the bastard that killed Claybucket and his old woman. Why, hell yes—that's who he is, all right," he said. "Hell, we ain't got time to play hide-and-seek with a crippled constable!" he blasted. Stepping off the porch, he remembered to avoid the loose board at the end, the one he always purposely stepped on when he wasn't in a hurry. It made a sound like a gunshot and never failed to send the porch gang scampering for cover, a scene that kept Clough entertained the rest of the day. But a stranger on the dock? That promised to be even more entertaining. He stomped his way toward the dock, kicking up patches of sand along the way.

In truth, federal agents rarely made it to Niceville, as even the best access meant lengthy boat rides through dangerous narrows in the sound or life-threatening storms along the Gulf of Mexico—and the only other route involved time-consuming tromps through thick wooded areas that foreigners were ill prepared to tread. Even if they survived irritated alligators as they stealthily sunned themselves along the sandy creek banks, the long list of poisonous snakes throughout the area was another cause for alarm. If the federal agent had made it through, he wasn't likely to discover a single moonshiner's still house in spite of the fact that one in five families in Niceville proudly owned one.

Most residents, whether moonshine makers or drinkers, saw the popular man-made brew as an elixir in spite of its esophagus-searing, gut-wrenching blow to those who partook of it. They thought no more of making moonshine than of making soup. As they saw it, both were necessities in life. Still, they kept their bootlegging activities secret, as a life in federal prison didn't appeal to them.

Protecting their moonshine stills was the main thing that kept this diverse, otherwise warring group somewhat friendly with one another. Many who inhabited the sandy-soiled terrain had ambled into the area, often accidentally, from other states, territories, or foreign countries themselves, some seeking asylum from the law. But once they were accepted by the suspicious long-term locals, they were, themselves, just as suspicious of future newcomers, not to mention long-term locals.

As for the recent murder of the lovable old Claybucket couple, that was another thing entirely. It was thought at first to have been a robbery, as the couple was rumored to be "sleeping on a ton of money" hidden in their mattress. As Niceville had no banking facility, hiding their money was the only option available to the old couple. But the Claybuckets were found bludgeoned to death in their home, their money untouched in spite of the fact that it lay between the mattress and springs, just as rumor had it.

The longer the killer was free, the more anxious everyone was to hang somebody. And many had no intention of waiting for a jury trial.

Niceville residents ached to see the Claybucket killer hang, not entirely because of his cowardly crime but for the opportunity to witness a hanging. A hanging party was seen as a party to outdo all parties, as it would be a rare chance to dress up and go some-where, to see friends and relatives they rarely saw, and to be seen in the new finery they intended to make or purchase from the mail-order catalog. There were a lot of variables, of course. Getting to Crestview, the county seat where the hanging would take place, was only one of them. Crestview was only twenty-something miles from Niceville, but the only cleared paths through the forest were rough Indian trails where horses often broke legs, forcing their riders to shoot them and return home. Those who attempted the trip via wagon were no luckier, as the rough surface was noted for breaking axles, rendering the cumbersome vehicle useless.

But since no one had been arrested for the crime, the com-munity remained focused on making, distributing, and drink-ing moonshine. Conglomerates of crude, handmade furnaces and rough-soldered barrels connected to spiraling copper tubing, these rough-hewed still houses decorated the area woods without fanfare. Although everywhere, they were nowhere as far as the eye could see. The crude monstrosities were hidden by little more than a shed built close to the ground and choked with undergrowth, felled trees, and thorny bushes. They were masterpieces of disguise, as were the workers who crawled their way in and out of the unsightly inventions, never taking the same trail in or out. They went to great lengths to leave no evidence for federal agents that any human be-ing had ever stepped foot there.

Clough Martin was one of the area's most dedicated producers of this sour mash, as well as the most suspicious. He welcomed this young stranger by poking a gun in his face while wearing a smirk on his own. "You've come to the end of your road, my friend!" he boldly announced.

Although the elderly group on the porch couldn't hear the goings-on, they easily drew conclusions when Clough repeatedly jabbed his rifle into the young man's face. The scene left the porch group in openmouthed limbo, a pose that prompted a generous flow of tobacco and snuff juices from chin to shirt.

"Bound to be the Claybucket killer," said one of the onlookers. The possibility created a deadly silence among the group and sent each of them clamoring to get a ringside stance near the boat dock.

"Odell ought to be here," one man insisted. "Clough's gonna—" he began, but he was interrupted.

"Yeah, Odell ought to be here," agreed another, prompting all to nod their approval. While no one trusted Clough to handle anything of this caliber, or any caliber, no one was willing to walk the mile or so to Odell's house, possibly find him gone, return empty-handed, and, in doing so, miss what promised to be a momentous occasion they seldom had a chance to witness in their isolated habitat.

"I'll get Odell!" declared one elderly man, who then pointed his rifle in the air and pulled the trigger. The noise startled a few, caused the stranger to shudder, and angered Clough to the point of threatening to "kill the son of a bitch who did that."

The shot brought desired results, however. "Hey! What's going on out there?" a voice inside the store rang out. Everyone in earshot rejoiced as they recognized Odell's voice. He had arrived through the store's back entrance and had scarcely settled on a feed sack when he heard the shot. Odell was dedicated to doing his job, but about the only duty he had on a daily basis was to keep drunks and hogs off the street. He would have arrived at the store much sooner if not for a batch of hogs having dug up the money he had hidden under his own house. As with the Claybuckets, hiding one's funds was top priority for anyone who had any as the nearest banking facility was in Wanata Springs, a lengthy and dangerous walk or horseback ride on a rugged trail.

Dead tired from the hog hassle, the crippled lawman pushed himself up from the feed sack and moved as fast as his injured leg allowed. "What's going on?" he yelled, but the scene at the boat dock took precedence over any comments and sent him in a hasty hobble toward the dock. He knew Clough Martin's reputation for firing first and inquiring a great deal later, if then.

When the lawman took the stranger's rifle and urged Clough to put his down, some folks on the porch stopped chewing tobacco and either swallowed their juices or allowed them to roll quietly down their lowered chins.

Few dared cross Clough, a beast of a man who had no scruples about harming a fellow human being, not even one with a physical handicap. There was one exception, and strangely enough it *was* a man with a physical handicap: Odell McNeil, the constable himself. Odell had been left partially lame from a logging accident, but that hadn't hampered his uncanny expertise with a gun. Although he had never killed a man since arriving in Niceville, his recorded reputation for accuracy and speed with a gun had followed him from Louisiana. No one, not even Clough Martin, relished a gun-fight with Odell.

Meanwhile, young Chuck Haley, the store proprietor's son, bounced among the group clutching his own loaded rifle. "Is Mr. Martin gonna kill that stranger, Pa? Is he, Pa?" When the boy's father made no reply, Chuck concluded, "He may as well 'cause somebody'll hang 'im anyway, won't they, Pa?" he tittered. The boy's father was spared a response as everyone's attention was centered on Odell, who had grabbed Clough's rifle and tossed it on the ground. When Clough bent down to retrieve it, the constable held it down with his foot while pointing his own rifle at Clough's head. "Folks hired me to protect the area, and I'm gonna do that, and I'm gonna do it within the law," said Odell. A sudden hush filled the atmosphere.

"You're a damn fool," spouted Clough, but he didn't move the rifle, a testament to his respect for the lawman's firearm expertise. "How much proof do you need? I betcha five bucks he's the man who killed the Claybuckets!" Clough boasted. "Or else he's a damn fed! Go ahead—turn him loose, and you'll see I'm right."

It did look suspicious, even to Odell, who was something of a master at determining a man's character with little to go on. The stranger's arms, face, and hands were marred with scratches, some deep and still bleeding. His clothes were torn, and his shoes were laced with weeds and other debris.

"You got family here?" Odell asked the young man, whose emotions had shifted from helpless to hopeful several times within a few minutes.

"Hell no, he ain't got no family here!" Clough scoffed. He strutted about, making certain that his growing audience could hear now that they all had moved within a few feet of the boat dock. "Don't you think I asked him that straight off? He come right out of them woods over yonder!" he raved. "He's been swimming rivers to throw the hound dogs off. Look at his hat. It didn't take to the water too good. He's been running for a while, maybe since he killed Claybucket and his old woman. Check his pockets." He paused while Odell checked. "So what if he left the money in the old couple's mattress. Hell, they had money stashed all over the house," he declared as if he had proof.

"Who is Claybucket?" questioned the stranger.

"Who is Claybucket!" laughed Clough. "We got ourselves an actor, Odell."

"I have to agree," said Odell. "You'd have to be hiding out to miss the Claybuckets' story, I'm afraid, especially if you came through Crestview. I wired the news to the sheriff over a month ago." He paused and then added, "Ain't hardly nobody talking about anything else these days, and ain't nobody been arrested yet. Yeah, you woulda heard the news unless you've been hiding out," Odell concluded.

"Well, sir, I haven't been hiding, but I have been out of pocket, I guess you'd say. Been traveling through the woods for weeks now. You don't get much news in the woods," he pointed out without being sassy. "I come from up in Alabama and—"

"Enough of his lies," Clough interrupted. "Let's see what's in that blanket he's carrying with him," he insisted while simultaneously grabbing the unwanted visitor's bundle he had tossed on the dock earlier.

When everything was laid out, Odell grinned with satisfaction. He had been suspicious at first, but no longer. The visitor's clean-cut appearance in spite of his recent bruises and scrapes didn't fit the image of a brutal murderer. The rolled blanket contained a couple of sharp knives, soap, a bottle of ointment obviously meant to ward off mosquitoes and chiggers, and a crumpled change of clothes that appeared to have been washed in a creek along the way.

"A man running from the law wouldn't likely be that organized," said Odell. "Of course, nobody could walk that forest unscathed by insects and thorns and a few natural enemies. That could explain the cuts and bruises." But Odell's assessment didn't satisfy Clough. He was already examining the knives, snorting joyfully when he discovered a speck of dried blood on one.

"What'd you find to eat out there?" asked Odell pointedly. "Squirrel? Turkey? I'll bet you saw lots of black bear and deer. The last time I went hunting, I must have seen a dozen red fox. Pretty animals," he remembered happily. "Ah, I used to spend weeks walking in the woods. There's nothing quite like it," he reminisced. Odell's logging accident had left him with a bad leg and hip that made long walks impossible and had put an end to his hunting days. Remembering the good days gave him a thrill.

Odell's kindness prompted the young man to relax a bit even though most of the onlookers seemed as anxious to see a hanging as young Chuck Haley had been.

Realizing the whole town was apparently as suspicious as the first person he had come across, the uninvited visitor began talking. "I saw all the animals you mentioned, sir, and a lot more. As for food? Well, I ate a lot of nuts and berries after I crossed over Shoal River, and there was plenty of water. I did roast a squirrel now and then, but it don't take long to tire of squirrel when you don't have gravy and biscuits to go with it," he added, daring to chuckle.

Irritated by their sudden chumminess, Clough burst out in gaudy laughter. "Threw your rifle and your belongings across the big, wide Shoal River and swam across, did you?" he smirked. Everyone knew the rivers were swollen and had overflowed their banks following recent heavy rains. An area shallow enough to walk across Shoal River wouldn't exist.

"Didn't have to swim," said the designated villain. "I walked across the bridge, sir."

Clough let go with a loud guffaw, and the audience joined him while Odell stifled an urge to do the same. "Son, a bridge across Shoal River has been talked about and prayed for ever since I came to this area, but it's still in the wish-and-pray stage," said Odell. "Maybe you have your rivers and bridges mixed up?"

"No, sir, it's the Shoal River bridge, all right. It's not finished yet, but it was already open to foot traffic when I came through last week," he assured everyone, most of whom had broken into personal whispers once the stranger made what they deemed a surefire hanging mistake.

Reaction to the possibility of a bridge's actually existing varied. Anyone involved in moonshine knew a bridge across the river would enhance distribution of the area's popular product, but they also knew it would open up isolated Niceville to federal agents who had been denied access to the little community by highway or even a cleared pathway. And entry via water was far too visible and, therefore, dangerous. Still, Clough had always viewed a bridge crossing Shoal River as a windfall. He had dreamed of souping up an automobile engine that would outrun the law, whether local or federal, in case the bridge ever materialized, and he planned to equip his vehicle with a secret tank for hauling moonshine. Yes, a real road out of Niceville and a bridge connecting it to Crestview would be a dream realized, but he resented being told by a stranger, possibly a fed himself, that the bridge was open to foot traffic. Like other big moonshine producers in the area, he paid Noland Hagood, the county sheriff, a sizable fee to make certain their moonshine stills in remote Niceville remained a secret, at least from the feds.

"That damn sheriff has more secrets than we realized," Clough grumbled.

"Musta slipped the sheriff's mind," offered Odell, whose tight muscles around his mouth revealed his own irritation with the sheriff's sudden love affair with secrecy. Crestview, a mere wide spot in an otherwise deserted road, was nevertheless the county seat of Okaloosa County, and folks in the south end of the county were obliged to ride horseback through the wilderness and swamp to get their business taken care of in the hard-to-reach county seat. Odell found it difficult to side with Clough on anything, but he had to admit that Sheriff Hagood should have notified them that a new bridge, if only for foot traffic, had been completed or was even underway.

"Aw, hell, it's a damn lie anyway," accused Clough. "Ain't no bridge been built across Shoal River! We've been sucked in!" he spouted.

Realizing he was in a tight, perhaps dangerous, situation, the stranger spoke up. "My name is Ecil Brighton. I have some paperwork in that envelope there to prove it. I'm a bookkeeper for Farber and Sons Hosiery Mills. Or I was until they closed it down a few weeks ago. I've been looking for work all over Alabama but haven't found anything. While roaming through the woods, I ended up in Florida before I realized it, and it was so beautiful … and I … well, I've heard stories about Niceville and its great fishing and hunting, and I decided to see for myself." He neglected to mention gruesome tales of wrongdoing in the area as he was still hoping those had been exaggerated. Sadly, the pendulum had swung in the opposite direction during the last half hour, but he saw no need to bring that up under the circumstances. "You folks sure are lucky to live here. Don't think I ever saw a prettier place than this," he said.

"Bookkeeper!" Clough mocked. "You don't believe that story, do you?" he roared at Odell and then turned to the crowd for reinforcement. But he didn't get it. While many hadn't made up their minds about the young stranger, the last thing they wanted to do was agree with Clough Martin.

By picking up the letter from among the young man's belongings, Odell let everyone know he wasn't ready to shoot the stranger. "I know for a fact that he's telling the truth about Farber and Sons closing the factory. David Stewart went up there last week to see about purchasing the mill." David was the son of the most successful lumber and turpentine businessman in the county, and that was not including an empire in moonshine stills. Stewart Enterprises employed virtually everyone in Niceville as well as a majority of residents throughout the county.

"Tell you what," said Odell. "I'll take you to see David Stewart.

He'll know if you're a bookkeeper. And if you are who you say you are, he might even have a job for you. While laborers are plentiful, David can't always find the help he needs in the office."

The onlookers were shocked, and Clough was livid. He motioned for Odell to step aside for a private conference. "Are you crazy? We either got to get this bastard out of town before he accidentally discovers something, or we got to shoot 'im and get rid of the corpse," he growled impatiently.

Odell shook his head. "He's no fed! The youngest one I ever saw was forty, and he looked sixty. The hassles they go through and the chances they take when they trespass on a moonshiner's property in these parts age them fast. I'd stake my life on this one. He's just a young man looking for a job."

"Bull!" blurted Clough, who followed the comment with a sinister laugh. "How many muscled-up bookkeepers have you ever seen? They sit at a desk all day and never lift anything heavier than a damn pencil." He was no longer whispering. He wanted to put fear in the minds of the growing audience.

Undaunted, Odell had an answer. "You shoulda shook hands with him—good firm grip, but soft like a bookkeeper's." He turned his back to Clough and faced the man who called himself Ecil Brighton with stern resolve. "Come on, Ecil. Let's go see David Stewart."

David would soon replace his aging father as president of the county's most prominent and highly regarded business leader. Unlike his father, however, David would also be the area's most polarizing figure. Folks either loved him or despised him. It wasn't his personality that turned folks away, as he was noted for his warm and friendly manner, his generosity toward his employees, and his unassuming attitude in spite of his wealth. It was his bride they had issues with.

When David's father, Clarence J. "Claffie" Stewart, first came to the area, he opened the businesses after creating forestry and turpentine jobs for families in the entire county. David, his only offspring and a handsome young bachelor, had been especially welcomed by parents of unmarried daughters.

The welcome mats wore thin, however, when David shunned all of them in favor of an Indian bride. If he hadn't been Claffie Stewart's son and the manager of the Stewart empire, he and his bride would have been run out of town, and quickly.

David welcomed the town constable and Clough Martin, both men's constant agitator, into his office and extended a warm welcome to the stranger. If Odell liked him, so did David, and if Clough didn't, so much the better. After lengthy questioning by himself and Mr. Jeffries, his own bookkeeper of many years, David reached a conclusion.

"I can tell you unequivocally that this man is an experienced bookkeeper. I can also tell you that the letter he carries with him came from Farber and Sons Hosiery Mill. What I can't tell you is whether he's in trouble with the law, but I would certainly give him the benefit of the doubt."

Clough fumed significantly in silence.

Odell was ecstatic. "I don't suppose you could use a—"

"Bookkeeper?" asked David. "As a matter of fact, I can, but it would only be as an assistant to Mr. Jeffries. I'm certain it would be a reduction in pay from what this man is accustomed to."

"No matter!" Ecil quickly responded. "I need a job." It was soon settled. The man who had almost been shot or, at best, run out of town would soon have a job in Niceville.

Clough kicked the wall of the office so hard that a sign tumbled to the floor. He made no apology but lowered his rifle for the first time and headed boldly toward the exit. Once his hand was on the doorknob, he turned to face the startled threesome and directed a threat to Odell. "Better watch 'im like you watch the hogs," he warned. "If I see 'im snooping around in the woods …"

Chapter 2

IT WAS OCTOBER, THREE MONTHS AFTER ECIL'S AGO-
nizing introduction to Niceville and its suspicious inhabitants.
Neither David Stewart nor his father, Claffie, had ever been totally
satisfied with the available bookkeepers in the area, and the company's advertisements for professionally trained people were rarely
fruitful. Prospective bookkeepers who had endured the rough and
lengthy voyage into the isolated moonshine haven were often quick
to grab the first boat out.

Except for the suspicious nature of the area's majority, the atmosphere in Niceville was to Ecil's liking. He spent every free moment enjoying the water and the thick wooded area, both of which
offered interesting and edible inhabitants. Word quickly spread that
Ecil was not only a trained bookkeeper but an accomplished one
who took his work seriously. David Stewart couldn't brag enough
on him, and he assured Ecil of full-time work as soon as Mr. Jeffries
retired, which was less than a year away.

Clough didn't like being wrong, and he had always been
above admitting it even if he were. He had kept a close eye on
Ecil from the beginning and was finally convinced he was not
a federal agent. "He wouldn't know a whiskey still if I showed
it to him. Probably would think it was an outdoor toilet!" he
guffawed to all who would listen. "But that ain't to say he didn't

kill Claybucket and his old woman," Clough had announced early on. "Hosie Buie better keep an eye out," he warned often.

Hosie was a well-respected, hardworking man in his fifties who owned a small fishing concern not far from Ecil's rooming house. Ecil had become friendly with Hosie, who, unlike most of the fishermen, had befriended him. While others mocked Ecil as a soft-handed bookkeeper, Hosie took him on nighttime fishing trips, and Ecil showed his appreciation by assisting the fisherman with engine repairs as well as lending a heavy hand with all the work involved in the business. Their relationship grew into one they both enjoyed.

Late one Saturday, Ecil and his new friend were working on the boat's engine when Hosie sent him to fetch a wrench. Just as Ecil came out of the engine room, he saw a young woman approaching the boat dock. In order to step onto the dock, she had to lift her ankle-length skirt to prevent tripping on it. When she didn't notice Ecil, he tried to turn away but found himself riveted to the spot, his mind having wiped its slate free of watching anything except her.

Tall and waspy-waisted, her face framed by soft ringlets of light brown hair peeking out of a blue-flowered bonnet, she floated along the dock in spite of its unevenness. Untied bonnet strings dangled sensuously over tiny pleats in a soft, silky vest that snuggled up to full breasts. She smiled sweetly when she saw Ecil, making him keenly aware of his own appearance—his hands, face, and arms smeared with grease, his bedraggled clothing fit for the work he was engaged in but not for the prettiest face he had ever encountered. Even the small scar below her left eye enhanced her beauty, as it was a reminder of her perfection elsewhere.

"You must be Ecil," she said in a voice as elegant as her movements and as soft as her nearly flawless skin. "I'm Connie Buie. I came to thank you for helping my daddy."

Ecil was quite taken that she knew his identity and more so that she had apparently made the trip just to see him, or at least to personally thank him. He knew Buie had a daughter, a school-teacher, as he often spoke of her, but the image Ecil had of school-marms in rural Alabama were old and ugly in comparison, and too strict for a student to attach any humanity to. "You're a teacher?" he stumbled.

Connie laughed softly, putting him at ease.

"Actually, I'm giving up teaching. I'm going into sales. I'm a bit nervous about it, but I think I'll be quite good at it," she beamed. "Of course, I have the whole community up in arms, you know. They say I'm deserting their children."

"Sales?" he questioned as his mind conjured up horrible images. He had seen the wrinkled faces of fishermen's wives hawking their husband's catches along the bayou, or worse, door to door, and he cringed to think this lovely young woman was destined for such a fate. "You dislike teaching that much?" he asked pointedly.

Before she could answer, her father poked his head out of the engine room, held his greasy palms up for viewing, and threatened, "I'll do a number on that pretty dress if you don't stop harassing my helper. I sent him after a wrench an hour ago!" he exaggerated playfully.

Ecil blushed violently, conjuring up a comical contrast on his grease-stained face. "Sorry, sir," he moaned. He was still reeling from the notion that Buie apparently planned to subject his lovely daughter to the kind of activities usually performed by toothless, snuff-dipping old hags. He stared at Buie with questioning eyes but kept his silence.

Buie, however, didn't notice. "Last day of school?" he asked his daughter. "Did you tell Ecil you're giving up teaching to sell wom-en's dresses?"

"Yes, I did," she said, "but I'm afraid he disapproves just as you do."

Ecil was relieved. "Women's dresses?" he almost shouted. "Oh, on the contrary!" he assured her. "I'd say that fits you perfectly. You'll surely make a good model for all of your customers," he rallied, but he realized immediately that the reference to her shapely body was a mistake. Deciding that any further comment would only make things worse, he dealt silently with the deep and embarrassing flush that surged through his body.

Hosie gave no hint of being angered. Instead, he attempted to ease Ecil's obvious discomfort. "I tried to tell her that women around these parts make their own dresses. Gonna be hard to convince them to order from a catalog and pay those high prices," he warned.

"Wait and see!" she insisted. "They made their dresses because they had no choice! Now they do. They drool over the ready-mades in my catalog." The whole notion energized her, sending her twirling about on the dock and skipping across the cracks between the boards like a little girl. There was clearly no regret on her part that her teaching days had ended. Best of all, she showed no anger toward him for his remark, and most remarkably, neither did her father.

Forgetting his hands were greasy, Ecil rubbed his neck to relieve the tightness, an unfortunate reaction as it left his neck smeared and his shirt collar smudged. Connie and her father laughed, and he laughed with them, easing the tension for all of them. Connie was all the things he liked in a woman: graceful, intelligent, attractive, friendly, and best of all, full of confidence.

"Come on, Ecil. Tell her what a mistake she's making," urged Hosie in good humor.

"Well, the way I see it, if you don't like what you do, you don't have much to look forward to," offered Ecil.

Connie thanked him profusely. "I suppose that means you like bookkeeping?" she asked.

"Yes, I do," he said, convincingly. "Of course, I'd like to make a living hunting, or even fishing, or both," he admitted. "Game and fish warden? Now that would fit me perfectly, but a job like that is hard to find." He gazed unashamedly into eyes so blue they appeared to be a reflection of the sparkling blue bayou that flowed by on its way to the Gulf of Mexico. Befuddled by the attention, Connie adjusted her dainty, meticulously stitched bonnet, a move that sent a mass of flowing light brown hair tumbling sensuously down her back. It settled there in soft, aesthetically pleasing waves that begged to be touched. It was all Ecil could muster not to oblige.

Get a grip, he moaned to himself, but he remained transfixed.

Realizing that Cupid had struck both of them with piercing arrows, Hosie tried to continue the conversation. "Tell you one thing—those big ol' boys'll be glad she won't be in the classroom anymore. You should have seen her using a hickory switch on them. Every one of them could have broken her back, but they didn't dare touch her! She had her bluff in on them," he bragged.

Ecil's mind was churning, his body trembling. Had he gone mad? he wondered. He had known this woman no more than fifteen, maybe twenty, minutes, and yet he was determined to have her for his wife.

Six months later, word spread that Connie Buie was engaged to marry David Stewart's new bookkeeper, a man who was yet to be fully accepted into Niceville's secluded clan. Incensed, Clough Martin renewed his efforts to prove that this "pretty boy" was a common criminal. He began his campaign with Ecil's boss, David Stewart. David, however, was not interested in Clough's suggestion to "either shoot the little bastard or send him back to Alabama."

"What you got against this young man, Clough?" asked David. "First, you insisted he murdered the Claybuckets, and then you claimed he was a federal agent bent on destroying our whiskey stills and seeing all of us rot in the Atlanta Penitentiary. What's the charge now?"

Clough snorted, a habit of his that intimidated helpless old men and children but had little effect on anyone else. "I ain't changed my mind!" he burst out. "He's a damn murderer! I guess you forgot that ain't nobody been arrested yet for murdering the Claybuckets, and that's going on seven or eight months now. No damn wonder! You're harboring the culprit right here under your nose. You're just like the others—bent on waiting till he kills somebody else. Did you ever ask yourself why he traipsed through the woods to get here instead of coming by boat like everybody else? He was runnin' from the law, that's why!" Pointing a big, thick index finger at David, he warned, "It ain't gonna set well for you when they find out you've been hiding a fugitive from justice."

David's temper had been tested from the moment Clough burst unannounced through his office door. Slowly and deliberately, he rose from his seat behind a big heart-of-pine desk. He forgot, temporarily, that he and his father had agreed to tolerate Clough as best they could, as he was a fellow moonshine maker and dealer with a short fuse and no sense of obligation toward others. If caught making, selling, or distributing moonshine, he would make certain that everyone else went to prison with him. David and the other moonshiners had struggled to keep that in mind when dealing with Clough, but David's own temper didn't always cooperate with him.

This was such an occasion. "I suggest you wire Crestview and tell Sheriff Hagood you've single-handedly discovered the Claybucket murderer and that I have been hiding him right here in my office for the last eight months." In outward calm, he opened the office door and waited silently for Clough to depart.

Clough recognized the comment for the insult it was. Sheriff Hagood himself was as involved in the moonshine business as the producers and distributors were, perhaps more so. All dealers in the business, including David and Clough, paid the sheriff a handsome sum to keep federal agents out of Niceville and to keep his mouth shut.

Red-faced and fuming, Clough kicked the door open, spouting insults of his own. "Well, I'll say one thing for this boy you're coddling: he knows how to pick a wife!"

It was, perhaps, the most cruel thing he could have said and one that was certain to infuriate David, said as it was in the company of a dozen or more employees who felt the same way Clough did, that David's marriage to a common Indian was an insult to the community and to all of its eligible white daughters and their parents. Other single white men who had migrated to the area looking for work had been forced to take Indian brides as demand far outweighed the supply of eligible white females. However, these women "knew their place." They went out of their way to remain in the background, never attempting to rise above their inferior station in life. David's wife, on the other hand, took center stage as if she were an equal!

As the only son of Claffie Stewart, the wealthiest man in the county and the man who employed a majority of its citizens, David could have had his choice of single women, and he had chosen Mary Sam and given her the same freedom and privileges as white women enjoyed. It was enough to start a war, and it often had.

The remark that Clough made in David's workplace and the support he received from David's own employees emboldened Clough enough that he stomped his way out the open door, head held high with a broad grin monopolizing his mammoth face. None of David's employees liked Clough, and Clough knew it, but he also knew they enjoyed seeing their boss get what most of them felt he deserved.

Meanwhile, the upcoming wedding of the newcomer in town to a highly respected old-timer's daughter was soon pushed to the background when Parnie, the supply-and-mail boat captain, returned from his biweekly trip to Pensacola with exciting news. "There's two of 'em. J.R. Klinger and his kid brother. The two bastards murdered Wally and Gertie Claybucket! Thank God they're in jail. We gonna have us a double hanging!" he crowed.

The news spread quickly. The biggest event Nicevillians had ever experienced was a come-one, come-all fish fry or an occasional rip-roaring, moonshine-guzzling hoedown. The thought of loading up the family for a trip to Crestview to witness a double hanging was far beyond anything most had ever hoped for. Nobody would want to miss it.

"How will we all get there?" was Odell's first concern. He posed the question to David Stewart, who made the trip more often than most.

David had no answer. Workers had begun to clear a road from Crestview to Niceville, but progress was painfully slow due to insufficient funds, bad weather, and the spread of the flu bug.

"Yeah," David agreed. "Hasn't been a wagon or buggy go through there yet without breaking an axle or destroying a wheel. The only way a majority can go, and the only way any woman or child can go, is by water, and if we're honest about it, we know that can be treacherous too." The truth left them both somber. "But maybe we're worrying needlessly. Truth is, we may never have a trial. Self-appointed hangmen have already bought the rope! And you can bet your long johns we won't get an invitation to that affair."

In spite of the odds, nearly everyone in Niceville continued to harbor hopes of attending the big event. Men shod horses, sharpened axes, and repaired wagons, while women canned and preserved foods from the fields and gardens to be shared on the harsh trip to Crestview.

Meanwhile, Connie Brighton walked the sandy streets, cut through thick woods, and rowed the swift waterways in canoes or john-boats, catalog and order blanks in hand. Every woman who could afford it, and some who couldn't, ordered a new dress and bonnet for herself, her elderly mother, and her daughters, as well as a Sunday shirt and hat for her unsuspecting husband.

Taking orders was easy; it was delivering them that made life difficult. While delivering a package one morning, Connie boarded a canoe and proceeded to cross a swollen creek. The unsteady boat capsized, leaving her scrambling to retrieve the packages and head for dry ground. She spread the merchandise over tree limbs and stumps. While waiting for them to dry, she lay on the grass and finally fell asleep.

A *chomp-chomp* sound awakened her to a devastating scene. Goats had destroyed everything in sight, including the paper the merchandise was wrapped in. Rather than cry, which she was not prone to do, she satisfied her anger by belting the stuffed goats with the biggest tree limb she could handle. In the process, she stumbled and fell, hitting her head on a tree stump. The blow left her unconscious.

The next thing she remembered was waking up in her own bed with her family and loved ones staring down at her with anxious faces. And there was Dr. Smythe, the area's only practicing physician, who was always either drunk or recovering from a drunken binge. He appeared, on this occasion, to be experiencing the latter.

The doctor motioned for Ecil to follow him outside the room. "Your wife has suffered a miscarriage," he said through labored breathing, unsteady motions, and heavily alcoholic breath. "She needs to take it easy for a while."

"Miscarriage?" Ecil questioned. He stared at Smythe, a mere piece of a man whose moonshine abuses had all but destroyed his ability to care for the sick. "But she wasn't ..." Ecil began to argue, but he realized the doctor was not capable of carrying on a meaningful conversation. *Connie pregnant? Wouldn't her husband be first to know?* he pondered. *Still, if she isn't pregnant, what then?*

Is she dying? Ecil gave the situation deep thought. He knew her only chance of survival depended on getting better medical care, but heavy blood loss had taken such a toll on her frail body. He knew she would never survive a rough and tumbling boat trip to Pensacola or a rougher buggy ride to Crestview where she could expect to receive better care. He was about to break down when Connie suddenly opened her eyes. "I'm sorry," she cried softly.

Ecil stared at her in disbelief. He had assumed Dr. Smythe had misdiagnosed her situation. "You mean you traipsed through the woods, paddled the boat, lifted heavy packages, and climbed fences knowing you were carrying our baby?" he asked in a tone unfamiliar to both of them.

"I know you can never forgive me," she sighed, turning away.

Ecil walked the floor in morbid silence for a lengthy moment before revealing his innermost thoughts. "The way I see it, the Claybucket killers have taken another life," he groaned in abject misery.

As it turned out, Nicevillians needn't have rushed their preparations for the hanging. Weeks earlier, attempted escapes from the flimsy Crestview jail had ended in failure and prompted officials to transfer the prisoners to a more secure facility in Pensacola. Alas, it too proved vulnerable. Both prisoners had escaped!

Chapter 3

IT WAS 1920, THE YEAR OF PROHIBITION. ALL LIQUOR sales, not just those of untaxed moonshine, were now illegal, and anyone caught making, selling, or distributing any type of alcoholic drink could expect to receive free room and board in federal prison. Liquor dealers all over the country were shocked, appalled, and looking for a way out, while Niceville moonshiners laughed in their white lightning.

"It's a windfall!" Clough Martin told his fellow producers. "Hell, we've never been legal anyway, and now we have no competition! We can raise our prices!"

David Stewart was a bit more cautious. "I'm sure the feds have a plan. I'd say they're likely to hire a new batch of agents, update their training, and issue better equipment. They're smart enough to know dealers aren't gonna give up on a moneymaking business like moonshine without a fight."

"I agree," said Odell, "but on the other hand, the whiskey dealers won't stand still either. They'll figure a way to sell their whiskey, and they'll be richer than ever because they won't be paying taxes on their sales either."

Clough's embarrassment was obvious. Truth was—he hadn't thought the whole thing through, but he would be the last to admit it. "Bull! They can't train those city-fied idiots to master these woods. And even if they did, how they gonna get out before we kill 'em?"

"I have no plans to kill anybody," Odell assured him. "But liquor dealers aren't going to disappear any more than moonshiners are, and they've got a lot more money behind them. How will they do it? I don't know."

It wasn't long before he found out. David was contacted by rumrunners south of the border, a name attached to people who distributed illicit whiskey on the waters. David passed the word to Odell, who arranged a meeting at David's house with the biggest moonshine producers in the area.

"We meet these so-called rumrunners in the Gulf, transfer the goods to our boat, and bring them back here where representatives from Atlanta, Birmingham, and other cities, including our own little Crestview, see that it is delivered to their customers. Once it's off our boats, we're safe, at least until the next haul. That's it," he explained in a very tight voice. "These boat runners are quick to point out that they're taking most of the risk as they have to cover a lot of water with the whiskey on board, and all we have to do is meet them at Yellow Bluff just a few miles into the Gulf." Making no eye contact with anyone in the room, David walked the floor of his own house in a nervous rendezvous with uneasiness, hands clutched behind him. "What's your pleasure?" he finally asked, his laboring stroll around the room having come to a halt and his eyes finally coming into contact with those of Ecil, Odell, and Clough, one by one.

"You make it sound easy," said Odell, who was adamantly against the idea. "We might not have to spend a lot of time in the Gulf of Mexico, but there ain't nothing to keep the Coast Guard out of the bay or the sound. Guess I don't have to remind you those are the only ways we can reach the Gulf?"

"The profit is astounding," said David, ignoring Odell's comment.

Clough, always anxious to get involved in any moneymaking scheme, appeared hesitant as well. "Distribution by water? Always dangerous. It's damn near impossible to escape the Coast Guard. Even if we happen to see them before they see us, our only option would be to dump our cargo in the Gulf and go back home empty-handed—rum and money gone," he added before slamming his filthy hat down on a massive head of unkempt hair and announcing with the fervor of a bull who had just been released from captivity that he couldn't wait to get started.

Rumrunners were born overnight, it seemed, and liquor dealers in Niceville were among the first in the Panhandle to become associated with them. Even as they continued to distribute their own home brew, they met the rumrunners at a designated spot in the Gulf, filled their boats with multiple cases of liquor, and distributed it to waiting crews in Valparaiso and Niceville.

Luckily for the Niceville distributors, a rough, sandy road had finally been cut from Crestview to Niceville. The opening left a lot to be desired as vehicles bogged down in the heavy sand, especially when loaded with jugs of moonshine and rum. The new opening had its merit, however. As tough as it was to maneuver the troublesome, sandy soil, Panhandlers prevailed while federal agents who had no experience with such a surface failed. The best the feds could hope for was to catch the distributors once they arrived in Crestview or later, when they headed east or north.

Meanwhile, with no news of the escaped Claybucket murderers, the Crestview hanging had been pushed to the background. Everyone began to worry that self-appointed hangmen had hanged the guilty parties, the Klinger brothers, privately, thus depriving the public its right to witness the event.

David Stewart paid Odell a visit. "Have you heard anything from the sheriff? Folks are getting restless," he said. Both agreed that Odell should contact Sheriff Hagood in Crestview.

A wire from the sheriff's office arrived before Odell could make the request:

Prisoners still at large. Source of escape tool unknown.

Escapees believed to be armed and dangerous.

Odell was quick to visit David's office. He tossed the wire on David's desk with a short comment: "Inside job. You can't hide a saw in a bowl of grits! And what about the noise? They must have sawed all night to open up a hole in the jail big enough for J. R. Klinger to crawl through. And any jailor who wasn't dead or deaf would have heard all that sawing," he pouted.

"Maybe not," said David, thoughtfully. "I was thinking about that the other night. Pensacola got the brunt of that hurricane that went through the night the prisoners escaped."

It was true. The hurricane itself hadn't hit the city head-on, but it had left its mark with the assistance of devastating tornadoes. Homes were destroyed, and streets were clogged by fallen trees, home appliances, furniture, and debris, making it impossible for anyone to pass through safely. The Klingers' biggest worry would have been survival, not the law. The question was, who furnished the saw?

While Odell and David bandied the notion about, Rhoda paced the floor at home, waiting for Odell's scheduled arrival. The scene he had left at home of huge pots of tomatoes simmering on the stove, and Rhoda in need of jars for canning them, had totally escaped his mind.

Irritated and frightened, Rhoda donned her bonnet, tying it tightly under her chin to hide thin, flyaway hair. She depended on the bonnet to soften an unattractive profile created by a nose much too large for her tiny face but necessary for supporting the thick glasses her poor eyesight demanded. Prodding heavily along the sand road, she stopped at Connie's house for assistance.

"Don't be angry with Odell," begged Connie. "He just got busy and forgot. Ecil does it all the time," she added in an effort to appease Rhoda.

"I know," agreed Rhoda. "When he sees all those tomatoes, he'll be full of apologies."

At the store, young Chuck Haley, barely fourteen now, was in charge. Chuck was always glad to see Rhoda and Connie as both women were well liked by all the young folks. He quickly abandoned his broom and dustpan and rushed to greet them.

"Miss Rhoda! Miss Connie!" he beamed. "How can I help you?" Pointing toward the front of the store, he encouraged them both to take a look at the new dresses. "They just came in yesterday."

The women chatted endlessly with the likable young man, inquiring about his family and any news he might have heard of late about anything and anybody. A visit to the store was better than reading the newspapers, which were filled with old news by the time Niceville received them. Chuck's only interest was centered on the Klingers, however, and the only news he had was also old.

Disappointed, Rhoda headed for the dress racks. She had never owned a ready-made dress, but to please Chuck, she began looking them over when a sudden scuffle in front of the store demanded her attention. A view out the window was especially disturbing.

"Did you see that? I've never seen poor old Mr. Ellerby move like that! Or any of the others for that matter," she added nervously. "You don't suppose it's the Klinger brothers? They're loose, you know, and they're desperate," she whispered in a tight voice.

"No!" Connie assured her. "They could never get through all those rivers and creeks and heavy woods. Why, they'd ..."

Chuck joined both women at the store's only window, where they caught a glimpse of a burly man wearing a broad-banded cowboy hat. A shock of reddish-brown hair appeared to have been slashed with a dull knife to keep it off his ears and out of his face, the remaining blobs left to their own bidding. He took a long look up and down the street and grinned, apparently at its emptiness, a situation he realized his presence had brought about. He reacted with wild laughter when the old men scampered off the porch without the aid of their canes or the security of their rifles. When he reached the open porch, the post he grabbed to pull himself up came loose at the bottom, causing him to lose his balance. He grabbed the post again, ripped the other end out of the ceiling, and slung it on the ground before heading for the door.

"Oh, Miss Rhoda, it's him and he's coming in!" cried Chuck, his face pasty white, his body shaking. He managed to get behind the counter, where he fumbled with the merchandise underneath as if he were searching for something. In any case, he never found it. "You both better go in back," he said, quivering.

Neither Connie nor Rhoda had ever seen the man before, but they knew his identity nonetheless. It was John Holder, a man it was said had run out of knotting space on his gun belt and a man who had never spent a night in jail—or even been arrested, as far as anyone knew—for all the murders he was said to have committed. He rarely came into town, at least in daylight hours. The last thing either woman wanted to do was stare at John, but that was exactly what both of them did. John's masculine build reminded Rhoda of her beloved Odell before the accident, but the likeness ended there. She wanted to hide behind the dresses, but before she could, she noticed a woman and a young girl entering the store, and the sight of the pitiable twosome left her traumatized.

"Has to be John's wife and little daughter," she whispered to Connie, who appeared as dazed as Rhoda felt. The shy twosome had followed behind John submissively, their heads lowered, eyes gazing at the floor as if they had done something to be ashamed of. It was said that John had managed to reduce the twosome to nothing long ago, at least in their own eyes.

Connie smiled at Jeannette Holder, whose frayed dress was disintegrating on her body, the cheap fabric having deteriorated many washings past and prompting her to hold her hands over her bloated stomach to prevent her bare skin from showing. Jolene, who appeared to be seven or eight, was dressed in equally shabby attire, her matted hair in need of a good washing and combing.

Everyone had heard the story many times of how John had nearly beaten his wife to death after she gave birth to Jolene. John had wanted a son, so the story went. Jeannette had been puny after that difficult first pregnancy, and to add to her dilemma, subsequent pregnancies—and there were many—had ended in stillborn babies. Nobody knew any of this for certain as John had never sought medical attention for his wife.

"Mrs. Holder? I'm Rhoda McNeil," Rhoda said warmly. "Would you like to join me here with the new dresses?" she asked sweetly, but immediately regretted the comment as it would surely remind the poor woman of how desperately she needed a new garment.

"I never buy ready-mades myself, but it doesn't hurt to look," Rhoda quickly added before laughing a thin, nervous laugh.

Jeannette nodded anxiously but didn't stir from behind a barrel of flour where she appeared to seek refuge. Young Jolene hung tenaciously to her mother's flimsy skirt tail. Meanwhile, John swaggered around the room, extracted an expensive pipe from a display, and flipped it up and down in his mouth. "Charge this," he told Chuck, who quickly bagged the item without writing a sales slip.

John pranced around the store, picking up a man's shirt and a pair of overalls, several pairs of socks, and a bag of undershirts. After piling them on the counter, he instructed Chuck to show him some boots in the largest size he had in stock. After settling on a pair, he went behind the counter and grabbed a hunk of cheese before stuffing a bag with crackers from the open cracker barrel and then ordering Chuck to get him a slab of bacon.

"What the hell are you doing?" he asked his wife, who remained behind the barrel of flour, her arms clutching her intimidated daughter. "Grab one of them dresses!"

As Jeannette moved timidly toward the dress rack, Rhoda cringed with fear that Jolene's tug on her mother's flimsy dress would rip the garment off her thin body. Meanwhile, Rhoda continued as she had been, nervously pulling the dress tails out and tucking them back in place, always without seeing a single one of them.

When Jeannette finally reached the dress rack, she stood there gawking, first at Rhoda and then at the floor. John bolted across the store, grabbed a handful of dresses, hangers included, and threw them on the counter. "Now go git the girl somethin'," he barked.

Seeing her distress, Connie led her to an area featuring children's clothes, quickly selected several dresses that appeared to be Jolene's size, and handed them to Jeannette.

As uncomfortable as Jeannette was, she gave Connie a grateful nod before taking one of the dresses her husband had tossed on the counter. Instead of returning to her safety zone behind the flour barrel, she fingered the smooth fabric of one of the dresses for a split second and almost smiled. The dress was a blue-and-white polka dot in smooth rayon, the only one not made of cotton. John, however, ordered Chuck to put the whole batch of dresses in the bag and add them to his account.

John laughed out loud at the fidgety boy, bear-hugged the mountain of merchandise he had piled on the counter, and swaggered out the door, the new pipe dangling from his massive lips. His wife and daughter followed submissively.

The episode left young Chuck as embarrassed as he was frightened. He had seen John Holder in action before but never when he was manning the store all by himself. He tried to apologize to the women.

"Don't you worry about that, Chuck," said Rhoda. "There's not a man in Niceville who will stand up to John Holder." She neglected to mention that Chuck's father, who was owner of the store, would have reacted the same way, totally giving in to whatever John said or did.

After discussing the whole thing numerous times, the women said good-bye and headed home. It was not until Rhoda walked in her kitchen and saw the washtub filled with cooked tomatoes that she remembered what she had gone to the store for.

Meanwhile, Ecil's efforts to pacify Connie failed. She went to bed that night knowing she would never close her eyes. Like Rhoda, it was her nature to see good in everyone, but she knew she would have a hard time continuing in that belief now that she had been introduced, so to speak, to John Holder.

Chapter 4

RHODA AND CONNIE'S EXPERIENCE WITH JOHN MO-
nopolized their thoughts until Odell received a telegram from
Sheriff Hagood:

Klingers back in custody. Security tight.

New trial begins next week.

Again, Nicevillians rejoiced. The time was riper than ever for
attending a double hanging as the new sand road to Crestview had
been completed. Traveling on it was still a struggle, but with the
whole town going, extra wagons would be used to haul new wheels
and axles so nobody would be left behind.

Everyone felt certain that the trial would move fast this time.
Sawmill owners announced to their employees that the mills would
be closed so that everyone who wanted to attend the hanging could
do so. Haley's General Store, the old silent movie house, and the
new hotel and cafe made similar announcements.

Only the turpentine stills would remain open. Everyone knew
why. Except for the supervisor's job, these were dirty, low-paying
jobs handled exclusively by black people, and none of them could
afford the trip.

With everyone anxious to plan the massive exit from Niceville,
Odell called a meeting at Haley's General Store. He had just begun
to address the crowd when a loud, vulgar voice familiar to everyone

demanded their attention. "Fools! All of you!" yelled a fuzzy-headed man who stood in the doorway after assuming a wide-legged stance, his right hand clasped firmly on a holstered gun.

It was Clough Martin. "Go home! All of you!" he demanded. "There will be a hangin', all right, but it won't be open to the public," he warned.

"Maybe you'd like to give us a date you plan to perform this illegal act, Clough," suggested Odell, who stood up and began a slow but determined walk in the direction of the bully, who resembled a bear standing upright.

"Oh, I won't do it myself," laughed Clough. "Romie Beavert will do it for me. But ain't none of you folks gonna witness it!" he promised.

The crowd groaned, almost in unison, but held their tongues so as not to miss anything.

"Don't you realize it was Romie who passed that saw to the killers in the Pensacola jail?" he said with a smirk, his eyes focused on Odell, who hastened his step in Clough's direction.

"Why would Romie want the killers to go free, Clough?" asked Odell, who had reached his adversary and stood face to face with him. "Everybody knows Romie wouldn't help his own mother escape." Beavert, who lived in the north end of the county, was a well-known troublemaker, hotheaded gambler, quick-triggered moonshine maker and distributor, and more recently a land poacher, specifically of Claffie and David Stewart's properties. Romie had no friends anyone knew of, but neither did Clough.

Clough's smirk broadened. "Why? Easy! He wanted them to escape so he could hang 'em!" he announced to the shocked crowd. Resting long enough to fully enjoy the attention he was receiving, he finally added, "That was the night a tornado ripped through Pensacola and tore it apart. Romie couldn't get to the jail to carry out his mission," he guffawed. "The damn coward. I woulda done the deed myself if I hadn't been sick in bed."

Most everyone was startled by the accusations, unwilling to believe anything Clough said, but as their only lawman appeared startled by Clough's remarks, they were confused.

Odell, however, was not confused, only frustrated. In spite of being across the room from David, their eyes met. As their gazes locked on each other, each felt the crumbling of the other's countenance. Still, they kept their silence and began where they had left off, encouraging the group to prepare for a public hanging in Crestview. Once the group dispersed, David, Ecil, and Odell held a private meeting.

"We've been a pack of fools," Odell began.

"How were we supposed to know Romie Beavert gave them the saw? And I have to tell you, I don't believe it anyway," Ecil admitted.

"You're right. Romie had nothing to do with the jailbreak or the gift of a saw to the killers," Odell assured them. "Clough did! He just admitted as much!"

Ecil remained quiet, hoping Odell would explain.

David, however, was no longer confused. "My God!" he yelped as he mentally pieced the whole episode together. "We *are* a pack of fools!"

"Maybe not," argued Odell. Eyeing Ecil, he asked if he could ever recall Clough missing a moonshiners' meeting.

"Can't say I have," said Ecil. But then he remembered something. "He did ask us to change a date for a meeting once."

Odell and David were immediately enlightened. "Willie May told us he was sick, and we took her word! Good grief! It was that very night, the night of the storm!" Odell raved.

"Yeah," agreed David with a groan. "He was likely in Pensacola already. He must have managed through some egghead in the jail to get the saw to the Klingers. The last thing Clough wanted to do was set the Klingers free, but he had to free them in order to kill them! He obviously planned to kill them the minute they sawed their way out, but he couldn't get to the jailhouse in that tornado."

"I feel like an idiot," admitted the nettled lawman. "But we got the last laugh. He told on himself tonight, and if he hadn't, I don't think we would have ever figured it out."

"Why did he blame it on Romie?" asked Ecil.

"Another story entirely," said David. "Clough has always wanted Romie dead! He thought if he could convince anybody that Romie had delivered the saw, the law would go after him and that would leave Clough free to get the Klingers." He was quick to add, "It might have worked too. Every lawman in the Panhandle would like to rid the area of Romie Beavert."

"Keep in mind that Clough don't have a lot of patience," offered Odell. "It's one of many flaws in his character. If we give him a little more rope, I'm pretty certain he'll hang himself."

Odell was quick to report the news to officials in Pensacola and just as quick to suggest that they fire all their jailers, hire new ones, and tighten security. Rather than arrest Clough, whose part in the escape would be difficult to prove anyway, officials agreed to follow Odell's suggestions.

With week-old newspapers from Crestview their only source of news, Nicevillians were constantly in an emotional uproar. The trial was underway again, and folks wondered if they should shoe horses, repair wagons, make new frocks, and prepare food for the trip to Crestview. Many looked to David Stewart for an answer. In the past, David had made an occasional trip to Crestview for the distinct purpose of keeping the community informed. But his father's semiretirement kept David busier than ever, leaving him precious little leisure time. He opted to send Ecil, his trusty book-keeper, to Crestview. "Keep us informed," David told him.

Ecil understood his assignment. He was to call the new hotel in Niceville, the only place in town with a phone, at a particular time on a daily basis. Odell and the community would be waiting for the call. For Ecil, a woodsman, horseman, and avid hunter, getting there was half the fun. Crestview was only twenty or so crow-flying miles from Niceville, but nonfliers were obliged to travel well over a hundred miles to reach what was commonly referred to as "a wide spot on the railroad track." Ecil chose to rough it on a popular Indian trail, but this time, he invited his horse along. Except for the horse, it would be the same trip that had landed him in Niceville on his initial visit.

When Ecil arrived in Crestview late the following day, the little community was in an uproar in spite of the lateness of the hour. Boisterous groups had gathered in the streets, in the tiny cafe, and in the railroad station. Right away he ran into Josh Tarrow, Okaloosa County's first school superintendent. *Something awful must have happened*, he thought, *for Tarrow to be hanging around so late*. Either the prisoners had escaped again, or worse, the jury had taken a bribe and let the criminals go free. He wished immediately that he hadn't come as he dreaded taking the news home to Connie, who had already taken dress, hat, and shoe orders for nearly every woman, and some men and children, in Niceville.

"Ecil Brighton!" yelled Tarrow. "If you're here for the hanging, you're a mite early," he joked.

Ecil hurled questions at Tarrow during their lengthy hand-shake. "What's going on? Why is everybody on the streets? Did the Klingers break out again?"

"No! They've been found guilty as charged!" Tarrow rejoiced. "You're just in time. Sentencing is today, but everybody's uptight. Word has it a hanging posse plans to bust open the jail, grab the prisoners, and hang them on the nearest tree. You know, make certain they don't go free." Before Ecil could get his bearings, Tarrow invited him to walk over to the sheriff's office with him. "Maybe he's learned something new since I spoke with him ten minutes ago," he laughed.

"You mean they haven't secured the jail?" asked Ecil as they walked along. "I think I'd be more concerned about that Bible-carrying governor." Word had it that the governor, a former Baptist preacher, had visited the prisoners and publicly announced that he believed in the prisoners' innocence. Many feared a last-minute stay of execution from the sympathetic governor.

Both men were duly welcomed by Sheriff Hagood, a smallish man who was nonetheless big in the minds of the people. He would be elected again and again for the job and was touted as a man who would uphold the law in spite of the fact that he continuously broke it himself by accepting bribes from big moonshine makers, distributors, and sellers, not only in Niceville, but all over the county.

The sheriff was quick to speak his mind on the only subject everyone was interested in. "That damn lawyer has already said he will appeal a guilty verdict. If he gets it, there will never be a hanging, at least not in public. It's all a travesty anyway," he said nervously. "If they don't get on with the public hanging, somebody's gonna yank 'em both out of jail and hang 'em on a tree."

"Yeah, Clough Martin tried that, and I wouldn't be surprised if he tries again. I'll tell you something else. This kind of thing is gonna happen again and again if we don't get a bank in the south end of the county. Folks have to hide their money in their mattresses or in a hole in the yard," he said with obvious concern.

Hagood burst into devious laughter. "I can't help but laugh at the Klingers," he said. "They thought that old couple would tear up their mattress and dig up their yard when they found themselves face to face with a loaded rifle." Still laughing, he plopped his hat on his bald head, straightened his gun belt, and announced, "It's time to head on over to the courthouse."

The sound of children playing in the streets demanded their attention. Most were involved in a make-believe "shoot 'em up," some posing as the killers and others chasing them with toy rifles. Still others walked behind their "captors" with a rope wrapped around their necks. All made their way to the real gallows.

"The kids are having a good time," laughed the sheriff, who stopped a moment to observe the activity. "Let's go in the side door. We'll never get past the drunks at the front door. It's been standing room only for hours now."

Just as they turned the corner, they caught sight of Judge James Aiken, who returned their gaze, a mournful attempt to seek comfort that he knew neither of them could deliver.

The judge's face was puffy from long, sleep-deprived nights brought on by a botched and antic-filled trial. Murder trials in Okaloosa County always brought out lawless individuals who had been known to hang their fellow man at the slightest opportunity or provocation, if any. In their minds, the accused were always guilty, and they wanted to make certain they died for their crimes.

Judge Aiken had learned early in his career that the fate of the accused rested more in the hands of the ugly minority than in the decision of the court. Those who had the luxury of a trial constantly feared being strung up by angry posses long before the trial ended. It was Aiken's greatest fear as he approached the bench.

While the sheriff stood watch along with many assistants who had been hastily hired to keep order, Ecil and Tarrow joined him in a corner, where they fought for standing room. Rowdy spectators quickly quieted down when Judge Aiken, a well-respected man in the community, made his appearance, but they forgot their manners once the prisoners came hobbling through in leg irons and handcuffs.

John Roy Klinger, better known as J. R., walked with his head thrust so high in the air that his Adam's apple appeared ready to burst through the tight skin on his neck. He brushed his attendants aside and pranced as best he could with leg chains clamoring to catch up with his movements toward the seat designated as his. Willie Earl Klinger, his younger brother, could scarcely stand without assistance. His head drooped to his chest, and his body shook as if he'd been incarcerated in a freezer. He entered the courtroom sobbing, creating mucus that ran down his face and onto his prison uniform, where it gathered in a soggy mass of collections from his mouth and nose.

Before uttering a sound, the judge made eye contact with several courtroom spectators known as troublemakers, all of whom were longtime acquaintances of the judge but not necessarily friends. All sat squeezed between their neighbors, struggling now and then to wipe the sweat from their brows and necks, but they soon realized that any movement on their part could be considered an insult to their neighbors.

Court attendants scuffled now and then with the defiant J. R., leading the judge to repeatedly demand order in the courtroom. Meanwhile, Willie Earl required assistance to rise from his chair. The feat had no sooner been accomplished than the young prisoner's legs crumpled beneath him, sending him to the floor. He fell with such force that attendants were forced to leave J. R. to himself in order to attend to the man he referred to as his baby brother.

With attendants still struggling with Willie Earl's listless body, Judge Aiken took the opportunity to call all attorneys to his bench for a short conference. Meanwhile, Willie Earl sat with his head dangling helplessly, as if his neck had already been snapped in two. Totally ignoring his devastated brother, J. R. jutted his strong jaw out in defiance, cursed his own lawyers, and shook a fist in the general direction of the prosecuting attorney.

After warning J. R. that a similar outburst would find him barred from the courtroom, Judge Aiken addressed Willie Earl, who was upright once again thanks to two strong court attendants.

"Willie Earl Klinger, you have been found guilty of murder. Have you anything to say before I pronounce sentence?" asked the judge.

A limp Willie Earl made no response.

J. R., however, was energized by his brother's silence. He jerked loose from the court attendants, shoved his distraught attorney aside, and plodded in the direction of the judge's bench even as his leg chains clawed at festered wounds on his raw ankles. "I got plenty to say!" he announced. The scene prompted a few women in the courtroom to cover their eyes or at least look away. Those reactions didn't last long, however, and the women soon joined the men in stomping on the floor in loud and disturbing unison. "Hang 'em now!" one yelled, and others applauded.

Prompted by lawyers on both sides, several bailiffs rushed to the judge's bench before the judge could order J. R. removed from the courtroom and began dragging the belligerent prisoner across the floor. With little alternative available, they attempted to press him into a chair that wasn't wide enough to easily accommodate his broad buttocks. "Be quiet until given a chance to speak, or the judge will remove you from the courtroom!" warned his attorney in a loud, frustrated whisper.

J. R., however, was up in a heartbeat even as his attorney and both bailiffs tried to apprehend him. "Bring him up here," ordered the frustrated judge, who wished above all to be done with the ordeal, lock the prisoners up, and go home, even though he knew there would be no peace there either, at least not until the hanging had taken place. "Take Willie Earl back to his seat and let him rest a bit." Once the switch was accomplished, Judge Aiken addressed J. R.

"John Roy Klinger, I find it difficult to have mercy on you. You could have been a role model for Willie Earl, but instead, you chose to lead him to destruction. You have been found guilty of taking two innocent lives and ruining a host of others." With sweat dripping from the judge's chin onto the paperwork in front of him, he made an irritated swipe across his face with his bare hand, flicked the moisture onto the floor, and continued. "And yet the only regret you have is regret that you were caught!" he bellowed, his voice so strained from overuse that it cracked, giving him a hint of weakness. In a milder tone, he continued. "Now, you may address the court," he said, "if you do so with a civil tongue!" Pointing a demonstrative finger at the prisoner, he added, "Don't make the mistake of thinking I won't throw you out of here."

Instead of bursting into a rage as everyone expected, J. R. remained silent, almost as if he had taken ill. When he finally opened up, he responded in a soft, mellowed voice, declaring his innocence. "Your honor," he began, "we've been railroaded by this court. Look at 'em out there," he said of the spectators. "They just want to see a hanging, and they don't much care who hangs."

Folks were disappointed as they were prepared for a rowdy story of abuse and innocence. Instead of continuing his physical fight, J. R.'s shoulders drooped to a new low, and his facial features followed suit. He suddenly appeared pale and weak, his labored steps a testament to a complete change in his demeanor. Mumblings circled the courtroom as everyone tried to make sense of what was happening.

The judge took advantage of the lull. "John Roy Klinger, I sentence you to hang by the neck until you are dead," he announced.

The courtroom erupted. There was a scuffle in the hallway caused by a drunk trying to retrieve his gun from the array of assault weapons that officers of the law had confiscated from spectators as they entered the courtroom. Rather than give up their guns, hundreds had opted to remain on the courthouse grounds, where they stood shoulder to shoulder with their fellow citizens in the nearly unbearable August heat. Those inside had been kept busy relaying the proceedings to those outside. When word spread to the outside that the judge had ordered J. R. Klinger to hang, screams of joy erupted.

The most ardent supporters of hanging had their own plans for the occasion. While some banged on tin pans, others climbed atop a tin-roofed building near the courthouse and beat the metal with ax handles and baseball bats. When spectators inside began to join the rally, Judge Aiken made his intentions clear. Since threats of emptying the courtroom hadn't worked, he tried another tactic. "If one more person carries the news of courtroom proceedings to the folks outside, I'll have the doors and windows in this courtroom barred shut and the fans turned off with all of you in it!" he bellowed, his nostrils dilating like a snorting bull's. His demeanor told them he meant it even though such a move would be dangerous in the already stifling atmosphere. They were quickly calmed by the possibility.

Meanwhile, court attendants had managed to get Willie Earl on his feet. With his broad shoulders slumped severely, he appeared much shorter than his once-lanky six feet, three inches. His slim hips swayed helplessly to one side. Wavy jet-black hair, wet from the perspiration created by the intense heat as well as by his emotions, spilled sensuously over one side of his high forehead and called attention to unblemished skin, sun darkened just enough to soften its glow. Except for that, his physical attraction was hampered only by his languishing body language, the full, soft lips muttering in anguish, the strong chin perched limply on his chest, his usually dancing black eyes and high-spirited smile quelled by disillusion and hopelessness. He was known for his modesty and warm, outgoing personality. Those who knew him best never imagined that he would harm anything beyond a house rat.

But twelve jurors said the public's assessment of young Willie Earl was wrong. He and his brother, J. R., had been found guilty of murdering an elderly man and his wife in a botched effort to take the couple's life savings.

In anticipation of Willie Earl's response, the sheriff and his assistants, attorneys for the defense as well as the prosecuting attorneys, and every spectator in the stuffy courtroom maintained a catlike silence. Those who had been fanning themselves, and that was virtually everyone, stilled their paper fans in spite of the misery it wrought.

It was all for naught. Willie Earl was incapable of putting a single thought into words.

Like his older brother, he too was sentenced to hang.

With court dismissed, Ecil glanced at Josh Tarrow, who attempted to wipe the sweat from his face with a handkerchief that was already soaked with it. "Think the prisoners will make it to Pensacola?" he asked. "Or will they hang on the way?"

"They may or may not," said Tarrow. "The sheriff does have a good plan. Nobody, not even the driver of the car, knows when they're going to leave here. Won't know until five minutes before they leave," he explained.

As it happened, the small caravan arrived at the Pensacola facility without incident. At the urging of his brother, Willie Earl had kept his emotions under control during the trip, but the minute they were locked in their cells, he fell apart, finally slithering off his bunk onto the dirty floor and then lying there sobbing.

"Aw, shut off your spigot, baby brother. We'll get a retrial, and if our stupid lawyers can get it moved to another county ..." J. R. thought out loud. "Yeah, it'll be different in another county where nobody knows us and nobody knows that old Claybucket couple either."

By morning, a grinning jailor stuck a newspaper through the

Klingers' jail bars. "Folks are buying new frocks to wear to the party you guys are throwing!" he laughed.

J. R. grabbed the paper and read the front page headlines: *Klinger Brothers to Hang* shouted the written words. "You son of a bitch!" J. R. yelled at the jailor.

Meanwhile, Willie Earl had dragged himself onto the cell's lower bunk and fallen into a deep but disturbed sleep.

J. R.'s periodic banging on the cell bars throughout the day failed to wake his ailing brother but always brought an irate jailor into the hallway.

"What time is it?" asked J. R. every time the jailor appeared.

"What difference does it make to you? You ain't goin' nowhere," growled the jailor.

"Maybe not today, my friend, but one day." He shook his fist in the jailor's face. "Me and my brother's gonna leave this place, all right!" he promised.

"Yeah, when they string you up!" laughed the jailor as he headed for the exit.

J. R. pounded on the bars with such force that Willie Earl's eyes finally popped open. The deep sleep he had entered into had removed him from his worries, and for a fleeting moment, he had dreamed of better times. He sat on the side of a thin mattress, his hands grasping the flimsy bed frame, and glared at the bare wall in front of him.

"Maybe you should take it easy, J. R.," he warned. "You know your condition. You had that bad spell when we were on the run. If they hadn't caught up with us when they did, you would have died!" he said as he wiped emotional tears away. "And I saw what happened to you yesterday in court. You didn't take your medicine, did you?" he wailed.

J. R. had been diagnosed with a diseased heart valve, something doctors knew little, if anything, about and knew even less about treating. A doctor in Mobile had treated him as he would an invalid, ordering him to take it easy and get lots of rest. When J. R. asked, "How long?" the doctor had responded, "For the rest of your life." He had also prescribed a pill that J. R. was to take for the same length of time, but J. R. was not one to adhere to rules. He made no effort to control his activities, and he took his medicine on an irregular basis, if at all.

"Say, baby brother, that gives me an idea!" he rallied. "All we have to do is let the public know about my condition—yeah, that's it. The publicity ought to get that preaching governor's attention again, and when he hears about my bad heart, he'll convince the public to turn me loose and let me die in peace," he fluttered. Turning to face his fractured brother, he tried, for the first time, to console him. "They ain't gonna hang you either, Will. They'll feel sorry for you what with your only brother dying," he promised as thoughts surged through his mind faster than he could put them in order. "Yeah, that preaching governor we got, he loves sob stories," laughed J. R. "He'll grant a stay of execution when he hears about my condition, and as soon as we get out of here, I can start taking it easy and I'll get well again and we'll be free." He took a seat on the cot with his brother, patted him on his back, and broke out laughing. "We're gonna get out of this, Will!" he railed.

Ten days later, headlines in the Crestview newspaper shocked everyone:

J. R. Klinger Dead!

The atmosphere in Niceville was glum. J. R. had deprived them of a double hanging, perhaps of any hanging. *Would the death of his brother lead to a new trial and a new jury that might set the emotional Willie Earl free?* they worried.

They needn't have. In a few short weeks, Odell received a wire from Crestview:

Willie Earl Klinger to hang. Courthouse steps
Crestview, Florida. September 2, 2:00 p.m.

Chapter 5

WITH ONLY THREE WEEKS TO PREPARE FOR THE BIG event, Nicevillians were panicky with fear that an angry mob or some overanxious fool like Clough Martin or Romie Beavert would succeed in hanging Willie Earl before the official hanging committee had a chance to do it. And none of them would be invited!

Still, everyone planned to get to Crestview by September 2, whether by wagon, horse, boat, or foot. Those who planned to tackle the tricky white-sand road through the wilderness packed enough food for four or five days as well as home medications to be used against ticks, chiggers, mosquitoes, and dog flies.

Travel in the south end of Okaloosa County was always a struggle unless one took to the water, and even that came without a guarantee of safety. With no unforeseen storm or other catastrophe, it was, however, quicker.

The constable, his friend Ecil, and their wives had settled on taking the boat. Like others who could afford it, they would board the *Helma*, a passenger, supply, and mail boat captained by Parnie, considered one of the safest boat captains in the area for maneuvering the difficult narrows. However, if the captain met with a strong head tide, it was entirely possible they wouldn't arrive in time for the hanging.

But that wouldn't stop anybody from trying. Only the very sick and the poorest of the poor would miss this event. When the day came to depart, the unusual activity in the bayou spoke for the excitement everyone was feeling: an array of fishing boats, combination passenger and supply boats, wind-powered craft, tugboats, steam and motor launches, and tiny john-boats. Some owners had dry-docked their boats or at least had them secured, but most were plowing through the water in a feverish effort to complete their work in time to make the hanging.

Docked beside the *Helma* was the *Charles Palmer,* a schooner loaded with twenty-foot lumber stacked crosswise on its sixteen-foot deck. It was a tricky and sometimes scary haul, and not always a successful one. Rough waters determined whether the boat would make its haul with or without its lumber intact. The sailing vessel's other cargo included cross ties and wooden barrels filled with turpentine produced at local turpentine stills. The schooner's captain planned to deliver the goods to Pensacola and then join his crew on a train ride to the hanging.

Rhoda and Connie's excitement had reached a peak by the time they boarded the *Helma.* Thoughts of fingering local arts and crafts as well as manufactured surprises at Buck's Store in Camp Walton, their first stop, kept them both entertained even as they stowed their belongings and chose their seats.

"I wish I had one of those ruffled bonnets at Buck's Store in every color," squealed Connie.

Never one to worry about fashion, Rhoda asked only for a moment in one of those "pretty white rocking chairs at the Gulfview Hotel at the landing or a chance to lounge on the wraparound porch at the Florosa Inn." The inn was located in a community that bore the same name and would be the last stop before they reached Pensacola. It had a reputation for boarding famous, and often infamous, criminals from Chicago. Several months back, Al Capone and his cronies had rented the entire inn under assumed names, kept a low profile, and departed without incident. But when the owner of the inn learned who her guests had been, she had new locks installed throughout, placed a "Closed" sign at the boat dock, and remained holed up in the building until a newspaperman from Pensacola came calling. Fortunately for the hanging enthusiasts, the Florosa Inn was finally open for business again. Among other pleasures, it would offer a last chance to hide in the bushes and relieve oneself.

The *Helma* was much more than a passenger boat. It was partially loaded with naval stores (essential products for producing and maintaining wooden ships), salted-down mullet, food for the crew, and outgoing mail. Niceville and other waterfront communities depended on the ship and other supply boats for their entire inventory, and merchants built along the waterfront for easy access to these supplies. Of course, Nicevillians produced an ample supply of moonshine, but as it was illegal to make, sell, or distribute the product, they seldom took a chance on distributing it on the open waterways, where all watercraft was fair game for the Coast Guard.

With more and more passengers arriving with their umbrellas, tin-bucket lunch pails, croker sacks, and pasteboard boxes stuffed with their essentials, Rhoda and Connie abandoned the popular upper deck where they had originally settled and opted for the lower deck that promised a bit more privacy.

With everyone aboard, fares collected, and the gangplank pulled, they were about to depart, and not a minute late—an unusual occurrence. It wasn't a guarantee that their arrival in Pensacola would follow the pattern, but everyone aboard saw it as a good omen.

They were still cheering their imminent departure when a troubling land-based noise demanded the attention of even the deafest. It was a deep, roaring bellow with a powerful reverberating sound that prompted everyone to search for its creator. Moving hurriedly down the sandy pathway was a repulsive-looking figure with sprawling reddish hair protruding from all sides of a dirty hat. A thin little girl with unusually broad shoulders struggled to keep up with his massive steps.

It was John Holder! Trailing behind him was his reluctant little daughter, Jolene.

"My God!" murmured Odell. "Never thought I'd see the day when John would attend a public hanging." Both crew and passengers eyed Odell as if expecting the lawman to protect them by denying this feared man a seat. Some tongues remained locked inside nervous lips, while others twisted and turned in an unsuccessful attempt to calm themselves, and still others, including the boat captain, said a quick prayer.

John pranced along the dock as if he owned it, a smug grin spreading across his bulbous face, his clothes so wet that he appeared to have been swimming in them. Jolene walked with her eyes rooted to the loading platform and then kept them glued to the floor once she stepped on board. Noticeably missing was John's wife. Only a few passengers would have recognized Jeannette Holder as she was seldom seen with her husband, or even in public, but when she did accompany him, Jolene was always present and vice versa. With the image of a glorious trip erased from their minds, Connie and Rhoda sat in rigid misery.

Captain Parnie was at a total loss for words, an anomaly for a man known for his bubbling chatter. Everyone had questions, but nobody dared ask them. John seldom left Niceville for anything. He didn't have to. If he wanted something, whether it was a pair of shoes or a milk cow, he approached the first man he saw, usually in the pool room, a bar, or even the man's home, and demanded whatever he wanted—and he received it.

Most everyone complied with John's wishes no matter what strain it put on the family's finances. Those who refused often disappeared from the area and were never heard from again. No one was ever quite certain if they left out of fear or if John had done away with them, but as no dead bodies were ever discovered, nothing could be done.

Fully expecting John to flash a daring grin in his direction, Parnie made no mention of any fee. But to the shock of everyone on the boat, John handed Parnie a half dollar, the one-way fare for two passengers. All aboard wondered who had been hit for the money, and they cringed to think what John might need from each of them before the trip came to an end. Questions abounded, but there were no answers. Why was he taking his daughter on a one-way trip? Had he killed the child's mother? They worried.

Rhoda was clearly the most disturbed by the new passenger, not out of fear for her own safety but for Jolene Holder's. The Holders were said to reside deep in a wooded area called Bolton, an undeveloped bayfront community connected to Niceville by Rocky Bayou, another wide body of water much like Boggy Bayou. An early morning trip from swampy Bolton to Niceville would be a difficult excursion, especially for a little girl.

Jolene stood in the aisle, her head hung so low that her chin touched her chest and made breathing difficult. Her right hand was pressed hard against her face, and tears had begun to drop from her eyes and land directly on her thin cotton dress.

As John had boarded with no belongings, and therefore had little to do other than take a seat, Connie and Rhoda marveled that he still hadn't done so. His eyes had settled on the quiet young man who had been the first to board and who sat in a corner by himself. The young man struggled constantly with an odd-shaped package, which was wrapped in old newspapers and held together by a rope. Although everyone had attached a name to this young stranger and was somewhat content with his presence in the backwoods, Odell was one of few who had ever seen him. He and his package had created greater interest among passengers and crew than John had, something previously unheard of. The young man had raised eyebrows when he refused the captain's offer to place his package in a storage area designed for passengers' belongings and rejected Odell's suggestion that he place the unwieldy package under his seat.

With John's attention centered on the young man with the package, Connie and Rhoda had a rare opportunity to take a hard look at John himself. His eyes were narrow slits, and his hair was a tangled mass of dull red straw. Both horrified women were convinced that it hadn't been washed or combed since they last saw him. He wore a stained and mutilated cowboy hat over the tangled mess and had crammed the unruliest blobs of hair underneath his filthy headgear.

John finally chose the seat he wanted, a bench shared by a family of four and already crowded. Ignoring the family, he pushed his way onto the bench, knocking two of them off the other end. The family quietly sought seating elsewhere. The bench was the closest seat to the young man with the package and directly across the aisle from Rhoda and Connie. Once settled, John noticed for the first time that Jolene had rested her head on Rhoda's shoulder. "Sit up straight!" he growled after giving the child a harsh pop on her bare leg.

Rhoda and Connie had been quick to notice that Jolene was in some kind of pain, so they had questioned her while John was occupied with deciding on the best seat for his purpose. Jolene had timidly explained that she had a toothache and that they were going to Pensacola to have it pulled.

In hopes that John would allow the sick child to rest in her lap, Rhoda insisted, "No, no, it's no bother, really." Jolene, however, had been quick to do as her father demanded and dealt with her pain in silence.

The women's excitement for the trip had quickly turned to muck, both of them having been subjected to silent misery. They couldn't get past the look of despair on Jolene's face, the same expression she had worn at the store that infamous day that John raped the place.

It occurred to Rhoda that John intended to have the child's tooth pulled and then proceed to the hanging, perhaps even hitch-hike as there wouldn't be another train until the next morning. The thought of it made her quite ill and brought her to silent tears. "We can look after her at the hanging if—" she began.

"We ain't goin' to no hangin'!" bellowed John. "The girl's teeth ain't no good. Pulled some of 'em myself but it takes both hands to hold 'er down. I reckon I can hold 'er while the doc pulls 'em out," he said without a hint of pity for the child. "Gonna get 'em all out this time."

"No! You mustn't do that!" screeched Rhoda.

"I mustn't?" laughed John, clearly agitated. "Get the picture, lady. Every tooth in the girl's head is coming out!" he assured her with an angry shout, apparently having reached his low level of tolerance.

Rhoda realized she had only made things worse, but she couldn't stop herself. She tried pleading with John while Connie sat back in silent panic. "Surely you don't mean that, Mr. Holder? What about her schooling?" she tittered.

"What about it?" he guffawed. "Her mama teaches her every-thing she needs to know."

Realizing that John had no humanity whatsoever with which she might deal, Rhoda's hopes of easing Jolene's misery faded, but she didn't give up. "It doesn't hurt so much to have a tooth pulled, honey." She bit her cheek just remembering her own experience with the dentist. Truth was, dental work, especially in remote ar-eas like theirs, was still in its early stages. Dentists were known for breaking the patient's teeth off at the root, leaving pieces of bone buried deep in the jaw. They then had to dig them out, usually without painkillers except for a stiff drink of moonshine.

Recalling the pain of it, she turned again to her adversary. "Please, Mr. Holder," she begged. "So what if she's had two or three teeth pulled? I had four teeth pulled when I was young, but I've never had a toothache since then."

"Well, look at me," John rallied. "I ain't had no toothache in twenty years!" he bellowed before fashioning a big grin, purposely revealing an ugly, toothless cavern. With that, he stood up, prompting Jolene and her would-be protectors to cringe in fear, but it quickly became clear to them that his sudden move had nothing to do with them. Instead, he made an unwelcome visit to the wheelhouse.

The moment he was out of sight, the young man with the package moved quickly across the aisle and whispered in Rhoda's ear, "Please, madam. Leave him alone before he kills us all. He already killed my father!" Too nervous to continue the story, he put his finger over his lips and returned to his seat.

Jolene stiffened, a clue that she had heard. Rhoda snuggled the child to her breast before responding, "How do you know?"

But it was too late as John was on his way back. Rhoda managed to remain quiet, but only out of fear. In an effort to keep a tight lip, she left John to himself and focused on the young man. He accused John of murdering his father, Gus Genepri Sr., an elderly man who had also resided in Bolton. The area that housed John and Genepri was connected to Niceville by a wide, bridgeless bayou and thick forests with heavy, nearly impassable undergrowth. Most everyone knew that Genepri, or "Old Gus," as they referred to him, was a fugitive from justice himself, but with John being his only neighbor for miles around, they were satisfied that he had enough to deal with. They left him to himself. Few residents had ever seen Old Gus, and that included Rhoda.

When Gus Jr.—the young man Rhoda spoke with here—arrived in the area, folks became antsy. He had been interviewed, jailed, and monitored for days before being given permission to continue his journey to Bolton, only a couple of difficult walking miles away. His purpose for coming? He wanted to pay his father a visit, but when they learned his father was dead, suspicion was high even in Odell's camp. Folks named the young man Gussie as it was difficult to carry on heavy doses of gossip without a name to vilify.

And now Gussie was leaving the area with only one item in his possession: a poorly wrapped, odd-shaped package that offered no hint as to its contents. Gussie appeared oblivious to the main topic of conversation among the passengers, that of the hanging, but he had shown concern for Jolene's plight, albeit without comment. Noticeable to Rhoda and Connie was the fact that John appeared to be uncomfortable in Gussie's presence, a rare occurrence for a man whose survival had previously depended upon making others feel that way. *If John wanted Gussie's package, why didn't he take it like he did everything else he wanted?* Rhoda wondered.

When the boat reached the narrows, Captain Parnie had his hands full. "Narrows" was a name given the narrow opening to Camp Walton that continued all the way to Navarre, a tiny settlement midway between the landing and Pensacola. The captain was fighting a head tide. It could last an hour or six hours, and it could make travel very difficult, depending on whether the channel had been dredged lately. They could run aground or even be forced to anchor on the beach and spend the night along the way. The thought kept many a heart pounding and blood pressures rising.

Typically, Rhoda would have been hysterical at the thought of spending the night stranded on a boat or anywhere else with John, but to her surprise, she was not so much afraid as she was angry.

She found herself wishing the hated man was facing the gallows instead of Willie Earl Klinger.

Although there were some tense moments, the captain escaped the troublesome narrows without serious incident, and the passengers and crew relaxed a bit. When they docked at Florosa Inn, a scheduled stop where they could take a short walk through the longleaf yellow pines surrounding the inn, feast their eyes on locally made arts and crafts inside, or relax in one of the inn's big rocking chairs, they forgot about the young man with the strange package for a few minutes.

Rhoda and Connie had dreamed about this opportunity for months, but now that it had finally arrived, their minds were too troubled to enjoy it. Rhoda half expected that Florosa would be the end of the line for Gussie even if he hadn't planned it that way. Satisfied that he and the contents of his unusual package were hiding from the law, and with John apparently focused on the young man's every move, perhaps determined to relieve Gussie of his treasured package, it seemed appropriate that the troubled young man would seek refuge at the isolated inn just as Al Capone had. If he were hiding from the law, he certainly wouldn't want to appear at a public dock like the one they would be encountering in Pensacola, she decided.

Rhoda wanted to disassociate Gussie from the infamous Chicago gangsters whose harsh, battle-worn faces seemed to verify their lifestyles. The young man's skin was dark, suggesting a Sicilian background, but smooth and youthful, not pock-marked like Al Capone's and the other gangsters she had seen photos of in the post office.

While Connie ran her fingers through handmade smocks, bonnets, and ribbons inside Florosa's gift shop, Rhoda took a moment to discuss John's plan to have all of Jolene's teeth extracted with Odell, as well as Gussie's accusation that John had killed his father.

"Why don't you arrest him for murder? At least then he couldn't do that!" she begged.

Odell scoffed at his wife's concerns. "Don't worry, honey. No dentist is gonna pull a mouthful of good teeth. You have to know John Holder. He gets a thrill out of frightening people. The best way to handle him is to ignore him. He was just having a heyday with you women and the young fella. As to John murdering anybody, we have no proof."

Reluctantly, Rhoda joined Connie inside the inn but scarcely acknowledged her purchase, a book of paper dolls.

Connie laughed at herself. "I know it's crazy. For months I've been looking forward to buying some of the local arts and crafts, and I've ended up with a manufactured book of paper dolls. I just had to. You-know-who loves them better than anything in the world," she said with a grin.

Rhoda did, of course. They were for Casey, David and Mary Sam Stewart's little daughter, whom Rhoda and Connie, both childless, claimed as their own. The Stewarts had gone in advance of everyone else as David had to join his dad in another land dispute with troublesome Romie Beavert in Baker.

"What did Odell say about John having Jolene's teeth pulled?" asked Connie.

"The usual!" sulked Rhoda. As soon as she caught sight of Odell again, she pulled him close. "What about that package Gussie's carrying?" she asked.

"What about it?" asked Odell.

"Why, he's guarded that thing like it was gold! If we had a bank in Niceville, I'd swear he held it up! You owe it to the community to see what's in that package!"

"Honey, we're out of my jurisdiction, and even if we weren't, I can't go around grabbing folks' packages!" he reminded her. Fortunately for Odell, Parnie had started the engine and everyone was boarding, including new passengers. Folks were quick to notice that Gussie and his package were missing. His absence created a tense moment as everyone jumped to the conclusion that John had managed to do away with him.

A search of the inn and the surrounding area revealed no one, and neither previous nor new passengers had seen Gussie once he had left the boat. Although highly unusual, Captain Parnie was eventually forced to leave without him.

Everyone was tense, and that included Odell. Rhoda remained quiet the rest of the trip, only glancing occasionally, and sympathetically, in Jolene's direction. By the time they reached Pensacola, the episode with John and the mystery of young Gussie had created an atmosphere of gloom for everyone, so all were relieved when the trip ended. Rhoda and Connie hated the notion of leaving Jolene in the company of her dreadful father, but they were comforted by Odell's notion that no dentist would actually pull good teeth, not even for John Holder. And once the bad tooth was pulled, the little girl would get relief and go back home to her mother.

Once on the train to Crestview, there was only one subject on anyone's mind: the Klinger hanging. It monopolized the conversation of passengers from New Orleans, Biloxi, Mobile, and points in between, and they were all on their way to see the exciting event.

Rhoda and Connie were quick to peruse the train's wanted list of criminals, certain they would see a photo of Gussie. Instead, their eyes became fixed on an advertisement taped to the wall of the train. A Chicago industrialist was hawking the sale of lots in a proposed subdivision across the bayou from Niceville. He referred to the area as the Vale of Paradise.

"He must be crazy! Who would pay fifteen hundred dollars for a sandy lot in the wilderness?" Rhoda scoffed. "He'd better tell any buyers not to expect to raise anything in that sand or they'll be chasing him with a sharp hoe."

Folks from Mississippi, Alabama, and Louisiana perused the ad and asked questions of the Niceville group. Most of them had never heard of Niceville or its surroundings.

As the train carried them closer and closer to Crestview, Connie began to have second thoughts about seeing a man hang. She studied other faces on the train, all of whom had the same destination even though they resided in other states, places she had never seen. While most carried on lively conversations, the exhausted Niceville passengers remained noticeably quiet, even nodding off now and then, at least until they heard the conductor's call. "Crestview! Next stop is Crestview. Don't miss the hanging."

Every passenger on their car and those behind them reached for his or her belongings and eagerly lined up at the exit.

Exiting passengers were met with sounds of merrymaking from a huge crowd that included children in spite of the fact it was well past ten o'clock in the evening. David Stewart and Mary Sam, his unpopular Indian bride, were already in Crestview. Once again, David had been summoned to the area to help his aging father in dealing with Romie Beavert, the infamous land poacher. Since the hanging would occur only a few days later, Mary Sam and their daughter, Casey, had opted to accompany him.

"I hope you slept on the train because you're not likely to get any sleep in the rooming house," David warned the close-knit Niceville group.

When a loud pop sounded close by, a noise similar to a gunshot, everyone who had children threw them to the ground and covered them with their bodies. Only David and Mary Sam remained standing.

"Just firecrackers," Mary Sam assured them. "Of course, it could be a gunshot," she admitted. "Everybody's been playing around with their handguns all day and night. It's a nuisance," she added.

"Yeah, the sheriff and his crew have stayed busy, and the jail is already crowded. Niceville's own Bedlam brothers arrived drunk as usual," laughed David. "They're already locked up for the night!"

"Too bad!" grumbled Odell. "The sheriff knows the Bedlams never hurt anybody but themselves. He ought to save the jail cells for the real troublemakers. There'll be plenty of 'em."

"I'm sorry to tell you this, but your rooms are right here in the center of all of this," David told his guests. "The sheriff has enlisted every man, boy, and black bear to keep watch, but he can't control the noise. Do your best to get some rest because you're gonna need it to get through tomorrow," he added.

David had held rooms in his dad's rooming house for the Niceville foursome. Otherwise, they would have been obliged to join hundreds of folks who would be sleeping on the ground or in their wagons.

"I guess there's nothing new?" said Odell. "I mean, the prisoner could have escaped and we wouldn't know it in Niceville!" he complained lightly.

"Well, you probably didn't know Willie Earl finally confessed," David revealed to his shocked audience. "Yeah, Willie Earl finally got his interview with Governor Chattle, who stated publicly that he thought Klinger might be innocent. But when the stay of execution from Chattle didn't come as expected, Willie Earl apparently gave up hope and confessed. That's why they've waited this long to construct the gallows. That's not something you want to build if you have no use for it."

"Oh my," gasped Rhoda as her attention was drawn to the gruesome hanging apparatus. With only a few hours before the scheduled hanging, workers still pounded nails into the structure. Connie quickly looked away but not before capturing a lasting image of the unfinished structure. "I wish I hadn't come," she whispered to her best friend, Mary Sam.

"I *had* to come," declared Mary Sam, somewhat spitefully. She had always been her own person and had never allowed others to dictate her actions or change her beliefs. Her Indian heritage had brought a lifetime of constant rejection from white folks, but she seemed to have been strengthened by it.

"What do you mean, you *had* to come?" asked Connie.

"I think it's all been too much for my baby," said David as he wrapped his arm around his wife's shoulder in an effort to comfort her. "Look out there, would you?" Purposely changing the subject, he called attention to the courthouse grounds, where flickering lights from kerosene lanterns swung from tree limbs, makeshift tents, and wagons. "It's been like this all day and night. They've had peanut boils and candy pullin's too. But really, folks, I think you should check in your rooms. We reserved your rooms down the hall from ours because of Casey. If she heard your voices, she would be up all night. We left her crying to come with us because she wanted to see her Aunt Rhoda and Aunt Connie."

Neither Connie nor Rhoda had children, but both women doted on five-year-old Casey Stewart. To their chagrin, the child was often referred to as "David's other Indian" by those who jumped at every opportunity to degrade their high-society boss for taking an Indian for his bride.

The next morning, the Niceville group was up early, watching in amazement as crowded trains came in from three directions and streams of passengers exited, leaving the trains virtually empty once they left the Crestview station. Man-made footpaths, trails, and sand roads guided droves of people, arriving like armies of ants heading for a picnic. Those who came by wagon or horseback had to leave their belongings beyond the railroad track on the south side of the courthouse as the nearest livery stable was in Baker, several miles west.

Neither exhaustion nor insect maulings quelled the excitement of these local country folks and visiting city folks. Children jumped up and down either from sheer joy of going somewhere or from the pain inflicted by sharp-needled dog flies, long-legged mosquitoes, and stealthy yellow flies. Mamas stayed busy treating the wounds made by the blood-hungry intruders.

Ecil and Odell paid the sheriff an early visit while David opted to join his father and a few friends in a roped-off section near the hanging platform. He promised to mark off an area close by where the women could spread their blanket and wait for the main event, hopefully in the shade.

Making their way across the grassless common area proved to be quite a challenge for the three women. As they pushed their way through, a young boy struggled with a gallon bucket of water and a big dipper. When he bumped into Rhoda, much of his merchandise was spilled onto the ground as well as onto Rhoda's ankle-length skirt tail and laced-up shoes. The red-faced boy apologized profusely and offered her a dipper of water for free.

"Free?" she screeched. "Why, water is always … You mean you're selling water?"

"Don't knock it," said Connie. "With this heat, he may get rich and retire this very day."

The boy grinned appreciatively and kept moving in search of someone thirsty enough to pay for a drink of water.

"Let's hurry!" insisted Connie. "The way this crowd is pushing and shoving, somebody might fight David over that shady spot he promised to save."

They finally connected with David, who had spread a quilt in a nice shady area not far from where dignitaries, speakers, and eventually Klinger would appear, assuming the crowds didn't get too unruly. Only one thing was missing. It was Casey.

"She's shooting marbles!" David explained, shaking his head playfully. He was still trying to become accustomed to his little girl's choosing marbles over hopscotch or similar games considered feminine. "But she's all right. She's playing with some of the Niceville kids, and Dad and I can see her from where we've settled." With that, he left the women to their chatter.

The threesome treasured the opportunity. They regularly spent time together but mostly at home, rarely on "foreign" soil where they found themselves poised to witness something none of them had ever seen before. In spite of the goings-on around her, Rhoda couldn't free her mind of Jolene Holder, her disgruntled daddy, and her toothache. Concerns for the hapless child and her equally hapless mother had taken precedence over other thoughts throughout the sleepless night. She had longed anxiously for this moment, an opportunity to discuss the episode with Mary Sam.

Mary Sam had been toughened by the assaults she had suffered all of her life because of her Indian heritage. She was born in Eucheeanna, an Indian reservation just east of Niceville. There had been a time when being a relative of Chief Sam Gushingwater would get you places, but that time had passed long before Mary Sam was born. Chief Gushingwater was once known for welcoming desperate white families to Eucheeanna, where the chief and his people had settled. But it wasn't long after his death that the Florida Legislature banned Indians from the state!

Named for her famous relative, Mary Sam had escaped the ban by virtue of her mother, a full-blooded Indian princess who married a Norwegian immigrant who had come to the area seeking work. By the time Mary Sam was born, most white settlers at Eucheeanna had forgotten, or chose not to remember, that Chief Sam Gushingwater had paved the way for them and other white settlers in the county. Mary Sam had lived with rejection, but she had never learned to tolerate it, at least not gracefully. Both Rhoda and Connie envied her for her courage to speak up and defend herself when necessary, and that was often.

Mary Sam immediately became interested in her friends' story about John Holder as well as Gussie Genepri and his unusual package. "I know the boy's father," she said, shocking Connie and Rhoda, who moved closer so as not to miss a word. As well as they knew their mysterious and often secretive friend, they were never quite prepared for her astonishing revelations, and they assuredly never lost interest in them.

"Oh, it's nothing!" Mary Sam assured them. "I was hunting in Bolton, and I saw that little shack out there in the boonies. I assumed it was John's place. You realize I'm not always in the mainstream like you girls are. If David knew about this elderly gentleman living out there, he didn't tell me. And you guys never mentioned it either," she complained slightly. "Well, I was hunting out there one day when I saw a buck feeding, and I had him in my sight when a human head blocked my view. I figured it was John Holder, so I decided to pull the trigger."

"No!" screeched both women, their hands over their mouths.

"Oh, get a hold," Mary Sam fussed. "Didn't plan to hit 'im. Just wanted to scare him to death. Before I could do that, the wind blew the man's hat off, revealing a bald head! I knew immediately it wasn't hairy-aped John!" The story prompted Rhoda and Connie to giggle like teenagers, their hands still cupped over their mouths.

"Ah!" gasped Rhoda. "You don't know what we've been through on this trip." She made a quick search of their immediate surroundings to make certain no one was listening. "Gussie claims John Holder murdered his dad."

The news was obviously a blow to Mary Sam. Her voice was strained as were her features, revealing an internal pressure fighting to be released. She was already tense, and the news of John Holder—a brutal, intimidating man—preying on helpless people infuriated her. "John must be laughing in his boots. And he knows nothing will be done about it," she said, gritting her teeth.

"Oh, forget it," insisted Connie. "Young Gussie disappeared into the woods at Florosa without a word to anyone. Why should we believe anything he said? Maybe he killed his dad himself and was trying to blame John. We don't know!" She had learned early in their school days not to raise Mary Sam's ire, and she was still mulling over her friend's spiritless announcement that she "*had to*" attend the hanging. *What was that about?* she ached to know.

"The whole thing is suspicious," said Rhoda. "We don't even know for sure that young Gussie is Mr. Genepri's son. If he loved his father so much and knew his whereabouts, why did he wait until he was dead to come here?"

"I agree," said Connie. "Well, we know Odell always figured that Old Gus was hiding from the law. Why else would an old man live out there in that marshy wilderness with all those snakes and alligators and … John Holder!"

The girls enjoyed a quick laugh before Mary Sam suggested in earnest that Old Gus didn't fit the mold for a criminal. "He could have been framed, and I wouldn't be shocked if John was the culprit who framed him. Makes you wonder if the old man and John knew each other before they came here." Such a notion shocked her listeners.

The women's private conversation was interrupted by old friends from Baker, and the Niceville threesome was pulled into an unwilling discussion of the still-unfinished gallows. "It's gonna separate Willie Earl Klinger's neck from the rest of his body," one man put it.

"They've hammered and sawed all night," complained Rhoda. "I doubt anybody got any sleep. I know I didn't. I'm beginning to agree with the newspaper writers in Miami: we really are barbarians up here in the Panhandle."

When the Baker group moved on, the Niceville women became silent, each with her own thoughts, at least until Casey came screaming through the crowd, her arms outstretched in pursuit of her mother. "Mama! Mama!" she screamed.

David, having witnessed his daughter's sudden exit from a marble game, struggled to work his way through the crowd. "Casey! What's wrong?" he yelled out, but Casey couldn't hear him above her own screams and the noise of the crowd.

"She stole my marbles!" shouted a young boy who had chased Casey into her mother's arms. He then stood before them with an ugly scowl on his face.

"Casey?" David asked his terrorized daughter.

"No, Daddy!" she screamed. "I won the marbles, Daddy. Honest I did. He called me names!"

"What kind of names?" David asked. While Mary Sam comforted her daughter, David grasped the boy by the shoulder. "Tell me about the marbles and about the name calling."

The boy, finding himself surrounded by grown-ups, none of whom appeared to be on his side, tried to wiggle free of David's grasp. He was especially mindful of Mary Sam's stern demeanor when she entered the fray. "What did he call you, baby?" she asked.

"Half a breed!" screamed Casey.

"Half-breed, stupid!" the boy corrected with a laugh. With that, he attempted to run, but David tightened his grip. "Wait until we settle this," he told the child without threatening him.

Mary Sam grabbed her sobbing daughter, who wrapped her arms and legs around her mother in a fierce grasp. "Where did you get these marbles, honey?" she asked.

"Clete gave them to me," she squealed, pointing a finger at the boy. "He wanted me to play marbles with him, but I had no marbles.

He gave me some so I could play with him," she explained between sobs. "He said I could keep them if I won the game. And I did win—honest, Mama," she cried.

It was a believable story for a mother who had taught her daughter the game and watched as her five-year-old became known for her expertise in the game. "Even so, honey, you shouldn't keep them. Calling you a half-breed is quite another issue," she added angrily. She held the marbles in front of the boy but closed her hands when he tried to take them.

"I'm gonna tell my daddy," the boy threatened.

"You do that. And while you're at it, tell him how a little girl beat you at your own game," said Mary Sam as she dropped the marbles one by one in his hand. He closed his hands tightly over the marbles and ran like a wild boar.

"Don't worry, honey," she told Casey. "He lost his pride. No male, no matter how young, can bear for a female to beat him at anything considered a man's game. Believe me—it'll hurt a lot more than losing his marbles."

With the boy gone, Rhoda tried to calm everyone. "We can't blame the boy. Kids only know what their parents teach them. That poor kid is paying the price for his parents' ignorance."

"Who is that kid?" asked David.

"One of the Cogbill clan," said Rhoda, rolling her eyes in disgust.

"You mean Homer Cogbill?" he scoffed. Her affirmative nod caused David's eyes to flash with anger. "That damn thief?" he swore under his breath. "Of course!" he raved. "A thief is still better than a little girl with Indian blood in her, right?" he raved.

When Casey finally caught sight of Rhoda, she threw her arms around her legs, the only part of her body she could reach. "What's half a breed, Aunt Rhoda?" she begged to know.

"Well, since you're the sweetest thing I know, it must have

something to do with sugar," Rhoda told her. She forced a smile in spite of feeling the child's pain.

Socially, it had been somewhat to Mary Sam's advantage that she bore more physical likeness to her Scandinavian father than to her mother, an Indian princess. Such was not the case with black-haired, black-eyed, dark-skinned Casey. Mary Sam worried constantly for her little daughter, who would likely suffer even more than she had among self-appointed, white-skinned superiors, and it frightened her immensely.

David was still seething over the Cogbill boy's comment. "'Half-breed!" he mocked over and over. Although Mary Sam and Casey often suffered racial slurs and rejection, it was rare for David. Since he and his father's businesses had created jobs for much of the population, not only in Niceville but throughout Okaloosa County and beyond, he had mostly been spared, at least face to face.

To comfort the child and hopefully take her mind from the episode, Connie told her about the gift she had bought. "When I saw it at the Florosa Hotel, I knew it was meant for you."

"What is it?" asked Casey, jumping up and down and clapping her hands. "Mama, Mama, I think Aunt Connie brought me some paper dolls!" she squealed. It was a favorite of hers, and everyone close to her knew it. She always assigned family names to her dolls and carried on conversations with all of them, even producing three- and four-character dramas now and then. Mary Sam sometimes worried that she would become so enamored with her fictional characters that she wouldn't be able to distinguish between fact and fiction, but friends had scoffed at such a notion.

"Well, I think you're wrong. I think your Aunt Connie brought you a new dress," David teased.

Casey studied her father's face. "I already have a dress," she grumbled.

Realizing a new dress was not a high priority for Casey, David acquiesced. "Well, I'm certain Aunt Connie chose something very special and you'll love it."

Casey wanted to pursue the conversation in hopes of learning the gift's identity, but a sudden loud shout directed everyone's attention to an area near the scaffold.

"Look! It's Willie Earl!" screeched an old man whose voice had nearly abandoned him just when he finally had something to yell about. The eerie sound that erupted from his aging throat was enough to corral the crowd, reducing them to whispers and a few muffled gasps. By the time an official appeared on the platform, the atmosphere was soundless except for a bit of squirrel chatter and the occasional buzz of a horsefly. Even unhappy babies seemed to sense the need for quiet as there was not a whimper in the bunch.

A much-thinner-than-usual Willie Earl Klinger stood on the platform talking to the officials and occasionally waving to the screaming crowd. "Anyone who wishes to speak with Mr. Klinger or shake his hand should line up at the courthouse entrance," the official announced.

"Oh my God. Who would want to do that?" asked Connie, and Rhoda quickly agreed. In a moment, however, a few men began lining up, and within minutes the line circled the courthouse. Ecil and Odell were among them. David was not. He had joined his father again, leaving the women alone. As soon as he was out of sight, Mary Sam made an announcement. "I'm going to shake hands with Klinger."

"Sure you are!" mocked Connie, who thought it a joke. But that was before she saw the thrust in Mary Sam's jaw. She had seen it many times before, and she knew what it meant: Mary Sam was going to shake hands with the killer!

Rhoda hadn't grown up with Mary Sam like Connie had, but she had become accustomed to her determination. Once Mary Sam made up her mind, it didn't matter much what anyone else thought. "We'll keep an eye on Casey," she said without further discussion.

"Casey's going with me," said Mary Sam as she reached for her daughter's hand. Standing straighter than usual, she tossed her head back and tugged on her daughter's reluctant arm.

"I want to stay with Aunt Connie!" the child pleaded.

"Shouldn't David go with you?" asked Connie, who hadn't come to terms with the notion of a woman and a small child greeting a convicted criminal. It was unheard of, and it would be condemned by basically everyone.

"No! Just Casey," said Mary Sam, giving her daughter's arm a jerk. The two headed for the end of the long line. Again, Casey begged to stay with Connie and Rhoda, but her plea was denied.

Mary Sam moved as swiftly as she could through the crowd, wiping sweat from her brow with a once-white handkerchief, now stained with sweat. When a young boy offered to sell her a hand-made paper fan, she gladly paid him the penny he required and then continued toward the long line of men waiting to speak to Klinger.

"I have to pee-pee," Casey declared, but her mother was convinced that she was using every ploy she could think of to avoid taking part in her mother's mission.

"Not now, honey. We need to pay our respects to Mr. Klinger because he's going to die." She spoke firmly, and Casey realized her pleas were useless.

Mary Sam's presence in the line caused an immediate stir among the women and no small number of men. Some remarks were purposely loud enough for her to hear, and one in particular stung a little: "They ought to hang that damn Indian too!"

Mary Sam came to realize that she was demanding more attention than the convicted killer. Casey was unaware that the insults and innuendos were directed at her mother, especially as Mary

Sam talked incessantly to her about whatever came to her mind, an effort to drown everyone else out.

Meanwhile, Mary Sam's determination never faltered. She did worry the crowd might become abusive and that Casey might get hurt. In response to those fears, she tightened her grip on the child's sweaty hand. As they neared the entrance to the courthouse, antsy folks began pushing forward, trying to catch a glimpse of the condemned man. When Mary Sam got her first glimpse of Willie Earl and the people who hovered around him, she stood still for a fleeting moment. "My God, you'd think he was a soldier who just returned from winning the war single-handedly," she mumbled to herself. Perspiration began to bead on her forehead and quickly spread over her entire body, leaving her moist and sticky. Casey fidgeted and complained about being thirsty and hot. With everyone in line much taller than her, she was denied the slightest breath of fresh air. Desperate, and in spite of her mother's admonitions, she pulled her ruffled bonnet off and crumpled it in her hand.

With only three men separating her from Klinger, Mary Sam's grip on Casey was so intense that the child let go with a scream before jerking her hand loose and wiping it on her new dress. The new stains would scarcely be noticed, however, as they were intermingled with those from the marble game in the dirt.

Klinger appeared miserable in a stiffly starched, high-collared white shirt and black Sunday suit. An equally stiff white handkerchief had been folded neatly and left partially exposed in his jacket pocket. Apparently, he had given his attire the attention usually set aside for a funeral. This time it was his own.

His tall frame rose high above the security men who stood on either side of him. His shining black hair lay in deep waves on top and hugged the sides of his head before forming well-shaped sideburns. He had been blessed with good looks.

He was noticeably startled when he spotted a woman in the line and only inches away. Scarcely acknowledging the man who was in the process of greeting him, the condemned man's exhausted demeanor suddenly came to life. He stood up and eagerly reached for Mary Sam's hand, cupping it in both of his.

"I'm Mary Sam Stewart, and this is my daughter, Casey," she said.

After thanking her profusely for coming, he sat down again so he could acknowledge Casey, who twisted from one side to the other, obviously bored by the whole thing. Mary Sam suddenly worried that she really did have to pee.

"Casey?" Klinger asked. "What a perfect name for a pretty girl like you."

Casey was delighted by the attention as noted by her giggle.

"My, my, look at all those curls," bragged the condemned man. "You must have dipped your head in a bucket of shiny black paint with sparkling glitter mixed up in it," he teased, a comment that sent Casey into a titter.

"And what a pair of eyes!" Klinger continued. "Black diamonds!" He fought an urge to pick her up, finally deciding against it. His shackles had been removed for the occasion, but scars from having been handcuffed so often were noticeably ugly and might frighten the child, he thought. Still, he yearned to make some kind of physical contact with her. "Would you shake hands with me, Miss Casey?" he asked.

"Yes, sir," she said, eagerly thrusting her left hand toward his.

"No, honey. Use your right hand," her mother reminded her.

"No, no, no," insisted Klinger. "I'm left-handed too." He quickly extended his left hand and shook hers gently. Casey was delighted. Most everyone else growled at her when she tried to do anything with her left hand. They didn't seem to care that she felt awkward and uncomfortable when she used her right hand. She took an immediate liking to the man everyone seemed intent upon hanging.

"My mama said you were going to live with Jesus, Mr. Klinger," she said with total innocence.

Mary Sam attempted to shush her, but Klinger encouraged the child. "You bet I am, and I want you to be a good girl so you'll go there too some day. You know what? I'll bet Jesus is left-handed too."

Casey's big, black, deep-set eyes danced with pleasure.

The men next in line began to grumble. When one man at the end of the line yelled, "Who let the Indian Squaw in?" Mary Sam buckled inside but held her temper. Rather than make life more difficult for the condemned man, she shook Klinger's hand and said good-bye.

As Mary Sam and Casey made their exit through the back of the building, chants and yells from the jail competed with noises from the crowd. The disturbance from the jailhouse had been initiated by Niceville's Bedlam brothers, who had become aware of the notion that they might miss the hanging, their sole purpose in coming. They began to beat on the walls and barred windows, seeking freedom. Communicating with folks through one of those windows, they promised free moonshine to anyone who would help release them. With that in mind, one man had backed his mule wagon up to the jail, threw a rope to the prisoners to tie around the iron bars, and then gave the mule a whack on his hind side. The mule, however, wanted no part of the scheme. He reared up on his hind legs and gave the whine of a very frightened and irritated animal.

One of the sheriff's deputies had been summoned and had quickly put a stop to the scheme. Inside the jail cell, the Bedlams had begun to discuss their dilemma when Lucifer suddenly landed a hard right fist into Billy Bob's unsuspecting stomach. The blow sent his brother to his knees, prompting Lum to throw a hard right into Lucifer's cheek, a blow that separated a good portion of his cheek from the rest of his face. Instead of continuing the fight as was his usual move, Lucifer screamed with delight.

"Get the deputy in here!" he ordered. "He'll have to take us to the hospital to get sewed up, and then we'll be free to see the hanging!" he railed. With all in agreement, Billy Bob landed a fist in Lum's mouth, a blow that broke the last front tooth he had. Lum understood. Without a problem of his own that needed attention, the officials might leave him behind.

Unfortunately, the boys' plans fell through. Within a few minutes, a grumbling Dr. Phillip Azore, the only doctor in Crestview and surroundings, arrived at the jail. A quick glance at the bleeding threesome aroused the doctor's ire. "My God! If you intend to kill each other, I wish to hell you'd go back to Niceville to do it. I've got sick people all over the county waiting to see me."

"Aw, hell, Doc, we'uns was just foolin around," moaned Lum. "Didn't mean no harm a tall."

"Hey, Doc, get us out of here. We won't cause no more trouble," Lucifer promised. He gestured with his hands, forgetting for a moment that one hand had been holding parts of his face together. Blood poured down his face and onto his shirt before he could grab his facial part again. "Guess you'll have to take me to the hospital, won't you, Doc?" asked a hopeful man.

"Hell, no," said Dr. Azore. "The hospital's full of sick people. You ain't sick. You're just stupid."

The boys were stunned. "How would you like it if you come a long way and couldn't see the hanging, Doc?" Billy Bob asked poignantly.

"Well, now, that's an easy question. I wouldn't come a long way to see a man hang. I try to save lives, not take them. Now you lie still if you don't want a crooked nose on your face. I'm gonna sew you up, and it's gonna hurt like hell." He pulled out a surgical needle that appeared big enough to sew up a wounded rhinoceros, threaded it with a coarse-looking twine he might have salvaged from a kite outing, and began to attach Lucifer's cheek to his face.

To the doctor's amazement, Lucifer made no sound, not even a whimper.

"Okay, so you're tough," Dr. Azore ridiculed. "I'm not impressed. Smart beats the hell out of tough. Look at your faces—all scarred from knife wounds and knuckle sandwiches." He noticed that their arms were just as scarred. He shook his head in disgust and left the room without another word.

The boys began to realize for the first time that they truly might not see the hanging. After the doctor left, they sulked in their corners, reluctantly accepting their fate.

Once outside, Dr. Azore took a moment to survey the crowd before heading for his horse and buggy. He again shook his head in disgust. The tall, square-shouldered, straight-backed man with his ever-present ten-gallon hat reaching for the sky made a striking figure as he stood on the courthouse steps.

When Josh Tarrow and his friends spotted Dr. Azore, they quickly sought his company. The doctor was popular as a healing physician, a position he filled without ceremony and little pay, and as an entertainer, which he accomplished without effort, forethought, or desire for recognition. Ecil had heard many fascinating stories about Dr. Azore but had never had an opportunity to see him in action as the good doctor rarely had the leisure to tackle a difficult trip to Niceville. Ecil's interest was piqued.

"Where are you off to, Doc? Ain't you gonna pronounce the prisoner dead?" teased Odell, who vigorously shook the doctor's hand in warm friendship.

"I've no part in this drama," Dr. Azore said in a belittling tone. "Just sewed up your Bedlam boys. Take all three of them home when you leave," he begged. "I've never seen a family get such pleasure from mauling each other. I should have told them to go to hell. On second thought, maybe I did. I should be halfway to Ovid Switzer's house by now. Mamie Ruth's having another baby. Poor woman," he sympathized. "It'll be her ninth if you don't count the three stillborns." Large families were the norm, and who knew better than Dr. Azore? Still, he seemed unusually troubled by this one.

"What about the old darkie?" asked Tarrow. Reference was to a black woman who worked for the Switzers and that included baby sitting, cooking, cleaning, and working in the fields. That was not to mention satisfying Ovid's sexual needs when Mamie Ruth was disabled.

"It's a little more than Marge can handle now. Mamie Ruth's been in poor health for years. No business having any more babies," Dr. Azore grumbled. The doctor had warned Ovid again and again that another pregnancy might take his wife's life. He had stopped short of suggesting that the farmer abstain from having sex, but he often hinted to Ovid that he could prevent a dangerous pregnancy by withdrawing just prior to reaching a climax. Ovid had obviously ignored the doctor's advice.

"Man, you've got a good ten-mile trip ahead of you," Odell commiserated.

"And a dangerous one," added Tarrow.

"Dangerous?" scoffed Odell.

"You betcha," chuckled Tarrow. "Remember the time Bessie, his old faithful mare, had to retrieve Doc's gun for him?"

Odell begged to hear the story. The three were totally caught up in their own little world, oblivious to the hanging for the moment.

Tarrow was always glad to meet someone who hadn't heard his story. "Well, Doc rode Bessie out to the old Simpson place, you know, delivered their baby, and started back home. On the way, he went to sleep, fell off his horse, and busted his head open. While he lay unconscious on the ground, the spry old mare took Doc's gun and shot a black bear."

"True, Doc?" asked Odell playfully.

"Left a little out and added a lot," declared Dr. Azore, giving everyone in hearing distance a hearty laugh. "Fell off old Bessie, all right, hit my head, and lost consciousness. When I regained my senses, Bessie was on her hind legs, pawing the air with her front legs, and whinnying like hell. Not far away was the biggest, hungriest black bear I've ever seen, just itching to eat the food I had in my croker sack, and he didn't care who he had to kill to get it. I reached for my gun, but the holster was empty. I didn't know how I got there or what had happened to my gun. I thought somebody had knocked me out and stole my gun and my hat."

The men careened with laughter. It was well known that Dr. Azore never removed his ten-gallon hat, not even in the operating room. It had become a joke among his friends and patients that he slept in the high-top monstrosity.

Dr. Azore was unabashed. "To get my attention, Bessie bumped me with her head and then spit my hat out of her mouth. She had picked it up somewhere on the ground, and when she did, she uncovered my .45. I grabbed that gun and shot it in the air, and that bear flashed his fast-moving backside in our direction."

Between peals of laughter, Odell remarked how happy he was that Dr. Azore planned to travel by buggy this time.

The buggy was necessary for another reason. Like most farmers, Ovid Switzer had no money with which to pay the doctor, but Dr. Azore knew he would be the recipient of a buggy full of cured meat and fresh canned vegetable. Best of all, he would likely receive a few bottles of moonshine, but he wouldn't arrive home with any of that.

Their little group attracted quite a gathering of men as Dr. Azore was well known and warmly received not only for his good works but for his antics.

"I'm out of here. You guys have had enough fun at my expense. Say, where is my damn buggy?" he asked after bidding everyone adieu. The crowd had grown so big during the doctor's jailhouse duties that Bessie and the buggy were no longer visible.

"Would you look at that?" yelled the doctor. "That fella's trying to sell a piece of rope. Claims it's a piece of the hanging rope! What a mess," he sighed. "Well, here comes the preacher. I guess he'll preach Klinger's funeral before and after he dies." He straightened his gun belt, cocked his hat to the side, and headed for Bessie and the buggy.

After the preacher delivered a lengthy fire-and-brimstone message, Klinger struggled to walk a few steps to the podium with his hands cuffed and his ankles chained. Armed guards stood on either side of him, circled the scaffold, stood watch inside the train depot, and jammed the courthouse interior. Others were stationed on top of the courthouse, the jail, and the Rice Building, the only other building in town except for Dr. Azore's private hospital across the highway. Most of the guards wore plain clothes, and since nearly every man present carried a gun, it was difficult to determine who was a guard and who wasn't. The sheriff had mulled over the idea of confiscating all guns except for those of the designated guards, but he decided it would cause more trouble than it would prevent. Gun toters considered their weapons to be part of their attire and were no more amenable to removing them than they would have been to removing their undershorts.

It was during the lengthy sermon that Mary Sam and Casey returned to David.

"What in God's name came over you!" David lashed out in anger.

"Daddy, Mr. Klinger said Jesus is left-handed just like me," squealed his excited little daughter.

David's temper was ignited. "Oh, I see. Mr. Klinger is our role model now," he ridiculed.

It was the angriest Mary Sam had ever seen her usually calm husband. Would he ever forgive her? she wondered. Still, she *had* to do it.

"You have obviously lost your senses," continued David, his anger rising with the speed of a sick baby's temperature. Too distressed to continue, and with friends standing by, he walked away, filled with anguish.

Connie had always admired Mary Sam for her courage, but there were times when she was puzzled by her actions. This was one of those times. Connie and Mary Sam had been roommates at Marshall College in Wanata Springs, Florida, an institution known for its advanced programs. The women's resumes would have landed them an upscale job anywhere, perhaps with the exception of Niceville, where upscale jobs didn't exist. Both were rebels by early twentieth century's strict standards for women and, as such, had filled a longing in each other to escape the ordinary. After marrying local men, both found life in Niceville as ordinary as it gets. Even so, they were grateful for each other and for their mutual friend, Rhoda, something of a mother figure to both of them.

Odell and Ecil stood side by side, arms folded, silently trying to understand what had happened. To Rhoda's dismay, tears began to wet her cheeks. The episode with John and young Gussie, and now the hanging, had taken their toll. For her, Jolene's dilemma had taken precedence over everything else. She longed to discuss it with Connie and Mary Sam at length, but there had been little or no opportunity. When the reality of the moment set in, she became aware of Mary Sam's absence.

"Where's Sam?" she asked Connie. "And Casey?" Neither Mary Sam nor Casey was anywhere in sight. Rhoda and Connie studied each other's faces but found no answers. They looked to their husbands for reassurance but received none. Both men began to conduct a search within the crowd, each going a different route, but neither one caught sight of Mary Sam or her little one.

Connie tried to minimize the situation. "Maybe Casey had to go to the woods," she offered.

They laughed with thin, suppressed noises. Their friend's actions had stumped them all. Before they could find her, Klinger was given an opportunity to speak to the crowd, but he had declined. A morbid silence followed.

Families huddled together, and many who had struggled to get as close to the action as possible began to move back. Nobody seemed to be quite comfortable with their positions, and even the mockers remained quiet when the hangman tied a scarf around the convicted killer's neck. When Sheriff Hagood pulled the black handmade hood over Klinger's head and face, it was enough to quiet the drunkest man in the crowd, send schoolchildren hiding their faces in their mother's skirts, and induce others to faint or at least swoon respectfully. Within seconds, a loud, unusual noise pierced the ears of the gathered throng. The trap door had opened, and Klinger fell beneath the black curtain underneath the scaffold. Young boys who had rushed to the scaffold earlier screamed in horror at the sight of Klinger's bludgeoned throat. South Florida newsmen jumped at the chance to capture children's horrified reactions on film, shots they would use as proof that Panhandlers sacrificed their children's well-being in order to witness a man hang and were, indeed, barbarians. Frightened as much by newsmen's bright, intermittent flashes as by the bloody corpse itself, the children were captured on film running in all directions, desperately searching for their mamas and papas. It was something most Panhandlers had looked forward to but that many learned they did not enjoy.

While Connie struggled to breathe, Rhoda vomited everything she had ingested during the day. The grounds everywhere were mushy with vomit. Men loosened their ties and shirts in an effort to catch a fresh breath, while others turned their backs to the scene and planted their eyes on the ground to hide their tears. Babies cried as did young children, many of whom continued to hide their faces in their mama's skirts.

And Mary Sam was still missing.

The moment the hangman had appeared on the scene with the black hood, she had led Casey to the first wagon she came to, away from the crowd and the sight of the scaffold. The two played hop-scotch in the sand until Casey tired and eventually fell asleep in her mother's arms. Mary Sam fanned the flies off her sleeping daughter, and she wept.

Chapter 6

ON THEIR WAY HOME, CASEY ENTERTAINED HERSELF with her new paper dolls. After naming each doll, she created a lively drama among them, changing her voice for each make-believe character. The real people in the wagon, however, remained taciturn.

David had been unable to overcome the shock and embarrassment dealt him by his wife's actions. When he did speak, he directed his comments to Odell or Ecil, precluding any conversation with Mary Sam.

David had been drawn to Mary Sam in the beginning because of her fighting spirit and her indomitable courage, especially when her Indian heritage, or that of Casey, was attacked. He admired her ability to ignore society's strict, unspoken rules regarding women, especially Indian women. But this time, it was different. She had clearly gone too far. The whole episode reminded him of all the public warnings tossed his way about "that Indian squaw" he married. He didn't accept their opinions then, and he wasn't ready to do so now, but he was concerned. In the beginning, he had imagined that people would gradually realize, as he had, what Mary Sam's intellect and energy could offer the community. They had allowed her to teach their children but only when no one else was available. Except for Rhoda and Odell, and Connie and Ecil, she was not considered an equal to anyone except another Indian. *Is Indian blood too wild to domesticate after all?* David wondered.

While most of the crowd lingered within the town limits, Mary Sam's shocking actions had guaranteed there would be no fun-filled trip home for the Stewarts or their friends. David was in no mood for conversation. His wagon had been at the scene and ready to board while most attendees lingered outside the city limits, discussing the events of the last few weeks. Camping with the others by the river or other streams no longer interested him. And he made it clear he planned to go all the way home.

When Odell protested lightly, David explained, "Be serious, Odell. Can you imagine what the topic of conversation will be?"

Odell acquiesced.

As they plodded along the white sandy road, David festered. In spite of his misery, he broke into a smile when he heard Casey's make-believe conversation between well-known people in the area, names she had assigned to her new paper dolls. His smile withered, however, when she introduced Willie Earl Klinger, a newcomer to her usual clan, into her drama.

"No, honey. Mr. Klinger is dead," Mary Sam reminded her.

"I'm just pretending. Why did they hang him, Mama? He was such a nice man," she said.

A few tense moments followed, and Rhoda sought to ease the strained atmosphere. "Maybe you should put your dolls away now, honey. The road is getting bumpier, and if we hit a big root, your little paper folks might go flying all over the place."

"Yes, and it should be getting dark soon, honey," said Casey's relieved mother The women helped the child gather the dolls and their attire and watched with interest as she placed them neatly and securely in a box that had been emptied for that very purpose. Once done, the women moved to the back of the wagon, their feet dangling in a carefree fashion. In an effort to erase the hanging scene and Mr. Klinger from everyone's mind, they began to focus on Jolene Holder's plight. While planning a strategy for helping Jolene escape her mean-spirited father's demands, the wagon suddenly ran off the trail. When David tried to lead the horses back onto it, they danced around, tried backing up, and generally refused to go where their master directed them.

The mystery was soon solved. Piercing the quiet ahead of them was Dr. Azore in his dusty black carriage. Jugs filled with moonshine bumped against each other in spite of fresh vegetables and fruit having been stuffed between them. There was a croker sack full of sweet potatoes and another filled with peanuts jammed up against the driver's feet. In the seat beside Dr. Azore was a jug of moonshine that had been generously tapped into.

"Hello there!" said the good doctor with something of a slur. "You folks musta got a mighty late start. Did you have trouble getting the man hung?"

With an atmosphere of gloom still hanging over the Niceville group, they welcomed an opportunity to communicate with an outsider. They laughed in unison at the doctor's comment before questioning him.

"How's Mamie Ruth and the new baby?" asked Rhoda.

"Boy or girl?" added Connie.

"She must have delivered right away," noted Mary Sam.

They could see that Dr. Azore's eyes were cloudy, his eyelids puffy, and his face drained of color, but his audience attributed part of it to the long, difficult trip, lack of sleep, and perhaps too much drink. "Mamie Ruth was dead when I arrived," was the doctor's solemn reply.

The news prompted grunts and groans from the adults and sent Casey scrambling to reach her mother's waiting arms. "Will Miss Mamie Ruth live with Jesus and Mr. Klinger, Mama?" she whispered. Mary Sam lay her cheek on Casey's head in a comforting gesture before shushing her.

"Oh my! What about the baby?" asked Rhoda.

"Baby's okay. Got old Marge nursing it," Dr. Azore revealed. Mamie Ruth wasn't the first patient Dr. Azore had lost in childbirth, but her death would haunt him more than most because he knew beforehand that the pregnancy should have been prevented. Tending to a woman's chores on a farm while rearing eight children was, in itself, too much for the poor woman. "She survived longer than I expected," Dr. Azore admitted with a hint of anger.

"What about a funeral?" asked Mary Sam.

"Already buried," said the glum doctor.

"Poor Ovid," moaned Rhoda. "Whatever will he do with all those children and no mother? We'll go pay our respects."

The notion pleased Dr. Azore. "That's good," he said as he bopped Bessie on the behind and gave the group a slurred good-bye.

"Doc's taking it hard," noted Odell. He agreed with his wife that they should drop by the Switzer place. When they reached the cut-off leading to the Switzer house, David pulled on the reins but made no effort to direct the horses toward the Switzer farm.

"What's wrong?" asked Odell. But then he remembered. "Aw, don't worry about that," he insisted. "Ovid's forgot about that I'm sure. He'll be awful glad to see anybody right now."

David made no response.

Meanwhile, Rhoda had embraced Mary Sam. "Honey, we have to go," she whispered. "We couldn't live with our consciences if we didn't see about the baby and all those little ones and ..." She trailed off in tears.

"You don't understand," said Mary Sam, who stiffened noticeably in Rhoda's embrace. A lengthy silence ensued before David finally, and reluctantly, directed the horses toward the Switzer house. Meanwhile, Casey had begun to whimper. She felt the tension between her parents as well as that of their best friends, and it frightened her.

Ovid Switzer had been one of many fathers who had single white daughters when David Stewart, a rich bachelor, came to Okaloosa County. But no one had considered Ovid a likely contender for the prize because his eligible daughter was only twelve years old!

But in Ovid's mind, Ora May was approaching old maid status, and he was not about to let this opportunity pass. He had brazenly appeared at the sprawling Stewart waterfront home for the distinct purpose of introducing Ora May Switzer to the Stewart family. Having done so, he departed the Stewart mansion confident that David would be calling on Ora May and asking for her hand in marriage. When David chose Mary Sam for his bride, Ovid took it as a personal insult. Unlike most fathers of single daughters in the county, Ovid didn't depend on David Stewart or his father for his livelihood, so he was freer to release his anger every chance he got. And he always had!

Mary Sam and David had kept their distance from this angry man who was noted for his hatred for the red man, black folks, as well as a host of white folks who didn't cotton to his way of thinking. That was nearly everyone.

When the Switzer house came into view, David brought the wagon to a complete halt. Turning to face his wife for the first time since they left the courthouse grounds, he suggested that she and Casey could wait in the wagon.

When Mary Sam gave no immediate response, Rhoda spoke up. "No, honey. It's a great opportunity to show Ovid Switzer how sweet you are. Ah," she rallied, "when he sees you coddling his motherless baby the way I know you will ..."

Reluctantly, David signaled the horses to continue on the route to the Switzer home. Almost immediately, the trail narrowed, tree roots multiplied, and holes deepened, making travel slow and very uncomfortable. When they finally pulled into the Switzers' yard, children of both sexes, two colors, and several sizes peeked around the corners of the house, gathered on the front porch, or stood in the doorway, gawking. Several breeds of dogs barked incessantly, and just as many cats shimmied up nearby trees or scrambled under the porch. Chickens squawked and flapped their wings in an effort to vacate the premises, and fattened hogs grunted with curiosity and let loose with lengthy, ear-piercing squeals when the dogs chased them out of the yard.

When a young girl came racing around the corner with a basket of eggs, she ran into an equally excited sibling carrying a gallon bucket of hog slop. When they collided, both girls found themselves covered in a repulsive mix resembling vomit. When a boy of five or so set his gallon bucket of water on the ground, his older brother stumbled over it and fell broadside, emptying its contents on the ground. The boys scuffled for a moment, each blaming the other before they realized they were missing what they had come to see. Once they all reached their destination in the yard, they took their chosen positions, stood still, and stared at the visitors.

A black woman nursing a black baby on one teat and a newborn white baby on the other appeared in the doorway. Seeing the wagonload of people, she jerked her teats from the babies' mouths and covered her breasts with a ragged dishcloth. In a moment, Ovid came wobbling from around the back, spat an ugly stream of brown snuff juice on the ground, pulled at faded overalls held up by twisted galluses, and tugged on the bib that barely covered his exploding stomach.

With their source of nutrition taken away, both babies began to cry, prompting Ovid to yell for the black woman he called Marge to "quiet them younguns down," whereupon she quickly stepped out of sight. As expected, the babies cried no more.

Ovid instructed one of the older boys to water Odell's horses even though he surely knew the fashionable wagon and team belonged to David. When Rhoda and Connie began to exit the wagon, Ovid tipped his hat and made a point of assisting them, and then he walked away, leaving Mary Sam to make the descent the best way she could. "You folks come on in," he said. "The old nigger'll have supper ready in a little while."

They all offered condolences to Ovid and the children nearest them for their loss. "Can I show them Mama's grave, Papa?" asked one of the older girls. It was exactly what the women had in mind, especially as total darkness was imminent. When Ovid gave his consent, the men remained with Ovid while the older girl took Rhoda by the hand and led her and the others to the site where Mamie Ruth and her three stillborn babies were buried. At the head of a pile of fresh dirt was a quart jar stuffed with a massive bunch of flowering bitterweeds. The grave bore no marker, but the three tiny graves on one side of Mamie Ruth's were marked by weathered pine boards, each one darker than the previous one. None bore a name.

When Rhoda surveyed the faces of the teens, preteens, little ones, and diaper-clads who had gathered around the graves, she saw evidence of long-term sobbing in their swollen eyelids. While the women struggled to say something comforting, they fought their own tears and felt the pain of deep grieving. Casey squeezed her mother's hand so hard that she temporarily cut off the blood flow through her fingers as well as those of her mother. Unable to control her emotions, she began to cry, and others in the group followed suit.

Inside, Marge continued to struggle with the two babies while preparing a simple but massive meal for supper. When the white women came in the kitchen, Marge placed her own baby on a thin quilt on the floor but continued to hold the newborn Switzer. Heavy perspiration soaked her clothes so that they clung to her body, leaving nothing to the imagination as to her form. Huge droplets

of sweat dripped off her chin and elbows, but she made no effort
to wipe her face or arms. She did occasionally attempt to blow the
perspiration off the end of her nose. She gave orders to the older
children who assisted with the meal preparation and other chores,
and none questioned her authority. While one girl used her fingernails to scrub a cooking pot, another sat in a windowsill pumping
a handle up and down in a churn. Occasionally, she removed the
lid to check the progress of her butter-making job, and then she
solemnly replaced it and continued churning.

A young boy the women hadn't seen before came in with a
five-gallon bucket filled with fresh milk. Without a word from
Marge, one of the girls strained the milk, poured it in jugs, and
placed them on the table to be served with supper. Several girls
came struggling in with gallon buckets of water they had drawn
from the well. For a moment, it seemed that things were going remarkably well for a family that had lost the children's mother and
the head of the household's wife just hours before.

Rhoda took the newborn from Marge and made over it like
women do.

"How many children do you have, Marge?" asked Mary Sam.
"I mean, of your own?"

"Yes'm, I has five," she answered.

Mary Sam shook her head compassionately. Marge's baby was
a "yeller." It had likely been conceived at a time when Mamie Ruth
was too pregnant for sex. A look around the room revealed that
three of Marge's children were "high yellers," a term given babies
born by black women and fathered by white men. Society shunned
these children, and that included men like Ovid who had fathered
the children, often without permission from their black mothers.

"Go get Chris off the grave," Marge told one of the girls.

"Off the grave?" asked Connie with a hint of disbelief.

"Yes'm. He been staying there most all the time since Miss

Mamie Ruth passed," she explained without emotion. "Bring him in and clean him up," she ordered the girl.

"But Marge, he wasn't there a moment ago," Connie pointed out. "You don't suppose …" she said with a worried tone.

"No'm. One of the girls dragged him away, but he done gone back," explained Marge.

All three white women watched in horror while one of the girls dragged little Chris in the house as he pleaded with them to let him stay with his mama. It took three of his siblings to hold him down while another one cleaned his fingernails and attempted to brush the fresh dirt from his hair and clothes. When he noticed Casey staring at him. he stopped fighting his sisters long enough to explain to her, "My mama died."

Casey was startled but recovered in time to tell him not to worry. "Your mama has gone to live with Jesus and Mr.—"

"Your mother went to live with Jesus," Mary Sam interrupted. "She'll be able to look after her babies who died before her," she explained to Chris while pressing Casey's arm so hard, the child let out a whimper. Casey was confused. *Is Mr. Klinger doomed for hell?* she wondered. If so, apparently nobody told him as he had promised to see her in heaven someday. She yearned for answers, but the situation at hand called for her undivided attention as well as her silence.

When the meal was served, they were all seated on long, backless benches around an oblong table constructed of pine boards nailed crudely together. The older children held the young ones in their laps and saw to their eating. Marge stayed busy refilling service bowls and cooking more food as the supply got low. Her own children were sent to the porch to wait until the white folks finished their meal.

Rhoda held Casey, and Chris sat beside them in his sister's lap. The vegetables were tasty, cooked as they were with bacon grease, the soup with fresh tomato juice and oodles of equally fresh vegetables, the cornbread with fresh buttermilk. There was fried chicken, milk gravy, and mile-high biscuits accompanied by home-churned butter or sorghum molasses, for those who preferred it. Topping it all off were thick slices of country cured ham from Ovid's cellar. Everyone found it difficult to stop eating, everyone except Chris. He sat limp in his sister's arms and turned his face away no matter what she offered him.

Casey could scarcely take her eyes off him. All through the meal, she kept offering him a piece of her buttered biscuit with chunks of ham between the layers. When he refused her offer, she plopped it in her mouth, smacking with pleasure to indicate its good taste. "I think you should eat because your mother would want you to," she told him sweetly.

Chris kept his eyes focused on her every move but made no response. Her continued pleas finally prompted him to take a bite off her biscuit. Ovid jumped up from his chair, pulled his razor strap from a nail on the wall, and jerked the boy out of his sister's arms. He dragged the screaming child into the yard and began lashing him with the leather strap until the boy's thin shirt was shredded and pieces of it began falling to the ground. Between screams, Chris begged his dead mother to intercede, but Ovid seemed to gain strength as he went along. Everyone in the house sat helplessly by as they listened to the boy's screams.

"Why? Why?" screamed Casey who cried uncontrollably. She begged to know why Mr. Ovid was beating little Chris, who was already suffering from the loss of his mother. She finally snuggled her face in Rhoda's chest while reaching blindly for her mother's waiting arms. Nobody knew the answer to her question, but when Ovid had worn himself out and released Chris from his grasp, the mystery was solved. "Now get back in there and eat what your sister feeds you! Switzers don't eat out of a squaw's hands!"

David jumped to his feet and headed for the backyard. He jerked the leather strap out of Ovid's grasp and began delivering blows across the oppressor's back just as Ovid had done to his help-less little boy. Ovid attempted to fight back, but the tiring episode with Chris and the poor condition of his overweight body soon gave in to the younger, stronger, perhaps angrier man. Odell and Ecil tried to hold David back, insisting they "get in the wagon and leave right now," but David was not to be dissuaded. When Ovid begged for his life, David felt avenged. He left his victim on the ground and joined his friends, who were already boarding the wagon.

In spite of his wounds, Chris ran back and forth from the scene to his mother's grave. When his father fell to the ground the last time, Chris ran full circle around the house, screaming with all his strength for his mother. The sight of him sent Casey into a fit so violent that no amount of hugs from her mother or anyone else could calm her. When David joined them, he threw his arms around Mary Sam and Casey and held them for a long while. "I'm sorry, sweetheart," he told his wife. "Forgive me?" he asked.

She nodded consent.

The ride home was quiet, with Casey sleeping and the others deep in thought. The scene at the Switzer house had erased the horror of the hanging, especially for Connie. She managed to let go of the dreadful scene on the courthouse lawn long enough to mull over Mary Sam's ongoing battle with white folks' prejudices against her people. Connie knew better than most the trauma of prejudice. Her classmates in the Wanata Springs private school had bullied her for not having a mother. Only one classmate had come to her aid, and it was Mary Sam. "Better a dead mother than an Indian mother," seven-year-old Mary Sam had told her. "Nobody likes you if you're an Indian whether you have a mother or not."

"Don't you worry. I can solve your problem," Mary Sam had promised her friend. She called a meeting of all their classmates and announced to them that the Great White Father had chosen Connie's mother over all of theirs to help him take care of the children in heaven. Connie's classmates took it all to heart, and from then on, Connie was sought after by her peers.

Unfortunately, Mary Sam's problem had intensified in the private school. Her bloodline had become a target for elite parents who sent their daughters to the exclusive Wanata Springs school for a "proper" education, which apparently meant classmates who could boast of socially acceptable backgrounds. Wanata Springs was famous for its educational opportunities, a southern version of New York's educational seminars and entertainment. Officials from New York had chosen Wanata Springs for its winter site partly because the Pensacola and Atlantic Railroad lines connected the community with Pensacola and other gulf ports to Tallahassee and the Atlantic Ocean. The educational facility featured lectures by prominent speakers, performers, and educators from around the country; and it provided classes and workshops in politics, economics, drama, music, crafts, and more. Nobody seemed to notice that many of these experts who were invited to address the students and their families had descended from Indian tribes.

The whole educational experience in Wanata Springs was a world apart from the one-room schoolhouses, short summer sessions, and constant shortage of qualified teachers in Niceville and other remote communities in Okaloosa and other Florida counties. While socialite parents fought Mary Sam's enrollment and continuing residency at the school, their offspring didn't. Once the students became acquainted with their energetic, fun-loving, rule-breaking classmate, they idolized her and were quickly turned off by their parents' notions of nobility.

Young Mary Sam came to realize that children's minds were flexible, enabling them to choose their friends, totally unbiased by their skin color or background. But once they became adults, they too would be locked in the public mind-set. Frustrated, Mary Sam opted to prove them right, that Indian blood was bad. During her teenage years at the school, she began sneaking out the dormitory window at night and returning well after curfew. To prevent her being expelled, her classmates took turns slipping into Mary Sam's bed during curfew check. It became a game they eagerly looked forward to, but their fun came to an end when Mary Sam crawled out the window one night and never returned.

She had eloped with David Stewart!

The whole thing had left Connie devastated. Life would never be the same without her soul mate and best friend. Her only comfort was that Mary Sam's marriage to David, the son of the most powerful businessman in the county, would put an end to the racial atrocities her special friend had been subjected to all of her young life.

Or so she thought. After witnessing the episode at the Switzer house, she realized that discrimination against Mary Sam would never end. Instead of returning to her beloved Niceville bursting with fond memories of a trip she had anticipated for months, Connie was filled with anguish. She had the same worries that haunted David.

Chapter 7

ONCE THE SUBJECT OF THE HANGING GREW THIN, PAR-
ticularly the part that Mary Sam had played, folks in Niceville finally began to take notice of the highly advertised Vale of Paradise
development across the bayou. News that a Chicago developer had
purchased sixteen thousand acres in the area with the notion of
dividing it into residential lots he planned to sell to strangers was
met with ridicule. The land was worth only what the timber would
bring, knowledgeable locals said, and after the timber was cut, it
would be worthless. It would take a host of expensive equipment,
tons of fertilizer, and a lifetime of work to raise the simplest of gardens in the useless sandy soil. Hope of anything beyond that was
insane, everyone agreed.

Apparently, the purchaser, Mr. Hampton "Hamp" Etheridge,
disagreed with them as witnessed by the ads he continued to post
on railroad cars. It had all come about after Etheridge took a ride
down the Santa Rosa Sound on a government survey boat. He had
been obsessed by the natural beauty of intricate waterways mean-
dering through unspoiled forests of virgin longleaf yellow pines,
moss-draped live oaks, and stately hickory trees. Etheridge had
imagined young and old frolicking on the sugary sand beaches,
gathering hermit crabs, wading in ice-cold creeks, boating and
swimming in deep bayous and bays, and sunning themselves on

the snow-white sands of the Gulf of Mexico just minutes away by boat. With that image engraved in his mind, Etheridge purchased the property, subdivided much of the land into residential lots, built a hotel on the bay shore for prospective customers, and waited.

It was to be a very long wait. For fifteen hundred dollars and five hundred dollars down, a buyer could own a residential lot in Etheridge's Vale of Paradise and have his choice of ten acres of cane-growing property some distance away from the homesite, or he could opt for an interest in a stock farm. Prospective buyers were assured that either investment would create enough profits to make the mortgage payments on their lots.

Interested folks gladly left the crowded city for the open country and its beaches, waterways, and hunting grounds. Getting there was the worst part, as it required a thirty-one-hour train ride from Chicago to Pensacola and a five- to ten-hour boat trip from Pensacola to the Vale of Paradise, depending on the tide and a lot of other unknowables.

Once the visitors saw the beautiful open country and clean, undisturbed atmosphere, most thought the trip was worth the trauma of getting there. With Hamp Etheridge pampering them with three good home-cooked meals a day, they scarcely had time to take in all the activities available to them. Many opted to lounge in rocking chairs on the wide, screened porch and watch the steam- and gasoline-powered boats and lumber-laden schooners go by. Just as Hamp had promised, it was a vacation they wouldn't forget, but none of his guests wanted to reside permanently in his paradise. There were no sales!

The hullabaloo across the bayou was of little concern to Connie, Rhoda, or Mary Sam. The whereabouts of Jolene Holder and her mother took precedence over everything else. Odell could do nothing as there had been no evidence a crime had been committed, and even if there had been, he couldn't arrest John as he was missing too. John's appearances in public had always been rare, and until the episode with Jolene occurred, everyone was pleased about that.

Months passed and still, no one had seen the Holders. With family and loved ones trying to discourage Connie from continuing the search, Captain Parnie offered his own advice. "Look at it this way. John was last seen at the Pensacola docks. He could have stowed away on a ship to Cuba or Honduras or anywhere in the world. Nobody would know it until they were in the middle of the Gulf, miles and miles away. John likely was sent to jail or prison by now or somebody may have killed him."

"But wouldn't the men at the Pensacola dock notice a man like John? I mean, he looks like a vagrant, and nobody else looks quite like him, with that big, toothless cavern and those huge elephant ears, and that crab walk he's so proud of. And if Jolene's teeth are missing, wouldn't that be a clue? What thirteen-year-old girl is toothless?" It was the same argument the women had given on previous trips to the Niceville boat dock, one the entire crew could easily recite by now.

"Likewise, now, old John could have holed up in Pensacola or Florosa," Captain Parnie told them. "What difference does it make to him? He lives off everybody else no matter where he is."

The truth of the statement struck Connie.

Back home, Ecil noticed a soberness about his wife, a hint of self-control. Had she found Jolene? he wondered.

"John Holder will never leave this area," announced Connie. "Where else would people tolerate him?"

Ecil stared at his usually soft-spoken bride with renewed interest.

"Folks anywhere else would see him for what he is: a bully. And they'd chase him out of their area!" she said with growing confidence. "He likes the image everyone in Niceville has of him:

a dangerous killer with a lot of notches on his gun. Yeah, he'll be back."

"I agree," said Ecil with a sense of pride.

But they were wrong. Neither Ecil nor Connie would ever see John Holder again.

Meanwhile, Mr. Hamp Etheridge found himself struggling with his development across the bayou. With no sales, and visitors requesting additional amenities in their hotel packages, Hamp sought to pacify them. He approached Captain Parnie about doing a sightseeing boat tour of the area.

"Can't do it, Mr. Hamp," said the captain. "Between runs to Pensacola, the old boat keeps me busy repairing it for the next run. Talk to Odell. He's the constable, but about all he has to do is keep the hogs and cows off the streets," he said with a laugh.

Odell readily agreed to give the hotel guests a sightseeing tour of the waters on a weekly basis. He was returning to the hotel from a third tour when a streamlined cruiser had just docked on the opposite side. Happily, he had an uninhibited view of its passengers and crew as they disembarked.

The captain, who was first to exit, surveyed the area at length prior to boarding again. Next, two other crewmen did likewise, each canvassing the area before boarding again.

Finally, a threesome emerged, all men, two of whom were dressed in classy three-piece suits and colorful ties. The fat one wore a fashionable, creamy-white felt hat, while the other, a muscle-bound, broad-shouldered man in his early thirties, sported a sophisticated bowler several sizes too small for his head.

The third man followed submissively behind the other two, his attire a testament to either his lower station in life or his desire for comfort. He wore simple slacks and a short-sleeved shirt. No accessories adorned his simple attire except for a bandless hat that had seen a lot of wear. Coastal winds that gusted up to ten miles per hour kept all three men tugging at their head wear.

Finally, crew members exited with two small pieces of luggage that apparently belonged to the two well-dressed men. With no luggage to worry with, they were left free to observe the surroundings and hold onto their hats at the same time. The third man, much younger than the others, declined offers from Hamp's employee to assist him with two cumbersome pieces of luggage. With both hands occupied, he failed to catch his hat when a strong gust of wind carried it across the ground several yards before a crew member came to his aid. Odell, entertained at first by the hapless visitor, suddenly felt a tug on his memory. Even from a distance, he recognized the bareheaded man who insisted on carrying his own luggage.

It was Gussie. Yes, it was the same young man who had mysteriously disappeared from Parnie's passenger boat during a stop in Florosa. Except for John and Jolene, all of Parnie's passengers had been on their way to the Klinger hanging,

Before any of the three reached the hotel entrance, a noisy group of vacationers came bursting through the doorway, their excitement in high gear as they jostled about, apparently in anticipation of the sightseeing boat ride they had been promised.

By this time, Hamp had been notified of his guests' arrival and had rushed to greet the newcomers. He welcomed the threesome and asked if they would like to join other guests on a tour of the area.

"Maybe another time," said the fat one.

"If you're hungry, I can ask the cook to whip up something to hold you until supper time. Or maybe a glass of tea and some cookies?" With the new guests rushing past him, seemingly uninterested in what he had to say and demanding to be shown their rooms immediately, Hamp tried to rush through his welcome speech.

"If you like country cooking, you're in for a treat: corn pones, black-eyed peas, fresh ham, and all the vegetables you can eat," he rattled off.

"Maybe later," repeated the fat one. "Show us our rooms!" he demanded, obviously irritated with the chatter.

"Yes, of course. Just down the hall," said Hamp as he tugged on a big key chain attached to his belt. "Here you are: three of our finest rooms, all overlooking the beautiful bayou just as you ordered," he said proudly. "Dinner will be served at five thirty."

"We never eat earlier than eight," said the group's spokesman before stepping inside the first room designated as one of theirs. He closed the door in Hamp's face.

"Well, now, that might be a problem," Hamp called through the door. "You see, all the help goes home after they clean up the kitchen." He waited by the door for a moment or two, but as there was no response, he walked away, taking a glance behind him now and then. When two more doors slammed shut behind him, one of them opened almost immediately. It was Gussie's door. Gussie tiptoed in Hamp's direction and spoke softly once he was close enough to touch him. "Never mind about dinner. We have food on the boat, and Al, well, he hardly ever eats before midnight," he explained in a near whisper.

"Al?" Hamp wondered aloud. *Al Capone?* he thought. *He's got the fat cheeks; the ruddy, pockmarked face; and of course the money!* Al had siphoned off several big bills from a wad of cash in his pocket and gave the luggage carrier a bigger tip than the boy made in a year working at the hotel. *My God, what have I gotten myself into?* Hamp asked himself. He lingered in the hallway, befuddled by questions he had no answers to. In spite of the new guests' unusual behavior and the possibility that they were gangsters trying to escape the law, the developer of the Vale of Paradise was hopeful.

If they have that kind of money, he thought, *they must be planning to buy property. What else would bring them to the Vale?* He allowed his imagination to go wild. *Maybe they'll buy the entire acreage?* With a bounce in his walk, he rushed outside just in time to wish Odell's sightseers a good tour.

"Give them a good show," he yelled to the constable.

Odell's curiosity was piqued, so he left the boat to have a word with Hamp. "Who are the two dudes in the stiff collars?" he asked. "I know the other one. The name is Gussie. Last name is Genepri. Claims John Holder killed his daddy."

"Gus Genepri? Yes, that's the name given for the reservation. He reserved three rooms but gave only one name. He said he was coming in on the supply boat, but it looks like they chartered a damn ocean liner," he joked.

Odell's interest was growing. "I'll check with you when I bring your guests back."

Hamp was jittery. He begged Odell not to take the passengers on their tour but to remain close by the hotel. "You know something. I think one of them is Al Capone!" he fluttered nervously. "The others called him Al."

Odell shook his head. "I doubt it. He likely adopted a name just for this trip. These criminals change their names like they change friends. They have to because they keep killing the old ones."

"I see what you mean," said Hamp. "Saw the initials *J.J.* on one of the bags that Gussie fellow held onto. Maybe he don't go by Gussie anymore."

With his passengers complaining good-naturedly, Odell proceeded with the tour, but his thoughts remained with the chartered boat whose unlikely visitors to the backwoods of northwest Florida were suspect. He knew they were not the usual family grouping, nor did they fit the description of hunters, sunbathers, or stealthy government agents looking for moonshine stills.

After the tour, Odell returned his passengers to the hotel in time for supper, which was served promptly at five thirty. Cooks, servers, and the cleanup crew had gone home to their families before the threesome wandered into the lobby. Again, Hamp offered leftovers, which he promised to "warm up for you."

"We're not hungry yet," said Al, who had removed his hat and tie but remained formally dressed as if he intended to go out. Al had a habit of picking at his facial skin, an action that worsened his already scarred face and neck. His facial pockmarks were the first thing anyone noticed about him, but his jolly laugh tended to draw attention away from the disfigurement. A young man in his late twenties or early thirties, he was already overweight, his fat belly bouncing up and down with every step he took.

Shortly after the tour boat left the hotel, Al left his room and yelled at his companions to join him. As soon as they entered the lounge, his companion, a muscular man, loosened his belt, pulled his shirt out, and began doing push-ups. He followed those with a hundred sit-ups.

Odell had studied every bulletin he had ever collected from the post office walls as well as those from the sheriff's office in Crestview, and he had perused them as if he would be expected to pass a test on the subject. If this J.J. had ever been in serious trouble with the law, his name should be among them. But there was no J.J. mentioned in any of his bulletins. Dismayed, he had begun tossing the bulletins in a basket when he caught sight of two small capital letters in parentheses: J.J. True, the photo didn't look exactly like the man at the hotel, but he hadn't seen the man in question without his hat on. Further study of the pamphlet revealed that Johnny Jackson was one of many assumed names of J.J. Hoagland, a former heavyweight prizefighter turned gangster. That Al called him Hoagie was telling. He was best known in Chicago's gangland as J.J. Hoagland, but police referred to him as Two-Gun Hoagie.

Two-Gun's belt was coming apart from all the marks he had

slashed in it. His signature was a brimmed hat a size too small for his bulging head and gruesomely thick hair. His skin was so pasty white that it appeared to never have seen sunshine. His long, thin neck enabled him to wear the fashionable tight, wide-collared shirts with ease, while Al's short, fat neck denied him the same pleasure.

Al stuffed himself into a shirt two sizes too small and managed to stretch a size forty-two pants around his forty-five waistline, thus completing a picture of a man who refused to admit he was obese. Both men called attention to themselves whether alone or in a crowd, although neither seemed to understand that the attention he received was not of a complimentary nature.

While standing on the hotel's massive screened porch, Al's attention was drawn to a skiff moving along the water's edge. Two men had exited the tiny craft and were beating the water with boat paddles.

"What the hell are they doing?" he asked Hamp, who had followed them outside.

"Mullet fishing," Hamp told him.

"Fishing!" laughed Al. "What the hell? They beat the fish to death?"

They all laughed, including Hamp. "Well, as I understand it, they scare the mullet out of the tall grass so they have nowhere else to go but in their nets. Wait here," he advised. "They're coming this way. Maybe you'd like to ask them about it yourselves. I've lived in Chicago most of my life. I get these strange customs all mixed up in my head," he admitted.

The fishermen stared at the suit-clad threesome as if they might an alien from Mars, and then they exchanged glances with each other before staring at the strangers again.

The fishermen had a lot in common: they were ill shaped, and they had unkempt beards, dirt-encrusted fingernails, matted hair, missing front teeth, and gruesomely soiled attire. Their scarred faces bore signs of knife slashings and bone-breaking brawls.

It was the Bedlam brothers.

The whole scene, so remote from anything Al and Hoagie had ever encountered, fascinated them. Noticing an empty jug rolling around the floor of the craft, Al asked if that was some of "that moonshine you folks are noted for." Lucifer grabbed the empty bottle and cracked Lum over the head with it. "I told you not to drink it all up! Now we don't have none for the visitors!" he complained.

With Lum obviously in pain but showing no credible signs of dying, Al and Hoagie pursued information about the bottle's contents. "Must have such a kick it makes you want to beat the fish to death," laughed Al. "You know something? I like this place," he added with a cackle. They all enjoyed a spell of raucous belly laughter.

"Perfect spot for a gym," said Hoagie, who had kept his body in shape long after giving up professional fighting. "Maybe a spa and lots of running space. And a nine-hole golf course! Ah," he breathed excitedly. "Every sports-minded man in Chicago would kill for a vacation here if it offered all that."

Lucifer eyed his brothers, who exchanged knowing grins. "You want some moonshine?" he asked the city dudes.

"Hell, yes," said Al, and Hoagie readily agreed.

"You can bring it to the back entrance of the hotel," Hamp told Lucifer. Turning to his guests, he added, "The men are trustworthy. You can pay them now, and I'll see you get your merchandise," he told Al, and he agreed.

"We'll be back before you miss us," promised Billy Bob with a near toothless grin. His brawls had cost him so many front teeth that the spaces resembled blackouts on crossword puzzles. All three Bedlam boys boarded their man-made skiff and rowed across the bayou.

"I hear it has quite a punch," warned Hamp, who struggled with a constant cough. "I've never tasted it," he admitted between coughs. "As you can see, I have enough problems."

In less than an hour, Hamp knocked lightly on Al's door, but there was no answer. All three had gathered in Gussie's room to discuss their plans. When Al heard the knock, he stuck his head out, grabbed the package of home brew from Hamp, closed the door, and locked it. Al and Hoagie grinned at the sight of two full quarts of the southern mash. Each claimed a bottle of his own, screwed the top off and ran the opened bottle by his nose. Grinning broadly, Al declared, "This stuff ought to be good. These backwoods clowns ain't got much else to do but work on improving it."

"I'm hungry," complained Gussie. "Okay if I raid the kitchen?"

"Go ahead!" snapped Al, somewhat dismayed that the boy had no interest in sampling the brew. "With his first swallow of the concoction making its way down his esophagus, he screwed his facial muscles into a mass of wrinkles and squeezed his eyes tight in an effort to assist his digestive system in handling the shock. "Damn!" he yelled between choking sputters.

Hoagie made his own facial distortions after taking a big swallow from his jar. As their bodies learned to tolerate the onslaught handed them, both men drank until they passed out on the floor. Meanwhile, Gussie had eaten the food he discovered in the kitchen, drank some milk, sprawled out on the bed, and fell asleep.

In the wee hours of the next morning, Al began to suffer stomach cramps and diarrhea, along with a headache and dizziness. Unable to stand up and writhing in pain, he woke the others with his moans. When Hoagie heard the noise, he instinctively pulled a gun from his chest holster and searched the room, which was still dimly lit by an oil lamp no one had stayed awake long enough to snuff out. When he saw Al on the floor, he searched the hallway before holstering his gun and then tried to determine what ailed his companion. Awakened by the noise, Gussie sat straight up in the bed and let out a yelp.

"Get a doctor!" moaned Al. The usual bark in his orders gave in to a plea for help. He was not only in pain; he was obviously concerned about himself.

"Damn it, Al, they probably don't have a doctor in these backwoods," shouted Hoagie. He was clearly concerned.

"They have one," said Gussie, "but my father told me he's never sober."

"We'll sober the bastard up!" declared Hoagie. He ordered Gussie to "find Hamp and call on the boat crew and do whatever it takes to get a doctor in here now." Hoagie was to remain with Al. Talk about taking their chartered boat back to Pensacola where there would surely be better medical attention wasn't popular with Al, who feared he would never survive the trip.

Gussie took his job seriously. He knocked on every door in the hotel in an effort to locate Hamp. Sleepy-eyed, confused, and pajama-clad guests complained, while others sympathized. One of them finally directed the boy to Hamp's private quarters. Within minutes, Hamp was accompanying Gussie in a dinghy across the bayou, but an hour had passed before they returned with a very sober, albeit hungover, Dr. Smythe.

"Diarrhea, stomach cramps, dizzy, and a headache!" Hoagie yelled at the doctor.

Dr. Smythe took one look before touching Al on the forehead. "And a fever," he added.

"What is it, Doc?" Hoagie asked nervously.

Ignoring the question, Dr. Smythe took a wooden spatula from his bag and tried to take a look in Al's mouth. The doctor's hands shook so violently that he latched onto his patient's face with one hand in order to steady the other. Rather than embarrass himself further, he took a cursory glance in Al's nose and ears and then poked around on his stomach before asking a few questions about his recent food intake.

"Didn't eat nothin'," Al grumbled.

Smythe looked around the room. Spotting the moonshine jugs, he picked one up and held it to his nose. "Did you drink this?"

"Yeah. We both did, but I ain't sick," shouted Hoagie.

"You're lucky," said Smythe. "I'm afraid your friend was not so lucky. This stuff is poison."

"Poison!" Hoagie scowled. "What?"

Al struggled to get on his feet. "Get me to Pensacola," he ordered.

Smythe insisted that Al lie back. "He needs rest and lots of liquids as soon as he can keep them down," he advised Hoagie. "I'm gonna give you the same treatment you'd get in Pensacola," he said to Al, "and you won't have the trauma of getting there."

Turning to Hoagie, he added, "But he's gonna need your help. Keep ice packs on him if Hamp has any that ain't melted already. It's up to you to keep him cool."

"The cook is here already," said Hamp, who had stood in the doorway throughout the doctor's visit. "She'll get the water and towels and I'll send after some ice, but you know they may not have it made yet. It's four o'clock in the morning!" he reminded them.

"Have your cook make some mint tea. It'll help with his nausea and calm his nervous system. As soon as he can keep that down, give him these pills." He pulled a container of pills from his bag and tried to empty a few in his hands, but with his unsteadiness, it was all or none. He finally asked Hamp to count out ten pills. Even as the doctor spoke, Al began dry heaving and cursing everyone in the hotel. That included the doctor.

Remembering that the doctor had a reputation for drinking heavily, Gussie questioned him. "Dr. Smythe, I understand you drink this stuff? Does it ever make you sick?"

"All the time," admitted Smythe.

The comment infuriated Al. "Listen, pal, you don't have a monopoly on moonshine making here in this hog trough!" he blared with as much anger as he could muster between pains. "We make plenty of it in Chicago, but we don't poison nobody with it!"

Without a change in his expression, the doctor repeated what he had said before: "It's all poison. No matter who made it."

"Is he gonna make it, Doc?" asked Gussie, who had begun to shake uncontrollably.

"Depends," said Smythe.

"On what?" Hoagie bitched.

"On what kind of nurse you are," Smythe said without emotion. He struggled to close the clasp on his scrubby old medical bag, but his hands shook so that he gave up and grabbed the bag by its handles.

Gussie followed Smythe out of the room. "What if he don't get better?" he asked.

"I don't think you have to worry about it. He's got youth on his side. Now if he were older …"

"Al's not gonna want to stay in bed," Gussie said, worrying out loud.

"I'm afraid Al has no choice," said Smythe.

Back in the room, tensions raged. When the cook brought ice water and towels, Gussie began bathing Al's face and neck with them. Keeping them wet was a full-time job that both men gave their best effort.

"What we gonna do?" Gussie kept asking.

"Nothing right now," Hoagie said. "We may have to come again when Al's well, and we'll blow the head off the bastard who did this."

"I mean—"

"I know what you mean," he assured the young man. "We'll get it done, but right now, we have to look after Al. Nobody poisons Al and me and gets away with it!" he shouted.

"Yeah," Al moaned in agreement.

Leaving Gussie in charge of Al, Hoagie made one of many trips to the kitchen for more ice when the back door flew open and a bedraggled woman stepped inside, her bonnet perched lopsided over thin, unruly hair, her face flushed, her heavy glasses hanging on the end of a king-size nose.

It was Rhoda!

"Miss Rhoda!" yelled the cook. "What's wrong? Something happen to Mr. Odell?"

Rhoda and Hoagie exchanged anxious glances before he headed for the door. "Please, sir," Rhoda called out. "Are you here with Gussie? If you please, I'd like a word with him."

Hoagie was startled. In an effort to regain his composure, he repeated the name as if he hadn't heard clearly. "Gussie?"

"Yes, sir," said Rhoda. As Hoagie's and the cook's eyes traveled up and down her disheveled frame, she realized for the first time that she had thrown her ankle-length dress on backward. The wide collar, meant to lie down at the back of the neck, protruded over her chin and made natural facial movements difficult as well as hilarious. "Oh, I'm afraid I dressed in rather a hurry. I didn't want to miss Mr. Gussie." Truth was, she had dressed in the dark for fear of waking Odell, who would have talked her out of making the trip. "Please," she begged. "Gussie's dad was our neighbor, you know," she fumbled. Rhoda didn't like lying. She rationalized that in a small area like theirs, everyone was her neighbor. Her hope was that Gussie had seen Jolene and, if so, he might assist them in finding her.

"I'm afraid I don't know anyone by that name," lied Hoagie. He excused himself and waited in the hallway until he heard the back door to the kitchen close. He watched Rhoda make her way down the dock to a dinghy she had apparently rowed across the bayou before daylight. As soon as she was out of sight, he raced to Al's room in a frenzy.

"We gotta get the job done and get the hell out of here. Some ugly broad just came in the back door looking for you!" he yelled at Gussie. "What the hell is that all about?" he snarled.

Disgruntled himself, Gussie shot out of his seat and paced the tiny floor, mumbling to himself.

"I asked you a question," growled Hoagie. Al stopped groaning long enough to hear the boy's response.

"Just a nosy old woman," said Gussie. "She don't know nothing."

"The hell she don't!" grumbled Hoagie. "I shoulda shot the bitch!"

The whole thing didn't set well with Al. "I don't give a rat's ass about an old woman," he assured them. "Shoot her if you have to, and while you're at it, shoot every damn moonshiner in this rotten place."

"Gussie and me could do the job we came here to do, Al, and that way, we can avoid that nosy old bitch and get the hell out of here," suggested Hoagie. Al grudgingly agreed.

By the time Hamp arose that morning, the fancy boat was gone, the three hotel guests with it.

Two nights later, the McNeils heard a loud banging on their back door. Instinctively, Odell yelled, "Come in!" as the door was seldom locked, and everyone was welcome.

When there was no response, Odell opened the door and peeked into the darkness. The oil lamp in the living room afforded him enough light to distinguish the figure of a man who stood a respectable distance from the entrance. He knew it was a black man as any white man would have stood directly in the doorway. It had to be one of David Stewart's turpentine workers, and Odell knew it wouldn't be good news. "What's wrong?" he yelled through the door. Recognizing the fear in Odell's voice, Rhoda rushed to the door and clung to her husband. "Something happen to David?" Odell was asking

"No, sir, boss. Mr. David said I'm to fetch you out to Bolton," he gasped. As he inched his way a little closer to the door, Odell knew why he was out of breath. He had apparently run all the way through the heavily wooded, snake- and wild animal-infested bayous, creeks, and sloughs to bring some bad news.

The lawman didn't have a lot of calls at night. True, some disturbances happened during the evening hours, but they were seldom discovered or reported before morning. He knew it had to be something out of the ordinary. He donned his hat and fastened his holstered gun around his hips. All the while, Rhoda kept asking, "What happened?"

"You wait outside. I'll be with you in a minute," Odell told his caller. Inside, he grumbled to Rhoda, "Probably a nigger fight. They're always cuttin' on each other. Guess they musta killed a whole slew of them this time or David wouldn't have sent for me. I'll be back soon." It was a common occurrence for the blacks to get into a brawl, and unlike the Bedlams, the black people didn't usually stop until at least one of them was dead. Odell marveled that it didn't happen more often as they were all huddled together in miserably cramped lean-to shacks near the turpentine stills. No blacks were allowed to reside inside the town limits, so whites who hired them were obliged to furnish living quarters outside town, but there were no rules governing the condition of the workers' housing.

Odell begged Rhoda not to wait up, but his request was wasted. As always, she waited, finally falling asleep in a chair. It was well past midnight when her husband returned. In most circumstances, he would have turned the cover back and assisted her to bed. This time was different. He tugged gently at her sleeve until she awakened.

"What's wrong?" she asked. A glance at her husband's troubled face told her the news wasn't good. "What is it?" she cried.

"It's John Holder," he said. "He's dead!"

Chapter 8

JOHN'S BODY HAD BEEN DRAGGED THROUGH THICK, wooded trails with a rope around his neck, a ride that nearly separated his head from the rest of his body. Still, it was a painless ride for John. Prior to being dragged like a log to the mill site, his body had been riddled by hundreds of .45-caliber bullets, obviously pummeled into him at close range. By the time a turpentine worker found him, he was a blob of raw meat.

The news of his death gave Rhoda a feeling of contentment, but only for an instant. "You don't suppose … oh my goodness. What if Jolene did it? Or her mother?"

Odell was stunned by her remark. "Get hold of yourself, honey," he cautioned.

"Well, who could blame them if they did?" asked Rhoda, seeking to explain her accusation. When Odell turned his gaze to the floor, she feared the worst. "What is it!" she screamed. "No! They're all dead, aren't they?" Her fingers plowed into the loose fabric of the old chair whose arm she had been resting on.

"No, honey, we don't know anything for sure. We searched the house and the grounds, but there was no sign of the girl or her mother." He shook his head. "We couldn't see much at night."

Rhoda breathed a sigh of relief but held little hope. A lot of questions remained unanswered, but she was certain of one thing:

117

Gussie, the handsome young man with the odd-shaped package, held the secret to John Holder's death! "If he was determined to kill John, why didn't he do it on the boat that day?" she asked. "Did he really witness John killing his father? A hundred bullets?" asked a horrified woman. "Did he load his gun a hundred times and empty it into a dead man?" All were questions she wanted answers to, but mostly, she ached to know that Jolene and her mother were alive and safe.

Odell, always compassionate, was especially so now. He cuddled his wife in his arms and held her until she stopped crying, but it didn't last. A sudden thought occurred to her. Planting anxious eyes on her husband, she asked in a frightened whisper: "Where is John's body? You didn't bring it here?" It was more of a plea than a question.

"No. Still in the woods. Ecil and I tried to lift his remains onto my horse, but his flesh fell apart in our hands," he managed with some effort, his emotions quite unstable. "It'll take a dozen tow sacks to bring him in."

"Ecil?" she asked.

"I stopped by his house and took him with me. I really can't describe what we saw. John was riddled with bullets," he said, his voice tinged with emotion. He stared at Rhoda, who appeared to be in charge of her emotions again. "I tell you, honey, it was a nightmare."

"There's not one cemetery in this community where people would allow John to be buried, not even if you bury him in the middle of the forest, so why bother?"

"Exactly what Ecil said," he admitted.

Rhoda sought another avenue to comfort him. She knew from experience that Odell's brooding was best treated by her long-winded nature. She proceeded to use that ploy. "You know, I think young Gussie brought his friends back here to do what he didn't have the courage to do that day on the boat. He obviously lost his nerve and opted to traipse off through the woods when we stopped at the Florosa Inn. I wonder how long it took him to get back to Chicago?" she reminisced. "He really seemed like a nice young man. I still think if we knew what he was hiding in those old newspapers ... well, I think it would give us some answers to the whole thing—Gussie's father, John Holder, everything," she mused thoughtfully. "Say what you will, Odell McNeil, I think John's murderer was recently in the area, but he's not here anymore."

"I'm certain of it," Odell admitted quietly.

Rhoda eyed him suspiciously. "Are you laughing at me again!" she fussed. But one look at his pale face told her otherwise. She regarded him with renewed interest.

"I don't know who pulled the trigger," admitted Odell, "but I know now what Gussie was hiding in that odd-shaped package that day on the boat."

Rhoda held her breath.

"It was a tommy gun," he said with a quiet that only fear creates. Rhoda waited in terror for an explanation.

"It's one monster of a gun," said Odell in a whisper.

Chapter 9

ODELL HAD NO PROOF TO BACK UP HIS TOMMY GUN theory, but he was convinced that John had been mutilated by this little-known, but devastating, weapon.

"I've only read about the monster myself," he eventually confessed to his wife. "I saw a bulletin at the sheriff's office in Crestview. They claim it'll fire hundreds of .45-caliber cartridges a minute! It's the only weapon out there that could have pulverized John's body the way it was."

Rhoda was stunned. "How could that be? Wouldn't it take two or three men to handle a powerful weapon like that? How could anybody sneak one in and out of the hotel?"

"That's the amazing thing about the tommy gun, honey. According to the bulletin, it was created for the soldier, but the war ended before they could get them distributed to the troops. They're designed for one soldier to handle. Apparently they're not very heavy," he explained, astonished by his own words.

"The worst part? There's apparently no ban on sales. Chicago's worst criminals are having a heyday," said Odell. "Gussie's package that day on the boat was the right size and shape for such a weapon. He must have stolen the gun. Why else wouldn't he have a case for it?"

But from whom? they both wondered.

Odell reached the conclusion that young Gussie wasn't as innocent as he appeared. Still, the notion that a Chicago gang killing had taken place in their little isolated community? And using a gun few people had even heard of? It was too far-fetched for anyone else's ears, he decided.

Odell was in a quandary. Sheriff Hagood was on his way to Niceville. "If he sees John's bullet-riddled body, he will know what did it and he'll spread the news as far as Washington," Odell worried aloud. After explaining the situation to Ecil, he asked his opinion.

"Hagood's been fascinated with that gun ever since he received information on it. If he knew one had made it to our area and killed a man, he'd notify Chicago police and put Niceville on the map for every crook in Chicago."

Ecil agreed. "There'll be lawmen crawling all over the place, and it won't be any time before revenuers will be camped on our doorsteps," he worried out loud.

"On the other hand, wouldn't that be the last thing Sheriff Hagood would want to happen?" asked Ecil. "He'd be the first to go to jail, wouldn't he?" One of few men in Niceville who didn't deal in moonshine, Ecil nevertheless sympathized with those who did. He knew that for many of the little moonshiners, it meant the difference between eating and suffering hunger pangs.

"Maybe you forgot about Hagood's ego?" Odell countered. "He'd be famous. He would take a chance on the feds discovering our moonshine madness if he thought he could get his picture splattered in all the papers. Here's the way I see it: The sheriff is already on his way to Niceville, but his trip is based solely on capturing the men who killed that traveling salesman. If he gets this far, he needn't know about John's demise. The buzzards have called in all their kin, so there won't be anything left to identify him anyway."

The two agreed that silence was their best option. No mention would be made of John's death.

Meanwhile, Sheriff Hagood had run into problems unassociated with John Holder. He had left Crestview four days earlier with Josh Tarrow, who planned not only to assist Hagood in the search but to use the opportunity to visit as many Okaloosa County schools as possible.

In addition to Tarrow, Hagood had deputized a crew of men for the occasion, sending twosomes in different directions in search of Jinks and Hardy, two hitchhikers who were wanted for murder. Their victim, a man who was born in Okaloosa County, had just returned home from serving in World War I. A traveling salesman, he had graciously given the two hitchhikers a ride in his new car—and they had thanked him by bludgeoning him to death and stealing his car.

Hagood and Tarrow stopped at farmhouses, country stores, and public schools searching for the killers and warning everyone— adults and their offspring—to be wary of strangers in the area as they were likely armed and dangerous.

The road from Crestview to Niceville had improved, but swollen rivers and streams that separated the two communities often covered the road and the bridges, making transportation difficult, if possible at all. Hagood thought the isolation of the southern portion of the county might be very attractive to killers looking for a hiding place as they could arrive and disappear before residents knew they had been there. The two-man posse had traveled well over halfway without success or incident when they arrived at the last county schoolhouse on their route to Niceville.

The sheriff addressed the headmaster and the students, warning them about the dangerous murderers. While Tarrow waited his turn, he noticed a youngster in the back of the room writhing in pain. His arms, hands, and face were swollen and badly bruised. Tarrow approached the boy and sympathetically questioned him about his bruises. It occurred to him that Marvin Lovelace, the headmaster and a beast of a man who had a reputation as a brutal disciplinarian, may have gone too far.

When Tarrow spoke to the youngster, tears streamed down the child's swollen face. Hagood noticed the commotion and stopped in the middle of his talk to join Tarrow in the back of the room. Tarrow suspected the child was too intimidated to speak in the presence of his teacher, a sour-faced man with a massive build. Even the sturdy oak podium he leaned on seemed frail and inadequate to support his towering, muscular figure.

The sheriff commented that there were a "lot of empty seats" in the room. He wondered if there were other children who had skipped school because of similar bruises. In an effort to gain the boy's confidence, Hagood patted him gently on his back. The child cringed in pain from the light touch and again broke into tears. With all eyes planted on the youngster, the sheriff asked Lovelace to dismiss the other students for a short recess. When the last student had left the room, the sheriff posed a question to Lovelace: "Who is responsible for this?"

Lovelace shrugged his shoulders. "Musta picked on somebody tougher than he is," he said without a hint of sympathy. "What happens outside the classroom is none of my business."

"It is now!" raved the sheriff. He unbuttoned the child's shirt and drew back in horror when he viewed a tiny chest of raw meat! The boy's back had been equally bludgeoned, and even his stomach was multicolored from obvious blows he had sustained over a lengthy period.

In a moment of deep pity, Josh Tarrow closed his eyes. "God help us!" he moaned.

Noting the child's flaming-red face, Hagood felt his forehead. "This boy is burning up with fever. We've got to get him to a doctor."

"We're too far away from Crestview. We'll have to go to Niceville," said Tarrow.

The sheriff severely reprimanded Lovelace for neglecting the boy while Tarrow called to one of the boys outside to draw a bucket of cool water from the well. "Do it now!" he ordered. Using their handkerchiefs, the men bathed the child's head and face, but seeing the inadequacy of that, Tarrow removed his undershirt and used it the same way.

"Let's go!" said Hagood. "Give me your shirt," he ordered Lovelace.

"My shirt!" Lovelace protested.

Ignoring the teacher's outrage, the sheriff told Josh to wet the teacher's shirt and place it between him and the boy to prevent contact with Tarrow's hot body. When Lovelace made no effort to unbutton his shirt, Sheriff Hagood grabbed the portion covering the teacher's protruding stomach and yanked it off his body, sending buttons in several directions.

Standing with his arms folded across his bare chest, Lovelace pointed out that he would have to dismiss school for the day as it would be indecent to appear before the children bare chested.

"Don't worry about that," snapped Hagood. "Your indecency has already been bared." With the sheriff in charge of the reins, Tarrow handled the shirt-bundled child as if his life depended on it. As far as he knew, it did.

Before taking off, Hagood yelled back to Lovelace. "Who is this boy's father?" Lovelace, who had made a dash for the schoolhouse, made no response.

"Ovid Switzer," came a weak reply from inside the bundle Josh Tarrow was holding.

The sheriff fought an urge to lead the horses directly to Ovid Switzer's house with the intention of beating him to death. A bullet in his brain wouldn't be bad enough; he needed to suffer, thought Hagood. It was a feeling shared by everyone who knew the story of Switzer unmercifully beating his little son, Chris, for having accepted a bite of Casey Stewart's bread. According to Switzer, his family was above eating with an Indian.

The notion of doing Switzer harm was quickly put asunder as Hagood knew Chris' only chance of survival rested on getting medical help for him in record time.

The sheriff's department in Crestview had recently acquired a Model T Ford to assist the sheriff and his staff in carrying on their business throughout the county. Unfortunately for some areas, the automobile had arrived in advance of a surface upon which the vehicle could easily travel, particularly in the south end of the county.

Only a fool, or a city dude, would attempt to travel over the Crestview–Niceville road without carrying a crowbar and shovel for digging out of thick ruts made by shifting sands and heavy rains. Sheriff Hagood had considered driving the Model T to Niceville, but he had opted for the buggy because of its narrower wheels. Too, Josh Tarrow was accompanying him and they hoped that they would be returning with the killers they sought. The buggy was led by his faithful horse, Babbles, with two extra horses tied behind. It was his notion that the extra horses could pull the buggy out of any situation they might find themselves in as well as carry the fugitives back to Crestview, tied crosswise and belly down.

In an effort to save little Chris Switzer's life, the sheriff pushed Babbles as hard as he dared in the teeming hot weather. The mare seemed to understand the urgency as she made the trip in record time. It was a relief for the anxious men to finally reach the narrow street fronting the water as Dr. Smythe's home office was less than a half mile beyond the boat dock.

The bayou sparkled like a field of diamonds, a sight that usually demanded the attention of all passersby. Big-jawed pelicans fished from pole tops while a bevy of ducks fed in the high grass on the water's edge, and a hungry, long-legged crane crept stealthily in the shallow water in search of a meal. Mullet jumped three feet straight up or sideways as if they were evading a predator.

Tarrow and Hagood saw none of that. When they passed Odell's house, Hagood yelled as loud as he could but kept his eye on the pathway and the moving buggy. Minutes later, he pulled into Dr. Smythe's home office, and Tarrow quickly alighted with his precious bundle.

The noise of fast-moving horses' hooves and buggy wheels captured the attention of everyone on the main street. Many ran into the street and watched until the buggy came to a halt at Smythe's home office. After hearing the sheriff's cry for Odell, Rhoda ran as far as she could and then walked to catch her breath before running again.

Sheriff Hagood and Josh Tarrow were relieved to find the doctor at home and apparently sober.

"This little fella is nearly dead from an apparent beating!" the sheriff exploded.

"He's burning up with fever," Tarrow added.

Smythe examined the tiny victim's wounds, listened to his heartbeat, and felt his pulse.

"Will he make it, Doc?" Hagood begged, and then he began pacing the floor when the doctor didn't immediately respond.

Smythe's hands shook so violently that it was nearly impossible for him to place his stethoscope on the child's chest. The sheriff worried he might injure the boy more than he helped, but as there was no one else to call on, he fought an urge to scream.

"Hard to say. He's trying to hold on, but he's got a mighty battle. His wounds are infected in addition to a dozen other problems. I'll need some cheese mold," he told his anxious wife, "and some ice. One of you watch him every minute and let me know if he makes any moves. Don't let him turn over on his back. I have to help my wife make some packs," he told Hagood and Tarrow. "You might do well to get Miss Rhoda down here. The boy's gonna need a lot of mothering if he wakes up."

"I'll get her," promised Tarrow just as they heard footsteps on the doctor's wooden porch. "Here she is now," he announced.

Rhoda let herself in, a prayer on her lips for whoever needed it. When she heard the news, she had to leave the room in an effort to calm herself. Outside, she begged the Lord to spare little Chris's life and was still praying when she spotted Mary Sam running toward the doctor's office.

Mary Sam didn't hold back. "Maybe he'd be better off dead than living with Ovid Switzer!" she said with uncontrolled anger. "Where is Odell? He needs to arrest Switzer while he can. If this child dies …"

"Oh no!" cried Rhoda. "Odell and Ecil are both in Bolton! No telling when they'll be back, and Connie's by herself," she said. "She mustn't know about this!" Connie was in the early stages of another pregnancy and had already experienced some difficulties. Dr. Smythe had advised Ecil to shield her from any emotional strain as well as monitor her physical activity.

As word spread, Hagood and Tarrow took turns relating the story to concerned citizens who continued to gather in the doctor's yard. As they attempted to digest the shocking news, Dr. Smythe suddenly appeared on the porch. "The boy's in a coma," he announced with obvious hopelessness.

Sheriff Hagood, convinced the child would not survive, had moseyed outside, silently mourning. When he heard the news, he pounded his fists into the steel-lined wagon seat. "If that little boy dies, somebody'll have a hanging posse heading for Ovid Switzer's house in an hour," he announced. While everyone struggled nervously with that possibility, each offering his opinion but showing little interest in hearing anyone else's, the sheriff held his bruised hands gently against his chest. The sheriff was noted for craving attention but only in the form of praise or adulation, not for pain he had brought on himself.

"Oh no!" screamed Mary Sam, who was first to see a woman struggling to stay upright as she walked toward the doctor's office. Mary Sam sprinted down the pathway but failed to reach the woman before she slumped to the ground.

It was Connie.

Once Smythe completed his examination, he appeared in the doorway, his facial features drawn beyond the usual scourge of an alcoholic hangover. It was as if he felt the weight of the community on his debilitated shoulders. He knew how much the community loved Connie and Ecil and how they held hopes that she would carry this baby to full term.

"She better stay here tonight," said the doctor. "She's lost another baby."

The women were traumatized, even more so as Ecil had accompanied Odell to the backwoods of nowhere with the notion of ridding the community of John's body. Locating it alone would be time consuming, and disposing of it more so, they feared. And David was in Baker again, dealing with Romie Beavert, the constant troublemaker, who had once again planted cotton on fifty acres of Stewart Enterprise farmland.

While pondering what to do, Ecil and Odell were still plodding through marshy Bolton in search of John's remains.

Just then, a sudden noise pierced the quiet, prompting both men to snatch their guns from their holsters. They were somewhat relieved when they identified the source: the flapping of buzzards' wings as they lifted their stuffed bodies in the air, many struggling to hang onto chunky pieces of human flesh they no longer had space for in their bulging stomachs.

"There must be a hundred of them!" yelled Ecil.

The birds, disgusting as they were to Ecil and Odell, had led the men to the spot, a good hundred yards from where Odell had left it the night before. "They cleaned up the picnic table," said Ecil, who joined his partner with a handkerchief over his nose and mouth and began to breathe shallowly. As soon as they could, they dug a deep hole and buried the near-meatless skeleton before making their way home. When they reached Odell's house, Odell implored Ecil to come inside and rest for a bit before heading home.

Ecil was as reluctant as he was anxious, as always, to get home to Connie. But Odell insisted that he stop in long enough to quench his thirst "with some of Rhoda's popular iced tea." The silence that greeted them inside the house suggested that Rhoda was taking a nap, but the big chair she usually rested in was empty. Odell headed anxiously for the old library table by the front door, the spot where Rhoda always left a note if she had to leave the house for any reason.

But there was no note!

"Probably an emergency stork call, Odell," Ecil suggested. But except for black folks on the other side of Niceville, Connie was the only expectant mother in the tiny area, and she was only four months along. A miscarriage at this stage might kill her.

While surveying the area surrounding the house, they noticed the unusual activity at Dr. Smythe's home. They began as fast a walk in that direction as Odell's leg could handle, and both men began to crumble emotionally when they caught sight of Mary Sam on the doctor's front porch.

"Has to be Rhoda," moaned Odell. "She's been working too hard again. I kept telling her—"

"No, I'm sure it's Connie," insisted Ecil.

Glancing ahead, they saw Mary Sam coming to meet them. "Connie lost the baby," she wailed. "But she's okay, Ecil," she assured him with a warm hug. She made no mention of little Chris Switzer's dilemma.

Back at the doctor's office, Mary Sam led Ecil to the room where his wife lay unconscious. They were about to knock on the door when Rhoda emerged, her face disfigured from uninhibited crying. She reached out to her husband, a man who had always been able to comfort her, but this time, she knew he would fail.

"Little Chris Switzer is dead!" she cried.

Chapter 10

NEWS THAT OVID SWITZER HAD BEATEN HIS SON TO death covered the area with the speed of a tornado, and angry citizens began descending on the constable's residence seeking confirmation. Others needed no proof.

Sheriff Hagood knew not to waste time in warning Clough Martin of the consequences if he and his hotheaded followers murdered Ovid Switzer. He also knew that none of them would be satisfied until Switzer was dangling from a rope, and they had no intention of waiting for a lengthy trial or an equally slow-to-act jury. He enlisted the help of the only men in the area who would listen to reason—Odell, Josh, Ecil, and David—the minute he returned from Baker. They hastened to the head of Turkey Creek, where the only cleared pathway to Ovid's house began and where they knew Clough and his followers would gather.

Half the men in Niceville had arrived in advance of the sheriff's group, anxiously awaiting their leader's instructions. Sheriff Hagood tried to take advantage of Clough's unusual absence, but the minute he began his speech, Odell advised him, "Talk fast. Clough's in sight, and he's whipping that horse like he's trying to outrun a bullet."

With the sheriff and his men blocking the pathway, their guns loaded but not drawn, their opponents puffed on their hand-rolled cigarettes and mumbled to one another in growing anger. Within seconds, Clough was spotted atop a bareback horse that sprinted across the soft sand as if it were a smooth racetrack. The horse's rider had demanded the ultimate from the hapless animal in an effort to arrive at the scene before anyone else took charge.

And he was not a moment too soon. One man assured the sheriff, "We aim to kill Ovid Switzer, and we'll shoot every damn one of you if you try to stop us." Others rallied behind the threat. Significantly, the spokesman for the group rested his hand on an automatic weapon, his fingers clearly in reaching distance of the trigger.

"We're not here to stop you!" Hagood assured them.

"On the contrary. We need your help!" added Odell just as Clough led his battered horse through the middle of the group before coming to a halt.

Odell's weapon was nowhere in sight, but the blanket that lay across his horse had a suspicious lump in it, and Odell's hand was underneath that blanket. Odell knew Clough would never take a chance on drawing first without knowing the whereabouts of Odell's trigger finger. If Clough wouldn't, no one would.

"Go ahead, sheriff," said Odell. "Tell 'em."

"Don't you think we owe little Chris Switzer something?" Hagood began.

"Yeah, we owe it to him to hang his daddy for killing him!" yelled Clough, and nearly everyone agreed with loud and unsavory comments.

"I agree, but first, we owe him a decent burial," said Odell in a breaking voice. "What's it gonna look like if we just throw this little fella's body in the ground like Ovid Switzer did the boy's mamma and all of her stillborns?"

Grumbling decreased considerably. "If we do that, we're no better than Ovid Switzer," Odell continued. "If we rush off looking for Ovid, there's no telling how long it'll take to find him 'cause he ain't gonna be at home waitin' for our visit." A few light snickers could be heard among the group, an indication, Odell hoped, that they were rethinking their reactions. "What kind of men are we if we leave everything to the womenfolk? We need a grave dug, a casket made, a clear pathway up the hill, and a lot of volunteer boat owners to help us all get to the cemetery. We're gonna need lots of strong-legged men to carry the boy up the hill. Chris deserves to have every man, woman, and child crying, praying, and singing at his funeral. The women have enough to do. They'll be sewing up a nice burial suit and lining that casket with pretty cloth, and they'll be cooking vittles for everybody."

With an unusual quiet suddenly piercing the group, Sheriff Hagood took advantage of it. "There's something else I need to say, men. You know why I'm here. I'm looking for two desperate killers on the loose. You know the story. We'll get Ovid Switzer all right, but let's just wait till things cool off and he thinks we have forgotten about him. Right now we ought to be seeking revenge for a soldier, a man who fought for our freedom and returned to the area only to be bludgeoned to death by two hoodlums. Think about it," he insisted, his voice no longer cracking, his courage showing through. In an effort to make the men as angry at these bloody killers as they were at Ovid Switzer, he recanted the story. "These bastards beat the good man's brains out and left his body for the animals to devour. His devastated folks have nothing left to bury." As his own emotions rose, so did theirs.

Hagood continued. "We don't know where they're hiding, but what better place than this isolated area? Now if all of you go traipsing off searching for Switzer, you'll be leaving your wives and children at the mercy of these killers. If you do that, we may have to bury more than one little boy."

Realizing he was losing ground, Clough pierced the new quiet that followed the sheriff's speech with a warning: "Don't muddle your minds with hogwash. We're wasting time! Follow me!" he yelled, and then popped his horse on the rear and headed with a vengeance toward Ovid Switzer's house.

But no one followed. Without a word, one man led his horse out of the pack and proceeded in the opposite direction Clough had taken, one that would take him home to his wife and four children.

Odell encouraged the others to grab some of the latest "Wanted" signs that offered valid information about the brutal murder of a local war hero. "Based on what we know, we believe he gave two hitchhikers a ride in his car." The men's anger rose until they were as intent on hanging these killers as they had been on hanging Ovid Switzer.

Once alone, Ecil asked Odell the inevitable: "What you gonna do about Clough?"

"Nothing!" spouted Odell. "He would love for us to chase him, and that's why we're not going to." Laughing facetiously, he pointed in the distance where he could barely see the image of a horse and rider coming out of the wooded area that led to Ovid Switzer's house. The horse and rider were heading toward Niceville. It was Clough.

Every sawmill owner in the area offered wood for the casket, and a multitude of men volunteered to do the rest. The general merchandise store donated the finest cloth they had in stock for a burial suit and more for casket lining. Several women organized an assembly line at Rhoda's house, where they began measuring, cutting, and sewing.

People began to gather at the little church shortly after lunch the following day. Owners and employees at sawmills, turpentine stills, boat-building concerns, Niceville's only hotel and restaurant, and the general store closed their doors and halted business so everyone could pay his or her respects for a little boy most of them never knew. Even the black turpentine workers were given permission to attend as long as they remembered their station in life and stood at a reasonable distance behind the white folks. Miss Maggie, the church pianist, played softly on an old piano while early-arriving grievers sang hymn after hymn, stopping now and then to wipe their noses and dry their eyes.

The tiny church with its hard benches and rough, wooden floors offered only a small percentage of the mourners a chance to go inside, and mothers stayed busy inside the church trying to keep small children off the open path that led to the tiny casket.

When the designated hour arrived, pallbearers wept openly as they carried the blue satin–covered casket down the narrow aisle. Odell opened the service with layman's words of praise for "this innocent little victim." He purposely refrained from describing the trauma the boy had endured for fear of inciting the angry crowd to unwanted action.

Casey's emotions had been held at bay until David lifted her up for a view of the tiny corpse. The sight was more than she could handle. Her screams pierced the walls of the tiny church and re-verberated throughout the congregation inside and out. Folks out-side, mostly men and young boys, crowded the single doorway and struggled to get a peek inside from the tiny windows.

As soft cries became louder and a few screams erupted, Miss Maggie hit the old piano keys harder and motioned to the singers to raise their voices. By the time the pallbearers were given the nod to close the casket and carry it to the dock, everyone was either swiping at his own nose and eyes or those of his or her offspring.

Together the crowd walked behind the casket all the way to the dock. Once the casket was aboard, they all piled into a mul-titude of clean-swept boats and barges, all of which had been do-nated for the occasion. The funeral procession began at Niceville's boat dock, which was closed temporarily to all other traffic. The casket, now covered with homemade flower arrangements, was placed on a barge with the pallbearers and as many others as could find standing room. A long line of overcrowded boats followed in a somber procession along Boggy Bayou and a small portion of Choctawhatchee Bay before turning into Tom's Bayou, where Sunset Cemetery was situated atop a steep incline. When all boats had been docked, tied up, or anchored at the bottom of the hill, four pallbearers—Odell, Hosie, Ecil, and Clough—lifted the tiny casket onto their shoulders and began the ascent up a difficult, zigzagging path.

Nobody was in a hurry on this trip. When the men reached the top with their precious cargo, they looked back at the mourners, a steady stream winding its way slowly up the crooked path. From a distance, the scene brought to mind a cavalry of weary soldiers trudging unwillingly to battle. Below, the elderly and small children watched and waited.

Casey was one of them.

After releasing her emotions at the church, she began to show remarkable maturity. With all around her still shedding tears, she was dry-eyed. "It's okay," she told the other children. "Jesus wanted him to be with his mama. And Mr. Klinger will be there, and he's a nice man and he likes little children," she added, a notion that eased her pain considerably in spite of raising the eyebrows of some adults.

After the burial, everyone was urged to gather in the constable's yard to share a meal. But Clough Martin and his followers weren't hungry. The unpleasant emotions brought on by the funeral prompted a growing number of them to forget about the murdered soldier in favor of hanging Switzer.

"Where's the sheriff?" yelled Clough, noticing for the first time that Sheriff Hagood and Josh Tarrow were no longer among them.

"Should be well on their way to Crestview by now," said Odell.

"Son of a bastard!" Clough blasted. He suddenly realized why he had been chosen as a pallbearer, and it was not for his personality or his high standing in the community. It was to divert his attention from hanging Ovid Switzer long enough for the sheriff and Josh Tarrow to haul Switzer in to Crestview to await trial. Clough was so irritated with his own ignorance that he cursed himself instead of everyone else.

Weeks passed without a word from Sheriff Hagood regarding Ovid Switzer or the men who had murdered the traveling salesman. It was not until David Stewart returned from his trip to Baker that Nicevillians learned why.

"Switzer disappeared!" David explained. "Hagood and Josh Tarrow had searched Ovid's house and properties, questioned neighbors far and wide, all to no avail." The sheriff was in a tizzy. He had been forced to go back home empty-handed. "They figure Switzer went up north where he has some relatives. He'll be back, and we'll move in on him when he comes."

Clough began to snort like a porpoise, a warning to David and Odell that he planned to disregard all their warnings. He spat a bulbous blob of tobacco juice on the ground in readiness for his heated response. "Now you listen to me—"

"Before you go into your tirade, Clough, you need to know this," warned Odell. "The sheriff and his men haven't been sunbathing. Ovid's not the only man who has committed a crime in Okaloosa County. Maybe you'd be interested to know that we finally caught the two hoodlums who murdered the traveling salesman? It took a lot of cooperation from all of us."

Clough shouted a lengthy tirade of four-letter words before vowing that he would "hang the bastards before the court turns them loose." Ignoring Clough's threat, Odell continued. "Caught one of them in another robbery. Once in jail he came apart. Told on himself and his partner!"

"Think about it, Clough. Nobody had a picture or even a sketch of what these two men looked like, but we all worked together and we caught them anyway. And everybody knows what Switzer looks like, and we know where he lives! Just be patient."

"You got your way, and I got mine!" Clough bellowed.

" Like it or not, Clough, you're gonna have to put Ovid Switzer on hold for a while. We've got a run tonight." Clough knew, as did David, that no amount of pleas or warnings would get Clough's attention like a rum run would.

While most rumrunners dreaded the whole dangerous episode, Clough had exulted in them from the beginning. Meeting the illegal rum-laden ships twelve miles into the open Gulf, dodging Coast Guard ships, maneuvering their loaded boats through the moody East Pass, and arriving home without getting caught was a challenge he relished.

Like Odell, most of the men were involved in the illegal activity solely to put food on otherwise lean tables. They felt some comfort and safety in knowing that their leader, the highly respected constable, would be the last person anyone would suspect.

Odell had received a wire requesting "six to twelve darkies by tomorrow," and he had passed the message along to all involved except Clough, who had been on the chase for Ovid Switzer. Odell's message from an unknown sender in South America seemed simple enough, as turpentine workers were always looking for more black people. These folks were often referred to as darkies, and many of them collected sap from the pine trees. Only Odell and his fellow rumrunners knew the message had naught to do with black people or pine tree sap. The reference was to a loaded rumrunner boat, which would anchor in the Gulf of Mexico about four miles northeast of Yellow Bluff, the highest point of land near Destin, a small fishing village just a few miles from Niceville. The rum boat should arrive around nine in the morning, which was midway between "six and twelve" the following day. With Switzer still on the loose and Sheriff Hagood expecting him to be available twenty-four/seven, Odell was hardly ready for the run any more than Clough was, but as the group leader, he had no choice.

Even for the foolhardy, rumrunning was a nerve-destroying business. While moonshiners could hide their produce in thick backwoods on private property, rumrunners were obliged to work in the open Gulf, where gun-loaded Coast Guard ships plied the waters in search of them. Even if they escaped the Coast Guard, their worries were far from over. Transferring the cargo to waiting haulers along the bayous was equally dangerous. Even though these "little" guys assumed the same liability as all the "big" guys, their pay was minimal. Consequently, they came and went, often to prison, thus posing a major problem for Odell and other rumrunning crew members. When a new face met the rum-loaded boats that Odell and his team brought to Niceville, they could only hope it was not that of a revenuer. These were the times Odell dreaded most, as well as the times he kept his finger closest to the trigger. He often asked himself if he would really kill a man to prevent being caught. It was a question he had never had to answer.

The cargo from each Niceville boat was destined for different customers who delivered to designated customers from Crestview to Birmingham, Alabama. Much of Odell's cargo would go to Clifford Jones's restaurant in Crestview. Like dozens of others dealing in alcohol, Clifford had changed his bar into a soda fountain after Prohibition, ostensibly serving only tea, Coke, and coffee with restaurant meals. But longtime customers knew the truth. The real stuff could be enjoyed in the back room, at least as long as the rumrunners saw to its delivery.

Rumrunning delivery and pick up didn't always happen as

planned. Clifford's mostly white crew had been delivering smaller and smaller supplies of late, always blaming Moses, the only black man in their crew, for the discrepancy. On their last haul, they had arrived at Clifford's restaurant with less than half of the alcohol their employer had paid for, and again, they pointed their fingers at Moses. It was unheard of, and dangerous, for a black man to accuse a white man of lying, so Moses, though innocent, had no choice but to remain silent. He had a lot of mouths to feed.

Clifford and David often discussed the problem. "I trust Moses completely," Clifford told his friend. "The man would die before he would lie or cheat. I know it, you know it, and the white men who work with him know it. But if I side with a black man—well, you know what would happen." New furrows in both men's foreheads spoke for the strain they lived under. "It's a damn wonder either one of us has gotten away with hiring Moses at all," David lamented.

For years, David had trusted Moses to run one of his large turpentine stills in Baker. It was a job usually given a white man, as were all supervisory positions. Thus far, there had been no threats from the white sections, only bickering. "I see it this way," David told Clifford, his fellow business friend. "If the white men won't work with Moses and you don't make a profit when the whites run it, you either have to let Moses do the haul by himself or quit trafficking."

Clifford pondered the idea. "Yeah," he finally agreed. "Truth is, Moses does all the work anyway." He made up his mind to let Moses do the haul by himself.

On this particular run, the weather was a factor. Heavy rains often sent the rivers rising over the bridges and made fording the bridgeless streams, rugged trails, and thick sand roads between Crestview and Niceville impossible. If the haulers from the north end of the county couldn't get through to claim the cargo, David and the others were faced with tearing the walls out in their homes and barns to hide it until the weather improved.

None of these worries put a stop to the scheduled run. When morning came, local rumrunners loaded their boats with basic fishing gear and bait. It was a necessary ploy to make it appear that they were on a fishing trip, but at the same time, they were careful not to overdo the trick as they needed all the space they could muster for their treasured haul.

Odell's boat was first to leave from Joe's Bayou, and others were to follow at thirty-minute intervals, with David last to depart from his starting point in Boggy Bayou. A dark, threatening sky greeted the men, but they decided it was one of the area's frequent thunderstorms that would come and go, usually without incident other than the eerie cracking of a few trees split open by nerve-racking lightning bolts.

This time, they were wrong! Only one boat, the lead boat with Odell at the helm, made it through Destin's treacherous East Pass to the Gulf of Mexico. One by one, the others overturned in the East Pass, sank, or turned back. Odell's crew didn't know which.

Odell headed for the Yellow Bluff area, half-expecting the supply boat from South America to have turned back or capsized.

It had done neither. The heavily loaded rum boat was nearly beside Niceville's crew before they could see it in the blinding rain. As happy as they should have been, it was hard to be joyous with howling winds drowning out their voices and giant waves filling their boat with water. Crew members on the covered rum boat loaded Odell's craft with crates of rum until he motioned for no more. His own crew was furiously bailing water out of their boat.

"Take all you want!" yelled the captain of the rum boat. "Got a devil of a storm behind us. We can't turn back, and we can't go forward. What you don't take will have to be thrown out. We're headed for one of the bayous."

Odell shook his head. "We may have to do the same thing," he admitted.

Perhaps the worst was yet to come. "Keep bailing!" he yelled to his crew. "If we can get in the bay, we might make it home."

Somehow they did, but there was no opportunity to celebrate. A tornado appeared across the bayou before they could reach their destination in Tom's Bayou. The monster extended from Valparaiso to Niceville and beyond. If it touched the ground, the community would likely be destroyed. Their only hope was to anchor their heavily laden boat in the bayou and unload it before it sank. Even though it was midday, the sky had taken on the darkness of early nightfall. Lightning brought temporary daylight to the sky, enabling Odell to spot a familiar ship anchored in the very bayou they had turned into.

It was a Coast Guard ship!

It was too late to turn around. Odell knew that if he could see their ship, they could see his. He never changed his course, as he knew such action would create suspicion. As he headed into the bayou, he ordered the crew to throw the rum out. In seconds, the boat was empty, and he anchored it at the end of Tom's Bayou, not more than fifty yards from the Coast Guard ship. It was the boldest thing he had ever done but perhaps the safest. If the Coast Guard could find no rum on the boat, they could do nothing.

Fortunately, the tornado passed through without touching ground, but heavy rains in its aftermath made transportation of any kind nearly impossible. Most of the haulers headed home once their supply boats returned empty. Only Odell's customers stayed behind and battled the weather.

Some haulers resided in the area or at least had friends they could stay with until the weather improved. Others sought refuge in boat houses or storage sheds.

When Moses had spotted the tornado, he ran to a barn that

was attached to a rooming house perched on the edge of Tom's Bayou in Valparaiso. Weights had been installed at the site for dry-docking boats, ostensibly for repairs. Moses noticed, however, that the rooms were never occupied except for overnight stays that coincided with rum-running hauls. No black man would be allowed in the rooming house, nor would Moses make any effort to break the white man's rules, but when the tornado headed his way, he huddled in the corner of a horse barn that was adjacent to the rooming house. Even horses belonging to a black man would not be allowed shelter, but as no one was stirring outside, Moses tied his horse to a post next to the barn where an overhanging roof offered the animal some protection. From there, Moses hunkered down where he could keep a close watch over everything.

When Odell finally made it home, he and Rhoda had little opportunity to enjoy his safe return. Both of them sat glumly and silently, pondering the whole situation: crates of rum at the bottom of the bayou; haulers waiting through a dreaded storm and having nothing to show for it; while buyers in Crestview, Birmingham, Atlanta and other areas counted the days until they would receive a shipment. Already tense, Odell and his unsteady mate jumped when they heard a soft knock on the back door.

"Who in the world is running around in this weather?" asked Odell. Although thunder and lightning were at a safe distance now, rain continued to pummel the area. It was not what one would call visiting weather. While Rhoda tugged at her husband's sleeve, Odell tried to calm her. "Relax, honey," he insisted. It was with some satisfaction that he opened the door, fully expecting to see David or one of the other boat captains, and he was anxious to know what had happened to all of them.

It was Moses!

Wet as the crashing waves in the Gulf of Mexico and exhausted from a night of horror, Moses respectfully removed his rain-soaked hat and begged Odell's pardon.

"Don't worry about that," Odell kindly assured him. "Come in out of that flood!"

Moses declined. He begged Odell's pardon again and again before telling him his purpose in coming. You'll likely need some help bringing up that rum, won't you, Mr. Odell? It's mostly just heavy rain now, and that Coast Guard ship done pulled out."

Shocked by the comment, delivered matter-of-factly as if it were an everyday occurrence and an equally ordinary offer of assistance, Odell grabbed Moses by his shoulder and pulled him into the kitchen. Moses was reluctant to stay, but finding himself inside the house, he kicked his thin, loosely fitted shoes and rain-soaked, nearly threadbare socks off. He stood so close to the door that Odell had difficulty closing it. When his wet clothes began to form a puddle on the kitchen floor, he tried in vain to wipe it up with his bare hands, but seeing that only made things worse, he began to tremble. Again, he apologized without saying what for.

"I'd offer you some dry clothes, but if we're going swimming, I guess there's no need," Odell said in good humor.

Rhoda had begun to feel lightheaded. For fear of fainting, she took a seat and rested her head on the kitchen table. She knew the details of the rum business that her husband was involved in, but she had never discussed it with anyone, not even the men who accompanied him on his runs. She lived in a make-believe world, for the most part, a conscious effort to pretend the rumrunning business didn't exist in spite of the fact that their own walls were filled with rum.

Rhoda's reaction sent Moses reaching for the doorknob. "I best go now, Boss," he said, quivering.

Raising her head only slightly, Rhoda asked Moses, "How did you know the rum was in the bayou?"

"He saw us throwing it out, honey," Odell explained.

"Dear God," she moaned. "If he saw it, the Coast Guard must have too!"

"Beg pardon, ma'am," said Moses, who bent over double to show his respect. "They most couldn't see it 'cause it was throwed from the back of the boat, and it was dark as midnight outside." He dared not continue the explanation, afraid he had already gone too far by addressing a white woman without permission.

"Don't worry, honey. Moses was in the open shed at the rooming house where he had a side view and the help of the lightning. Don't think I've ever seen such lightning!" he exclaimed. "The Coast Guard was in front of us. As to those in the rooming house? You can rest assured they were crouched down in a corner somewhere or under a mattress. I doubt they saw anything."

Rhoda noted with sadness the look of desperation on Moses's face, his body shivering from a combination of fear and clinging wet clothes, his hand still clutching the doorknob. For a miserable moment, she faced the truth. If word leaked out that a boatload of rum lay at the bottom of the bayou, every dealer in the county would dredge that body of water. "Please don't do this," she begged. "You'll all be killed!" she cried.

But Odell knew what he had to do. "Stop by Hank's and the Caldwells' on your way back and tell them to get the word out," he told Moses. "We'll meet at the 'post office.'" It was a code name for the rooming house on Tom's Bayou where Moses and his horse had weathered the storm.

Moses delivered the messages and then waited at the site for everyone to arrive. Even in the protected bayou, the tide had scattered the merchandise, but everyone who had waited for Odell's run joined the search until every crate was found. By the time the rum was retrieved and loaded onto their vehicles, it was dark, this time from nightfall instead of a storm. Most of the haulers would have to wait till morning to begin their deliveries northward, and if the flooding continued, perhaps not even then.

Odell called upon his waning energies to help Moses load his wagon. As he did, a troubling thought presented itself. Where could Moses keep a whiskey-loaded wagon overnight? There was only one answer. "You'd better stay in my barn tonight. You can leave before daybreak," he said.

"Oh, no, sir, Mr. Odell!" said the frightened man.

"You must, Moses," said Odell. "Clifford Jones is a friend of mine. I can't allow his best employee to stay outside in this weather."

It was with great reluctance that Moses agreed to stay. With his loaded wagon safely inside Odell's barn, and with enough hay to feed his horse and make a bed for himself, Moses donned old clothes that Rhoda had given him and tried to sleep.

Exhausted, Odell slept soundly until the neighing of a horse awakened him. *Moses is moving out,* he thought, and then he turned over to resume his rest. When the neighing became louder and more persistent, he lit the oil lamp so he could check the time. It was only a few minutes past midnight. He lit a lantern and hastened to the barn in his nightclothes. The barn door was swinging back and forth, a sure sign something had gone awry as he knew Moses would never be so careless as to leave the barn door open. Too, the rain hadn't let up. *He surely wouldn't leave in this,* he thought.

Inside, Moses's horse stood over a pile of hay, jerking her head up and down and pawing at one section of it while whinnying mournfully. Odell pushed the horse aside to get a better view.

The scene before him sent him stumbling over buckets and other gear that he had stepped over on a daily basis without incident. Sprawled naked and belly up across a bed of hay lay Moses, his body covered in his own blood, his borrowed overalls scattered about him in shreds, and one of Odell's socks stuffed in his mouth. He had been pummeled by some kind of heavy instrument that left deep gashes in his skull. Odell felt for a pulse and a heartbeat but found neither.

Moses was dead.

For a few horrifying moments, Odell knelt beside the corpse and cried, making no effort to wipe the stinging tears away. Once in charge of his emotions, he began surveying the place. Moses's wagon had not been moved, but it had been entirely emptied of its cargo. Lying beside his body was a bloodied butcher knife. Although his skull had been laid open by some kind of heavy instrument, Moses had no knife wounds. It had to mean that Moses had managed to inflict a knife wound on his attacker. The discovery gave Odell hope that the killer would be found and would pay for the crime. But he knew the truth: nobody would pay. The color of Moses's skin guaranteed it.

He cursed himself on the way to the house and was still muttering self-contempt when Rhoda met him at the door. "Moses was afraid of this, and I ignored him," he complained bitterly. "Some bastard killed him."

"No!" screamed Rhoda.

"It's all my fault. He begged me not to make him stay!" he cried openly, finally relieving the awesome pressure by beating the kitchen wall with both fists.

"Why didn't they just take the whiskey?" Rhoda screamed.

"They did," Odell choked. "But that wasn't their motive."

"What?" she begged to know.

"Revenge!" he shouted. "They killed him because he took a white man's job, but it's more than that. They want revenge on me for putting him up in my barn."

"No!" Rhoda screamed. "Clifford Jones hired Moses, not you!"

"Yeah, but Clifford Jones was smart enough not to allow Moses to sleep on his property. Yeah, they left me a clear message." Odell wept.

By noon, David had arranged for some of his black employees at the turpentine still to return Moses's remains to his family in Crestview. In hopes of confusing the killer, or killers, Odell and David agreed not to publicize the crime.

"Maybe the suspense of not hearing anything at all will drive the perpetrators of this dastardly act to reveal themselves. At least then you'll know who your enemies are," said David.

Even though the majority looked upon Moses's killer as a bad man in general, most thought a sharp reprimand would be sufficient punishment. Odell didn't agree. "I'd like to know who was willing to sacrifice a man with a wife and a houseful of kids just to get revenge on me for letting him sleep in a pile of hay," he said with growing bitterness.

The whole episode reminded Rhoda that Jolene and Jeannette Holder were out there in this mad and cruel world, fending for themselves, perhaps enduring the rule of a madman. The notion prompted Rhoda to launch a new campaign to find the missing women. She had no sooner done so than word from Crestview shocked everyone. Okaloosa County had scheduled another double hanging.

Chapter 11

THE ARREST AND CONVICTION OF THE TRAVELING salesman's accused murderers bore little similarity to the Klinger fiasco. Within a few short weeks of their arrest, Jeremiah Jinks and Lawrence Hardy found themselves in Judge Aiken's courtroom awaiting sentencing. It had taken the jury only thirty-six minutes to reach a guilty verdict. The murderers were sentenced to hang, the date set for the latter part of October. Okaloosa Countians were ecstatic. They had another reason to dress up and go somewhere.

Connie Brighton wouldn't be among the attendees. She was pregnant for the third time! Ecil refused to leave her but finally agreed to attend the hanging when Mary Sam and Rhoda chose to stay behind with Connie.

Every able-bodied man in Niceville, and that included Odell, planned to attend. It was not so much the hanging that drove Odell to Crestview as it was a deep feeling of responsibility to Clifford Jones and a chance to discuss the murder of Clifford's trusted foreman. Odell was clearly in no mood to watch two men hang even though he agreed with the court that both should die for their dastardly crime. Burdened with sorrow, he tackled the long, arduous trip to Crestview via horseback.

Once there, he headed for Sheriff Hagood's office. The atmosphere was electric, just as it had been before the Klinger hanging.

A bustle of activity appeared on every corner and in between as crowds gathered around the train station and the courthouse. Odell walked past them all, determined to attend to the business at hand, perhaps view the hanging later, and then rest a spell before heading back home. Before he could reach the sheriff's office, he heard a familiar noise. There was no mistaking the sound—it was a gunshot!

From the corner of the courthouse, he could see a flurry of people, young and old, running out of the hospital as if the building were on fire. By the time he crossed the street, some were screaming for the sheriff and others were just screaming.

"What happened?" he yelled to the first man he saw.

"Doc Azore shot one of his patients!" yelled the man who kept running.

When an elderly man came hobbling out of the hospital, Odell sought details.

"Well, you see, this salesman was trying to collect money from Doc Azore for medical supplies the doctor bought but hadn't paid for. The salesman threatened to sue Doc if he didn't pay up. Doc told him he would pay as soon as his patients paid him," he chuckled.

"Surely Doc didn't shoot the man?" begged Odell. "Doc wouldn't shoot nobody unless it was in self defense, " he declared.

But the man who witnessed the scene, didn't agree. "Don't look good for Doc," he revealed. "True, the salesman kept threatening Doc and he refused to leave the premises without his money, but he never drew any kind of weapon. When Doc grabbed that old shotgun he keeps close by, the salesman hightailed it out the door! Well, sir, Doc chased 'im down the street, and shot 'im!"

"Oh dear God, no!" yelled Odell. Where is Doc now? Is the salesman..."

"Dead? Naw!" scoffed the old man as if such a notion were preposterous. "Doc? Why he's in the operating room. Been there ever since it happened. He's pickin' shot out of that salesman's ass."

The old man let go with a deep belly laugh while Odell breathed a sigh of relief.

Most of the townspeople had gathered outside the hospital by now, some of whom were would-be patients. Many carried croker sacks filled with garden vegetables meant for the doctor. The hospital grounds were covered with clucking chickens and squealing pigs, live food meant to settle their medical bills. While everyone entertained themselves with news of the shooting, Odell found a tree stump to rest his bad leg on. The horseback ride on rough Indian trails had wreaked havoc on it. And the walk across the highway to the hospital had been a task indeed.

Only a few minutes passed before a nurse appeared in the hospital doorway yelling for "all of Dr. Azore's patients" to come back inside. Without a word to anyone, Odell ignored the pain in his leg long enough to sneak into the private entrance of Azore's office. "Heard you shot a man in the ass," he said with a coarse burst of laughter.

"Yeah, and it put me way behind in my schedule," Azore grumbled as he pushed his ten-gallon hat back, affording Odell a view of sleep-deprived eyes and numerous other haggard features.

"Guess you're here for the hanging?" Azore said in a belittling tone.

"Yeah, seems everybody's going, except you," Odell replied, jostling him. "Apparently the sheriff don't know about the shooting yet. He's out on a call. I'll tell him your gun went off accidentally," he offered.

"No accident," Azore assured his friend. "I purposely put a bullet in his ass. I could just as easily have put it in his heart." With the nonchalance of a man discussing the weather, he opened the door and yelled at the nurse, "Either send me some patients or lock the damn door so we can take a nap!"

Odell left bouncing with laughter. He was still at it when he arrived at Clifford Jones's restaurant. The facility still posed as a simple restaurant, but old-timers, and nearly everyone else, knew it was where alcoholic drinks were sold. Clifford and Odell shook hands vigorously even as they gazed sadly into each other's eyes. Odell was quick to take the blame for Moses's death.

"No, it was my fault," insisted Clifford. "I knew it wouldn't work, a black man taking a white man's job. The worst part is that nobody will pay for the crime," he grumbled.

"Yeah," agreed Odell. "We'll probably never know who did it, and it wouldn't make any difference if we did. I'd sure like to know who my own enemies are, though. It was me they wanted to punish for allowing Moses to sleep in my barn. I'm convinced of that." To lift their spirits, Odell described the shooting incident at the hospital, and the two men enjoyed a laugh in spite of their misery.

Once outside the restaurant, Odell spotted Sheriff Hagood. As soon as they were close enough to communicate, Odell joked with the sheriff about the town doctor being so desperate for patients, he shot one so he could remove the bullets.

"I missed the whole damn thing," the sheriff spouted. "Had to make a run to Baker. I wish somebody would kill Romie before he kills David or his daddy or both. It's bound to happen."

Odell silently agreed. Like so many Okaloosa County residents, Odell had harbored the notion that either David or his dad would eventually get fed up with Romie's poaching and shoot him on the spot. But after all these years, he had given up hope. "Did you see the shooting?" asked Hagood, who wanted to clear his mind of the latest fiasco involving Romie. The whole thing was a severe headache for the sheriff as Romie was one of the biggest moonshiners in the county and therefore one of the biggest donors to Hagood's security fund. There was another drawback to shooting Romie: if the shooter wasn't successful with his first shot, he would never live to shoot again. Romie would never die without taking his agitator with him. That was a given.

"Wish I had," replied Odell. "It would have been a lot more interesting than a hanging."

Odell was quick to introduce a subject that everyone seemed to have forgotten. "Say, I stopped by the Switzer place on my way in. Didn't see nobody but old Marge and a bunch of younguns. Claims she ain't seen Switzer since Chris's burial. Of course, she's lying."

Hagood sighed, apparently in disgust, but Odell wasn't so certain.

"Probably thinks we'll forget about him and then he can sneak back home. We'll get him then," said the sheriff with little interest.

Determined to push Hagood into pursuing the search for Switzer, Odell offered suggestions as to how best to go about it, but the convicts had made their appearance on the courthouse steps. The outburst among the crowd guaranteed that nobody would be able to carry on a private conversation, at least until after the men were dead—and perhaps not then.

As there would be no further opportunity to discuss the matter with the sheriff, Odell worked his way through the crowd and left the hastily prepared hanging arena. He saddled his horse and began the long ride home in spite of the seething pain in his injured leg.

A bit of comic relief awaited him not far away from the crowd. Just outside the town limits of Crestview, he noticed an old barebacked mule standing under the shade of a hickory tree, her reins dragging along the ground and no rider in sight. A quick search of the area revealed a man lying face down in the tall grass. When several calls brought no response, Odell stooped down and turned the body over.

It was Lucifer Bedford.

He was in a drunken stupor. Lying more than fifty yards away in an open area and just as drunk was his brother Billy Bob, while

Lum lay snoring on the sandy banks of Shoal River not more than twenty yards from Lucifer.

It took some effort on Odell's part to arouse Lucifer, who managed with a great deal of difficulty to force his eyelids open, albeit to a narrow slit. "Mr. Odell?" he asked with mental dullness. As sensibility gradually returned to him, he propped himself on his elbows and took a look around. "Where are we?" he asked.

"On the banks of Shoal River just outside of Crestview," said Odell.

Lucifer rallied. "Oh, hell yes!" he shouted. "We're going to the hanging!"

"Not today," Odell assured him. "Maybe next year."

While Odell and his friends were attending the hanging, Rhoda and her friends had been experiencing a nightmare in Niceville.

It was the night before the Crestview hanging was to take place when the women heard a sudden pounding on the front door. With mostly black folks left behind, none of whom would have dared knock on a white man's front door, there was some concern among the women as to who it could be. Mary Sam picked up her loaded rifle and aimed it at the entrance before advising Rhoda to open the door and move away from it. "Identify yourself or take a bullet," she warned their visitor, but there was no response.

"The constable isn't here," Rhoda called in a friendlier voice, but she was quickly reprimanded by both of her friends for advising the caller there was no man in the house.

Without warning, Mary Sam moved to the open doorway and stood there, rifle cocked. As total darkness hadn't yet made its arrival, a survey of the yard revealed a slight movement behind a huge live oak tree just a few feet away from the McNeils' living room window. With her anger struggling to escape its imprisonment,

Mary Sam stepped outside. "Stay behind the tree unless you're tired of living!" she warned the intruder.

"Please don't shoot," begged Rhoda. "It's probably one of the niggers come to get Odell. Oh, Lord, I hope they haven't been cuttin' each other up again."

Harsh living conditions for the black people often created brutal fights, but they never bothered Odell with their confrontations unless one of them died in the battle.

"Dear God, what if it's somebody we know?" Rhoda cried. Connie remained silent except for a moan brought about after biting her lip. "Surely they mean no harm," Rhoda added.

"Maybe not to you or Connie," Mary Sam countered, "but some smart-aleck might see this as an opportunity to rid the area of one more Indian squaw!"

When another few seconds passed with no response, Mary Sam began walking toward the tree, her rifle still cocked and pointed.

"Oh no!" argued Rhoda, who always had difficulty seeing the bad side of anything. Rhoda began urging the reluctant visitor to identify himself while he still could. Within seconds, there was an unusual rustle of oak leaves as if they had been picked up by a strong wind. Shortly after, a tall, dark figure stepped from behind the tree and began a slow walk toward the open door.

Rhoda held up the oil lamp, which offered a dim view of what appeared to be a young boy, muscular but thin. "Is somebody hurt? Are they dead? Are you looking for Mr. Odell?"

"Yes'm," came a voice all had heard before but none could immediately identify. It was a long moment before any of the women realized that all of them knew their visitor.

It was Jolene Holder!

Chapter 12

JOLENE WORE A HEAVILY STAINED AND NEARLY threadbare felt hat over a mass of dull, tangled hair and a pair of overalls so big that she had pinned half the bib to her waist and wrapped the galluses around her neck so many times that she appeared to be wearing a neck brace. The pants legs had been cut off and left to frazzle and the extra fabric used as a belt, thus giving her tiny waist some semblance of wearing the garment instead of the garment wearing her. Her muscled, bare arms revealed a life of hard work, as did her calloused hands. In spite of her obvious reluctance to pay these women a visit, she stood tall and straight, a fact that both pleased and surprised Rhoda, who remembered the boat ride to Pensacola during which Jolene had never raised her head high enough to look anyone in the eye.

The girl remained solidly planted in the doorway until Rhoda gently pulled her inside and closed the door. It was an awkward moment even for Rhoda, who had prayed for this moment. For well over a year, she had imagined having an opportunity to dress Jolene up in a pretty dress and fancy shoes and maybe a flowered hat or something colorful that would give her life. So many images, thoughts, and remembrances coursed through her mind that she had difficulty communicating any of them. Fortunately, Mary Sam took over.

"Honey, if you only knew how long and hard we've searched for you. Have you been playing hide-and-seek with us?" she teased.

The comment brought a slight smile to Jolene's face, revealing a toothless cavern within. Everyone either openly gasped or managed to stifle one. Odell had paid the Pensacola dentist a visit shortly after the girl's ordeal, and the doctor had assured him that he had removed the child's bad tooth, nothing more. *Why would the doctor lie about it?* they all wondered.

Connie and Rhoda were made temporarily speechless by the news that John Holder had actually done what he vowed he would, and particularly that the dentist had been an accomplice in the crime. Finally, Mary Sam, perhaps angrier than anyone, took over and begged Jolene to take a seat and chat with them.

"Yes, please do," insisted Rhoda. "It's just us girls here tonight," she said, sensing that Jolene would be even more uncomfortable in the company of a man.

Casey, usually a bubbling fill-in for awkward moments, remained silent while nursing a feeling of inspired terror. She had heard many stories about Jolene, none of which painted the picture she saw before her. Her curiosity was spiked by Jolene's unkempt appearance, which was far more noticeable than that of the equally unkempt, poverty-ridden black children who lived in a swamp. Rhoda's loving description of the girl had given Casey reason to imagine Jolene with long, luscious hair and dreamy blue eyes not unlike those of a beauty queen. With her paper dolls in front of her, she pulled out the one she had named Jolene, a tall, curvy blond dressed in a fitted, ankle-length dress and matching broad-brimmed hat. Unconsciously, she crunched the paper doll in her hand until the thin cardboard finally separated into limp pieces.

"Come, come," Rhoda insisted, tugging playfully at Jolene's loose clothing. "You can't imagine how happy we are to see you. We were about to eat supper, and you can join us. And sweetheart, we want so very much to know all about your dear mother. Please tell us everything," she begged as Rhoda and Mary Sam anxiously awaited Jolene's story.

"I shot a man," Jolene announced while solidly rooted to the spot she had originally taken.

"You what!" gasped Rhoda. Her mind raced through the list of men she knew who hadn't attended the hanging. There were so few, and most of those were helpless old men who couldn't harm an insect.

"I don't know," she admitted.

"You don't know who you shot? Did you kill him? Where is his body?" rattled Connie. All three women harbored thoughts that someone had tried to take advantage of the young woman, perhaps sexually. But another good look at Jolene, the picture of a grungy-looking boy at best, convinced them nearly simultaneously that no man could be coaxed into having sex with her, much less fight for it.

Casey had let go with a low moan when Jolene made her announcement and then followed the reaction with a tight fist, permanently destroying her Jolene doll and its colorful attire.

Mary Sam motioned everyone into the kitchen where they could sit around the table, but it took some urging to persuade Jolene to move beyond the front door. It was not until the three women were settled in the kitchen that she made a move in that direction. Still clutching the crushed remains of her paper doll, Casey followed.

"Now tell us everything," Rhoda urged.

"There were three of them. They tore up Mr. David's moonshine still and Mr. Clough's too and maybe some more," she explained quickly and to the point.

Rhoda's first reaction was one of fear, but she managed to remain outwardly calm and steady. Mary Sam showed no such emotion and continued to stare mercilessly at Jolene, a peculiar child with an equally peculiar story. It went against Mary Sam's exuberant nature to sit still and listen, but she too, managed to accomplish the feat.

"I was in a tree trying to get my squirrel when I heard some voices," continued Jolene. "I was about half a mile from Mr. David's big still house, you know. They musta heard my squirrel drop because they turned around quick like, and when they saw me in the tree, one of them took a shot at me."

While the three adults and one little girl tensed up in anxious silence, Jolene stopped there as if she planned to keep the rest of the story secret.

"Please go on," Mary Sam begged. "If someone shot at you, we need to know. If the men are still out there, they may have followed you here."

"You dropped your squirrel?" asked Casey, who had abandoned her paper dolls for a seat close to her mother.

"Yes, he was my supper," Jolene said matter-of-factly, as if it were a common occurrence for young women to kill an animal for supper. "I shot 'im but he got hung up in the tree branches. I had to climb up the tree to get 'im, and while I was up there, these men came up and they were laughing about destroying Mr. David's and Mr. Clough's whiskey stills and—"

"Do you know for certain they destroyed my husband's still house?" asked Mary Sam. "And Clough Martin's? This man who shot at you—did he hit you?"

"No ma'am, but when the fat one saw me, he aimed a shotgun in my direction. I shot 'im in the hand. Didn't want to kill 'im."

Rhoda and Mary Sam found it nearly impossible to believe a whiff of a girl could shoot a man in the presence of two other men who were apparently armed and come away without an injury of any kind to herself. They glanced at each other often as each tried to relay her thoughts, albeit in silence.

"What about the others?" asked Connie. She had begun to worry about safety, not for herself, but for her baby. It seemed the forces of nature were determined to see her motherless, and she wouldn't wish that on anyone. Dr. Smythe had insisted that she pamper herself throughout the pregnancy so as not to lose another baby. Would stress affect her pregnancy? she worried. "Maybe we should secure the door," she told the others.

"If they break through these doors, they won't live long enough to pull a trigger," Mary Sam assured her, and Jolene nodded accordingly. Still, to please Connie, Mary Sam assisted Rhoda and Casey in pushing heavy furniture against both entrances to the house. With Jolene still in the kitchen, Casey jumped at the chance to whisper in her mother's ear. "Will they hang Jolene, Mama?"

"No, honey," her mother assured her with as much finesse as she could muster. Once they claimed their seats again, Jolene finally perched on the edge of one of the long benches.

"Let's figure out who these men are," Rhoda insisted. "It should be easy because nearly every man in Niceville went to the hanging."

"Maybe they're revenuers," said Connie. "They didn't go to the hanging!" That such a thing could have happened frightened her immensely.

"Calm down," insisted Mary Sam. "Let's hear the whole story before we come to a conclusion. Why would the feds destroy David's and Clough's still houses and no one else's? The feds don't play favorites. If they're in town, they won't leave a still house standing. I'm thinkin' they'll be looking for Doc Smythe to attend to those wounds Jolene gave them."

Connie stared at Mary Sam, shocked that she had apparently accepted the whole story as related by this child who always appeared to have dropped in from another world. As for herself, she had held out hope that the girl was hallucinating or at least had concocted the story for attention or some other unknown reason. After all, she was John Holder's daughter!

Rhoda took a long look at Jolene, a pathetic specimen only vaguely resembling a human and a deprived child whose life had always been the pits. She was reminded of the questions she still had no answers to after all these months, and now that Jolene was present, she was determined to know the answers. With this immediate problem facing them, they would need to spend more time with Jolene, and considering the girl's talent for disappearing, they couldn't afford to let her out of their sight until they had made some kind of plan to help her.

Jolene was bent on leaving, so the women tried, apparently in vain, to instill in her the dangers of a young girl's being out at night, especially when those very men she had wounded might be waiting for her. They soon realized the scare tactic wouldn't work on her. She hadn't knocked on Odell's door to seek protection but to report a crime. Having reported it, she was ready to leave.

"Okay, so you're not afraid, but we are! We need you to protect us," said Rhoda in earnest. "You saw us pushing the furniture against the door? That's because we are afraid!" she said with nervous emphasis. "Our husbands are not here, so we're especially frightened. And there's Miss Connie and her unborn baby to consider," she thought to mention.

Jolene showed signs of sympathy, but she stood her ground when it came to spending the night. Dismayed by the whole thing, Casey pulled out her only remaining paper doll and began a drama between herself and the female doll. She clipped colorful dresses, hats, and shoes on the doll and paraded her around make-believe palatial grounds.

Jolene was captivated. She took the doll in her hand, turned it over, and pulled its dress off. The sight of the doll wearing only bloomers and a tight-fitting bodice caught her off guard. She stifled a giggle and was clearly fascinated. She asked Casey for a pencil and paper, and when Casey obliged, she began marking on it. When finished, she handed the paper to Casey and giggled again, apparently at herself.

Casey followed suit with her own giggle before running to her mother with the drawing. Jolene objected, but the deed was done.

"Jolene! Where did you learn to draw like that?" asked Mary Sam.

"It's awful," Jolene insisted. "My mother tried to teach me, but I was a poor student."

While Connie and Rhoda perused the sketch, Casey revealed her thoughts. "If you'll stay, we can sleep on the floor in Aunt Rhoda's room," she told Jolene. It occurred to her that Jolene would be very uncomfortable in fancy bedding. Too, with Jolene's hair matted in filth, her body odor offensive, and her dirt-encrusted fingernails sharp weapons of destruction, Casey knew no one would be asked to crawl into bed with her.

Jolene seemed pleased by the notion of sleeping on the floor. She didn't agree to stay the night, but she appeared eager to join Casey and her paper people. The two eventually fell asleep on the floor and were allowed to remain there. Before daylight, however, Jolene woke everyone when she began dragging the furniture away from the kitchen door. All the women sprang from their beds and began pleading with Jolene not to leave.

"I'll get breakfast, and you get those paper dolls out again, Casey," said Rhoda in a frenzy.

"But I don't have another doll with me!" the child protested. "If we could only go to my house?" Remembering that she had destroyed the Jolene doll, she turned to their guest with a story. "I named one of my dolls Jolene, but I left her at home." To atone for lying, she crossed her fingers, a signal to God that she meant no harm.

The comment brought a broad smile to Jolene's face, one she hid as best she could with cupped hands over her mouth, an obvious attempt to hide her toothlessness. When the women saw the camaraderie the two had developed, they agreed to pack up and head for the Stewart house where a host of paper dolls awaited them.

Once there, Jolene and Casey were inseparable in spite of their age difference—Casey six and her new friend nearing fifteen. Jolene fingered the doll's faces and then began sketching their images on anything she could find to make a mark on. While Casey played house with her dolls, Jolene drew faces. Her first subject was Casey, followed by Rhoda, Connie, and Mary Sam. Having exhausted the images of those around her, she began other sketches.

Fascinated by the image of herself, Casey studied it at length before perusing the entire stack. One drawing particularly caught her eye. Without a word to Jolene, she jumped up and ran to her mother with it. "Look, Mama! It's Mr. Ovid!"

With no indication that she had heard the comment, Jolene proceeded with another sketch before casually announcing, "I shot that one in the arm."

Connie studied the sketch. "You shot Ovid Switzer! Nobody's seen or heard from him since little Chris died. Have they?" she asked, quite mortified. Her eyes met Rhoda's, who took a quick look at the sketch and agreed it was Switzer.

"Except for a revenuer, he would be the most likely to destroy David's still," said Mary Sam. The thought angered her, but she was too overwhelmed by Jolene's talent to allow her emotions to get out of hand. Quickly, she began studying the other sketches. "Your mama must have been quite a teacher. Do you have any of her work?"

"Lots of them," said the girl proudly. "Papa brought men to the house so Mama could sketch them. They paid Papa money," she added with obvious pride.

All three women were temporarily speechless. They knew the

sad truth. There was no man in Niceville who had the courage to refuse John Holder anything. At the same time, no man would admit to succumbing to John's demands, so the men who posed for Jeannette apparently paid John for the privilege and then left the premises without the merchandise they were forced to pay for. It was a typical John Holder fiasco and one the demoralized men kept secret from everyone, including one another.

While the women pondered the situation, Casey begged Jolene to "Draw the other men who destroyed my daddy's stuff." Without comment, Jolene reached for her newest sketches and handed them to Casey.

Casey screamed with delight when she saw the first sketch. "It's Mr. Homer!"

"Why am I not surprised?" asked Mary Sam, peeking over Casey's shoulder. "We should have known Homer Cogbill would spend the rest of his life seeking revenge!"

"Revenge? For what?" asked Connie.

"For what? Have you forgotten the marble game at the Klinger hanging? When Casey had a fight with Homer Cogbill's boy over marbles? Think 'half a breed,'" Mary Sam spouted, an unusual show of irritation toward her friend.

"Oh my," said Rhoda apologetically, unaware that the episode still aroused Mary Sam's emotions.

"In any case, I think the drawing looks like Homer," offered Connie. "And we all know Homer will stop at nothing."

Doubt had begun to sneak into Rhoda's mind, however. Was Jolene mistaken? If Homer wanted revenge on David, why did he also destroy Clough Martin's whiskey still? Too, it bothered her that Jolene hadn't actually witnessed the destruction of the stills but had only heard the men brag about it. "Do we know for certain the still houses are destroyed?" she asked.

Mary Sam, however, was satisfied, and she was consumed

with anger. "You should know by now that there's nothing Homer Cogbill won't do, and with all the men gone to Crestview for the hanging, he didn't figure on getting caught!"

"What if they come here?" Connie worried. While the women checked the door locks for the third time and made certain all the guns were loaded, Jolene completed a sketch of the third man and handed it to Connie.

"This was one of the men? Doesn't look familiar," she said after studying the sketch at length before passing it to Rhoda.

"Did you shoot this one too?" asked the startled woman.

"Got him in the shoulder," said Jolene. "I aimed for his arm, but he turned around just as I pulled the trigger. I'm afraid he got the worst of it," she said with apparent regret.

The women marveled at the girl's expertise with guns, as well as her compassion, even for those who meant to harm her. And they all pondered the same question: *Can she really be John Holder's daughter?*

"Well, let the menfolk worry about it. Let's talk some more," Rhoda insisted. "To tell you the truth, we have worried about you, young lady, since that day on the boat when you went to Pensacola with a toothache." She grimaced just thinking about it, especially with Jolene's empty mouth a testament to her father's heartlessness. "We always wanted to know why your mother didn't go with you. We could only assume she was not well."

Jolene shifted uncomfortably on the hard floor. "That man on the boat—he killed my papa," she announced without lifting her eyes from her sketch.

"The man on the boat?" asked Rhoda. "You mean young Gussie?"

"You *saw* him kill your papa?" Mary Sam nearly shouted.

"My mama did," Jolene answered. "My mama was awful sick. I couldn't get her warm all day," Jolene began. "I put all the covers on her, but she still shivered. It was a hot summer, but I had to keep a fire going to keep her warm. We ran out of wood, so I went out to cut some. While I was gone, I heard a thousand gunshots and I ran back to the house. Mama was lying on the floor by the chest. I thought she had been shot, but ..." She raised her head for the first time and surveyed the startled faces of each one of her listeners before continuing.

Connie gasped. "He killed your mama too?"

Jolene paused long enough to wipe her runny nose with her dirty shirt collar. Rhoda wanted to offer a handkerchief but didn't for fear of embarrassing the girl. All three women and one little girl waited in tortured silence.

"She was still alive. I carried her to the bed and crawled in bed to keep her warm. 'He killed your papa,' Mama told me."

"'Who did, Mama?' I asked her, but she was dead. She died with one of her sketches in her hand. It was a sketch of the man on the boat, the one with the crazy package. Mama had used her last ounce of strength to pull the sketch she had once made of him out of the drawer.

"I knew Papa was dead because there were a million gunshots like in a war," she explained. "With so many shots, there must have been a dozen men shot Papa a thousand times, but Mama didn't see but one of them, and it was the one with that crazy package." She took a deep, disturbing breath before catching the eyes of three compassionate women and one startled little girl. She put her head in her hands and began to sob. Her friends sobbed with her.

So many questions hadn't yet been answered. The story she related had come about later, after the dentist had brutally pulled all of her teeth. *If only she would fill in the blanks,* each one of her visitors thought, but no one had the courage to ask. *Where was Jeannette that awful day? Was she too sick to make the trip to Pensacola, where she might have prevented the massacre of her little daughter's mouth? And what happened to John and Jolene after the visit to the dentist?*

Odell had made a special trip to Pensacola to question the dentist, but the doctor assured him he had only pulled one tooth. He registered surprise when Odell told him that neither John nor his daughter had been seen since that day. Odell's dozen or more trips to the Holder shack offered no answers as there was no evidence that anyone had resided there for months. Also, there were no fresh graves in the thickly wooded surroundings.

"Sheronda," Jolene whispered mournfully. "She took care of Mama."

"Sheronda?" questioned Rhoda. "You mean the black woman?"

Jolene continued her story as if she hadn't heard the question. "Papa left Mama with Sheronda."

Everyone knew, with the exception of Casey, that Sheronda was an untrained black woman who assisted women of her race in childbirth. A majority of these babies died, as did their mothers. The same was often true in the white community, but no one talked about that.

Unspoken questions pierced the thoughts of all three women. *Was Jeannette Holder pregnant again?*

Their questions went unanswered as Jolene had said all she intended to. She stood up without warning and began a hasty move toward the door.

Pretending not to notice, Mary Sam jumped up and insisted they make an effort to find the men Jolene had wounded. "We need to check with Dr. Smythe and even Doc Holbrook." Holbrook had long since closed his practice, but many still sought his services. The doctor's mind was good, but he had lost his eyesight early in his practice. These guilty men would likely be encouraged by that as the doctor wouldn't be able to identify them. "I'll pay both doctors a visit," Mary Sam announced. Jolene, meanwhile, had moved all of the furniture away from the door and was on her way out.

Trembling at the thought of Jolene's leaving, perhaps never to return, Rhoda began whimpering. "We must think of Connie and her delicate condition, and there's Casey, a helpless little girl. And I'm an old woman," she cried. "What if the men come here?" The drama won Jolene over. She agreed to stay until Mary Sam returned.

With Mary Sam away, Casey carried on a conversation with her dolls while Jolene stretched out on a pallet and soon fell asleep. When she awoke, she was startled at first but was quickly pacified by Casey's playfulness. "You were sleeping," said Casey. "I'm glad you're awake now because I was thinking maybe you could draw a picture of my great-great-great-grandfather. Maybe there's one more *great*; I'm not sure now. Anyway, he was a famous Indian chief," she bragged.

Jolene did a quick survey of the room, apparently in search of anyone bearing the resemblance of such a man. "Oh, he's dead now," explained Casey, "but Mama has a picture of him. We could surprise Mama with a copy!" Excited by the idea, she ran into her parents' bedroom and soon returned with a box covered in deteriorating gold velvet and secured by an equally deteriorating velvet ribbon. Casey struggled with the knot at length before Rhoda offered to help.

"Are you sure it's okay with your mother to open this?" Rhoda questioned, but Casey assured her it was fine. "It's my mama's favorite photos, but she shares them with me," she assured them. "She keeps them in here so nothing can happen to them." Once the ribbon was untied, she eagerly took the box and placed it between her and Jolene on the pallet. "You're gonna love my *greaaaaat*-grandfather," she promised. Rummaging through faded tin types, she squealed with delight when she found the one she was searching for. "Being chief is like being the president," she proudly informed Jolene.

The gray tin type of a heavily wrinkled, dark-skinned man in feathered headgear captured Jolene's undivided attention. She ran her hands over the photo much as a blind person might a human face.

"Please! Could you draw him now?" squealed Casey. "I can't wait for Mama to see it."

Jolene appeared reluctant but nodded consent. While she concentrated on the job at hand, Casey began leafing through the other photos, handing them one by one to Connie, who passed them to Rhoda.

"Oh, look!" Casey shouted. "Here's Mr. Klinger." Instead of passing the photo as she had the others, she studied it. "Poor Mr. Klinger," she moaned. "They hung 'em. But he's in heaven now. Do you think he plays with little Chris?" she asked no one in particular as she pressed the photo lovingly against her chest.

When Connie took a look at the photo, she turned pale, a faint shadowy semblance of herself. It was indeed a photo of Willie Earl Klinger, a photo that couldn't have been taken more than two or three years earlier which would have been only months before he was arrested for murder.

Rhoda tried hard to think of an explanation for its presence in Mary Sam's keepsake photos, but as nothing came to her, she sputtered a few senseless words.

Paying little attention to the adults, Casey continued her perusal of the photographs. Mary Sam's brazen visit with Klinger the day of the hanging had remained a topic of conversation among the entire community, thus allowing no one the pleasure of forgetting about it. Children were quickly made to understand that Casey and her mother were to be scrupulously avoided as a result of their behavior, and her schoolmates responded by bullying her for "talking to that murderer." Casey, however, was not so easily bullied. She held fond memories of Klinger, and she was comforted in knowing he was in heaven, where nobody would make a fuss if he chose his left hand over his right. The would-be bullies not only failed to send Casey home in tears, they secretly admired her for her courage.

Rhoda was still holding the photo of Klinger when Mary Sam burst through the back door.

"No one has come to Dr. Smythe with a gunshot wound," she announced. "Doc Holbrook was already in bed, but Mandie assured me no one had been there seeking help. I explained everything to Doc Smythe so he can be on the lookout."

Rhoda quickly placed Klinger's photo in the pile everyone had already studied. No one made a comment, not even Casey, who was focused on Jolene's drawing. The quiet was intense, so unlike the gabby group Mary Sam had left only minutes earlier. Her attention was quickly drawn to the open box, its ribbons untied, its contents scattered in piles here and there.

"Casey!" she screamed. "What are you doing?" She grabbed the piles and began stuffing them in the box, but in her haste, the photo of Klinger fell on the floor, face up. She quickly retrieved it but realized it was too late; Rhoda and Connie had seen it, and that explained the morbid quiet they had greeted her with. Changing her pace, she pulled herself together long enough to exit the room, Klinger's photo in her hand. Everyone could hear the soft cries emanating from her room.

Jolene jumped up from the floor, her eyes fearful and her hands trembling. After tossing the chief's photo on the table, she tore her unfinished sketch into several pieces and stuffed them in one of her deep pockets.

"It's all right," Rhoda assured her. "Miss Mary Sam is upset, but it has nothing to do with you." While she comforted Jolene, Connie headed for Mary Sam's bedroom. They had embraced for a long moment before Rhoda had a chance to join them.

"So now you know," said Mary Sam, who gazed poignantly into Rhoda's stunned eyes before switching her gaze in Connie's direction.

"So now we know what?" asked Rhoda.

"Willie Earl Klinger was Casey's father!"

Chapter 13

WHEN ODELL RETURNED HOME LATE THE FOLLOWING night, he wasn't surprised to find Rhoda wide awake and anxiously awaiting his return. He knew she would be aching to hear all the details of the hanging.

As it turned out, his wife had more news to share than he did.

He wouldn't have the pleasure of meeting Jolene, however. During the night, she had slipped out of the house without a word. Rhoda was beset with worry. What if the injured men returned to seek revenge? Had Mary Sam's outburst frightened her away forever?

As to the news of Switzer and Cogbill's destruction of the moonshine stills, Odell immediately began plotting his strategy for dealing with them, as well as their unknown accomplice. It was not a crime that could be reported to any authorities, as the whiskey stills were themselves illegal. Also, nobody, not even lawmen, tattled on fellow moonshine makers. Odell was on Ecil's doorstep before dawn the next morning.

"I never went to sleep," declared Ecil, his swollen eyelids verifying his words. "I see you didn't either," he added after taking a good look at the tiny community's weary constable. "How will we handle Clough?" he begged to know.

Odell had the answer. "First, I'm gonna deputize you but only if you agree to it. I know Connie's condition—any time now, so I didn't want you involved but …"

"Don't you worry about that," Ecil interrupted. "The busier I am, the better."

"But this job is dangerous, and Connie's gonna know it. I tried to get David, but he's tied up again with Romie, that damn poacher," he fussed. "God, I wish they would get rid of that man!"

"Have you heard from David?"

"Yeah, the sheriff finally locked Romie up, but of course he paid the fine and went home and started plowing the Stewart land the next day! He'll be poaching on the Stewart land until they agree to sell it to him, and you know that ain't gonna happen!"

"I don't get it. Why don't they buy someone else's land?" asked Ecil.

"Because he wants the Stewart family out of Crestview! Romie thinks he can buy the Stewarts' unblemished reputation if he owns all their land. He's too stupid to realize his standing in the community is at the bottom of the pit no matter what he owns."

"Bad timing," moaned Ecil. "David needs to be dealing with Ovid Switzer and Homer Cogbill right here in Niceville now."

"Exactly. I'm tired of sheltering Switzer myself, and I'm in no mood to listen to Homer's lies either." He neglected to say what he planned to do about it.

"I'm thinking we should be the ones to tell Clough about his whiskey stills' being destroyed. He's gonna think we're hiding something from him if we don't," said Ecil.

"Maybe so. But let's not tell him who destroyed the stills. At least then, we'll have an opportunity to verify Jolene's story before Clough can get the whole thing screwed up."

At Clough's house, Willie May told them her husband had arrived home from the Crestview hanging only minutes earlier. "He's sleeping off a devil of a hangover," she added with the vulgar laugh she was noted for.

This was good news for Odell and Ecil as it would give them time to confront Homer before Clough had a chance to.

Homer's wife was already milking the cow, and his two teenage daughters, one harnessed like a horse, pulled a plow while her sister walked behind and guided the heavy plow in spite of being too short to easily reach the plow's handles. Young Clete, Homer's only son, chopped firewood and had apparently been at it since dawn as the pile was already high.

"You know who that is, don't you?" Odell asked.

"I know," said Ecil. "It was one of few times either of them had seen Clete since the episode at the Klinger hanging. "He's a good kid. He just hasn't had a chance with Homer Cogbill for a daddy," he said discerningly.

Odell agreed. "He's building up some muscles. I expect him to beat the hell out of his old man one of these days. I hope he does it before Homer beats the boy's mother to death!"

Homer was known for beating family members during his drunken stupors, but none of them dared reveal the source of their trauma. They didn't have to as everyone could see for themselves the family's bludgeoned bodies.

Having reached the entrance to the Cogbill house, Ecil noted that Homer was nowhere around. "I wouldn't be surprised to find him in bed. If he is, we'll wake him up." There was no immediate answer to a knock on the door, but they did hear noises inside. They knocked again, louder.

Homer finally ambled to the door, shirtless and in baggy pants that hung well below his belly. His shoulder had been loosely bandaged, and his arm was in a sling made of dingy long-john pieces. His near nakedness revealed an ugly zigzagged scar running from his chest to his waist and part of his belly, but it was obviously not a new wound. His uninvited guests paid little attention to it as Homer was noted for his drunken brawls. His fresh wounds, however, were of great interest to both men.

The sight of Odell and Ecil standing in the doorway played havoc with Homer's already weakened condition. His features were drawn and haggard as if he had spent the night in a drunken fight or perhaps a painful and sleepless tussle. He struggled to stay upright, finally grabbing the door frame to steady himself as the men walked inside, albeit without a formal invitation.

"Something wrong?" asked Homer. He made a point of positioning his arm sling across his chest so as to hide as much of it as possible.

"What happened to you?" asked Odell.

"Damned revenuer came through here while you guys were at the hanging," he explained. "But you don't have to worry—I killed the son of a bitch, but he got me in the shoulder."

"And apparently not before he destroyed a few still houses?" asked Ecil. He pushed Homer aside, making room for Odell to enter behind him and leaving Homer standing in the doorway.

Realizing his visitors weren't going away, Homer reluctantly offered them a cup of coffee. Once in the kitchen, he grabbed the tablecloth off the kitchen table, tossed it awkwardly over his injured shoulder, and tucked the loose ends in his baggy pants, a move that covered most of his scarred belly. Obviously unnerved by their visit, Homer talked a steady stream, tossing question after question at both men about the hanging but never waiting for their responses. In an effort to avoid his visitors' eyes, he focused on the pan of boiling coffee. Once the coffee settled, he picked up the boiler and attempted to fill a mug, but his hands shook so that he let go, allowing the pot to fall heavily on the stove top. "Well, maybe you can pour it," he said weakly as he plopped into his seat, obviously in physical, as well as mental, distress.

"We didn't come for coffee," Odell assured him. "Who helped you and Switzer destroy the moonshine stills?" he asked bluntly.

The accusation brought Homer to his feet in spite of the pain such a move created. "What stills? Why, I ain't seen Switzer in a coon's age," he protested. "You gotta admit it, Odell. It was a perfect time for the feds to come in with all the able-bodied men in Crestview for the hanging."

"We have a witness, Homer—the one who shot you in the shoulder, and it wasn't a revenuer. Don't make me any madder than I already am," cautioned Odell.

Homer was quick to change his story. "Okay. Switzer told me this revenuer was gonna raid some still houses, you know, but the fed said if me and Switzer would lead him to the big ones, he would pass ours up. I pretended to go along with it."

"Pretended?" mocked Odell. "David's and Clough's still houses are in ruins! Maybe you better tell me if you took any others down."

"No, that's all. Honest!" he assured them. "And don't worry. That damn fed will never take his report back to Washington. Like I told you, I killed the bastard," he bragged, his confidence somewhat restored as evidenced by the steady hand that finally succeeded in pouring himself a cup of coffee.

Ecil reached in his pocket and pulled out a sketch that Jolene had made of the third man and showed it to Homer. "Is this the man you killed?" he asked.

Homer's face suddenly lacked color. He began to wonder if Odell and Ecil had attended the hanging after all. "Where did you get that?" he yelped.

"Where's Switzer?" the constable asked.

"No telling. He's always on the run. He appeared out of nowhere one night with this scheme, but now that it's done, he's likely gone again."

"No more lies, Homer," warned Odell. "Where is he?"

"In his cellar most likely," said Homer, whose shoulders drooped from a mix of pain and utter hopelessness.

"I don't think so," said Odell, angered. "We've looked there and never saw any evidence he has been there. I think Switzer's a little smarter than that."

"He's got a cellar deep in the woods, maybe two, three miles from his house. I'd show you, but you can see I'm in no shape to ride a horse." He tried to lift his coffee mug again but quickly put it down without taking a sip. He smiled within, certain the men would realize he was indeed too sick to ride a horse.

"We'll give you time to saddle your horse or you can ride bareback, but you're going to take us to Switzer." When Homer made no effort to move, Odell continued. "You can go with that tablecloth wrapped around you or you can throw something else on. I don't care! How bad is Switzer's wound? We know he took a hit too."

The comment sent Homer into a slump from which it appeared he might never recover. "Nothing but a flesh wound. Went straight through his arm," he mumbled in obvious despair. No one knew better than Homer that he was not in an enviable position. Revenuers were the most hated men in Okaloosa County, and they were hated because they destroyed moonshine stills. And now, Homer was guilty of the same crime. Realizing this, the slump in his body deepened.

The men assisted Homer onto his bareback horse, and the three were off to Switzer's cellar. An hour passed before they spotted a man in the distance coming their way. "Is that Ovid?" asked Odell.

"Don't think so," said Homer. "Ovid covers a lot more horse than that." They all had a big laugh, the first of the day for all of them.

The horseman was nearly upon them before they finally recognized its rider.

It was Clough.

Clough greeted all three men in his boisterous and arrogant style, his personality echoing that of Homer in many ways. The main difference between the two was that Clough had material wealth to boast of; Homer didn't as he had always squandered his.

"What in the world? Your wife said you were sleeping off a hangover!" yelled Odell as soon as they were in speaking distance. "How'd you get way out here so fast?"

"That damn woman drinks too much juice," said Clough. "I'm just getting back from the hanging. She's right about the hangover though. I've been sleeping it off along the way. Still don't feel none too good. Damned horse ran me through a thornbush while I was napping." His face bore fresh scratches as did his hands and arms—nothing unusual for anyone riding horseback through the thick forest, ripe with briers and thornbushes the area was known for.

Odell and Ecil were suspicious for other reasons. Who was telling the truth: Clough or his wife? He couldn't have known about the whiskey stills if he was just arriving home, but *was* he just arriving home? He certainly would have learned in Crestview that Ovid Switzer had not been apprehended. Did he wait for morning so he could pay Switzer a visit? If so, what was the result? They had a multitude of questions but, thus far, no answers.

"Where you guys headed?" asked Clough.

"Just making another run out to Switzer's place," Odell answered. "Don't expect to find him, but we have to make an effort. Want to come along?" It was an invitation he hated to extend but a necessary one to hold down suspicion.

"I'd like to, but I'm so damn tired right now, think I'll pass. It's all I can do to keep from falling off this horse," he told them. He did appear exhausted.

Odell was satisfied that Clough knew nothing about his whiskey still being destroyed. If he had known his still was destroyed and that Homer Cogbill had taken part in it, he would have shot him on sight. On the other hand, he asked no questions about Homer's shoulder wound even though it had begun to bleed through the bandages. All of this coursed through Odell's mind. He stole a glance at Ecil, whose slight thrust of the jaw indicated that he too was concerned. But Clough gave his horse notice that he was ready to go, and just like that, he headed toward home, leaving a stunned lawman and his friend, as well as their captive, totally confused.

Less than a half mile later, Homer pointed toward a narrow trail. "Take it," he said weakly. "It's a shortcut that bypasses Switzer's house. It'll take you to the cellar."

"Let us know when we're within a hundred yards or so from the cellar. We'll tie the horses up and walk in. It looks pretty thick in there. If these horses run up on a snake, they'll wake the dead folks with their neighing. Of course, you never know what kind of welcome Switzer might have for us if he spots us first," said Odell.

"I'd say you're close enough right now," Homer said weakly. His plea to stay behind and wait for them to return was ignored. Odell and Ecil tied their horses to a tree, assisted Homer in his dismount, and walked behind him.

"I'm afraid somebody's beat you to 'im," Homer soon noted, pointing straight ahead. Dangling from the end of a rope that had been tied to a many-armed black gum tree was a lifeless body.

It was Ovid Switzer. His body was warm, but there was no life in it.

The flesh wound that Jolene had given Switzer wouldn't have rendered him helpless, but the hangman had apparently shot his victim in both legs, disabling him enough that one man could easily accomplish a deed normally calling for two or three strong men.

Homer shed no tears for his partner in crime. Self-preservation was his only concern. "I don't have to tell you guys Clough's gonna kill me too!" he bellowed pitifully. "And when he does, it'll be on your conscience!" When neither Odell nor Ecil showed any signs of pity, he began to wail uncontrollably.

"I have a question for you, Homer," said Ecil. "If you planned to kill the revenuer anyway, why didn't you do it before he destroyed the still houses?" he scolded.

"When you're with Clough, you do everything his way," he blubbered. "It ain't no secret that Switzer don't like David, the Indian lover, and don't nobody like Clough," he reminded them.

Odell and Ecil rather enjoyed watching Homer squirm. They had their own problems to take care of, problems Homer had helped create. With that in mind, they escorted him home and left him there in his misery.

In the wee hours of the night, David Stewart started beating on Odell's door. "Homer Cogbill's house burned to the ground!" he announced. "Whole family's dead except his boy, Clete, and he's burned pretty bad. I took him over to Doc Smythe."

Odell stared at David. "How did you—"

"I was just coming in from Baker. I could see the fire miles away. It lit up the sky, man!" he exclaimed.

"Clough?" Odell wondered out loud even as he struggled to get dressed.

"Clough? You think? But they're good friends. Could be an accident," said David.

"No accident, David. I don't have time to fill you in, but I'll tell you this much: Homer Cogbill and Ovid Switzer destroyed your still house, the big one. Clough's too. But right now we got a murderer and an arsonist on our hands."

"My God!" David yelled angrily. He took a moment to digest the bad news before reliving the last few moments. "I raced over there, but the walls were already coming down. I heard the boy moaning and found him lying on the ground."

"Is he gonna live?" asked Odell.

"Doc couldn't say," was the response.

Meanwhile, Odell couldn't get his mind off Homer's pleas for protection against Clough. "I never dreamed the bastard would kill the whole family," he groaned. It was nearly impossible to make Odell angry, but Clough had managed to do it. Odell grabbed his loaded rifle and filled his pockets with extra shells. All the while Rhoda was pleading with him, "Take David with you."

"Don't worry. I'm going with him," David assured her.

Clough greeted his visitors with a grunt and offered them no invitation to enter his home. "I guess you had your reasons for not telling me my still house was destroyed? Did you come to apologize?" he snarled.

"Guess you had your reasons for not telling us you hanged Ovid Switzer just before we got to him yesterday!" Odell retorted. "As for the still house? Apparently you already knew about that, Clough. With Ovid hanging from a tree and Homer and his family dead from a house fire? You don't leave much for the law."

"The law!" mocked Clough, who pushed the door wide open but remained staunchly settled in the doorway. "The law has had more time than it needed to take care of Switzer!" he shouted. "It don't take a mind reader to know Switzer and Homer destroyed our stills. I heartily congratulate whoever killed both of them." He had appeared at the door with his own weapon of destruction, and he made eye contact first with David and then with Odell, solidifying the fact that he intended to protect himself if need be.

Distraught with anger, Odell lashed out at him. "You've gone too far this time, Clough! Sheriff Hagood tried to warn you before, and I can tell you that—"

"Yeah, and we all made the mistake of listening to the great sheriff's promises, didn't we?" Clough interrupted. "Look what happened. Switzer should have been hanging from a tree long time ago, and if he had, David and me wouldn't be faced with building new still houses!" he announced with vulgar intensity.

"Not the point," snapped Odell. "Neither you nor anyone else has the right to take a man's life anymore than Switzer had the right to take little Chris, his own son's life."

"You boys better read the good book. The Lord says, 'an eye for an eye,'" said Clough with a great deal of satisfaction just before slamming the door in their faces.

Clough's mention of the Bible irked Odell for he was relatively certain that Clough had never opened the holy book. He was just as certain that Clough had either set Homer's house on fire or hired someone to do it for him. Homer was a thief, a wife beater, and a drunk, but he had never killed anybody. "'An eye for an eye,' you say? Who did Homer kill?" Odell yelled through the closed door.

Clough yanked the door open long enough to respond. "You mean you don't know?" he said with a smirk.

"I don't," admitted Odell. Clough was bluffing.

"Who the hell do you think killed your old nigger Moses?" he asked with a distinct air of satisfaction.

The area's only officer of the law had walked away from Clough, a murderer, without making an attempt to arrest him. Niceville had no jail! Odell's barn had occasionally substituted for a temporary jail but only for drunks who were ready to call it a night but couldn't find their way home. It wouldn't hold Clough Martin long enough for Odell to lock the flimsy door.

"I don't know about you but I'm not going to take Clough's word on that. If he was going to squeal on Homer, why did he wait until he was dead?" grumbled David.

"I hate to tell you this, David, but Clough's telling the truth. Moses left his signature on Homer's belly, a knife wound halfway across it. Ecil and I got a good look at it yesterday when we went to his house," he grimaced. "We were looking for fresh wounds from the night before and we overlooked the most telling of all, the one Moses left us."

"Don't beat up on yourself," urged David. "We knew Homer was an evil man, but murder? Sometimes we get stuck in our mind-set. Homer would never have killed a white man, but in his mind, black lives don't matter."

Odell was struck by the truth of it. They shared a moment of grief for Moses before discussing any plans.

"I think I'll hold off wiring the sheriff. If he takes Clough in, we're done for, David," Odell told him. "Clough will never hang nor go to prison without spilling the beans on everybody who ever made a crockpot full of moonshine. Every fed in Washington will have his own moonshine map of Niceville, and that will end our rumrunning too."

Both men walked along with their heads down, lifting them only when they noticed unusual activity at Dr. Smythe's place. "Must be Clete," mourned David. "I was afraid the boy wouldn't make it."

They straddled their horses and made a hasty ride to the doctor's home office. Rhoda came running out of the house, her eyes red from long-term crying.

"It's Connie!" she screamed. "She's having birth pains, and Dr. Smythe is out cold! No, don't' even think it!" she yelled to her husband. I can't deliver Connie's baby. She's high risk, and she's my best friend. What if—" she bawled.

Connie had lost two babies already, and now her pains were coming too early. "It's not good," Rhoda explained, her voice a quiver. Rhoda had subbed for Dr. Smythe on many occasions when the doctor found himself disabled.

Odell snuggled her close. "I know," he said with compassion.

"Mary Sam can do it, but we don't know where she is. We've been to the house, but she's not home. David, where is she?" It was clear to everyone that Rhoda was indeed in no condition to assist Connie.

"She's bound to be home or not far away," David assured her even as he straddled his horse. "Probably walking in the woods again," he called as he rode away. "I'll bring her back in a heartbeat," he promised. Everyone remained tense as David's house was more than a quarter mile away. *What if Mary Sam isn't there?*

Intent on bringing his wife to the aid of her best friend, David pushed his horse. Once inside the white picket fence that surrounded their sprawling waterfront mansion, he began calling Mary Sam. "It's Connie, honey!" he yelled. "She's delivering! Hurry, honey!" As there was no answer, he raised his voice and continued to yell as he ran from room to room. In the kitchen, he stopped to catch his breath and grab a drink of water. The moment of quiet revealed voices coming from inside the house. They were in Casey's playroom, which was isolated from the other rooms. The voices he heard turned out to be only one, that of Casey speaking for numerous paper doll folks. He was about to open the door when Casey's drama grabbed his attention.

"No, Daddy Klinger," he heard.

Daddy Klinger? He thought.

"Please, Daddy Klinger. Please go with Mama and me to visit her great-great-grandfather in Eucheeanna. It's Mama's wish," Casey continued, obviously speaking for the Casey doll.

"If it is truly your wish, my darling," she purred, speaking for the Klinger doll.

"Yay!" she screamed, speaking for herself again. "Daddy Klinger's going with us!"

David was stunned beyond anything he had previously experienced. Still, he tried to let it pass, at least until he could send

Mary Sam to assist Connie. But he found himself too emotionally paralyzed to do anything. He had known for some time that Casey had named one of her dolls Mr. Klinger, but *Daddy Klinger?* Wasn't it enough that his little girl had clung to pleasant memories of a man who was hanged for murder? With his hand already on the doorknob, he finally managed to turn it.

"Daddy Klinger?" he asked.

Casey tossed her dolls aside and went screaming toward her father. "No, Daddy! Please don't tell Mama. I promised!" she pleaded, her arms wrapped around his legs as if to keep him there until he promised to keep the big secret.

"Don't tell Mama?" he asked.

"About my other daddy," she cried. "But I didn't really tell you, did I, Daddy? I didn't know you were in the house. Promise?" she pleaded as tears covered her agonized face.

Equally agonized, David questioned his daughter. "When did your mother tell you this secret?"

"I don't know. Oh yes, I do. She never really told me. I heard her tell Aunt Rhoda, and Mama was angry because I listened to grown-ups talk." David was left speechless while crippling thoughts muddled his mind. Casey took his silence to mean he was okay with the secret and that he wouldn't tell.

"Mama said if I told you, you wouldn't love me anymore, but you will, won't you, Daddy?' she pleaded.

"No, I won't tell," David managed before leaving the room. He had caught a glimpse of Mary Sam through the kitchen window as she shooed squirrels away from her flower garden. Without making his presence known, he left the premises. During his rush to find Mary Sam, he had seen Jolene sketching along the creek. He jumped on his horse and pushed the animal to its limit again. As soon as he caught sight of Jolene, he screamed at her, "It's Miss Connie! It's Miss Connie! Can you … I mean, have you …" he stumbled.

It was unheard of for single girls to be in the presence of a
woman giving birth. What would people say if one were allowed in
the delivery room? He worried, but he was desperate.

"Many times!" Jolene yelled back. She abandoned her artwork
and mounted the horse behind David. On the way, she confessed
that she had been her mother's only assistant during the many
births the poor woman had endured. The thought of such a thing
made David quite ill.

Rhoda stood watch at the doctor's fence gate. No one had to tell
her the woman who was riding with David was not his wife. And
when his passenger alighted, there was no mistaking the familiar
walk—a jerky, almost crablike motion—or the layers of odd-shaped,
oversized rags and loose headgear that defied definition aside from
the fact that they had seen more time than was expected of them.

"Where is Mary Sam? What are you doing, honey? You mustn't
come in here," Rhoda insisted. With David riding away without
a word to anyone, Jolene unlatched the gate and walked briskly
up the pathway, covered two porch steps in one, and entered the
doctor's home office. "Where can I wash up?" she asked of all three
handwringers: Odell, Ecil, and the doctor's wife, who whispered to
one another as if the patient had already succumbed. Seeing that
Jolene had obviously come to deliver a baby, the doctor's wife nervously led her to the kitchen and pointed to a kettle of hot water,
clean cloths, and soap.

Once scrubbed, Jolene entered Connie's room, threw back the
covers, and took a look at the patient before breaking into a wide
grin. "Miss Connie, you're doing fine. That baby'll be here in no
time. Now I ain't never given birth myself, but I know that if you
could relax, it would make things a lot better for you and me and
that baby. And I have to say that if you do relax, you'll be the only
one in Niceville who is," she said with a hint of stark sarcasm.

Meanwhile, Rhoda and Odell were in near panic, still wondering what happened to Mary Sam.

"She'll be here," promised Odell, who no longer believed it himself. Like Rhoda, he had decided something terrible had happened to her.

With Odell and Ecil pacing the floor and Rhoda's body twitching all over, Jolene finally appeared in the doorway holding a screaming baby, bathed but still wearing his birth suit.

"You have a son, Mr. Ecil," she announced. Ecil followed Jolene and his new son into the birth room and stared at his pale-faced wife before moving nervously toward her bedside, his hand over his mouth in a fearful pose. "Oh my God, honey, let's don't do this again," he pleaded.

Connie was unresponsive. Death during childbirth was common, a fact that had haunted Ecil from the beginning of Connie's first pregnancy. The joy he felt from having a son was all but canceled by the trauma of getting him there. Was she going to be like so many others who appeared to be fine once the baby arrived and then took a turn for the worse and died?

"Miss Connie needs to rest now, Mr. Ecil," said Jolene, who placed the newly dressed baby beside his mother.

But Ecil heard nothing as fear had taken over. "I'll get Dr. Azore!" he shouted, but he made no move to carry out the threat. The trauma of childbirth in an isolated area where the only practicing physician was rarely capable of caring for the mother or the baby had suddenly gripped him. He stood up and sat down repeatedly, all without releasing the grasp he had on his wife's cold hand. Connie hadn't spoken a word nor moved a muscle. Why did Jolene insist he leave? Did she know something he didn't?

"I'm either taking her home, or I'm staying with her. That damn doctor ought to be shot!" he raved bitterly.

"It's not his fault, Mr. Ecil," Jolene offered. "He's a good man.

He went to school half his life learning to take care of people, and then he came to this desolate area where he must have known most folks could never pay him for his work. What he didn't know was that they would keep him supplied in their homemade moonshine and now he's hooked on it. We made him what he is, sir," she said without apology.

Ecil was stunned, his face having lost its color and his mind almost as bare. She had spoken the truth, and he knew it.

"But you're not to worry about Miss Connie. I've delivered for the doctor more than you know," she confided. The news came as just one more shock to his tortured system, and she hadn't finished. "Of course, you must know I attended to my mother on several occasions." It was, perhaps, the worst thing she could have told him as none of Jeannette Holder's babies, except Jolene, had survived.

"What happened to them? Your siblings?" he brazenly asked.

"Drowned," she said without a show of emotion.

"All of them?"

"All of them," she repeated.

Ecil asked no more as he could easily fill in the blanks. With Jeannette always in poor health, most everybody assumed her babies were stillborn or, worse, allowed to die of starvation. Now he knew the truth: John had drowned them!

The reality of it all struck Ecil hard, but it also strengthened him. He and Connie were facing a new problem neither of them had given any thought to. He knew there wasn't a kid in Niceville who hadn't tasted alcohol by the time he was old enough to enter first grade. Some were alcoholics by the time they entered high school, and for many of those, addiction to alcohol had led to suicide. Would Yancy, their newborn son, be a victim too?

Chapter 14

UNKNOWN TO MOST RESIDENTS, YANCY BRIGHTON'S birth had caused quite a stir among Niceville's most elite. After David delivered Jolene to the doctor's office, he had ambled along the pathway toward home, but he never arrived. Less than halfway there, he turned around. He knew he could never go back.

When a week passed without a word from David, Casey was forced to tell her mother about the incident. "But I really didn't tell him, Mama, honest. I didn't know he was in the house."

When David returned more than two months later, he did so with a solemn message for his wife: "The townsfolk were right, it seems. I scoffed when they warned me against marrying a squaw. Said I'd have to keep a lid on 'er. Unfortunately, they were only partly right. Somebody lifted the lid before I had a chance." He spoke in monotones, void of compassion.

"I'll give you a divorce, David," Mary Sam solemnly offered. "Casey and I will go our own way, and we will ask for nothing," she added in a cracking voice. She kept her distance throughout the difficult conversation and made no attempt to make eye contact with her husband.

"No divorce!" said David with unusual resolve. "Couldn't tolerate the *I told you so*'s." He walked down the hall to the bedroom they had shared, closed the door, and turned the lock.

It was a signal to Mary Sam that she was never to enter his bedroom again.

David single-handedly annulled the marriage as far as companionship was concerned. He had sentenced both females to a life of silence while all three essentially occupied the same square footage they had been accustomed to. In the beginning, Mary Sam held hopes that her husband would eventually tire of this self-imposed loneliness. But she had long since given up on that and refused to harbor their deep, dark secret from the public any longer. She applied for and received a teaching position in the Baker school system.

Baker could boast of progressive-thinking town leaders with liberal views. Even blacks had been allowed to own their own land in Baker as long as they worked it, and their success had encouraged white men to look more closely at crop growing as a means of survival. Teachers were hired for their qualifications, not their backgrounds. It was a very moderate and unusual policy, especially for the Deep South, but one that paid off as the little community was the first in Okaloosa County to grow. It had been the first community in the county and many counties to have its high school accredited, and parents were quick to show their appreciation. Students traveled all the way from Allentown, Florida, and Foley, Alabama, to take advantage of this superior educational institution.

With Mary Sam and Casey leaving Niceville, David was left to face a horde of pouting parents who still harbored hatred for his choice of an Indian squaw over their white daughters. But only Connie and Rhoda were privy to the reason for the Stewarts' separation. Eventually, the two women confided in their husbands, but all four of them agreed the story would never go beyond their consciences. The general public was left to stretch their imaginations to their exhausting limits. And they did.

Connie was the most devastated by Mary Sam's dilemma, especially with her college classmate leaving Niceville for Baker. It was only thirty-five miles away, but it still took a lifetime to get there.

For Casey, the move was heartbreaking. Now ten years old, she had kept her promise to herself never to play with paper dolls again in spite of its being her favorite pastime. Before she and her mother left Niceville, she had replaced the dolls and all the drama that went with them with a real live "doll" named Yancy Brighton. Young Yancy had quickly learned to love the attention that this high-spirited, uninhibited little girl had given him as far back as he could remember, and Casey's feeling of closeness from the day Yancy was born had only intensified with the years. It was of little comfort to know that Casey would be allowed to return for visits with Ecil and Connie Brighton, Yancy's parents and Casey's honorary aunt and uncle.

In spite of the public's view of her ancestors, Casey had always taken pride in them, and she eagerly studied their rituals, habits, and beliefs, most of which she learned from her mother. Young and inquisitive, Yancy was a perfect student as he was too young to have formed any prejudices against the Indians. The fearlessness Casey displayed as they traipsed through the heavily wooded, wild-animal-infested area surrounding Niceville delighted and entertained him.

Her detailed information about the local herbs and plants her people used to make healing potions bored him in the beginning, but there were times when her enthusiasm stimulated his young brain enough that he began to ask questions. During one of their treks through weed-tangled growth and sticker vines, Casey stopped to admire a flowering black gum tree. "This tree is one of our many gifts from the Great White Father, Yancy," she said with unusual passion for someone so young.

Yancy had heard of the Great White Father, but he confused

him with God the Father, whom his Christian parents often spoke of as having powers over their lives. Yancy came to accept Casey's belief that there really was a Great White Father somewhere too, either above the earth or below it, but he had difficulty believing he had anything at all to do with the black gum tree.

While on a trek through the woods one day, Casey ran her hand across one of the tree's glossy green leaves. "This leaf will turn into a beautiful red in the fall, and it will brighten up the entire woods with its brilliant color," she told her little friend. "My mama says it saved many of our people who would have died without it."

"That tree can save your life?" Yancy ridiculed, cocking his head in a questionable pose and raising a suspicious eyebrow. He approached the tree, studied the bark, and rubbed his hand over the surface of a big leaf just as Casey had. "Who told you that?" he demanded.

"Everything has a purpose, Yancy. You need to understand that. Look at this cedar tree. One just like it saved my mother's life—and lots of other folks'," she added. "My people boil the bark and make a concoction that makes their pain go away."

"It saved your mother's life?" The thought of Mary Sam, who was one of his favorite grown-ups, being dead if not for the bark on that tree demanded his full attention. Casting doubts aside momentarily, he listened.

"They say my mother's blood was too thick. You know, everybody's blood has to flow through small veins to take it all over our bodies," she explained patiently, "but if the blood is too thick, it can't go through and you die. My people learned that the potion they get from boiling the bark from this tree will make the veins bigger so the blood can get through."

Convinced at that point that Casey was a genius, Yancy began to latch on to her every word.

Casey noticed the change in her little companion and took

advantage of it. "Some of the plants are used to season foods, some for food itself, some for construction, and many for medicine."

As they continued along the shores of Turkey Creek, the swift-moving waterway was marked on either side by thick, sharp-pointed briers; viburnum shrubs that formed dense tangles of arching trunks and branches; sabal palmettos; and overhanging live oak, black gum, and bald cypress limbs. It was a jungle of sorts, too thick for all but the hardiest to penetrate. Yancy gleefully followed Casey's lead in spite of the discomfort it wrought, at least until a sudden noise broke the quiet atmosphere and sent them both scrambling for cover.

Casey shushed him with a contagious fear in her voice. As they crouched in the bushes beside each other, she noted a strange phenomenon. "That bush is moving," she told her startled little friend. "I'm afraid we've ventured out of my daddy's property and happened upon a moonshine still house."

Yancy peered through the heavy brush. "Where?" he asked. "You can't see the moon in the daytime," he said condescendingly. But then he remembered something. *Moonshine* was a word he heard often, but he never really knew what it was. Judging from the conversations, he had come to think of it as one of those elixirs like the man in the covered wagon sold. He had always wanted to taste it but was never allowed to.

"Quiet," Casey shushed. But it was too late.

"Come out of there with your hands up!" an angry voice yelled. "Now!" he bellowed as he waved a rifle in the air.

"Put your hands up, Yancy," ordered Casey, who had already done so herself.

"Please don't shoot," she begged. "It's only me and my little friend." Following orders from the man with a rifle in his hands, the two youngsters made their way as best they could through a thicket of prickly vines and other unfriendly wetland growth with their hands held as high in the air as they could manage while unmerciful limbs whipped them in the face and belted them on their backsides. By the time they made it to a clearing, both were bleeding from scratches and tears. Both remained dry-eyed, albeit frightened.

When they were close enough to identify their enemy, Casey was so startled that she allowed her hands to drop to her sides. The gunman stood his rifle butt on the ground and began laughing. It was Clete Cogbill, the boy who was still known in the area as "the one who burned his own house to the ground with his parents and siblings inside." Most everyone knew in their hearts that Clough Martin had planned the horrific crime and had publicly blamed young Clete for the whole thing. Many believed Clough had nailed the doors shut, lit the fire, and left Clete to burn to death with his family. And most believed Clete had tried to save his family.

The majority thought Clough had never intended for Clete to die in the blaze as he needed him to build a race car. Like most folks, he was beginning to understand that continued success in moonshine marketing would depend on one's ability to build an engine that would outrun the feds. Clough was convinced that young Clete could build such an engine.

But for Casey, Clete was still the boy who had invited her to play marbles with him at the Daddy Klinger hanging and who, when she had beat him at his own game, had called her a half-breed. She had since learned the meaning of the term, and it had left a scar. Through their subsequent school years, Clete had apologized and had explained to her that his dad would have "skinned me like I was a rabbit" if he hadn't come home with all of his marbles. He had no choice but to break his word to Casey.

Casey had believed Clete's story as she had seen his battered body on many occasions after that. Everyone knew it was the work of his brutal father, Homer Cogbill, who was noted for beating his wife and children.

Clete's bludgeoned body had always reminded her of little Chris Switzer and the beating his father had given him. She hated Clete's father with the same intensity she hated Ovid Switzer, even though she never really knew either one of them.

After the death of Clete's entire family, his continued association with Clough did little to enhance his reputation in spite of the fact that he had nowhere else to go. He grew up in that atmosphere and was considered a bad influence on young people, most of whom made no effort to associate with him.

"Well, now, the federal agents are getting smaller and smaller these days," teased Clete. "Is this a raid? I give up!" he said, tossing his gun aside and raising his hands high in the air. "Before you haul me in, please let me take care of your wounds. Follow me into the doctor's office?" he teased.

With that, he ambled toward a large clump of bent-over saplings and evergreen branches and lifted an unattached bush, the same one Casey had seen "walking." Underneath it all was a sand pit with a log ceiling. "Come on in," Clete invited.

"Wow!" Casey yelped once she stepped inside. "A turnip-still boiler! It's the smallest one I've ever seen!" Big moonshine producers like Clough and David spent a great deal of time hiding their massive moonshine equipment, and if it was discovered, it was usually destroyed and they were faced with rebuilding. Small producers had no such problem. They used turnip-still boilers or simple crock pots from the kitchen, which were small enough that one man could grab it and run with it if caught.

"It's not a still house—more of a hideout," he explained. "Although I do have what you might call mash, I guess, but I never drink the stuff myself," he quickly added. "The kid is bleeding, and so are you, girl and it's my fault. Let me doctor your wounds," he said apologetically.

"Does it burn?" she asked, but she agreed to try it.

Opened mouthed and anxious to try it, Yancy begged to go first. "You can make medicine? Just like Casey and her mama?" he asked.

"You could say that, I guess," laughed Clete. "I learned from my mama too, and I know this stuff works. Now hold still so I can cover all of your wounds," he told him. Yancy was hooked when he saw Clete take a mouthful from the dipper, swirl it around in his mouth, and spit it on as many of his sores as it would cover before taking another mouthful. "Now it may burn just a little, but if you don't treat these things, they can get infected and then you'll have to see the doctor."

Yancy squirmed a bit from the burning sensation but made no fuss, so Clete managed to cover every visible scratch on the child. Casey was taken by Clete's warm and caring demeanor as he carefully applied the mixture and then blew on each one to ease the sting, all the while assuring Yancy that it wouldn't hurt long. *How could the offspring of Homer Cogbill have an ounce of caring? It had to have come from his mother,* she decided. He began to treat her own cuts, and once the burning sensation subsided, she felt an urge to talk. "How often do you come here?" she asked.

While they talked, Yancy made a beeline to the covered sandpit where Clete had left the crock pot. He took a long look inside the pot, lifted the dipper, and filled his mouth just as Clete had. Liking the taste, he swallowed it. The mix set his esophagus on fire, and the burning sensation lasted long after the mixture reached his unprepared stomach. The expression on his face was not easy to interpret as it appeared to be a mix of pain and pleasure. He gulped, coughed, and beat on his chest in an effort to deal with the consequences. His struggle brought Casey running to his aid, but she was met with the broadest grin his little face could muster. "It sure tastes better than quinine," he managed between explosive sputters.

"What have you done!" she screamed. "I thought you were playing in the sandpit!" she yelled while confiscating the dipper. With fear and anger gripping her, she turned the pot upside down, emptying its contents on the ground.

"I ought to boil some poison ivy leaves when we get home and make you eat them!" she shouted. "You too!" she spouted at Clete. Quickly, she began gathering bitter herbs, broke them in small pieces, and attempted to stuff them in Yancy's mouth, but he fought her. "Chew and swallow! Chew and swallow!" she demanded, but Yancy continued to fight for his freedom while keeping his mouth clamped shut.

Casey was insistent. "You have to get that poison out of you before it makes you really sick," she explained once she succeeded in prying his mouth open and filling it with bitter herbs. "Chew and swallow! Chew and swallow!" she demanded. "Okay, then, if you won't do as I say, we'll go home and heat up some onion juice. That'll bring it up!"

"Okay, I'll chew it!" he spouted.

"Let me carry the little fellow," pleaded Clete.

"No. He needs to walk," said Casey. "It may take another batch of these bitter herbs to make him vomit," she said, worrying. She needn't have. She and Clete watched in misery as Yancy lost everything he had put in his stomach that day.

"I'm so sorry, Casey," moaned Clete. "I'm so sorry," he kept repeating.

"Never mind. It wasn't your fault. Or his. It's mine. I shouldn't have brought him here."

Meanwhile, the vomiting had taken its toll on Yancy's usually energetic mind and body. Casey splashed his tortured face with cold creek water and attempted to wash the bitter taste from inside his mouth. "I'm sorry," she said, cuddling him close to her, "but you had to learn a lesson I never want you to forget. You are not to drink this stuff. It's poison!"

When Yancy began to feel better, Casey began to think about the whole, strange episode she found herself in, and it disturbed her. "Exactly what are you doing here, Clete? A covered sandpit? A pot of moonshine?"

There was a bite in her voice, one much different from the beginning when she graciously accepted his offer to medicate their wounds. He turned away for an embarrassing moment to hide the flush in his face. "I used to bring my mother here when my daddy was on a rampage. I guess you could call it our hideout."

Yancy was exhilarated. "You mean like a real hideout? Like criminals hiding from the sheriff?" he squealed. "Can we come back and play here sometimes? Please?" he begged as he jumped playfully on Clete's back after seeing him nod affirmatively.

Suddenly, Clete let go with a terrifying scream while attempting to remove his shirt. Thinking he had been bitten by some creature of the woods, Casey tried to assist him in removing his shirt but screamed herself when she saw the problem. The shirt had become enmeshed with large, bloody scabs that broke loose on his back, revealing fresh knife wounds and blackened bruises.

"Present from Mr. Clough," said Clete, who continued to wince from the pain.

Yancy closed his eyes and buried his head in Casey's shirt. When Casey burst out in tears, he snuggled closer and squeezed her hand so hard that she whimpered. "I'm so, so sorry," she told Clete. "I've poured all of your potion out!" she bawled.

"Not to worry," he told her. "I poured it all over me before you got here. And I can get more," he said, completely free of self-pity.

Casey had always sympathized with Clete even as others her age had shunned him. Though four years older than she, he was only two grades ahead of her in school, but she knew why. Schooling was far from a priority with many area families, and that included Clete's father as well as Clough Martin and his gruesomely ill-bred wife.

"Don't cry," he insisted once the pain began to ease. "This is my healing place. I know it sounds crazy, but I come here to see my mother. Oh, I don't actually see her, but I feel like she's here, anyway," he told his captivated audience of two. In an effort to quell his own emotions, he sought to lighten the mood. "You're so lucky, Casey. I mean—"

"Yes I know," Casey interrupted. She knew what he was about to say, that she had the good life with a nice home and nice parents, but she was in no mood to tell Clete what the public itself did not yet know: that David was not her father and that her family of three hadn't sat together for a meal or shared anything except a physical house for at least five years. Rumors that Mary Sam had finally obtained a teaching position at Baker High School had surfaced, but little else. Gossipers were busy trying to put two and two together, but thus far, no one had come up with a total of four.

In spite of her own family dilemma, Casey grieved for Clete. She made a mental note to seek help from the Great White Father the moment she arrived home.

As the threesome neared Yancy's house, Clete offered an apology to Yancy. "Sorry I introduced you to white man's medicine. You're not to get Casey's medical herbs and plants mixed up with this mash. It's not for little boys."

Yancy was deeply disappointed. "If you leave them bitter herbs off, that white man's medicine tastes pretty good," he insisted. "If we ever get sick and need some medicine, you take that bitter stuff and give me the poison."

Chapter 15

IT WASN'T LONG AFTER YANCY'S INTRODUCTION TO white man's medicine that Mary Sam and Casey left Niceville for Baker. Yancy was left to struggle with the disappointment of his young life. He lived for summer vacations when he was allowed to accompany Odell in his continuing efforts to keep the drunks locked up in his barn and the hogs run off the streets. With Hamp Etheridge's development across the bayou entertaining more and more visitors from Chicago (referred to locally as foreigners), Odell had begun to keep a close eye on the goings-on in the Vale of Paradise.

For the most part, nothing out of the ordinary had presented itself, but that would soon change and Yancy would have the distinct pleasure of taking part in it. The day began with Odell, still the area's only lawman, and his new sidekick riding the waves in Boggy Bayou, a weekly run that coincided with the arrival of newcomers to Etheridge's new hotel. On this particular day, the twosome took two or three trips past the hotel and in and out of the smaller bayous and back again before a passenger boat arrived from Pensacola.

Odell was quick to notice that it was not the weekly passenger and supply boat. Rather, it was a showy, chartered number that only the rich could afford. Odell purposely docked next to the fancy boat in time to watch two suit-clad passengers exit, and he immediately tried to suppress a yell quite foreign to anything Yancy had ever heard.

Yancy's heart raced so fast that he pressed hard against his chest in an effort to quiet it. "What is it?" he squealed.

"It's Gussie!" cried Odell. "At least it sure looks like him."

"Who's Gussie?" asked Yancy, but Odell had no time for questions. He wanted answers.

"Listen to me," he told Yancy. "I want you to run inside the lobby and make sure the man in the gray suit don't leave that lobby before I get there even if you have to trip 'im."

Yancy asked no questions. He ran inside the hotel set on throwing his body in front of the designated man if he had to.

Inside, a small group of people had gathered in a circle, fascinated by something Yancy couldn't see. Since the man Odell called Gussie was one of them, Yancy moved closer to him and then took every step the man took. A quick peek inside the circle revealed a small child perched in a young woman's lap, apparently his mother, wiggling and whimpering, obviously reluctant to have his portrait drawn.

Onlookers were captivated by the scene, many making positive comments about the artist's work.

"Who is she?" questioned the visitor Yancy had been told to keep an eye on. He seemed captivated from the start, scarcely taking his eyes off the artist's work more than the few seconds hotel registration required. Her face was half hidden by a grungy hat whose brim had crumpled and clung loosely to one side. Faded, torn, and clownishly roomy garments hung loosely around her body as none of them had hooks, snaps, or buttons.

Nearly everyone heard the visitor question the artist's identity, and that included the artist. Meeting his gaze, she gasped audibly and quickly began gathering her paraphernalia. "I'll finish this at home," she told the child's bedraggled mother.

Shocked and disappointed, everyone stared at Gussie. "What did you do to her?" asked the child's mother, and others chimed in with snide remarks.

"I just wanted to know who she was," he explained. "I meant no harm. I will apologize," he promised. "Does anyone know her name?"

"She's the lawman's daughter," said Mr. Hamp, who had just come in to welcome the newcomers. "Well, not really. Her parents are dead, but Mr. Odell and Miss Rhoda kind of adopted her."

"It's Jolene," announced Yancy.

"Jolene? Jolene Holder?" yelled Gussie. "Where did she go?" he yelled again. Pushing his luggage out of the way, he ran out the back door, with Yancy close behind.

"There she is," said Yancy, pointing toward a skiff that was tied to the trunk of a pine tree. "I would approach her cautiously if I was you. I've seen her drop a bear from two hundred yards with one shot—and he was running. If you don't mind me saying so, she didn't seem to take to you any more than she did to the bear."

Shocked by such a warning, particularly as his memory of Jolene was of a frightened young girl who would have been afraid of her own shadow, he slowed his step but only momentarily. He watched as Jolene threw her art supplies in the general direction of a basket tied to the end of the skiff before pushing off and jumping in. When he reached the spot she had abandoned, he pleaded with her, saying, "Wait up. I would like to talk to you."

Jolene grounded her paddle and lulled the skiff by dragging one foot in the shallow water. "What did you want to say? That you killed my pa?" she snapped.

With all the noise from other craft, Gussie assumed he had misunderstood her. Seeing her standing there, tall and thin but apparently strong and resolute, he took in a deep breath and smiled contentedly. "You have no idea how much I've worried about you," he said with a sense of joy. "And you still have your teeth," he fluttered before blushing an embarrassing red. In truth, he really couldn't be certain, but she didn't have the sunken mouth syndrome that identified the toothless.

"You think so?" spouted Jolene. She stuck her hand in her mouth, pulled out two dental plates, and stuck them into a loosely held-together pocket on her ill-fitted shirt. "I'm gonna assume you didn't chase me down just to say that," she grumbled.

It was a violent blow for Gussie, who was left temporarily speechless.

"What do you care?" she queried. "The way you disappeared into the woods that day and left everybody wondering what happened to you. But after you killed my pa, I didn't care."

Realizing he had heard her the first time, he could only stare at her. "Well," he finally stammered, "I did wish your pa was dead, but I couldn't kill him. I couldn't kill anybody," he admitted. "Anyway, it seemed to me you had enough trouble without me killing your daddy." Having said that, Gussie's passionate demeanor quickly turned to stone. "But let's not forget one thing. I had reason enough to kill your pa, all right, 'cause the truth is, he killed mine."

Jolene's lips began to twitch noticeably. She glared at Gussie as she might her worst enemy and then pointed a stiff index finger in his direction. "You killed my pa all right. My mother saw you! But you can rest assured my pa didn't kill yours. *I* did that!"

Chapter 16

JOLENE'S CONFESSION SENT GUSSIE INTO A SILENT RAGE. *How can this be? How many sleepless nights have I endured in mourning for this pitiful child? And she murdered my father?*

While Gussie seethed, Yancy had his own emotions to deal with. The shock of Jolene's confession to murder had sent him tumbling into the bayou before he could get his balance. Splattered with wet sand, he struggled to get his breath and regain his composure.

"You admit to murder and brag about it?" Gussie shouted. Glancing helplessly toward the only witness to her confession, he accused her of confessing in the presence of a kid who was too young to testify to her admission of guilt.

"Him?" Jolene laughed. "He's no kid! He was born one day and grew up the next!"

"And she oughta know because she delivered me!" spouted Yancy, but in truth he was too uptight to enjoy what he considered a compliment. He liked Jolene immensely. Unlike some of the kids who poked fun at her—admittedly a crude, ungainly, boorish woman—he held a totally different image of her. In many ways, she had taken Casey's place in his heart. He had been in Jolene's company when she dropped a deer as it sped across the forest in lightning speed and then watched her throw the animal on her shoulder and carry it through the lengthy forest unassisted. He knew she was equally adept at hitting a tiny squirrel in midair as it flitted from limb to limb. He knew grown men who couldn't match these feats. "If she killed your pa, she had a reason," he told Gussie.

Meanwhile, Jolene's agitation had grown. "If you have anything else to say to me, you do it in the presence of Mr. Odell." She plopped her plates back in her mouth and belted out a whistle that folks across the bayou could easily discern. Both Yancy and Gussie flinched when the unrestrained whistle sent their skin crawling.

Odell had already headed in their direction when Jolene began her exit. Moving as fast as his crippled leg allowed, he arrived in time to stop her.

"What's the problem here?" he asked. When nobody responded, he turned to the visitor.

"What's your business here this time, Gussie?"

"Well, sir, I sure didn't come to accuse Miss Jolene of killing my dad, but she has just confessed that she did just that!" Gussie responded with a newfound haughtiness.

"Jolene? You know better than that," Odell scolded.

Yancy took in a deep, audible breath upon learning that Jolene's confession apparently was not true.

"And who confesses to a murder falsely?" Gussie said condescendingly.

Yancy began shifting his weight from one leg to the other, unsettled in his mind about a lot of things. He had grown up among foul-talking fishermen whose vocabulary consisted mostly of four-letter words. He figured their lifestyle had trained him for anything he might encounter, but he was clearly not prepared for the hard stuff.

"Are you saying you witnessed my father's murder?" Gussie snarled. When Odell's response was a silent lowering of his head, Gussie took it as a confession. "I thought not! You people are no different from the gangs in Chicago. If a stranger comes into the area, you see that he goes out, feet first." He turned his back to all three of his listeners and began a slow but determined walk across an uneven path toward the hotel.

"Wait a minute!" yelled Odell. "Jolene, you go on across the bayou and see after Rhoda," he said in a fatherly manner.

Gussie turned to face Odell and stared at him for a taunting moment before slowly retracing his steps. On the walk back, he glanced in Jolene's direction. While struggling to organize her scattered paraphernalia, the unfinished drawing of the reluctant young child surfaced, and Gussie was astonished by her raw talent.

He recalled the comments made by some of the art-ignorant onlookers at the hotel. A group of women admired Jolene's sketch, but most agreed in private that she had failed to capture a likeness of the child. But Gussie knew her talent went much deeper than that. A camera could produce a likeness, but it couldn't capture the child's personality as Jolene had done with one brilliant stroke of her brush. He had no artistic talent himself, but he had been exposed in depth to art studies in the private school back east; and for the first time, he realized the advantages of his studies. This rusticated woman was capable of producing a masterpiece. *What might she have accomplished given a real opportunity?* he wondered. But then he chastised himself. How could he think good thoughts about a girl who admitted to killing his father?

"About the girl," Odell began, "she's easily the best thing that ever happened to this area. She was still a teenager when she delivered this boy here, and she's been delivering babies ever since. She was God-sent our way. As to your papa? He had a bad case of flu that turned into pneumonia. She found him lying in his yard nearly frozen. She managed to roll his helpless body onto a quilt and drag him into the house. She was just a little girl, mind you, but she nursed him like she was a grown woman. When the inevitable happened, she cried like the baby she was. She blames herself for not saving him."

Odell had a knack for lying when the need arose. The only thing he knew about the death of Gussie's father was what Jolene had told him, but he had never questioned her story.

Gussie appeared relieved. "I can't tell you what I've been through or what I've put my friends through because of that girl. Finally, my good friend allowed me to return to Pensacola. I found the dentist and questioned him. I just had to know if he had pulled all her teeth and if she survived such an onslaught."

Odell gasped. "My God, man. Why didn't you let me know? What did he tell you? I paid him a visit too but he lied to me. Said he pulled only the bad tooth! You can see that wasn't true. I'm sorry. Please go on with your story."

"Yes, he told me the same thing, but I didn't believe him. The man was in emotional pieces. I mean, his body began to shake as if he were freezing, and it must have been eighty degrees that day. I point blank asked him if he had killed the girl and her daddy, and the poor man broke down. When he finally gained control, he told me that when he applied pressure to the girl's aching tooth, it broke into pieces, leaving the root. When he tried to dig it out, she began hemorrhaging. He begged John to take her to the hospital, but John refused. John forced the dentist to take him and his daughter home with him until she recovered. He told me it took weeks to remove the shattered bone from Jolene's jaw, and every time he tried, she started hemorrhaging again." Just remembering the episode sent Gussie into an emotional rage. After regaining his composure, he wiped haphazardly at his nose and made several swipes across his eyes with his bare hands. Odell and Yancy did the same.

"I think he told the truth as far as it went. Somewhere along the line, he did John's bidding. He pulled all of the child's teeth!" he shoutly angrily.

"The poor man must have been so traumatized with his family in the hands of John Holder, he was afraid to tell anybody anything," Odell sympathized. The story had left him drained of his usual energy, but he forced himself to brush it aside. He needed to know something about Gussie's companions and their reason for being there.

Somewhat emboldened by Gussie's show of weakness, Odell delivered a blow to the young man's raw emotions. Instead of beginning with a question, as was the usual protocol, he delivered a startling comment. "I see you're traveling with Mr. J. J. Hoagland, a noted Chicago criminal," he said as if he knew the man personally.

Obviously shocked beyond comment and unwilling to respond anyway, the muscles around Gussie's mouth tightened. He couldn't have known that Odell was only guessing at his companion's identity and that his reaction had verified it.

Odell made the most of it. "Your friend is better known in Chicago's gangland as Two-Gun Hoagie, of course," he added as if to substantiate his knowledge of the notorious criminal. A short silence ensued during which Gussie struggled to remain in control of his emotions. He couldn't have imagined that Odell, a small town constable would have access to bulletins describing famous gangsters in Chicago or that Two-Gun Hoagie, a man famous for the corpses he often left lying in the streets of Chicago, was one of them. Although known as Two-Gun, Hoagland never left home without three weapons, and every policeman in Chicago carried descriptive details of all three. So did the sheriff's office in Okaloosa County.

Gussie had always managed to stuff these truths in the back of his mind. But Odell hadn't. Still, he knew the consequence of dealing with an infamous Chicago gang leader. He planned to walk and talk softly, and he had no intention of removing his gun from its holster except to save a life, including his own.

"Whether you killed John or not, I can't say, young man," he added brazenly, "but you were apparently with the man, or men, who did kill him. In the eyes of the law, that makes you as guilty as they are."

The more the lawman talked, the tighter Gussie's lips became. With no comment as yet from Gussie, Odell continued.

"Fortunately, folks in this town were so delighted to be rid of John, a murderer himself, we left him for the buzzards and went about our business," Odell admitted. "We never really knew much about John's background, but we always suspected he was hiding from the law for unsavory deeds. We believed he had earned the endless notches on his belt. As to your dad? Well, we didn't trust him either, but as John was his only neighbor out there in the wilderness, we figured Mr. Genepri had enough to contend with. We pretty much left him to the big bad wolf."

"I don't remember when I didn't know Two-Gun Hoagie," Gussie began, surprising Odell, not to mention his sidekick. "Before you go any further, you need to know something about my father. He was a poor tenement dweller in the slums of Chicago when Two-Gun demanded that all tenants in his apartment houses make rot gut mash—or moonshine in their kitchens. Chicago doesn't have the leisure of hiding their produce in densely wooded areas like you folks have here, so criminals force these poor helpless tenants to either make it at home or die," he explained with obvious bitterness. "Any tenant who refused to make the rot gut disappeared from the face of the planet, sir. Forever!" he emphasized with obvious and lingering bitterness.

Odell kept silent, desperately hoping this young man would reveal the reason for the dreaded visit of a Chicago gang leader to the Vale of Paradise.

"In spite of that, my father refused to make the poisonous mash because he didn't want to bring me up in a gangster's world. Nobody pleads with hardened criminals, Mr. Odell!" Gussie continued. "And yet my daddy dared to!"

"Why? I'm sure you're wondering. It has to do with Mr. Two-Gun's own daddy, who abandoned him on the dangerous streets of Chicago when he was only twelve. And there lies the answer. My dad's willingness to give his own life to save me made quite an impression on Mr. Two-Gun. In short, he arranged an escape for my dad. It called for breaking his own harsh rules, something unheard of in Chicago's unforgiving gangland. Of course, once on the gang's hit list, always on the gang's hit list, so the only way out for my dad was to disappear. That's how Gus Genepri, my daddy, ended up in this swampy backwoods you folks call Bolton."

The story held Yancy in such a spell that he swallowed the small piece of chewing tobacco he had lifted from his grandfather's pocket the previous day. With the tobacco caught in the middle of his esophagus, he began beating on his chest in an effort to dislodge the wad. Instead of chastising the boy, Odell turned on himself for not sending him home. A youngster like that should never have heard the story of brutal Chicago murderers, and who knew better than he? But it was too late.

"Frankly, sir, I'm having a little trouble believing your story about Jolene taking care of my dad," Gussie revealed. "She couldn't have been more than a small child. Why would she need to look after him, anyway? Mr. Two-Gun has always paid a caregiver to look after my dad."

Stunned, Odell pushed himself up from the tree stump he had been resting on. "A caregiver! Who?" he shouted.

"John Holder," was the reply.

Chapter 17

NEWS THAT JOHN HAD BEEN ENTRUSTED WITH THE care of anyone at all shocked Odell. His mind was bombarded by thoughts of his mistakes, as well as opportunities he had missed to prevent these disasters. He would gladly turn in his badge if only someone would accept it. He might have continued these self-destructive thoughts if Yancy hadn't fallen out of the tree he had recently scampered up. He now found himself on the ground gasping for breath.

Gussie rushed to the boy's aid. "It's okay," he assured Yancy. "The fall just knocked the breath out of you." But Yancy needed no reassurance as the accident had dislodged the tobacco and sent it through to his stomach.

As far as Odell was concerned, he too had been robbed of his breath, not to mention his pride. "I guess that explains the letters," he mumbled, his mind hurtling through mistakes he had made. "It also explains why we never saw your dad in town. John probably wouldn't allow him to leave the house," he realized out loud as his self-esteem took a beating. "I did worry that John would steal your dad's money. And, of course, he did in the long run," he revealed.

"What?" asked the surprised young man.

But Odell continued thinking out loud. "And John's poor wife was a prisoner out there in the wilderness, forced to give birth and watch all her babies die except for Jolene. Yeah, I see it all now. Your dad's caregiver? What a laugh that is! He collected your dad's supplies at the general store using Two-Gun's money, but he never paid for them. It's that simple."

"But wouldn't the store owner complain?" asked Gussie.

"Not to Mr. John!" Yancy assured him.

Odell took a good look at Gussie, a tortured young man whose facial expression hadn't changed since that day on the boat when he vehemently protected his odd-shaped package. He must have lived his whole life without peace, constantly worrying about his father.

"As to the letters, John had never received a single letter here in Niceville, and then suddenly he was getting a letter every two or three months. Yeah, and he even sent one out himself now and then. It got to be a joke around town, most folks thinking John had mailed letters to a make-believe person just to make it appear he had friends somewhere. Mr. Haley runs the post office, right there in the old store, you know? He showed me the letters. They were all postmarked in a little town called Cattle Rock or Callie Rock."

"Calico Rock," Gussie corrected. "Little village in the Arkansas Ozarks. All a ploy. They were addressed to John, placed inside another envelope, and then sent to the village. The postman there was instructed to open the envelope, postmark the envelope inside, and mail it to Niceville."

Odell hung his head. "They think of everything, don't they? Who would be suspicious of letters coming from a tiny hamlet in Arkansas? If only I had opened one of those letters," he grimaced.

"It wouldn't have mattered," Gussie assured him. "The letters were in a code that my dad was familiar with, but John wasn't."

As mind-boggling as the story was, Odell had finally concluded that Gussie was telling the truth. "What exactly did John Holder do that landed him in Bolton?" asked Odell.

"He committed the ultimate sin, Mr. Odell," Gussie began.

"He sneaked in a speakeasy in Chicago that was guaranteed protection by Two-Gun himself. John torched the place and bolted the doors on his way out, killing a mass of people, including a few highly ranked members from Two-Gun's organization. Well, sir, no Chicago gang is gonna trash a place that's protected by another gang and live to brag."

"Yes, I know," said Odell. "I'm familiar with the protection code, and I know what happens to anybody who destroys that protected property. How could a jerk like John escape the inevitable?" Odell had no sooner begun to trust Gussie than he began to lose faith again. But Gussie had worked himself into a spiel, anxious, it appeared, to share the story. He continued.

"It *was* a miracle. The torching of the 'protected' speakeasy caused an all-out war among Chicago's underworld, each spying on the other to determine who was responsible. When nothing turned up in their enemies' ranks, Mr. Two-Gun and all the other bosses began searching within their own organizations. John escaped in the beginning because nobody thought he was capable of planning such an attack or of going through with it without being caught or killed.

But John had fooled them," Gussie explained. "He had been seeking a name for himself in Chicago's underground far too long without success. Destroying the speakeasy brought fame, all right, but not the kind John had in mind.

"News that the initials *JH* had been etched on the sidewalk in front of the gutted speakeasy caught the ear of the most feared criminals in Chicago. Finally, all of the flamboyant kings of crime sought John, but only to put a bullet in his brain.

"Scared for his life, John had nowhere to go except to Mr. Two-Gun who was as anxious as anyone to see him dead. He had to kill him, of course."

"What?" squeaked Yancy.

"Well, same as," said Gussie. "He sentenced John to this isolated community, where he could never realize his goal of becoming an underground king of organized crime. For John, it was a death sentence."

Odell and his sidekick had stood spellbound throughout the tale—Odell skeptical and Yancy twitching in his pants, unwilling to relieve himself behind the nearest tree because it was out of hearing distance.

"Well, Mr.Two-Gun gave John a car with a fake license plate, but even that wouldn't have been enough if John hadn't kidnapped the first woman he saw on the street, a schoolteacher who was forced to pose as his wife. It was enough to throw the police and other criminals off his trail. They have always assumed he killed the woman once she was of no use to him, but they've never found her."

When Gussie concluded, the most alarming story yet, Odell felt overpowered with grief for the woman everyone referred to as Jeannette. She was obviously the victim that John had snatched off the streets of Chicago and made to endure pregnancy after pregnancy with only Jolene, the firstborn, to assist her. Apparently, Chicago had long since stopped looking for the teacher. While attempting to digest this latest news, Odell caught sight of Yancy, who appeared to have grown up in a matter of minutes, his curious appetite for news of underground criminals having been voraciously fed.

Again, Odell chastised himself for not sending the boy home, but the whole episode had left him unmindful of the norm.

"And the tommy gun?" asked Odell, whose skepticism was growing.

"John spotted the gun's empty case in my dad's house, and he knew what went in it. Every criminal in Chicago knows! John tore the walls out of my dad's house searching for it. My dad had hidden the gun outside the house and had sent a coded message telling me where it was. John stole the case, so I had no choice but to carry the tommy gun out of here wrapped in newspapers," he explained.

The notion of how utterly frustrated John must have been, knowing that gun was within his reach and not being able to find it, gave Odell a brief moment of satisfaction. "That reminds me," said Odell. "I've always been confused as to why you left the area on the same boat that John took that day when everyone was going to the hanging. When you saw John boarding, why didn't you just take the trip the following day?"

"Because John would have exited the boat the moment I did. I had left my dad's house the night before and spent the night in the bushes near the boat dock. That way, John wouldn't see me leave my house. The minute the boat captain showed up, I boarded. Fortunately, my plans called for me to exit the boat in Florosa." He paused, his demeanor having taken on a look of contentment. "I'm sorry, Mr. Odell, for any stress I've caused, but you can rest assured that Mr. Two-Gun's not here to do harm to anybody. He's here to settle a real estate deal. Surely you know that Mr. Grendle's exercise farm is for sale? It's been highly advertised in Chicago newspapers. Mr. Two-Gun Hoagie was once a heavyweight prize fighter," he said proudly. "He wants to settle down here, and when he heard about the exercise farm, he couldn't wait to make an offer. If not for Mr. Two-Gun, the exercise farm would have to close, and that would mean the loss of jobs for a lot of the people here, wouldn't it?" Gussie seemed hopeful that the news would guarantee a better reputation for his friend.

Odell, however, was irked by Gussie's praise for a hardened criminal. "As to the exercise farm, it does offer a few jobs to locals, but other than that, folks here won't miss it. None of us like the way Grendle works those poor people to death, running them around a brutal path and following that with a massive weight-lifting routine and a host of other indignities. Then he gives them a few string beans and an invisible slice of turkey. If those city folk worked for a living like we do here in Niceville, they would have no need for an exercise farm."

"Yeah," agreed Yancy. "They leave here pooped, and before you know it, they're back again, fat as ever." His comment brought relaxing laughter, but Odell wanted to end the conversation on a serious note.

There was something about the whole story that bothered Odell to the point that he could no longer remain silent. "I have had little experience with brutal criminals like they have in Chicago, but I do know something about their mind-set. I find it hard to believe that an underground king like Two-Gun Hoagland would give a blundering idiot like John a second chance. Frankly, your story has a ring of untruth to it," he finished. Odell and Yancy waited anxiously for Gussie's response, a look of triumph on each of their faces.

"I agree it's rare, sir, but it's even more rare for a hardened criminal to punish his own flesh and blood." Gussie's voice took on a milder tone. "John Holder's real name was John Hoagland. He was Mr. Two-Gun Hoagland's brother."

After saying good-bye to Gussie, the limping constable and his energetic sidekick boarded the lawman's boat for a ride across the bayou.

At home, Odell was eager to talk. "We have a problem," he announced. "First of all, Young Gussie is innocent!"

"How do you know that?" Jolene bristled.

"Honey, Gussie has been brainwashed by one of the most brutal criminals in Chicago! The boy thinks Two-Gun is here to buy the Grindle exercise farm! But he's wrong! He's here to create an alibi for himself."

"Seems to me Gussie needs an alibi more than Two-Gun does!" she pouted.

"Is Sheriff Hagood coming here?" asked Rhoda in a frail outburst.

"No. The last thing we want is to have the sheriff rolling in here with a bunch of untrained deputies. Truth is, none of us have deputies trained to deal with Chicago's monsters or their equipment or their mind-set, but Hagood don't seem to understand that."

His listeners hung tenaciously to his every word now. "These men from Chicago are ruthless. They think no more about killing than they do of brushing their teeth. If we raise a ruckus and try to arrest one of them, they will gun us down. It would mean total disaster even for the few who survive their attack."

"It would put an end to the moonshine business," explained Yancy. The comment shocked the women, but Odell quickly told them the boy was right. "The notoriety that would hit Niceville would put us on the map, and every federal agent in the country would camp out here. We can't allow that to happen."

Chapter 18

GUSSIE AND TWO-GUN LEFT THE VALE OF PARADISE without further incident. The infamous criminal returned to Chicago, confident that his alibi would exonerate him of any involvement in the bloody massacre of his known enemies. He was also confident that Gussie, an innocent witness with a spotless reputation, would verify that his longtime benefactor had indeed been on a business trip to purchase an exercise farm in sunny Florida when the recent Chicago massacre had taken place.

With that in mind, Two-Gun Hoagie eagerly prepared to step off the train as it approached the Chicago station. The moment he did, his body was mutilated by a tirade of bullets, sending him sprawling across the dirty platform and begging for his life in much the same fashion as those whose lives he had ended.

Like all criminals, Two-Gun Hoagie made one mistake: he always traveled by train. Rival gang members did not know his whereabouts, but they knew he would return to Chicago and that when he did, it would be by train. So they met them all. Apparently the gunmen, equally as brutal as Two-Gun himself, had no interest in hearing his well-planned alibi.

Back in Niceville, things had returned to normal before anyone heard the news about the Chicago massacre, and even then, only Odell associated the Niceville visitors with the crime.

Even Rhoda's fear of the Chicago twosome eventually weakened enough that she was able again to focus on Jolene's safety. Her energies had deteriorated in recent years, and she was no longer able to fight for Jolene the way she once had. She and Odell had "adopted" the girl years earlier and had tried to integrate her into their society. They had begun by having her fitted for dentures, which she mostly carried in one of her many pockets, often misplacing them for days. And Rhoda's handmade dresses, meant to identify Jolene as a female, hung unused in an old, deteriorating chifforobe.

Rhoda feared constantly that Jolene would just disappear one day and never be heard from again. She was more like a visitor, arriving unannounced on occasion and departing the next, rarely waiting for daylight. After Rhoda advertised Jolene's drawing talent on the hotel's bulletin board, the girl had stayed busy, mostly drawing children's portraits. The money that her drawings brought was a trifle, but it was enough to enhance the girl's self-image as well as renew Rhoda's dreams of Jolene's talent developing to its fullest.

The sagging economy, however, had taken a severe toll on Mr. Hamp's venture, and word was that Mr. Hamp was going bankrupt. As it happened, it was worse than that. The project's failure wrecked havoc on Mr. Hamp, whose weak heart couldn't withstand the pressure. His sales office had been abandoned, its signs left to deteriorate in the weather and the flyers that promised great things left crumpled on the floor. It was just one more sign of the times.

With the Vale of Paradise venture dead, Rhoda felt that any opportunity for Jolene to improve her situation in life had died with it. The thought of the girl growing old in a dirt-floored shack and killing squirrels for supper made her quite ill. Without Jolene to nurture and with her own health deteriorating, she rarely left the house.

Months later, when a letter addressed to Mr. and Mrs. Odell McNeil came from a women's college in Tallahassee, Rhoda passively handed it to Odell. Unexpected mail had captured her attention in the past, but no longer.

"This is for you, honey," Odell insisted. When Rhoda responded with a wave of her hand, he opened the letter and began reading it aloud.

"An anonymous donor has offered your adopted daughter, Miss Jolene Holder, four years of college studies at the Florida State College for Women in Tallahassee," he read.

Rhoda pushed her idle sewing basket aside and grasped the chair arms as if she intended to escape the bounds of a chair that had almost imprisoned her for too long.

"It says here that Jolene's expenses will be paid in full, including spending money for clothes, transportation, health issues, and room and board," Odell continued. "And listen to this:

> If Miss Holder wishes to accept the offer, she should come in person for an interview and bring proof of her completed studies in education and samples of her artwork. We look forward to meeting Miss Holder and viewing her work."

Rhoda's joy was unbridled. "I knew it would happen! It's one of those foreigners who came to the Vale of Paradise!" she squealed. "I knew somebody would finally see the potential in this girl and open up their pocketbooks!"

Odell couldn't remember the last time his wife had been so animated. She reached for her bonnet, tied it securely, and struggled to get out of her easy chair. "Let's go find her," she said with a sense of urgency. But before she reached the door, she stopped and began to cry.

"Now you've done it," Odell fussed. "You know better than to jump up quick like that! You're likely to fall and really hurt yourself.

Get back in that chair!" he ordered, and he assisted her in doing so. "I'll find the girl myself."

When Rhoda broke into sobs, Odell tried to comfort her. "You just got up too fast, honey. You'll be okay," he said in a mothering tone.

"It's not me," she bawled. "It's Jolene. She won't go. I know she won't."

And she was right. Jolene not only guffawed at the notion of attending college "way off in Tallahassee," she refused to read the letter.

Rhoda was not one to pass up an opportunity without a fight. While Connie gathered the girl's patchy school records, Rhoda gathered her strength and spent her days grilling Jolene for information on any background studies she could attest to beyond drawing. "People who are talented in one thing are usually talented in many things. What else did your mother teach you?" Rhoda begged to know.

"Arithmetic, history, English, literature, geography," Jolene said, rolling them quickly off her tongue and splattering saliva on her rugged paraphernalia. With her bottom dental plate resting in one of her grimy patchwork pockets, it was impossible for her to emit clean sounds. But poor enunciation failed to hide her excitement. She appeared happiest when talking about her mother, often recalling her many talents with the greatest show of admiration. "My mother went to college," she reminisced.

As sad as the occasion was, Rhoda and Connie rejoiced. All they had to do was convince their protégé that she would be honoring her mother by earning a college degree. "It would be the greatest compliment you could pay your mother," Connie told her. "Not only because you are her daughter, but because she prepared you for this. She must have hoped that somehow you would have a chance to develop your artistic talent."

Jolene sat with her head down, apparently unwilling to make eye contact with her would-be saviors. "No," was her only comment.

Devastated, Rhoda turned to her usual source of comfort. It was with great physical pain that she walked the long block to the little church and knelt to pray.

> Lord, I'm as guilty as the worst sinner. I have been ruining my health and that of my beloved husband over something I can do nothing about. If it be your will, the girl will take advantage of this opportunity. If not, I know you will look after her in some other capacity. You gave her the talent. And yes, you gave her the fire. It's up to you when, and if, it is to be ignited. Forgive me, Lord. And thank you for comforting me.

Rhoda's mental health improved in spite of the fact that Jolene continued her usual lifestyle and made no plans to apply for enrollment at the Tallahassee college. With the spring semester ended, time was running out for enrolling in the fall semester. Neither Rhoda nor Odell had seen Jolene for weeks, and both of them had solemnly allowed the idea to fade in their memories. Then one Sunday evening, they were attending a rare service at the little church when a sudden burst of excitement among the jammed-to-capacity congregation directed everyone's attention to the church's front entrance. Standing in the doorway was a human being dressed in a man's undershirt, scrubby hat, and roomy overalls. It was Jolene.

She had made a trip into town to see Rhoda and Odell, but when she saw the activity at the church, she stopped there as she knew they would be in attendance. It was her first visit to the church, but she was no stranger to Christianity as Jeannette Holder had conducted daily Bible studies with her daughter. Since John had never allowed his family to appear in public without him and since he had never entered the church, there had been no opportunity for Jolene to publicly worship God. She bolted through the aisles, pushed her tall frame through row after row of occupied seats, and generally disassembled the entire service until she found her adoptive parents.

"I'll go," she announced with a broad, toothless grin.

Chapter 19

THREE YEARS HAD PASSED SINCE JOLENE INTERRUPTED the church meeting. She had been accepted in the college but only on a trial basis, as her recorded background in education was not only sketchy but basically nonexistent. But her entrance exam was impressive, and she soon proved herself, excelling in all of her undertakings, and now she had completed three years of study. Her happiness was marred by only one thing: The Great Depression.

The sagging economy took a severe toll on everyone, and it was particularly true in Niceville. The death of the Vale of Paradise development was just one example. The economic downturn was universal, so only a few could afford a vacation.

Lumber mills closed, as orders for lumber from northern states were no longer the norm. When lumber mills closed, so did turpentine stills. The industries were owned by whites, but black men worked and depended on them for their livelihoods. Jobs were almost non existent, but one former resident of Niceville was comfortably employed. It was Jolene. After graduating from Florida State College for Women, she took a position teaching home economics in a Tallahassee high school. As such, she often had opportunities to use her artistic talents in the home decorating classes associated with such a position. She was still in her first year of teaching when she received a telegram from Chicago:

Mr. Two-Gun Hoagie, the man who killed your father, was killed in a blast of bullets that sent his body bouncing in the air and ended up lying in a pool of his own blood. That was four years ago. I hope you can think of him as I do: a good man who did some bad things. He was your benefactor. Regards, Gussie

Chapter 20

IT WAS 1934. WITH THE ECONOMY WORSENING ALL over the country, the government began creating what were commonly referred to as poor farms for families who were hungry, homeless, and without means of support. Those who qualified for residency in a poor farm soon learned that they were ostracized from those who didn't. Too, children of poor farm residents would have no schooling, thus guaranteeing that most would always be dependent on the government or starve. Residents of poor farms who became ill would either survive on their own or die, as they would receive no medical attention. Poor farm housing was subpar at best, and all members of the families residing there were obliged to raise their own food on farmland designated for that purpose. Death was their only hope of escaping their misery, and that was often welcomed, even hastened, as many committed suicide.

Even the rich felt the pinch of the economic times. That included David Stewart and his father, Claffie. They had to let many of their employees go, and one of them was Ecil Brighton. Claffie Stewart, however, still had power, and he used it to help his closest friends. He managed to have Ecil appointed as the overseer of the local poor farm. The Brightons would be furnished a house to live in, a truck, and a small paycheck. Best of all, they could hold onto their pride. There was something of a dark side, however. The family would have to leave Niceville and their lifelong friends and families and move to Baker!

Ten-year-old Yancy was, perhaps, the most distressed. News of the family's upcoming relocation prompted him to move swiftly. He had been working on just the right words and the right moment for delivering them, but with the family's moving away from his familiar stomping ground, and the very spot where he intended to launch his career as a tugboat captain, the time had clearly come to act.

"Mom, I'm quittin' school," he announced one morning. When Connie made no response, he rejoiced, assuming she had no objections. "Not here and not in Baker either," he added bravely.

"Five grades are enough for you, are they? Getting married or something?" Connie cajoled.

"Not funny, Mom. I can learn everything I need to know right here on the tugboats. I can live with Grampie. Who knows more than he does about making a living without wasting a lot of time in school? Baker, ha!" he laughed. "Folks there have to come to Niceville to get something to eat."

Connie was amused by her son's notion of Niceville's superiority over Baker. Truth was that Baker was noted for its ample vegetable crops, as their soil was rich and plentiful, unlike the sandy, nutrient-free soil in the south end of the county. True, Baker had no mullet, but ample waterways throughout the area offered a variety of delectable fish to accompany their luscious, homegrown vegetables.

"The truth is I'm glad you won't be hanging around those tugboats anymore. All those men—well, they're either drunk or in the process of getting drunk!" She stopped short of mentioning that Captain Herb, Yancy's hero, was a professed Christian and church elder who hogged the front pew every Sunday and then spent the remainder of the week hanging over a bar getting drunk. "If you're so anxious to learn from adults, the situation we face now is a good lesson for you. Times are tough, Yancy. We have to go where your dad has a job, and we're very lucky he has one. And this move to Baker? Well, it's not all bad, Son," she said, her own voice cracking. "We'll be close to Mary Sam and Casey again. I can remember when you cried yourself to sleep because you couldn't play with Casey every day," she said.

"I was just a kid then," he grumbled, although he did have fond memories of Casey, and the thought of traipsing through the woods with her in Baker was temporarily titillating.

"Mary Sam is one of Baker's most popular teachers, and Casey is one of the top students in high school," she told the uninterested young boy. "Both of them can help you with your schoolwork. You're going to like Baker, Son. Folks are more open-minded there," she said with some satisfaction. Her reference was to the genuine welcome that folks in Baker had extended to Mary Sam and Casey when they had first arrived from Niceville. The principal at the only accredited school in Okaloosa County had been quick to recognize Mary Sam's superior educational background, intellect, and talents, and he wasted no time brooding over her Indian heritage.

Realizing that his hope of leaving school and of staying behind with his grandfather was not to be, Yancy kicked the already battered screen door in a fit of anger. The blow loosened one of the metal attachments that had held it together. With the door scraping the floor, he was unable to open or close it. A quick glance at his mother told him the incident had changed her mood considerably.

He made the most of it. "There ain't a teacher in the whole school who could teach me how to repair that door like Mr. Odell could," he pointed out. "But if I moved to—"

"On the other hand," his mother said, "if you go to school, you will learn how to control your temper! And that would save you the embarrassment of enrolling in the Baker school with a blistered backside!"

Yancy cast his eyes toward the ceiling in a show of frustration. Once outside, he grabbed a rake that leaned against the wall on the back porch and swung it hard into the porch's corner post. Then, while his hand was still stinging from the blow, he threw the rake as far as he could send it. Connie raced to the door with unusual quickness and then struggled to open the screen door Yancy had damaged, finally tearing it off its hinges. "Don't take another step," she warned her son as she approached a hickory tree, broke off a sizable limb, and dressed it down to perfection. She then grabbed her startled son by the arm and began a lashing neither of them would ever forget. Each lick jolted his thin body and was still stinging when she landed the next. He had always been amazed by his mother's strength, a holdover from her teaching days when she had corralled a roomful of robust boys. Any one of them could have tossed her tiny body out the window, but none did. For an instant, he contemplated jerking away from her grasp, but just as he was about to follow through with the idea, he caught a glimpse of her face. Her eyes, already swollen from a lack of sleep, dealt with a steady stream of tears that gushed down her face and onto her neck and shoulders. It explained why the last blows she delivered were weaker than the others. Exhausted, she allowed her switch to fall to the ground, her weary body following suit as she landed haphazardly on a wooden doorstep.

Instead of walking away in a pout as he usually did, Yancy remained rooted to the spot she had left him in. Forgetting his own discomfort, he began concentrating on hers. The scar on her cheek, the one she had sustained early in life, always seemed to resurface when things weren't going well. Yancy had never seen it so prominent. He realized for the first time how devastating the thought of moving away from her aging father and tightly knit, lifelong friends must be. Still, she had accepted her fate and tried to instill in her equally devastated son the necessity to follow suit. The pain must have been awful for her, he thought, but she chose to bear it in silence for the sake of her family. He picked up the hickory switch and tossed it on top of the house.

"There's plenty more where that came from!" spouted his exhausted mother.

"I know, Mom, but you ain't gonna need it no more," Yancy promised. He moseyed toward the toolshed with a little wobble in his walk and began loading tools in the wagon in preparation for the move to Baker.

Chapter 21

ECIL AND CONNIE IMMEDIATELY FELT AT HOME IN Baker, where newcomers were welcomed and even sought after. In spite of Baker's isolation in the backwoods of Okaloosa County, its leaders were open-minded, flexible, and ahead of the times. For years, they had allowed black men to own their own land, and black men had responded by working the land and producing successful crops in cotton, corn, peanuts, sweet potatoes, velvet beans, and blueberries. White folks had paid little attention until the timber industry began to die, threatening a majority with the loss of their jobs. Succinctly put, the white men hadn't planned for the future. They had cut the ample supply of yellow pines indiscriminately and failed to replace them with new growth. The supply was running low, and it was too late for their generation to recover.

While jobless whites bemoaned the approaching death of the lumber industry, black farmers continued to work the fertile ground just as they had in the past. Whites eventually began to raise enough fruit and vegetables to feed their families, and even David's father, still the biggest landowner in the county, resorted to working the land to compensate for the inevitable loss of timber and turpentine returns. With some of the Stewart property still idle, an occasional farmer planted an acre or two in hopes of making a much-needed extra dime. Claffie was aware of these encroachments but opted, for the most part, to look the other way.

Except for Romie Beavert. Romie had spent much of his adult life poaching on the Stewart land, and none of the warnings, threats, and even lawsuits had discouraged him from continuing. When Claffie learned that Romie had recently planted over a hundred acres of Stewart land in cotton, he and David vowed it would be the last time. To their surprise, Romie declared that the property was his and that if anyone were caught trespassing on it, he would "blow them apart."

A few days later, Romie surprised his adversaries by agreeing to meet with them at one of their turpentine stills in Baker. It was a first, and David and his father were hopeful.

The Stewarts arrived early and had waited twenty minutes past the agreed-upon hour before Romie appeared. David and Claffie greeted him warmly, both extending their hands, but Romie kept his in his bulging pockets. Overlooking the insult, David opened the conversation. "Romie, we brought a survey so we can better determine the property's boundaries," he began.

"Why? Don't you know where your property is?" laughed Romie. Motioning toward Rufus, the Stewarts' black foreman, Romie ordered, "Get rid of the nigger!" David kindly asked Rufus to step inside the facility.

Meanwhile, Romie strutted about, wallowing a cigar around in his mouth before removing it long enough to spit a piece of it on the ground.

The Stewart men knew immediately that they had made a mistake. "This pint-sized idiot has no intention of listening to anything we have to say, son," Claffie whispered.

In an effort to ease tensions, David spread the survey of their land over the hood of his truck. "We can settle the dispute right here," offered David hopefully. He began pointing to the property's borders as indicated on the survey, while Romie continued to tumble the cigar from one side of his mouth to the other, never coming closer than three feet from the survey, a distance that precluded his viewing it.

"I don't need no picture to tell me where my property is," Romie scowled. Finding the cigar too much to handle, he finally stuck it in the front pocket of his shirt and then bit off a chunk of Brown Mule chewing tobacco. Having bit off too much, he proceeded to switch the tobacco back and forth just as he had the cigar, finally lodging it firmly to the roof of his mouth. No amount of tongue-struggling would release it. He was forced to swallow his pride and pop the troublesome wad loose with his finger, a move that landed it in the dirt several feet away.

The Stewarts pretended not to notice the drama that backfired on their cocky adversary and tried to continue the business at hand. "Romie, we all have to depend on professionals to survey our land and tell us where ours ends and others' begin," said David. "It's the only way we can make certain we don't encroach on someone else's property."

Romie responded with a spurt of dirty brown juice, some of which reached the survey.

"Let's go home!" Claffie huffed. "If he won't listen to reason, we'll take him to a higher court! Come on out, Rufus!" he yelled to his faithful employee. "You can get on with your work now. I never should have stopped you in the first place!" he grumbled. "Come on, let's drop in the store," he told David, totally ignoring the warnings Romie had begun to throw out.

David grabbed the survey and began following his dad, his back to Romie. He hadn't gone far when a shot rang out. Claffie turned around in time to see David fall to his knees and crumple to the ground. Before Romie could aim his rifle at Claffie, Rufus rushed out of the building, kicked the weapon out of Romie's hands and

threw him to the ground. While Rufus and Romie struggled over
the gun, Claffie used every ounce of his strength to drag his helpless
son to the Baker Mercantile Store just a few yards away.

Horrified, the owner of the store and his young son, the store's
only occupants, pulled David's wounded body behind the counter
and left him lying on his stomach, bleeding profusely. Grabbing his
own rifle, the proprietor told his son to run across the road to the
hotel and call the doctor and the sheriff. Before the boy could act,
Romie appeared in the doorway and began pounding bullet after
bullet into everyone he saw moving, this time with an automatic
rifle he had grabbed from his truck. He didn't stop until no one
remained standing, his gun empty. Neither Claffie nor the proprietor managed to get a single shot off. With Claffie, the proprietor,
and his son lying on the floor in pools of their own blood, Romie
pulled a .45 pistol from his gun belt and began searching for David.
"Come on out of your hiding place, Mr. David Stewart! The big
wheeling Stewarts' days are over!" he raved as he kicked at flour
sacks, overturned cracker barrels, and used his empty rifle to push
stacks of dry goods off the counter and disengage dresses and other
readymades from their racks. When none of that revealed David's
whereabouts, Romie sneered knowingly and began a stealthy walk
toward the back of the counter, the only place left for the wounded
man to hide.

Sudden noises coming from outside the building interrupted
Romie's mission. A peek out the window revealed armed people of
both sexes and several ages gathering on the grounds, each hiding
behind anything they came to in an effort to make their way to the
front door without being spotted. Romie fled the scene through a
partially blocked back entrance that had escaped the notice of the
hastily formed group.

With Romie gone, David managed to drag himself to the area
where his father lay. Huddling as close to his loved one as his own

injuries allowed, he managed to touch his father's face before collapsing onto the bludgeoned chest of the man he loved most in the world.

The men spread out, some remaining with the dead bodies and attempting to comfort those who appeared to be breathing. Others left in pursuit of a doctor or at least a nurse. A hastily formed angry mob left in pursuit of Romie Beavert, one of the least liked men in Okaloosa County.

Fortunately, the hotel proprietor across the street had called the Crestview hospital when she heard the shots and was told that Dr. Azore was delivering the Cutchen baby. The proprietor felt all was not lost as the Cutchens lived near the poor farm and Ecil Brighton, its manager, had a phone, still an anomaly in rural Crestview and Baker. Ecil promised to bring the doctor in. Meanwhile, students who lived in the hotel across the street were locked in their rooms, many in hysterics in spite of their teacher's cautioning them to remain quiet. All had heard the gunshots as well as the heart-rending silence that followed.

Casey Stewart was one of them. She had been chosen to tutor students who had been falling behind in math. Her class met in her hotel room three days a week. She left her frightened students with specific instructions: "Stay put while I see what's happening." She ran to the hotel's front entrance in time to see Rufus beating his fist against the metal building, filled with apprehension for his part in the fray.

"Rufus! What happened?" she screamed.

Rufus ran in place, too unnerved to stand still. "Mr. Romie! He done shot Mr. David—and likely everybody else by now," he managed to say, still moving in spite of not going nowhere. "They're still at it, Miss Casey. You best go back inside!" he cried out in obvious terror.

Ignoring his warnings and those of everyone else, Casey raced to the store and threw the door open. Bodies, young and old, lay on the floor in pools of their own blood. She let go with an ear-piercing scream before bending down to examine each one. Only one had a heartbeat. It was her daddy.

Others who had gathered watched in shock as Casey fled the scene as quickly as she had appeared, seemingly in hysterics, and disappeared behind the hotel. Struggling for breath, she returned with a bundle of ugly weeds, roots and all, dirt still clinging to them. She stuffed her mouth with the tops and began chewing. Women gasped in pity when they realized the scene had been too much for her as she had clearly lost her senses.

"All dead except David," Casey heard someone say.

"Don't touch him!" she shouted, and then she fell on her knees beside David, whose body was still resting on his father's chest. She covered her mouth with both hands to suppress a deep gasp of horror. "Shot in the back!" she moaned as she chewed the weeds with frightened fury.

"Daddy! Daddy!" she cried. "It's okay, Daddy. The doctor is on his way," she promised in spite of having no guarantee whatsoever that anyone had located Dr. Azore.

When the crowd parted, making a pathway for someone to come through, she breathed easier, certain it was a doctor. She gazed at the opening just long enough to catch sight of a familiar face, that of a tall, skinny kid. It was Yancy Brighton!

He had shoved his way in, bent on reaching the scene no matter how appalled the women were or how insistent the men that he stay put or, better yet, return to his classroom.

"Yancy!" Casey yelled. "Get me some scissors!" Many helping hands had been offered, but she knew most wouldn't sanction the use of Indian medicine; Yancy would welcome it. He had never forgotten the episode he had endured that day in the woods when Casey forced him to eat bitter herbs, a ploy to rid his young body of deadly moonshine. The lesson she hoped he would learn had backfired: he hated bitter weeds, but he had developed a keen liking for moonshine. Still, the two had formed a lasting friendship from their early scouting days in the woods, and Casey was always grateful for Yancy's belief in her and her people's medicine.

Asking no questions, Yancy grabbed scissors from the store's supply and returned in a heartbeat to watch Casey cut David's bloody shirt off and then spit a mouthful of chewed weeds onto his wound.

David began to shiver even though the atmosphere in the store was quite humid, especially on the floor where precious little fresh air could reach him. "Get out of here, all of you!" Casey screamed at the crowd, and Yancy quickly herded everybody out the door as if he were the doctor on duty. When David moaned, Casey promised him again that the doctor was on his way even as she stuffed her mouth with a new batch of weeds.

Word had spread quickly, and residents from near and far began to gather on store grounds, but none of them were medically trained. Casey busied herself checking David's wound while periodically pulling sheets and brooms from the shelves. "What's keeping the doctor?" she asked bystanders who had no answers.

Again, folks opened a pathway for someone. *It has to be a doctor*, thought Casey. It was Mary Sam! "Butterfly weed?" she asked her daughter.

"Yes, but if the doctor doesn't hurry, Mama …" she whispered. "If only we had a poultice."

"Dr. Azore is on his way," her mother told her. "Ecil tracked him down. You're doing all you can, honey," Mary Sam assured her. "Let's finish the gurney." She doubled several sheets Casey had grabbed from the store shelves and cut slits on both sides to secure handles. "Start tying," she told Yancy, who quickly followed her orders. "Never mind. I'll do that. You find a broom and cut the straw off." Yancy grabbed the brooms and quickly cut the straws, leaving only shortened handles. In no time, it seemed, they had fashioned a gurney for moving David's body with as little damage as possible.

A sudden motion outside the store demanded everyone's attention. An open path was quickly created, and a bull of a man came bursting through. It was Dr. Azore!

Azore knelt beside David. "Anybody else got a pulse?" he asked.

"No, sir," said Casey. As soon as he had examined David, he began spraying orders. "Let's get him on that gurney as fast as we can, but careful." he cautioned. "Got to get some blood in him," he said with urgency. The doctor spoke under his breath, an anomaly in itself for a man known for his booming voice. "Let's move him to the gurney, on his right side," he said. He called no names, but everyone sensed that his words were directed at the threesome standing nearest the victim: Mary Sam, Casey, and Yancy. The doctor pushed his hat back and used his sleeve to wipe away sweat so heavy that it had begun to obscure his sight. "Move out! Move out!" he ordered the onlookers, finally raising his voice. "Give him some fresh air!" His tortured face spoke for a life of trauma he had endured, often brought on by hotheads like Romie Beavert.

Once David was on the makeshift gurney, Azore quickly checked for signs of life in Claffie, the store proprietor, and his son, and he broke several commandments while cursing Romie. Azore had moved up in the world, now sporting a four-door sedan with a full-sized rear seat, purchased more with tragedies such as this in mind than for family outings. "I want all of you in the lab the minute we arrive at the hospital," he announced. "I pray to God at least one of you has the same blood type David has." Yancy was energized by the possibility that he would be called on to give blood.

"Dr. Azore, please let me ride in the backseat with him?" begged Casey, who had already settled on the floor of the backseat and was eagerly stuffing her mouth with more butterfly weed.

"All right, but if you start crying, I'll take your tonsils out!" promised the doctor with no hint whatsoever that he was joking.

Once inside the hospital, the doctor began barking orders to nurses and other employees to find a match to David's blood. "Try them first," he ordered, pointing to Casey and Mary Sam. "If that doesn't work, drag some of those curious onlookers in here and test them. If they balk, test 'em anyway. If they match, knock 'em out if you have to, but get me some blood."

Yancy coughed and cleared his throat endlessly but to no avail. His shoulders took on a deep and unusual slump, his whole demeanor one of sudden devastation. "What about me?" he railed, but he was ignored. Youth was the pits, he decided then and there, and he reiterated a promise to himself to grow faster.

As Azore issued orders, the crowd that had gathered drowned him out with their wailing and high-pitched chatter. Without warning, Azore pulled out his holstered pistol and shot straight up, landing a bullet in the hospital ceiling. Deadly quiet came over the lobby, waiting room, and admittance area. Even a restless baby stopped whimpering.

"The only voice I want to hear is mine!" bellowed Azore as he pulled his hat halfway down his wrinkled forehead, inadvertently trapping a wad of hair underneath his monstrous chapeau. With the hospital quieted, he holstered his pistol and disappeared behind a door, shouting orders as he went.

After David's blood type was identified, a freshly scrubbed Azore entered the operating room, his clean hands high in the air. A nurse pulled his surgical gloves on, tied his mask, and replaced his cowboy hat with a surgical cap before replacing his favorite headgear on top of that.

"You're in charge of the anesthesia, Gertrude," he said to a startled young nurse who appeared to be a teenager.

"But Dr. Azore, I've never … I mean, I don't …" she stuttered.

"I know your damn shortcomings, Gertrude, so don't remind me of them. I'm busy right now," he warned her.

Indeed, Gertrude had never administered anesthesia. However, the only nurse who had any training in the procedure, most of which came from Azore himself, had been working around the clock for several days, only catching a short nap in the hospital waiting room now and then. Azore had sent her home with orders to get some rest before she returned. The hospital was full.

With no trained anesthetists available, Azore was obliged to perform surgery while keeping as close a watch as possible on the administering of anesthesia, arguably the most dangerous part of a surgical procedure. The doctor had to divide his time, energy, and thoughts between removing the bullet and keeping tabs on the patient's blood pressure and other vital signs. Stopping the tedious surgical procedure with an order to drip the ether was nerve-racking and dangerous business. It was a job for several professionals, but only one was available to perform them.

Following surgery, Azore met with the family in his private office, his wild and wasted appearance reminding his audience of someone who was terminally ill. He used a surgical towel to wipe his crumpled forehead and then momentarily closed his eyes, bloodshot from too little rest. With his monstrous cowboy hat pulled sloppily over an overused surgical cap, his overall appearance put fear into everyone. All stood up, but Casey was quick to sit down again. She was still dizzy from giving blood. Hers had been the only match in their little group.

Azore's expressions were always hard to read, a frown often indicating shock rather than irritation, a smile indicating irritation rather than joy.

Casey began to cry softly. "He's never going to ride again, is he?"

"Not on a horse, maybe," said Azore. "With your blood in him, he'll likely be riding a tiger from now on." The outburst gave him the momentum to say what he had hesitated to say earlier. "I have to tell you they didn't teach us in medical school about the healing power of butterfly weed, but they did say that if anything works, use it." They all enjoyed a laugh as Azore made his way down the hospital corridor barking orders, his surgical cap still bulging outside his coveted cowboy chapeau.

Hours later, when the family was given permission to visit the patient, Mary Sam was faced with a decision of her life. She and David hadn't spoken to each other for years. Instead of following the nurse into David's room, she turned to Casey. "You go, honey," she insisted.

"No, Mama," said Casey. "You go. It's time you told him the truth," she whispered.

"What? No! Not now!" Mary Sam argued.

"Maybe not this first visit, but soon," Casey said, her demeanor one of distinct firmness.

Mary Sam stood up but fell back onto the bench she had been sharing with Casey and Ecil. Ecil grabbed her as she appeared unsteady. Casey, however, stood rigidly aside. "Come on, Mama. Stand up! You didn't give any blood!"

Mary Sam got the message. She stood up and walked down the hallway toward the intensive care unit, unassisted. When the attendant opened the door, Mary Sam stood in the doorway, shocked by what she saw. David appeared more dead than alive, lying on sheets scarcely whiter than he was. He peered at her with tired, partially opened eyes but gave no indication that he knew her identity. He appeared to have little interest in seeing whoever it was. She wanted to accommodate him by walking out without a word, but noises came out of her mouth before she knew it. "Did Dr. Azore tell you that Casey gave you blood?" she began. "She's boasting that you'll be in demand as a keynote speaker at the next Indian powwow!"

When David offered no response, her countenance fell to a new low, and she could think of nothing but escaping.

Before she could act on that, David's lips began to move, however subtly. She recognized the effort as an attempted smile. "Guess I'm part Indian now," he finally managed.

Within a week, David was able to sit up in bed and talk easily with his visitors. Casey insisted on accompanying her mother on the next visit, but Mary Sam had other ideas. "I'm not going back," she announced.

"Mama!" Casey quarreled. "If you don't tell him, I will."

The slightest wrinkle appeared on Mary Sam's forehead. "I told him!" she revealed. "Believe me, I wish I hadn't."

"He didn't believe you?" shouted Casey.

"I don't know what he believes. He talks a lot about how we saved his life, but he seems unwilling to discuss anything else. I'm sure he'd like it if I would leave him alone, and I intend to do that. You visit him if you like," she said.

Casey's restless eyes, always expressive, bore a startled expression. "You bet I will," she promised in a fit of anger.

When she visited David the next day, she found him lying on his stomach, obviously the most comfortable position. When he heard her voice, he lifted his head straight up, a move that put a strain on his neck and blurred his vision. Her intention had been to pounce on him with all her anger, but when she saw him struggling to get a clear view of his visitor, her natural instincts took over.

"Daddy? Are you all right? Lie back on the pillow and relax." She stood by his bed, gently stroking his hair. "Daddy, it took a lot of courage for Mama to tell you. I had to make her do it! Surely you don't blame her?"

"To begin with, she shouldn't have been with Klinger," he mumbled before burying his face in his pillow. Casey had to move closer in an effort to understand him. "Why didn't she report it? Rape is a crime, you know."

Casey could have tolerated the anger and frustration, but the doubt in his voice was more than she could bear. "And what if she *had* reported it, Daddy? Who would care if an Indian squaw was raped?" she burst out with bitter anger. She left the room, too angry to cry. To avoid contact with anyone, she exited the hospital through the back.

Several days later, word reached Casey that David had been asking for her. When she entered his room, he used all his strength to sit up in bed without assistance, a first since the accident, and he spoke with resolve. "Let's not allow Mr. Klinger to run our lives any longer. As far as I'm concerned, you are my little girl and I am your daddy."

Chapter 22

ALTHOUGH DAVID AND MARY SAM HAD NOT REACHED an understanding, Casey insisted that the three share a house and "live like a family again, at least until Daddy is on the mend." The adults agreed, although neither seemed comfortable with the idea.

Meanwhile, David's focus was on seeking revenge for the death of his father. While there were no witnesses to the final gunshot that killed Claffie Stewart or the store proprietor and his son, there was at least one witness who saw Romie shoot David in the back. That witness was Rufus, the Stewarts' faithful black employee. Although Rufus had been ordered inside the turpentine concern, the boards that held the outdoor facility together left wide cracks that enabled the employee to see the action outside. He saw Romie shoot David and then carefully aim his rifle for what surely would have been a fatal blow to the already immobilized man. Unarmed, Rufus had raced outside and thrown his body against Romie, knocking the rifle out of Romie's hands. A shot rang out as Romie had already pulled the trigger, but the bullet landed in the grass not far from his own feet. Stunned, Romie was slow to react, giving Rufus time to take the rifle. Unfortunately, Rufus was not familiar with the rifle and was unable to fire it before Romie retrieved an automatic rifle from his truck.

Sheriff Hagood quickly put Rufus under twenty-four-hour

protection, not only for the witness's safety but to ensure that he would live long enough to testify against Romie. Black witnesses' testimony was often discounted by white jurors, but with Romie being the accused, this witness's skin color had a good chance of being overlooked. For once in his life, the sheriff silently agreed with the multitude that Romie should pay for his crimes with his own life, and they didn't want to wait for a judge and jury to get the job done.

Panhandlers, the people who lived in the panhandle of Florida, were still viewed as "illiterate lowlifes," especially in the southern part of the state, where one newspaper reporter noted that the electric chair, Florida's new instrument for capital punishment, "might not be to the panhandlers' liking since it deprives the rednecks a chance to join their neighbors, friends and enemies in a rip-roaring celebration of de-heading a man."

Panhandlers scoffed at such talk, but the truth was, private hanging posses had already been formed, each intent on hanging Romie Beavert. Clough Martin was first to form a posse and the first to learn the disturbing news that Romie was not incarcerated in Crestview or Pensacola.

"If he ain't here and he ain't in Pensacola, where the hell is he?" demanded Clough, who muscled his way through an angry crowd, determined to get an answer.

"I can assure you he is securely detained by the law," said the sheriff, who demanded that his assistants break the crowd up and see that they go home, "even if you have to shoot somebody!"

Those were not soothing words for Clough or his cohorts. "Old Romie paid you off, did he?" Clough shouted at the sheriff.

Hagood knew how far he could go, and he also knew he was almost there. "He's in Tallahassee," he finally admitted. He tried to tell them he was as disappointed as they were, but his words failed to appease a single person. With the trial set to take place in Leon County, Romie stood a much better chance of going free as there would be no juror that far away who would know that he, clearly one of Okaloosa County's most dangerous people, had murdered anyone.

There was no question in the court's mind that Romie could not get a fair trial in Okaloosa County. He had already been found guilty by everyone, including his immediate family. Nobody knew it more than Romie did. He secured the best lawyer that Florida's capital city could boast of: Charles Kohlscrieber, a hard-nosed German-American lawyer who was undefeated in court. To Okaloosans' delight, Kohlscrieber did the impossible: he arranged bail for his client. But Romie knew that if he stepped on Okaloosa County ground, he was a dead man. He refused to leave the Tallahassee jail cell.

Before the trial began, David was given an opportunity to speak in person with Rufus. As youngsters, David and Rufus had played together while Rufus's mother washed, ironed, and sewed for David's mother. The two youngsters had developed as close a friendship as blacks and whites were allowed to.

When David entered the tiny room where Rufus was housed in secret, they embraced for a long and silent moment. Both of them wept. Few words were exchanged as neither could say more than their emotions had already said. Before leaving the cell that housed his friend, David thanked Rufus profusely "for everything."

The legal system moved rather quickly in Tallahassee. The jury was selected within days, and the trial was about to begin. David, while still healing, insisted on making the long, arduous trip to the capital city for what everyone believed would be a lengthy trial. They had the comfort of knowing that Rufus could put a nail in Romie's coffin, but there was still good reason for worry. Romie's money had bought a powerful Tallahassee attorney who had the distinction of never having lost a murder case!

When David and Mary Sam arrived at the Leon County

Courthouse in Tallahassee, they were quickly herded into the private quarters assigned to Zemery Noble, the prosecuting attorney. Noble's confidence and expertise comforted his clients and assured them they would prevail. Mary Sam and David walked with confidence into Noble's office.

But all was not well. Slumped in a chair behind a desk that appeared to engulf him, Noble made no effort to greet his anxious visitors. Instead, he motioned weakly toward seats surrounding the desk he used to support much of his upper body.

"What's wrong, Zem?" asked David. A quick search of the room revealed Zemery was the only person in the room; therefore, no one else could explain his condition or assist him. Bent on finding a doctor, David left Mary Sam in charge of looking after his friend.

"Too late," said Noble as tears welled in his eyes and then overflowed onto his distraught face. "Rufus is dead."

Chapter 23

THE VEHICLE THAT RUFUS AND TWO OKALOOSA County sheriffs had been traveling in from Crestview had turned over and burned so badly that none of the occupants were immediately identifiable. With no witnesses to the murder, the jury debated less than an hour before declaring Romie Beavert "not guilty."

The man who killed two adults and a young boy in cold blood was free to return to Okaloosa County, but Okaloosa Countians weren't anxious to receive him, at least not alive. They kept their guns loaded and they depleted the hardware store's supply of hanging rope. Unfortunately for them, Romie didn't make himself available for their public crucifixion. Weeks passed, and then months, and still, no one had seen Romie since his release from jail. His distant relatives appeared in public now and then, but all declared they had not seen Romie or members of his immediate family, and all were believable as they seemed as anxious as everyone else to see Romie dead.

As for David, the thought of his father's killer going free was more than he could bear. He began to lose interest in work, family, and friends. With all the stress, he and Mary Sam had little opportunity to rebuild their relationship, and he began to reject his wife's efforts to comfort him. He finally broke and had to be hospitalized again.

Dr. Azore knew that medicine wouldn't heal David this time, so he tried reasoning with him. "I'm not a lawyer, but I know that every profession has flaws and that includes the legal profession. They've botched this case and freed a cold-blooded murderer. I'll give you that, but be patient. Romie will die for his crimes. This community will see to it." When David tried to object, Azore cut him off.

"I know, I know!" the doctor shouted. "The bastard has flown the coop, but he'll be back! If nothing else, the repeal of Prohibition guarantees it."

David wasn't so sure. True, the repeal of Prohibition in 1933 had enhanced moonshine sales considerably. It was no longer illegal to sell whiskey as long as the sales tax was collected, but moonshiners were notorious for overlooking that small detail as it ate up their profits. With legal whiskey taxed, thus raising its cost to the consumer, the drinking public sought cheaper, untaxed—and therefore illegal—homemade brew as never before.

Even so, David remained listless and as well as skeptical, but Azore continued. "And therein lies his downfall, David! Moonshine is gonna hang Romie Beavert," he promised with gusto. "You have to admit that he takes pride in the quality of his product. Some fools add dangerous ingredients to speed up the process, and in so doing, they produce an inferior, ill-tasting, sometimes fatal concoction. Big businesses in Crestview, Montgomery, Birmingham, and Atlanta seek the best, and they know who produces it: you and Romie and a handful of others."

"You're forgetting something," David reminded him. "The feds are raising their monetary incentives to local officials. How long do you think it will be before the sheriff and all of his comrades accept one of those offers?"

Azore was shaken by the comment. "Get hold of yourself, David.

You sound like Clough!" he shouted. "Sheriff Hagood, a turncoat? Never happen," he insisted.

Revenuers had always offered monetary incentives to local officials in exchange for information leading to the location of still houses, and there were occasions when they doubled the offer for anything leading to the capture of a "gouger." It was a term federal agents pinned on moonshiners who were seen as "gouging" millions of dollars from government coffers by not paying taxes on their moonshine sales.

Thus far, local officials had continued to turn them away. Truth was, officials collected their money from the bootleggers themselves, who paid a hefty fee for that security. As a result, it was next to impossible for revenuers to succeed in destroying a whiskey still or arresting an owner of one even though experts estimated there were more than three thousand moonshine stills operating in Okaloosa County.

Azore's efforts to convince David that Romie would eventually pay for his crime had failed. "You seem to forget. Romie could live comfortably the rest of his life if he never made another dime. Why should he take a chance on moonshining again?" The doctor agreed in silence as the two parted company.

Meanwhile, David's health continued to deteriorate. In desperation, Azore called on Casey.

"Have you any idea of how sick your father is?" he asked point blank.

"Mama told me," she grieved.

"Why not move back in with your parents? You healed him before. You can do it again," he insisted.

"He will never heal as long as Romie Beavert is alive," she said with a sense of certainty. "Somebody needs to kill him," she added. "And by the way, I *am* living with them."

Azore pushed his big sombrero back and stood staring out the office's tiny, dirt-splattered window. He rubbed the window hard with a sleeved arm, but as most of the dirt was on the outside, his vision was not enhanced in the least. He grabbed a pan of water that he usually washed his hands in, splashed some on the window, and rubbed the surface again with his sleeved arm. His attempt to steal a view of the comings and goings in the circular driveway in front of the hospital not only failed, but his efforts left the window dirt-streaked, his sleeve soiled, and his temper heightened. "How long has it been since somebody cleaned this damn window?" he wondered out loud, and then he quickly remembered he had given strict orders that no one was to enter his private office in his absence. With Azore preoccupied with the window, Casey rose to go, but the doctor demanded that she "stay put."

"I think you're right, Casey," he began. "But how's anybody gonna kill him if they can't find him? What are you hearing out there?" he asked pointedly.

Casey understood. The doctor had good rapport with the young folks, who admired and trusted him and often shared their concerns and misgivings with him. Azore recognized their point of view as unhampered by greed, prejudice, or preconceived notions of good and bad. Adults tended to skirt the truth, enhance it, or avoid it completely when the truth might have saved a life or solved a problem.

"Not a lot going on right now," she admitted, "but I can tell you where to find Romie. All you have to do is find his still house."

Azore was visibly irritated by the remark as finding Romie Beavert's still house might well be more difficult than finding Beavert. Before he could pound the atmosphere with a booming response, Casey continued. "Yancy Brighton can take you there! And to any other still house in Okaloosa County," she added, uncertain the doctor was still listening.

Azore was quick to realize that he had been put down by a

pipsqueak of a girl whose mother was considered a second class citizen as was she herself, all because Indian blood ran through their veins. Casey was one of the most remarkable young women he had ever known. She was a genius, free of pretentiousness; a warm, glowing personality; and a delightful sense of humor that matched his own. And now she had possibly come up with a solution for doing away with Okaloosa County's worst criminal. Even so, what could he do with the information? What she didn't grasp was the problem of time. Put simply, he didn't have enough of it. Before he could think beyond that, he was called to the Cowlick Inn, a sleazy bar hidden in Crestview's countryside and known for its scummy patrons whose tempers flared in direct relation to the amount of alcohol they had inhaled.

When Azore arrived on the unkempt grounds surrounding the disreputable establishment deep in the backwoods of Baker, he found the victim lying on the ground in near darkness. A dim stream of light coming from a tiny window at the back of the bar was the only thing that prevented his running his car over the victim. The slamming of his car door brought the bar owner to the door, but only for a fleeting moment as a noisy brawl inside demanded his attention.

Using a flashlight, Azore examined the patient, who was bleeding from a gunshot wound to the chest. Brawls were commonplace at these sites, and with everyone carrying a gun, arguments often led to serious injuries and even death. Azore knew immediately this one fell in the latter category.

The victim struggled to say something to the doctor, who bent over to accommodate him. "What is it you want to say?" Azore asked.

"I killed Ru …" the victim struggled.

"You killed who?" yelled Azore, whose blaring voice made no impact on the drunken bar patrons.

After several attempts, the victim finally managed to make himself understood. "Rufus. I killed him and ..."

"Rufus who?" asked Azore. The only person the doctor knew by that name was a black employee at Claffie Stewart's turpentine business and the only surviving witness to Romie's shooting rampage. He was also the only person whose testimony could have sent Romie to the electric chair. "Now what the hell did you do that for?" Azore cried out. It wasn't Azore's first "dying confession." He once told a jury that every murderer was innocent until he was in the process of drawing his last breath. This was just one more example of that truth.

The victim had a lot more he wanted to say but managed only two words, "no money," before loosening the grip he once had on Azore's arm.

Just then, Bog, the owner of the bar peered out the back door. "Is that you, Doc?" He bolted through the weeds after taking the high wooden steps to the stilted shack three at a time. The hastily thrown-together wooden structure that housed his business had been built fifteen feet off the ground as it was located in a swampy area. During the rainy season, the only access to the place was by boat.

"You know anything about this?" Azore asked.

"I know somebody musta been waitin' for 'em," said Bog. "He was hardly out the door before I heard a gunshot. Hell, Doc, he musta shot himself. "Gotta go, Doc. I hear glass breaking inside. Wait up. I might have another one for you. Been a helluva night!" Sprinting across the weeds again, he manned the steps two at a time.

Azore had seen enough bullet-bludgeoned bodies to know it would be a miracle if this one ever regained consciousness. While attempting to revive him, he heard a suspicious noise in the tall bushes behind him. He grabbed his rifle, aimed it toward the bushes, and issued a threat. "I'm gonna start shooting. Might miss you, but then again, I might not." The moment he cocked his rifle, a high-pitched voice yelled, "Don't shoot Doc!" A tall, thin boy came bursting out of the bushes with his hands in the air.

Azore shined his flashlight into the pale face of a kid whose color had temporarily gone south. It was Yancy Brighton.

Azore was almost as shocked as Yancy was. "What the hell are you doing here?" he demanded, grasping the boy with a firm grip.

In spite of the doctor's grasp, Yancy made no effort to escape. Like most youngsters in Baker and beyond, Yancy had known the doctor all of his young life. "Well, I had to be somewhere, Doc, and this seemed like a good place, at least it was…," he explained without being sassy. "'Course, now I'm having my doubts," he admitted.

"If you don't tell me what you're doing here, guess I'll have you arrested for shooting a man," said the annoyed doctor. "Aren't you Ecil Brighton's boy? I thought your family moved back to Niceville. Does your daddy know where you are? I'm going to repeat my first question: What the hell are you doing here?"

"I'm spending the weekend with Herm. You see, Doc, Herm and me, we was just peeking in the bar you know. Suddenly Mr. Billy Joe came out of the bar to take a pee. Me and Herm hid in the bushes and all of a sudden we heard a shot and Mr. Billy Joe was on the ground right where he stood pissing," explained Yancy quite unabashed.

Billy Joe Harbeson was a man who was known for frequenting the bars, but he had never been in serious trouble. Azore administered a shot in the arm of the victim, who appeared to have lost consciousness. "I'm gonna get you to the hospital where you'll be more comfortable," he lied. Although the victim was still hanging onto life, Azore was virtually certain he would never survive the rough-and-tumble ride out of the parking area, much less to the hospital. Medical science hadn't determined if comatose patients could understand what folks were saying, but Azore always assumed they could so he did his best to comfort them with words as well as medicine.

"Now tell me about this Herm," Azore told Yancy. "You mean Delbert Woods' boy? Where is this elusive friend of yours?"

"He ran away when he heard the shot," Yancy explained with a snicker.

"In other words, your friend is smarter than you are," piped the irritated doctor. "He's home in bed while you've got yourself involved in a murder. As long as you're here, help me get this man in the car. Don't suppose you happened to notice who shot him?" he asked, knowing full well the boy had no clue or he would have rattled it off already.

"Mr. Romie," Yancy said without hesitation.

Azore tried to stand up, but the shock of Yancy's statement and the uneven ground in poorly lit surroundings denied him the pleasure. He lost his balance completely and found himself prone on the ground alongside his patient. The dim bar light no longer shone on Yancy's face as he had quickly moved forward to assist the doctor. Once upright, Azore retrieved his flashlight and shone it in Yancy's face. Satisfied he wasn't playing a joke, Azore asked, "Romie who?" in spite of the fact he knew only two, one of which was a character in a Shakespearean play.

"Beavert," said Yancy, shocked that the doctor had to ask.

"My God, boy! Why didn't you say so?" bellowed Azore.

Yancy shrugged.

"Is there anything else you haven't told me? Like where Romie's been hiding all this time?" The tone of the doctor's voice told Yancy how agitated he was, but it didn't tell him why.

"Before you came, Mr. Billy Joe was talking real fast like he was in a hurry to get it all said. Me and Herm, well, you see, we didn't know he was hurt that bad cause he was talking like he was okay.

He told us Mr. Romie owed him money—a lot of it," he added. "And he said Mr. Romie told him he didn't have no money."

Azore was hopeful. "Makes sense," he said. "The last words Billy Joe uttered were 'no money.' Romie must have told him he had no money to pay him for killing Rufus. What other lies did Romie tell him?" he asked Yancy. "Romie has more money than the whole of Okaloosa County could count in a lifetime," the doctor grumbled. Tossing his stethoscope and other medical supplies in his bag, he began making low, unintelligible sounds that grabbed Yancy's attention.

"Mr. Billy Joe's dead, ain't he, Doc?" he asked as a tremor bolted through his body, a feeling unlike anything he had ever experienced.

"I'm afraid so, son. He died like he lived," Azore mumbled.

The twosome observed an unannounced moment of silence, each dealing with his own perspective of things. Yancy had always been comfortable in the grown-up world, but this was quite another thing. He had never seen a man die.

For Azore, it was far from the first time, and he knew it wouldn't be the last. He had spent much of his adult life trying to save lives, and he had little sympathy for those who willingly took the lives of others. Billy Joe had taken a life, and now he had paid for it with his own. Azore could deal with that, but for the first time in his medical career, he had abandoned his medical oath long enough to wish a man dead. It was Romie Beavert.

"I'm gonna need your help getting him in the backseat," Azore finally said, breaking the silence.

"Yes, sir!" agreed Yancy. "But it's gonna be tight, ain't it?"

"I just don't get it," Azore thought aloud, unaware of Yancy's question. "Why didn't he just pay Billy Joe like he promised? He'd never miss the money!"

"Maybe he would and maybe he wouldn't," Yancy replied.

The comment had Azore's full attention. With Billy Joe's

extremities dangling from under the blanket the two had rolled him in and Azore trying to tuck the victim's loose parts inside, he found his oversized body stuck in the car door. In spite of a thick lining in his massive cowboy hat, his head took a pounding on the vehicle's door frame. For a moment, he thought the blow might have interfered with his senses as he suddenly heard water running on the ground and there was no source for such a thing. A moment passed before he realized the noise was created by Yancy. With one foot in the car, the other on the ground, he held Billy Joe's dead body at bay long enough to relieve himself.

Azore rubbed his pounding head for a brief moment before pressing Yancy to explain his comment. "You're an expert on Beavert's personal wealth, are you? Now I'm willing to admit a man would spend his last dollar to save his own life, but Romie didn't have to." The doctor's tone revealed a growing weakness in his confidence, and Yancy detected as much.

"Well, he couldn't gamble no more because he knew everybody had a bullet with his name on it. He was some gambler, all right, but if he couldn't gamble—well, that would be like having a hole in your pocket, wouldn't it?" he asked before realizing too late that he had revealed another habit of his, that of hanging around gambling halls. The slip didn't escape Azore, but he had suddenly come to realize that this was the very boy Casey deemed capable of doing what no other human being in Okaloosa County had been able to do: find Romie Beavert!

Azore wanted to search his young companion's face to determine, if possible, if he was just playing grown-up or if he had spent half of his young life peering through dim gambling hall windows. Unfortunately, the dark, moonless night denied him any opportunity to study the boy's expression. For the first time since arriving at the scene, Azore took a long look at the bar and shook his head in disgust.

"Now if you've got your private parts tucked in, we'll get on with our work," he spouted to Yancy. In spite of promising the boy he would deposit him on Delbert Woods's porch, the doctor sailed past the turn that would have taken them to the Woodses' house, and Yancy pretended he hadn't noticed. It was not until they arrived on the hospital grounds that Azore realized his error.

Instead of reprimanding Yancy, he let go with a frustrated laugh. "You pulled one on me, didn't you, boy? Don't know what you were thinking, though. The minute we deposit this man's body, I'll be driving you back to the Woodses' house. I ought to make you walk!" he grumbled.

In an effort to appease the doctor, Yancy quickly exited the car, grabbed the blanket that Billy Joe's body was rolled up in, and pulled it out of the backseat before Azore had a chance to stop him. When a hospital attendant appeared at the back door, he stood fixed for a moment as he witnessed a human body rolling out of a blanket and onto the dirty driveway. He braced himself for the unknown when a dim light from the hospital's open door revealed a youngster in charge of both.

"Long story, Bernie," a weary Azore explained to the mortified attendant. "It's okay. The man's not feeling any pain. Take him to the drugstore as soon as somebody shows up over there." The drugstore doubled as a morgue.

"You figure on reporting all this to the sheriff?" Yancy queried as the two stood facing each other once again in dim, scattered light.

"Why? Do you think I should keep it a secret?" Azore yelped.

"Well, it don't matter none 'cause the sheriff ain't gonna turn Mr. Romie in no way," Yancy said with the conviction of a jury in total consensus.

"You think not?" Azore humored.

"Well, if the sheriff wants to catch Mr. Romie, all he has to do is feed him to the feds," Yancy tossed out. "He knows where Mr. Romie is. Course, tattling to the feds ain't none too healthy."

Azore grabbed Yancy by his shoulders and pulled him into a stream of light. "Say what you want to say, boy!" he demanded. Yancy tried to wiggle out of Azore's grasp but found the doctor had no intention of letting him go.

"Come on!" Azore insisted, nearly certain that he had been taken in by this devious little clown who entertained himself by telling tall tales to gullible adults like him. He was equally certain the young man had formed his opinion based on loose talk among grown-ups and that he had no more personal knowledge regarding Romie's whiskey stills than he did. He decided the best thing to do was to play a trick on the boy.

"You know what? You've cleared up a number of things for me. With the sheriff and Romie enjoying a good buddy system like you describe, do you suppose the sheriff saw to Romie's still house production while Romie was locked up in Tallahassee?" As ridiculous as the notion was, he issued it with all the sincerity he could muster and then waited for Yancy to confess his story had been a ruse.

Yancy chuckled at such a notion. "Never happen. Mr. Romie would never let anybody else run that booger!"

Azore eyed the boy suspiciously. *Who is this kid? Is he, like Casey said, the key to catching Romie Beavert? Or have I been on my feet too long?* He was beginning to think the latter. On the ride back to the Woodses' house, he issued his passenger a warning.

"If you let me pass the turn to the Woodses' house again, I'll sew your balls together."

Yancy made no response but kept his gaze on the narrow country road, showing no sign of intimidation by the tall medical man whose hat rubbed the top of the vehicle's lining. Throughout the ride, however, he kept his legs squeezed tightly around his private parts.

Meanwhile, Azore continued to pummel the boy with questions throughout the bumpy ride. By the time they reached their destination, he was convinced that this young teenager knew Okaloosa County better than the elected officials who had been designated to run it.

Chapter 24

AZORE DIDN'T BOTHER TO GO HOME. HE RETURNED TO the hospital, lay on a makeshift bed in his office, and spent the rest of the night deep in thought. By morning, he had a plan. To carry it out, he would need the cooperation of David Stewart, Ecil Brighton, and of course, Ecil's son, Yancy. He had reached the conclusion that Yancy's idea of using federal agents to rid the area of Romie was the only one that would work in Okaloosa County. He also knew the feat could never be accomplished without the help of a tall, skinny, thirteen-year-old boy with the curiosity of a fearless tomcat and a knack for making adults look stupid. Who else knew the exact location and habits of the Beavert clan? As foolish as the whole scheme sounded, he arranged a meeting with David, Ecil, and Yancy.

David, still ailing and listless, was first to lose his temper. "I can't believe Romie has been in Okaloosa County all this time without being spotted by somebody!" he shouted. Quick to share his misgivings, he was nevertheless unwilling to turn down the remotest opportunity to see Romie dead.

"How can you be certain Romie will be there?" he continued, his eyes piercing those of their youngest member. "Does he sleep and eat there? Do you understand that if we try this cockeyed scheme and he's not there, we're likely to get caught traipsing through his territory and this man who murdered my dad will walk free?" he raved. "Hell, he could step outside to take a pee the minute we walk in," he added out of frustration.

Everyone was fearful. That included Yancy, but only for fear the men would change their minds about going through with the plan. "I can't say for sure Mr. Romie won't have to pee, but if he does, he'll stand right in the middle of those fifty-gallon rigs of his and spurt it everywhere and laugh like a maniac. It'd be a mighty good opportunity to take 'im down."

The comment eased the group's tension enough that they all joined in high-spirited laughter—except for Ecil. He was still trying to digest the news that his teenage son had been deemed an expert on the county's moonshine stills as well as those who ran them. "Have you actually seen Romie working his still houses?" he asked, hoping to hear a no! In an effort to ready himself for the boy's response, he took a seat but quickly abandoned it, tried another, then rested momentarily on the edge of Azore's cluttered desk before electing to pace the floor again.

"Well, have you?" Ecil asked with a grimace. Fearful of the answer, he didn't wait for one. "There's something you need to understand, son. Romie is not to be toyed with. He has killed a lot of men and will kill a lot more, and he wouldn't hesitate to add your name to his list!"

Seeing Ecil's distress, David and Dr. Azore began to ponder the integrity of carrying out a dangerous mission under the leadership of a boy barely into his teenage years.

"I have concerns myself," barked David. "How did you happen to enter that private property undetected? If we're caught at this job, none of us will live to brag about it."

The thought of such a plan really hit a nerve for Ecil. He stood up and looked every man in the eye, one at a time. "It's insane!" he yelled. "How can a mere spit of a boy locate well-hidden moonshine stills when only a handful of federal agents can find them in spite of their intense training for the job? I'm beginning to think this is my son's idea of entertainment."

"I agree," Azore said, surprising everyone. "I'm beginning to wonder if you have ever laid eyes on Romie's still house," he said, pulverizing Yancy's gaze with his own. He was suddenly so disheartened by the whole thing that he was about to walk out of the meeting and head for his private office when he remembered that the foursome was meeting *in* his private office and was doing so at his request.

With an anxious lull pervading the room, Yancy stood up from a crouched position on a footstool and began reeling off what he had been trying to say but hadn't been given a chance. "I've seen the still houses, all right, and once you've seen them, you don't never forget them. Three fifty-gallon rigs that stand twenty-eight inches high, twenty-eight inches long, and twenty-eight inches wide," he described with energized hands and the pride of someone who had constructed the rigs himself. "I might never have found it if not for a bad storm that went through Crestview a couple years ago. It destroyed part of the setup where Mr. Romie had been working, but that same storm partially downed one of the monstrous live oaks, landing it over the gully where all the equipment was set up. The tree trunk never surfaced even though the top part of it remained visible. Perfect for the Beaverts," he declared. "They trained live saplings to grow over the big tree, giving them near-perfect privacy. It's a masterpiece!" he squealed.

Ecil stiffened. With his colleagues obviously impressed and assuming a sense of renewed belief in the boy, it appeared more and more as if his young son was really going to be singled out to lead US federal agents to a fellow citizen's private whiskey still. That such an act was one of the worst things a man could do for his health and well-being had been instilled in him from the day he had appeared uninvited on the Niceville boat dock more than twenty years earlier.

"Never squeal on a moonshiner, least of all to a fed!" said Ecil. "It's one of the first warnings I received when I arrived in Niceville."

"Even if this gets out, it won't reflect poorly on your boy, Ecil," said David. "It's a good thing your boy's doing. He's helping us rid the area of a murdering coward."

"And as bad as we want Romie dead, we'll forgo the whole scheme before we'll take a chance on Yancy getting hurt," Azore promised. "Once the boy points us in the right direction, he'll remain in the background, away from any action. In fact, except for the agents, all of us will. As much as we would like to get involved in the fight itself, we mustn't. We don't want anything traced to us. We have to make it look like federal agents snuck in here and pulled off a strike!"

Yancy slumped in misery. "But, Doc, how you gonna find it if I don't go with you?" It was the team's first indication that their sprightly leader was not willing to take a backseat in this exciting mission. In an attempt to release his anger, he pulled so hard on one of the stool's spindles that he dislodged it from the stool, sending the seat crumpling to the floor with him in it.

Nobody reprimanded him; they were too overwhelmed with laughter. In spite of the doubt and potential problems, all agreed to give it a try. Weeks passed before David called a second meeting. "I've heard from Washington, and I'm convinced they're the dumbest people in the universe. They wanted to send a mob of federal agents to Crestview. No wonder they never catch anybody."

"Yeah," laughed Azore. "What hotel did they plan on using? The one next door to the sheriff's office?" The men enjoyed another laugh as it was the only hotel in Crestview.

"They finally agreed that each agent would stay in separate hotels in Pensacola or possibly Mobile, eat at different restaurants, and appear to be traveling alone so as not to arouse suspicion. The four of us will meet with them only once prior to the event."

"They've been warned not to bring more than three agents. If they break the rules, we'll call it off. Romie should be in the middle of a run, according to Yancy. But if he isn't and we don't see him, we get the hell out of there. Right now, we're set for eight o'clock sharp Wednesday night. Weather signs are good according to the almanac. Not too clear but not too dark, just a little overcast with a half moon fighting to make its entry," he explained.

"Is there anything anybody has to offer about Romie's kinfolks? I mean the ones who work at the operation?" David asked.

"I can tell you what I heard," offered Dr. Azore. "As a physician, I get an earful about every topic you can think of, and I get it on an hourly basis. Talk has it that Romie's wife and her brothers sleep with their fingers on the trigger and that every one of them can shoot the balls off a fleeing raccoon two hundred yards away. I don't believe the story myself, but you can probably assume from it that Romie and his kinfolks can severely wound a man, especially if their own lives are in danger. And if I'm right, Romie and his family are gonna massacre those stupid cowards from Washington, and we'll all be run out of town if Romie don't kill us first."

The doctor's sense of humor was enough to calm everyone, at least until the time came to act on their plans. Everyone arrived on time, safely hid their vehicles, and lined the john boats up along the creek. There was nothing anyone could do to ease the tension within the group itself. In spite of their agreement to work together, there was an ocean separating the two sides emotionally, and everyone knew it was deep enough to drown in. In spite of that, they all nodded their heads in cool and temporary friendship. Both groups had agreed to rid Okaloosa County of a brutal murderer, but that would have no effect on their bitter hatred for each other, and even if they were successful in their endeavor, no lasting friendships would come from it.

Although Dr. Azore didn't make, distribute, or sell moonshine himself, he was elated that others did, and he showed his appreciation by imbibing in it frequently. Like most Panhandle residents, he had difficulty standing face to face with a fed without spitting in his face. All three men and the boy restrained themselves but fell short of extending warm greetings.

As was agreed upon, Yancy occupied one boat while David and two feds followed in the second. Ecil shared the remaining boat with the third agent.

As they floated along, sounds of crickets tore into the atmosphere with such vengeance that the brashness of the frogs' brattle seemed mild in comparison, with neither species yielding to the nervous boaters' unspoken call for silence. Unknowingly, David, Azore, and Ecil shared some of the same thoughts. Aside from the dangers of such a mission, they knew that if they failed, they would be the laughing stock of the county for allowing a young boy to lead them on a futile nighttime path with companions that most Okaloosa Countians had spent their lives steering clear of.

But it was too late to turn back. Just as the almanac had promised, the sky was slightly overcast, a quarter moon sneaking in and out of the clouds often enough to warn them of impending danger. It also meant the enemy had a better chance of spotting them, but that wasn't likely as long as they could maintain quiet. Tension throughout the group mounted when Yancy's boat turned toward the shore but eased somewhat when he moved out again. Was he lost? they all worried, but they had their answer seconds later when he stopped again just a few feet farther down the stream.

When everyone had exited their boats and pulled them onto the sandy bank, they followed Yancy a few yards along the edge of the water. Their leader bent over now and then to pull on a shrub. If it was attached to the ground, he moved on until he found one that had been uprooted but left in its original spot. Like most moonshiners, Romie had placed the bush there to hide one of the many pathways the group used to enter the hidden still house if they came by water. Yancy lifted the bush and passed it down the line just as he had instructed the men and then began a slow, stealthy walk that required the occasional removal of other uprooted, but still green, bushes and vines without making a sound of any significance.

Although it seemed like a lengthy trespass, fewer than fifteen minutes had passed when they began to hear faint voices in the distance. Moving along slowly, they finally reached an opening where they could see dim lights underneath the fallen oak. The whole scene was exactly as Yancy had described it. The problem was that they couldn't distinguish one person from another as the live oak's thick growth and the bent-over saplings left them no viewing spaces of any significance. Although the plan called for Yancy and his dad to turn back the moment they reached the hidden still house, Yancy made no effort to do so. Any raid on the property from that angle would be a blind one, possibly yielding a few dead people but not necessarily the one they wanted. As it was too dangerous to carry on a conversation at that point, he took matters in his own hands.

He took a different path, one that appeared at times to lead them farther away from their target, but the others soon learned that Yancy had simply circled the area in order to reach an Indian mound. On their climb to the top, Azore was about to complain when the lights came into view again. It was all the startled men could do to maintain silence. They could see inside Romie's layout! There was a problem, however. They still weren't close enough to distinguish one person from another. They had come to kill Romie, not his wife or her brothers, and they knew that if a single shot were fired that didn't hit their intended target, Romie would escape again.

While mulling over the situation, Yancy suddenly fell to his knees and everyone followed suit. He pointed to the still house's entryway, where a fourth figure had come into sight. The minute the figure took a step, Yancy knew it was Romie. *Still walks like a four-year-old,* thought Yancy. Tiny steps were Romie's unwanted trademark, and he despised it. The public saw it as an indication of femininity, but it was a rare person who dared tease him about it.

David had dreamed of this moment, of Romie's being caught off guard. He instinctively raised his rifle, thus breaking the rules all had agreed upon, but he trembled so badly that he quickly lowered it and attempted to get control of himself.

Meanwhile, the federal agents and their local assistants took in the scene. They were close enough to determine that the designated man was well armed; the protrusions on his hips were obviously a gun belt loaded with guns. And they could distinguish the rifle hanging by a strap over his shoulder. He may have assumed that nobody knew the location of his hideout, but he clearly was not taking any chances.

Sadly for Yancy, the time had clearly come for him and the other locals to return to their john boats, leaving the federal agents in charge of nailing Romie. The agents understood and were about to move in when a loud gunshot came from within their own group! One agent had tripped on a vine and fallen forward, taking the shocked doctor with him. The shot sent Romie, his wife, and her brothers scrambling for cover, but Romie had mysteriously fallen to the ground and was unable to get up!

A single bullet from the fallen federal agent's Winchester had pierced Romie's heart, rendering him helpless. The agent, however, had no part in Romie's demise. His gun had downed the enemy, but Yancy had pulled the trigger. When the agent had fallen against Dr. Azore, both men and their rifles had gone down, causing one of the guns to fire accidentally and the bullet to pierce the ground in front of them. Yancy had grabbed the Winchester and fired a bullet into Romie's chest. He was down but still moving.

Realizing his condition, Romie began pleading with his wife and her brothers not to leave him, but it was too late. His family had fled the scene the moment they heard the first shot. When Romie realized they had left him to die, he cursed his wife and her brothers and vowed to get even with them in hell. The other federal agents pumped bullet after bullet into the dying man, who never had a chance to fire a single one of his many weapons.

News that Romie Beavert was not only dead but had suffered a painful death similar to those of his victims, created quite a stir throughout Okaloosa County. His demise was welcomed, but the news of the destruction of a whiskey still in the county by despised federal agents was not. Folks were nervous until word began to spread that Sheriff Hagood himself had led the attack and had seen it through without incident or injury to anyone other than Romie. Hagood was an instant hero.

Only Dr. Azore and the embarrassed feds knew the truth, that a teenage boy had fired the first shot at their target, disabled him, and prevented him from escaping. Yancy's bullet had landed in Romie's heart. Since all the bullets fired at Romie had come from federal agents' guns, there was nothing to tie Yancy or his exuberant friends to the raid. It was exactly what they wanted.

Sheriff Hagood was as confused as anyone. He couldn't enjoy the praise and accolades for fear of being shot in the back by those who didn't see his actions as heroic. He was left to wonder the rest of his life who really deserved the credit—or blame—for removing the county's most hated criminal from their area.

Chapter 25

THE DEMISE OF ONE OF THE MOST SUCCESSFUL MOON-shine makers and distributors in Okaloosa County did not discourage a single bootlegger from continuing to work his own still houses. Moonshine stills continued to dot the countryside in the Florida Panhandle. While many remained jobless, homeless, and hungry, they never felt hopeless as long as they could sell a jug of homemade whiskey from their kitchen crock pots or creekside still houses.

While income from moonshining had made a difference in the lives of many families, it fell far short of supporting the masses. People all over the United States were suffering from hunger and had nowhere to turn. President Roosevelt had come to realize that. He knew that some states and local charities could no longer carry the load of recovery from the Depression, and Northwest Florida was one of them. Poor farms across America had saved many a family from starvation and a few from suicide, but none were saved from a loss of self-confidence or a growing feeling of shame and inadequacy.

The president and his cabinet came up with a massive new agency, the Works Projects Administration (WPA), which was designed to increase employment that would benefit all of society. Ecil Brighton had been one of the first in Okaloosa County to benefit directly. On the local level, he had David Stewart to thank for it as David had been appointed to oversee the hiring for this new project. Once again, David had saved the Brighton family from disaster. He named Ecil Brighton foreman of a road-building project leading into the new bombing and gunnery range right in Niceville's backyard!

It not only meant a better lifestyle for the Brightons; it meant the Brightons would be returning home to Niceville and their friends. As for the new bombing and gunnery range, folks could thank James Poppell, the Chicago developer who had seen potential in the Valparaiso property that Hamp Etheridge had been forced to abandon. Poppell's development had been far from immune to the economic pinch, but he used what funds he had to improve the area and advertise it in Chicago as a clean, quiet, waterfront getaway. To help entertain the visitors who came, Poppell built a nine-hole golf course that meandered through the woods and hills before skirting Niceville's side of Boggy Bayou. It wasn't long before pilots from the Air Corps Tactical School at Maxwell Field, Alabama, discovered the serene waters, luscious beaches, and Poppell's elegant four-cornered Paradise Inn with its central gathering room and wraparound porch overlooking the busy waterfront. The pilots came, and they spent their money drinking moonshine and gambling in hastily built backroom bars. With the popular area contiguous to the Gulf of Mexico as well as the huge Choctawhatchee National Forest, the commandant of the Air Corps Tactical School soon saw the area's potential for a bombing and gunnery range for this growing military school.

Poppell also saw the potential for a regular Army payroll for the area. To aid the movement, he donated 137 acres for an airport, an area that was eventually accepted by the commandant of Maxwell Field. It meant regular weekend military flights to Valparaiso, and any activity in Valparaiso meant opportunities for employment for Niceville and Valparaiso residents.

Meanwhile, the real hero in Romie's demise had no problem entertaining himself. He ached to roam the waters with his grandfather again, especially as he was often allowed to occupy the treasured captain's chair on his aging relative's fishing boat. Too, his grandfather had a new crew member, albeit part time, whom Yancy admired. It was Clete Cogbill, the boy whom a majority still thought of as an unruly boy who set fire to his family home, an act that took the lives of his parents and all his siblings.

Clete was twenty-one now, a talented young man whose reputation for souping up engines that could outrun the law had long since made him the talk of Niceville. Yancy's many visits to Niceville during the family's tenure in Baker had him dividing his time between the auto repair shop and his grandfather's fishing business. His friendship with Clete had grown rapidly. There was only one problem as Yancy saw it: how could he convince his mother that these valuable experiences with his grandfather and Clete were far more beneficial to his maturity and his future than conjugating a verb or diagramming a sentence? More than ever, he sought her permission to quit school.

Clete, meanwhile, had his own problem. He wanted an auto repair shop of his own in a place far away from the clutches of Clough and Willie May Martin. He wanted to build a reputation as a top-notch automobile mechanic known for his quality work on automobiles and boat engines, and he didn't want to break any laws doing it. He also wanted to marry a girl he had known since his elementary school days.

In spite of Clete's reputation as a murderer, girls were attracted to him. Standing more than six feet tall in a muscular frame and sensuously tanned skin that highlighted a full head of sun-streaked hair, Clete had long been difficult for the girls to overlook. Clete, however, had made his choice early in life. He had neglected thus far, however, to reveal the would-be bride's identity, even to the would-be bride.

It wasn't stubbornness on Clete's part; it was fear of rejection. The truth was, he never really intended to reveal this long-held secret.

As for girls, Yancy had little or no interest in them, and he was especially glad that Clete apparently didn't either. In the past, the two had shared their innermost thoughts, so when Yancy suddenly noticed a change in Clete, he began to worry. Clete was gloomy and dispirited and far from forthcoming with any explanation for the sudden change.

Never one to hold back, Yancy confronted his friend using the only tactic he was familiar with: bluntness. "I hope you ain't gone and got lovesick!" he fumed. "Always screws a man up so he can't think clear."

When Clete met Yancy's anxious gaze, he drew his lips together tightly, an apparent effort to hold back tears. Embarrassed, he made no effort to respond to Yancy's inquiry.

Having sensed that Clete's silence confirmed what Yancy feared, he slumped in misery. "I'm never gonna let that happen to me!" he shouted out of frustration. When Clete made no effort to deny the charge, Yancy gave up. "Who the hell is this bitch who's ruining your life?"

"Casey," said Clete.

"Casey? Casey who?" asked Yancy.

"How many Caseys do you know?" asked the burgeoned lover.

"You mean our Casey? Casey Stewart?"

Clete blushed violently. "Now you know what a fool I am." He pumped his right fist into his left and cringed from the pain it caused. Clete's muscles weren't to be toyed with. Engine repair required heavy lifting, pushing, and pulling. He had created a

---

physique men envied and women admired—broad chest, muscled arms, slim hips.

"You want to marry Casey!" Yancy yelped, as if such a thing were preposterous.

Clete made a few poignant gestures, all of which begged for understanding. Having confessed, he felt like sharing everything, and Yancy was probably the only person in the world he would trust with his story. "She's always been the one," he began. "It pretty much started at the Klinger hanging. She was only five years old or something, but she was already the prettiest thing I ever saw. Tough as nails too, not like most girls. She could beat any boy at his own game then and she still can, but she never brags or comes on like a smart-aleck. She's the best, Yancy," he purred.

"Why, you crazy bastard!" laughed Yancy.

Clete cringed. "I know. It's a stupid idea. She would never be seen with me, and even if she would, Mr. Clough would never allow it." He fumbled nervously with his shirt sleeves, rolling them up and then pulling them down.

"What the hell! Forget about Clough. He's gonna end up in the gallows one day anyway. He's taking too many chances of late," said Yancy.

Clete sat up straight and eyed Yancy suspiciously. "Didn't you just say the whole thing is stupid? I mean girls and love and all that?"

"Well, if you're lovesick, you're lovesick," said Yancy, "and there ain't nothing nobody can do about it. I've seen it a hundred times." Disgruntled, he bade his friend good-bye and hastily began forming a committee of one to get Clete and Casey together. He entered the project as if he thought it would be easy. Casey, however, was not so easily convinced.

"You don't understand, Yancy. I've never thought of Clete Cogbill as anything but the boy who—" she began but was interrupted.

"I know!" Yancy growled. "The boy who burned the house down with his family in it? Come on, Casey. Everybody knows he didn't do that!" he snorted.

"Don't put words in my mouth, Yancy!" she spouted. "I think of him as the boy who promised me a bright, shiny set of marbles if I won the marble game. Well, he didn't keep his promise. Sure, I know he was just a little boy, and I didn't need the marbles, but I was just a little girl, and my mama always said folks are only as good as their word. Clete's word was no good, Yancy."

"Yeah, he definitely needs to pay for that the rest of his life," snapped Yancy.

Irritated, Casey jumped out of the porch swing they had been sharing, jerked the hotel screen door wide open, and then slammed the solid door hard enough to rock the porch timbers on her way to her room.

Yancy left devastated, not only because the wedding would apparently never take place but because he had failed utterly in what he had viewed as an easy task. *Clete and Casey belong together,* he told himself. *Men know those things, but women never seem to.* "Women!" he bellowed, and he promised himself all over again that he would never allow one to interrupt his life.

Of course, Clete was quite another story. Yancy planned strategy after strategy for bringing him and Casey together. Weeks disappeared into thin air, and still he had come up empty. Finally, he received a letter from Baker. There was no return address, but the pretty handwriting identified the writer's sex. It had to be Casey. It was a lengthy letter, nearly two pages, much of which he would not remember, but there was one line he would never forget: "It's okay for Clete to call on me Saturday evening at the Baker Hotel," she had written.

News that Casey had agreed to see him threw Clete into a working frenzy. The big day for testing the new engine he had been designing for Clough was just weeks away. The engine would not only make history, it would make Clough the richest moonshiner and bootlegger in the South! If successful, it would outrun anybody's wheels, federal agents' and other lawmen's included. As expected, Clough planned to accompany Clete on this exciting test. Clete's plea to take Yancy along was scoffed at.

Clete was bitterly disappointed. When Clough refused to give in, Clete began working nights in an effort to complete the project and test his work in advance of the expected date. The date for this secret run finally arrived, and Yancy was invited to take part in it.

When the time came, Yancy pretended to go to bed when, in fact, he lay on the bed fully dressed and ready to fly out the door the moment he heard Clete rounding the corner near his house. He jumped out of bed and started running in spite of a full bladder calling for his attention.

"How fast will it go?" he squealed as he jumped in the car, sockless with his shoes in hand and a fly zipper that refused to move up or down.

"That's what we're gonna find out," said Clete, who careened around the corner of Park Street and Bayshore Drive. Once the little settlement was a few miles behind them, he pressed the accelerator almost to the floor and laughed out loud when he noticed Yancy's white-knuckled fingers clutching the seat as doors and windows shook and fenders rattled.

Clete was about to push the pedal all the way down when he hit a clump of gravel that sent his lone passenger's head bouncing against a metal pole meant to support the vehicle's cloth top. "Hold on, partner!" he yelled at Yancy. "It's not made to travel empty. It's built to carry a load. It'll stay down once it's loaded with moonshine!" he rallied.

Rather than admit he was shaken, Yancy tightened his grip with one hand, pinched a bladder full of urine off with the other, and tried to erase the fear that monopolized his face. He pretty much failed at all three. "What if we had a revenuer chasing us?" he asked in a high pitch.

"I'm glad you asked," Clete said with a big smile. "It would give us a chance to play some tricks on 'im!" Before he could act on that, a black Model A Ford came screeching out of the woods, its siren screaming. "Would you look at that! It's a revenuer!" yelled Clete. "You wanna outrun 'im?"

Yancy was too caught up in the moment to worry about the consequences. He urged his friend to "leave 'im in the dust." For an exuberant moment, it never occurred to him that they might lose the race.

"Watch this!" yelled Clete, who braked a bit for a steep curve ahead of them. The revenuer didn't.

Clete was ecstatic. It was his first chance to test his work. While Clete and Yancy rode the sharp curve on two wheels, the fed, not knowing that the road curved, went sailing through the air, coming to rest after crashing into a huge live oak tree.

"Definitely not a fair race, Yancy," Clete admitted. "We locals know the roads so well that we can drive in total darkness. But the feds are forced to ride their brakes for fear of the unknown or press the accelerator to the floor and take their chances on the road being straight. Not many have that kind of courage. To worsen matters for the fed back there? I installed a switch that turned my taillight off so he didn't know I was braking a bit for a steep curve."

"Ahh!" he yelled as he beat his fist against the steering wheel in a moment of pure joy. Pushing the pedal as far as it would go, he warned Yancy to "Hold on!" And without further warning, he slammed the brake hard, successfully manipulating the vehicle into a complete turnaround and heading it in the direction they had just traveled.

Yancy had gripped the door with one hand, grabbed a rod in

the ceiling with the other, screamed with utter delight, and peed in his pants, simultaneously.

In a short moment, they reached the curve where the federal agent had sailed into the woods. The oak tree had sustained little damage, but the fed's vehicle had likely taken its last trip. They saw no sign of the agent, but Clete switched the light off of his own license plate just in case the agent was still able to read. Otherwise, he would have replaced the license plate with one of the many Clough had collected from other vehicles.

"Clete!" Yancy screeched. "How did you do that turnaround? Did you do it on purpose?"

"How? You have to have a lot of luck, Yancy. Of course, it helps if you have one brake wheel like this one does so that when you hit the brake, it spins the car around. But even then, if you don't have an experienced driver at the helm, somebody's likely to get killed. I don't want you to try it—not ever!" he insisted.

Yancy could only gasp.

"It's designed for use when you absolutely cannot lose the fed any other way. At a high rate of speed like we were going just now, you suddenly find yourself turned completely around and headed right into the face of your enemy," Clete explained.

Yancy pulled in a deep breath of fear. "But wouldn't both of you die?" he whispered.

"Well, you hope the fed wants to live bad enough that he will dive into the ditch. He knows the moonshiner ain't going to." He laughed heartily, and Yancy laughed with him, though void of the confidence Clete was armed with.

"Help me keep a lookout. We got rid of that one for a while, but you can rest assured the woods are full of these guys over here in Crestview," Clete reminded him.

"Why?" asked Yancy. "Ain't Prohibition over? It ain't against the law to sell whiskey anymore, is it?"

"Not if you pay taxes on it," Clete laughed. "Course ain't nobody paying taxes on moonshine. And you know Uncle Sam. He wants his money!"

"You mean if they paid taxes, they could sell it anywhere?" asked the stunned young man.

"That's right, but if these folks around here paid taxes, they wouldn't make a profit. And they ain't in this dangerous business for fun," Clete assured him.

With Yancy's mind bubbling with questions and struggling to understand most of the answers, he sensed that Clete had lost interest in small talk. His mind was apparently on the performance of the speeding monster he had created and nothing more.

"What do you say to another spin before daylight?" Although it was put in the form of a question, it was more of a warning as Clete had the accelerator floorboarded before he had completed the question. "Ah, I can't really get a feel for this without the car being heavily loaded. I've increased the suspension so the car can carry heavy loads and still outrun the feds!" He was yelling now so as to drown out the noisy engine. "But I know it'll work!" he said confidently.

"Pretty sure I need to triangle those leaf springs, but I can't do it until Mr. Clough's ready for a run," he added after a short pause. "If I make the suspensions too stiff, the rear end would stand up in the air so we could never leave it parked where folks could see it, at least not when it's empty." Yancy strained to listen but knew so little about the automobile's mechanism that he could make little sense of Clete's explanation. However, it left him ample time to concentrate on holding on. Bumps along the road often sent his head to the ceiling before depositing him against the car's hard, unforgiving interior.

The car itself was nothing to look at, desperate as it was for a good paint job, with its hard top already rusted in spots, its windows cracked, and its fenders decorated with the usual nicks. It was a ploy meant to suggest that it was on its last run.

With their wheels departing the earth now and then, Yancy held his breath when they found themselves temporarily airborne, breathing only when the vehicle hit dirt again. As they approached the Shoal River Bridge just a few miles from downtown Crestview, a sudden noise pierced the quiet. It was a siren, and there was no friendly source from whence it could come.

Clete hit the brakes.

"Can't you outrun 'em?" asked Yancy, who imagined himself handcuffed and thrown into a cold jail cell. And he would have to begin his sentence in wet pants.

"Don't worry!" Clete told him. "The only thing he can do is give us a speeding ticket. We're not carrying any moonshine, and he wouldn't care if we were. Likely got a still house of his own."

But Yancy wasn't so sure. "What if he finds out about that fed we ran off the road?" he worried. "What if he's dead?" There was no time for Clete to respond as the officer had already approached the driver's side of the car.

"You boys in a hurry, are you?" asked the deputy sheriff.

"Sorry, sir. It was so quiet and no cars around, I guess I got heavy-footed. It won't happen again, sir," he promised. The deputy shook his head in disgust, pulled out a pencil and traffic citation booklet, and began to write a ticket when another car pulled up behind them. Sitting in the passenger's seat was the federal agent whose vehicle had been wrapped around an oak tree. He appeared to be wincing with pain. He had been rescued by another agent, who pushed past the deputy and quickly ordered Clete and Yancy out of their high-speed vehicle.

"I'm afraid I was trying to impress my friend here when the gas pedal got stuck and I couldn't stop the car," Clete lied to the agent.

"Well, you impressed both of us, and if that ain't moonshine dripping off the seat, your friend has rewarded you by pissing on it," laughed the fed. He clicked both their hands and feet together with metal braces and ordered them into his vehicle. He asked the deputy to "keep an eye out while I search this hot rod."

While the deputy completed his citation, the federal agent searched the trunk of the car. Finding it empty except for a mass of tools, he resorted to pulling the trunk's interior siding off to check the space underneath. To his chagrin, the search revealed nothing. He hopped onto the car's fender and bounced up and down, listening for the unusual sloshing of liquids beyond the gas tank. Disappointed, he completed his search with a cursory glance in the limited space behind the seats.

"Well, now, what have we here?" he grinned after catching sight of a corked jug peeking from behind the passenger seat.

"Oh God!" gasped Clete, whose outburst confirmed his guilt as far as the fed was concerned.

Clough and Willie May had warned Clete to remain calm in the presence of a federal agent no matter what. "Fear in the face of the accuser is equal to guilt," Clough reminded the boy often. And now that Clete had an opportunity to use that valid training, he had clearly failed the test.

Unknown to Clough, Clete had been filling a jug with moonshine from Clough's supply and delivering it to Dr. Smythe on a weekly basis. The doctor had convinced Clete he needed it to assist his patients during childbirth. Clete had never forgotten the horrible screams and obvious pain his mother suffered during the birth of his four siblings and two others who were stillborn. He jumped at a chance to prevent other mothers from suffering as she had.

He had always carried the jug of moonshine on the floor of the passenger seat, but in order to make room for Yancy, he had squeezed it in the limited space behind the seat. The ups and downs he had put the vehicle through had rearranged everything in the

car, including the jug. He decided not to embarrass himself by relating a story the authorities would likely find laughable.

The agent removed the cork and sampled the contents of the
jug, an act that sent him squinting from strong fumes and struggling to survive the burning sensation of white lightning raping his
digestive tract all the way down.

"What do you know about this mash?" the fed asked the boy
whose pants were wet even though he hadn't been swimming or
caught in the rain.

Yancy shrugged his shoulders at first but finally came up with
an answer: "I know you don't like it much," he offered.

The federal agent enjoyed a laugh at that one and then promptly
advised the sheriff's deputy to see that Clete's car was immediately
hauled in for evidence. "I'll take him and his jug and his little companion to the sheriff's office. You might want to slip those pants
off and hang 'em outside the window," he told Yancy. "They should
dry by the time we get to the sheriff's office," he added, grinning.

At the Crestview courthouse, Clete and Yancy came face to face
with yet another angry man. It was Sheriff Herman West, the area's
new sheriff. The last thing West wanted to see in his office was a
federal agent who had caught one of his fee-paying moonshiners
distributing the stuff, especially one who worked for a hothead like
Clough Martin. He ordered his assistant to get in touch with the
boys' parents and "tell them what's going on here."

The federal agent made it known he had no intention of waiting
around for anybody's arrival. He demanded that Yancy and Clete
be locked up immediately.

"Lock up a couple of kids?" raved Sheriff West.

"Kids, my ass!" the agent screamed. "These vermin ran my partner off the road and damn near killed him. Don't try to downgrade
the charges against these young criminals," he warned. "We'll be
conducting a thorough search of the vehicle the boy was driving.

Your boy Clete over there has been caught with a jug of moonshine in this souped-up monster, and I plan to have the car impounded."

The sheriff was as furious as the federal agent was. He knew Clough would have his hide if he allowed the federal agent to see the car, much less search it. To get the fed out of his face, the sheriff agreed to lock Clete and Yancy in a secure jail cell long enough for the agent to get medical help for his injured partner.

"What the hell happened?" screamed Sheriff West the minute the door closed behind the agent. The sheriff's brain was stuck on fast-forward, tossing out more ideas than it was bringing in. He hadn't yet been informed of all the new modifications on the car as Clough wanted to surprise the sheriff once he'd had a chance to test them with Clete. If the sheriff had any notion of the truth, that Clete had devised a method for hauling moonshine that would take the federal agency a lifetime to uncover, he would have set the car on fire, or at least ordered it stolen.

By the time Clough arrived at the sheriff's office, West had succumbed to his weary body's call for rest and had fallen asleep in his chair. Clough slammed the door with the same vengeance he always slammed doors and then gave the sleeping sheriff a tongue-lashing.

"Where's the car? You can't let them examine that car!" Clough roared. He gave West an insolent stare before belting him with a threat. "If they take that car apart, the moonshine party in Okaloosa County is over, Mr. Herman West, and its gonna lighten them big, fat pockets of yours considerably." Too uptight to sit down, he began pacing back and forth in a space hardly big enough to accommodate movement of any kind, especially by a giant of a man who took up the space of three ordinary men.

"Like it or not, Clough, we're gonna be dealing with the federal judges now. And Clete's going to spend some time in prison," a fully awakened Sheriff West warned. "And he might do more talking than that souped-up car of yours will," he added.

"Horse hockey!" yelled Clough. "Ain't nobody gonna listen to that stupid kid. I should have canned that boy way yonder when he killed his whole damn family. He's got some bad blood in 'im." He let loose with a gruesome laugh.

It was perhaps the worst thing he could have said to the sheriff, who held a distinct dislike for Clough as well as his equally disagreeable spouse. Too, the sheriff belonged to the majority who knew that Clete had nothing to do with his family's deaths, and yet it appeared that Clete might have to pay for yet another crime that Clough had committed.

Certain that Clough would want to speak with Clete, perhaps to warn him to remain silent, the sheriff told the deputy to "show Mr. Clough to his boy's cell." But Clough declined the invitation. "I don't give a rat's ass what happens to Clete Cogbill. Whatever he has done has nothing to do with me. He ain't got a drop of my blood in 'im."

Meanwhile, the boys had been busy. They had been thrown into a locked facility and left alone, and Clete had used every second of their time together to pummel Yancy with information he was told to memorize.

Clete had begun in a whisper. He cupped his hands around Yancy's ear, imparting a great deal of detail in a few short minutes. Once finished, he repeated it and then ordered Yancy to repeat it over and over. Usually emboldened by brassy secrets of the lawless, this one left Yancy struggling to recall every shocking detail that Clete had imparted.

"What if I forget …" he begged on occasion even as he struggled to memorize it word for word. Clete filled in the blanks when Yancy became confused, corrected him when he made mistakes, and reminded him often that he mustn't fail. "Remember, you are not to repeat it to anyone until such time … until, that is … unless I go to prison."

The boys exchanged anxious glances when they were hustled into a private room with a huddle of stiff-faced men. Clete took the seat offered him and remained morbidly quiet while Yancy busied himself mentally repeating the secrets Clete had whispered in his ear just moments earlier. He had never felt so helpless or forlorn. It was as if he had been forced to grow up in a matter of minutes, and he was no longer certain that adulthood was all he had imagined it would be.

Yancy was sent home, but Clete was officially jailed with the understanding that he would be tried in federal court in Pensacola. With Clete in jail and possibly headed for prison, nothing comforted Yancy. The entire episode had such a devastating effect on him that he was allowed to attend the trial with his grandfather, Captain Buie.

While on the stand, Clough managed to capture the judge's sympathy. "I can't tell you how disappointed I am in Clete," he declared as he swiped at a steady stream of tears that appeared to flow from genuine disappointment and painful regret. "Just about anybody in this courtroom can tell you I took the boy in and nurtured him after his entire family met with a fatal accident that he was responsible for himself."

Those who knew Clough were shocked by the tears he managed to produce. They would eventually learn that he had punctured his body with a sewing needle at opportune times. Once the pain began to wear off, he jabbed the tiny instrument into another sensitive part of his body, creating excruciating pain to keep the tears flowing. It kept his facial features gnarled from what the judge mistook for emotional pain and misery Clete had supposedly dealt him.

Clete was given three years in federal prison.

Yancy's Grampie made every effort to comfort his grandson on their return trip to Niceville, but Yancy was inconsolable.

"I know you're in no mood for me to tell you there's a lesson to be learned here, but I'm gonna tell you anyway," announced his grandfather. "If you hang around folks who flaunt the laws like Clough has—well, you're likely to end up in trouble while Clough, the actor, goes free. He has never paid for killing Ovid Switzer, and he likely won't pay for this dastardly crime either, son."

Yancy had always valued his grandfather's notions and, for some reason unknown to him, he never resented his grandfather's advice like he did that of his parents. But at the moment, he was in no mood for listening to anyone. His thoughts were solemnly planted on the courtroom experience he had just witnessed, where heavy shackles had rubbed his friend's legs raw and sent blood oozing out of the wounds they made. Two armed men had stood guard by the entrance while two others clutched Clete's arms like a vice even though he was already restrained by chains. While Clough Martin acted out his dramatic tale of made-up woe, Clete hung his head so low that his chin rested on his chest in a hopeless fashion.

"Mr. Clough's gonna pay this time, Grampie," Yancy announced. "I'm gonna see to it, but I'll need your help. I would ask Mom and Dad, but I know they won't believe a single word I tell them. But you have to believe me, Grampie," he insisted.

Realizing his grandson was fighting a mix of anger and pain he hadn't been able to deal with, Captain Buie openly wept with him. "Just try to get the anger out, son. If you don't, it will eat you alive," he warned.

"Don't worry, Grampie. We don't have to kill nobody. All you need to do is write a letter. I'd do it myself, but you know I can't write pretty, and anyway, they wouldn't pay no attention to a kid. I'll tell you what to say."

Buie choked off a laugh to prevent embarrassing his grandson and responded with a bit of advice. "They'll find out eventually, son," he assured him. "Try to let it go, now. Don't spend your life seeking revenge," he cautioned somewhat ill-naturedly, not so much for his grandson's immaturity but for a sudden weakness of his own. By the time they arrived in Niceville, he was quite dizzy and wasn't at all certain he could stand up without falling. Once outside the car, he felt so faint that he leaned against the fender and slithered to the ground.

Yancy hadn't noticed as he was on the opposite side of the car. "You gotta listen to me, Grampie. We have to help Clete! The feds' minds don't work like a bootlegger's. They ain't never gonna catch Mr. Clough without our help and … Grampie!" he shouted once he spotted his grandfather lying on the ground. "Grampie! Grampie!" he moaned.

"You just hold on, Grampie. I'll get Doc Smythe," he promised, but he realized immediately that he mustn't leave his grandfather alone. He yelled in all directions, hoping that someone would hear him, but before anyone did, his grandfather touched him gently on the arm.

"Don't worry, son. I feel better now. Help me up, and let's talk about this. But first, I need to ask you a question. I want to know if you led the feds to Romie Beavert's still house?" The shock of his fallen grandfather suddenly recovered and the bombshell question that came out of his mouth dealt Yancy quite a shock.

"Did you put the first bullet in Beavert's body?" his Grampie brazenly questioned.

Yancy's prolonged silence pleased his grandfather. "Well, I'll be doggone," he said proudly. "Now if you'll help me up, I'll write that letter for you."

"Not now, Grampie," insisted Yancy. "You stay put while I get Doc Smythe."

"No! It's nothing," his grandfather insisted. "I have these spells now and then. Just a little dizziness now and then. Now that I know you can keep a secret, I want you to promise you will keep this one from Doc Smythe and everyone else. If they find out, they will insist I stay home in bed, and I would rather die than do that. Let me rest for a bit and then I'll write that letter."

Six months later, Clough and Willie May Martin were making one of their usual trips from Niceville to Birmingham, both perched sassily in the vehicle that Clete Cogbill had single-handedly designed for them. Their personal car was ordinary as far as anyone could see, bringing to mind a junk yard heap with no hint whatsoever of any speed-enhancing modifications. There was a reason for this. Their slow-moving, lackadaisical attitude as they drove along in a botched-up junkie attracted little attention. They planned it that way. Most everyone still looked upon Clough as a wild and lawless murderer who would kill his own mother to make a dollar, but his new attitude since Clete's demise seemed to indicate that fear had taken its hold on Clough's activities. Why else would he and Willie May live a common existence like nearly everyone else?

Clete's imprisonment had indeed brought about changes in Clough's moonshine business. He knew that federal agents would be staked out in big numbers along the Niceville–Birmingham route looking for speeding night runs in Clough's enhanced vehicles. He didn't disappoint them. On occasion, he allowed the feds to catch his vehicles, but only when they were empty. While the feds busied themselves examining one of these monsters, a second one, loaded to the hilt, passed by in a tornado-like whiz in spite of carrying six hundred pounds or more of bottled moonshine. The feds never came close to catching one of Clete's personally designed vehicles, and Clough's ownership of empty vehicles gave the feds no opportunity to arrest him.

Chugging along well behind the speeding runners were Clough and Willie May in their seemingly unremarkable vehicle. In spite of its innocent appearance, it too was loaded with moonshine! But no one knew that except Clete, who had designed the Martins' personal vehicle to include secret holding cells for carrying moonshine, just as he had done with the hot rods. The feds had never searched Clough's private vehicle and probably wouldn't have discovered the new hiding place if they had.

On this particular trip, the Martins weren't far past Crestview when they were flagged down by a three-man team of federal agents.

"Must be a bunch of new bastards," grumbled Clough. He and Willie May had become familiar with many of the federal agents, some of whom didn't bother to stop the Martins now that they always drove the speed limit and were both friendly and helpful with the agents during their searches.

Clough quickly brought his car to a halt and offered a friendly greeting to a federal face he hadn't seen before.

Ignoring Clough's offer of friendship, the agent ordered him and his passenger to "Get out of the car. Now! Both of you!" While two other agents kept an eye on the Martins, the agent in charge picked up a box that lay between the seats marked "Uncle Roy," opened it, and sampled one of the fresh, homemade molasses cookies. "Uncle Roy's gonna like these," the agent said as he rummaged through the other boxes and bags that had been placed on the floor or stuffed behind the seats. "My, my, you folks must be planning a feast for Uncle Roy. He live close by?"

"About another fifteen miles or so. In the country, you know," began Clough, who had planned a long tirade about an uncle who didn't exist. "Yeah, we try to look after our elderly. Uncle Roy's been awful sick, you know, so me and my wife—"

Clough's masterpiece was interrupted by two more agents who came out of the wooded area nearby, both with their jackets pulled back, revealing holstered guns.

"Step back away from the car!" said Clyde, the apparent leader of the threesome. "Okay, let's do it," Clyde told one of his assistants. "You take the front, and I'll take the back."

Both men crawled under the car and began a comprehensive search of the car's underside. After draining the liquid from the gas tank and finding nothing but gasoline, their disappointment was noticeable. They had reason to believe the Martins had turned the gas tank into a moonshine tank. Apparently they hadn't.

"Aw, come on, fellas. It's getting late, and we need to see after our sick folks. Why not have a piece of cake and some of my wife's fried chicken?" Clough coaxed as he reached for a large box in the floor of the passenger's seat.

"Back away from the car!" ordered Clyde. When Clough made no effort to do as told, one agent pointed a gun at him while another pushed him away from the vehicle. "You stay put," said the agent. Glancing at Willie May, he said, "You too!"

Suddenly the agent underneath the vehicle broke into laughter. "I found it!" he raved. "Right on top of the tank!"

Instead of turning her frustration toward the agents, Willie May turned on her husband, whose face had turned pale, his whole body slumped in sudden misery. She noticed for the first time how utterly ugly Clough was—his nose as flat as the bottom of a cast iron cook pot, his eyes hidden for the most part by puffy skin, and worst of all, big ears flapping like a horse's tail batting flies away. Instead of the strong, ruthless man she had come to think of as a fearless partner, she saw only weakness. She never imagined he would get caught and take her down with him.

All three agents who had been watching Clough and Willie May perked up considerably, each eyeing the others with a grin. "You need a siphon?" asked one of the agents.

"And a jug," added Clyde who had joined the agent underneath the vehicle.

"The old jalopy is about worn out," offered Clough, who had recuperated enough to continue his usual spiel. "We have to do a lot of soldering now and then, even on the gas tank. Soldering fills the hole in but it also leaves a pack of solder," he said, his voice tightening with every word.

Ignoring Clough, the revenuers waited anxiously for the sound of liquid hitting the bottom of the empty jug. Once the jug was full, Clyde scrambled his way from underneath the car, gasped for a good clean breath of air, and asked a simple question of Clough.

"White lightning?" he grinned. Clete had brilliantly built a moonshine tank inside the gas tank! "Pretty clever!" Clyde admitted. "Too bad you people don't use your skills for a better cause."

While Clough and Willie May gasped from pretentious shock, Clyde's assistant, who had continued to poke around underneath the vehicle, let go with a yell. "Yep! They've got a moonshine tank under the floorboard, all right."

"False underpinning," said Clyde knowingly. "You would have to know it was there," he admitted. "This car is loaded!" he said with a broad grin.

Clough began openly cursing Clete. "That damn son-of-a-bitch modified my personal car without my knowledge! We never should have taken him in after he killed his momma and daddy." This time, no body was listening to Clough's spiel.

Clough and his sullen wife soon found themselves facing the same judge he had encountered in Clete's trial—and the judge had a long memory. "You have both flaunted the laws of our country, pedaled your illegal wares across state lines, and perhaps worst of all, you forced a young boy into your home and trained him to break the law, all under the pretense of fathering him."

Clough and Willie May were sentenced to three to five years of hard labor in the federal penitentiary. Each entered a federal prison determined to get even with Clete Cogbill for inventing a system so simple "the stupid feds uncovered it." They never imagined that

a fourteen-year-old kid from Niceville, with the help of his ailing
grandfather, had been responsible for their demise.

Chapter 26

NICEVILLE WAS NO LONGER AN ISOLATED BACKWOODS moonshine haven. Publicity surrounding Clete's undoing had covered the front pages of newspapers throughout the South. When Clough and Willie May's story surfaced, newsmen had a heyday. Willie May was crowned the "Moonshine Mama of Not-so-Nice Niceville." One Miami reporter explained it this way: "Panhandle bootleggers encouraged their own children to create this dangerous illegal mash and then insisted they drink it. While under the influence of the concoction, these youngsters are expected to distribute the deadly mash in dangerous, self-designed hot rods."

While Niceville tongues wagged, Yancy made every effort to carry out Clete's plan. He approached his grandfather for assistance, but Captain Buie's health had worsened to the point that he was now bedridden. He did offer his grandson some advice: "I know how important this is to you, son, and I would gladly help if I could, but the truth is, I couldn't help you if I were in the best of health. You're gonna need a lawyer. I don't even know a lawyer, and I couldn't pay one if I did." In spite of delivering bad news, his ailing grandfather called on all of his strength to flash a firm thumbs-up.

It was all the courage Yancy needed. He met the challenge with the social graces of a wildcat. He hitchhiked to the hotel in Baker where Casey resided. "Clete needs a lawyer, a wife with a job, and proof he can make a living himself. Right now he's got one out of three," he blurted, then held his breath while awaiting her response.

Casey burst out in laughter. "So fill me in, Yancy. I'm to knock on the prison door and tell the warden I want to marry one of his inmates so I can make him a living? What do I need the lawyer for? Couldn't I just take a preacher with me to the prison?"

Yancy's face lit up like a heated stovepipe. She had made him look like the idiot he was. But there was a bright spot. There was no question that Casey was as frustrated as he was and as anxious to help Clete. The race to free Clete was on.

After extended correspondence between Casey and Clete, she finally took Yancy's advice. She approached David about hiring a lawyer to represent Clete. Since David had continued to accept Casey as his daughter, the two had enjoyed a closer relationship, but there was still a problem: the wedge that had driven David and Mary Sam apart had resurfaced. Mary Sam had made no mention of an apparent split between them, but she didn't have to. Casey saw for herself that the two never conversed with each other except for a few impersonal comments now and then.

Their split didn't deter her, but David quickly made it clear that he had no interest in assisting Clete. "The way I see it, honey, Clete broke the law," he said without a hint of sympathy.

"Daddy!" she exploded. "How can you say that? You have been making and selling moonshine all of my life! And you have stolen Clete's invention to soup up your own vehicles and hide the illegal mash that your own bootleggers distribute all over the country!"

David blushed violently, but made no comment.

Desperate, Casey continued. "Clete has made friends in prison, and I'm not talking about a friendship with other inmates. He has made friends with the prison officials—honestly," she added when David raised a suspicious eyebrow.

"I love him, Daddy, and he loves me," she uttered with a coo, a show of emotion that clearly shocked David. "We've been corresponding by letter, and, well, we plan to be married," she said with some hesitation. "I can tell you the warden has trusted him to repair his personal vehicle, and now he is working in the prison repair shop on official automobiles."

David was clearly agitated. His mind wandered back to the Klinger hanging when Clete, an obnoxious child, had called little Casey a half-breed. And there was Casey herself, derived from a mix of Indian blood and that of a murderer. He dared not say what he was thinking, that she was apparently destined to live the low life.

With David still harboring silence, Casey continued. "Daddy, if Clete had a lawyer—well, the lawyer could arrange for him to appear before the parole board. It would certainly be in Clete's favor that we plan to marry and that I have a teaching position that will sustain us until he can get a job in an auto repair shop. He is determined to have his own shop one day," she said proudly. "Oh, I'm sorry Daddy. I forgot to tell you about that. Well, actually I don't really have a job, at least not yet, but I looked into it and I have been promised a position as soon as there is an opening," she admitted.

David stirred uncomfortably. "Seems to me you forgot to tell me a lot of things."

"It was not intentional, Daddy," she apologized without losing a beat to her sales pitch. "It would assure prison officials that Clete will no longer be involved with bootleggers in Okaloosa County. Surely you know I don't think of you as a bad person, Daddy, but the truth is, you are involved in an illegal business of your own choosing! Clete, on the other hand, chose auto repair, a legitimate business and any illegalities he was involved in, were forced on him."

David struggled with the whole situation. Her accusation of him as a lawless man hit him hard until he admitted to himself that her description of him was accurate. Even his beloved father, who treated others as he would like to be treated, had been guilty of breaking the law, he reminded himself.

"All right then. I'll see what I can do." He stood up with the intention of leaving the room and then hesitated. "What will your mother think of your plans to marry this prisoner?"

The comment made it clear to Casey that David would always view Clete as a prisoner, nothing more. "Don't you ever talk to Mama?" she bellowed. David's only response was to avoid her gaze. "To tell you the truth, Daddy, I'm not certain anything would make Mama happy. I'm afraid she's too sick to give anything much thought."

"Your mother is sick?" he questioned.

"Isn't it time you woke up and faced reality, Daddy? My mother is hooked on alcohol—moonshine, white lightning, mash! You're familiar with it, aren't you?" she shouted. "She hates it, and yet she has embraced it as a way of abandoning society just as it abandoned her!" She stopped short of accusing David of the same offense.

In the beginning, Casey had intended a mild scolding of her stepfather, but the whole thing had taken a sinister turn. Certain she had spoiled any plans David might have had as far as helping Clete, she collected her personal items and left the room.

To her amazement, David followed. "I'll do my best," he promised.

Before the day ended, David had engaged an attorney in Atlanta who agreed to represent Clete.

A year passed before Clete appeared before the parole board. The warden himself spoke on Clete's behalf.

"Clete Cogbill has been an asset to this prison, not a liability," the warden told the parole board. "Our auto repair shop foreman recognized Clete's passion and talent for the craft early on, and with our permission, he spent quality time with the boy toning his already unusual skills. I might add that Clete has introduced subtleties and improvements in engine repair and design to the foreman as well." With his wife-to-be already employed in the Atlanta school system and Clete promised a job in an auto repair shop, the board voted unanimously for parole. Clete and Casey were given permission to wed in the prison chapel on the day he was to be released. David and Yancy were in attendance. Mary Sam was not.

Chapter 27

DAVID STEWART HAD BEEN THE FIRST TO INSTALL ILLE-
gal slot machines in Niceville. It was a daring move that sent a
hush-hush whisper throughout the community for a few days, but
within weeks, every store inside the city limits and out had its own
slots. Back-room gambling soon followed, as did specially made
wheels for rolling the gear out the back door when the sheriff sent
word of an upcoming raid.

The countryside was full of hidden bars, but the little bar on
Bayshore Drive, just a few short blocks from Yancy's home, was
the only one within Niceville's city limits. It had served as Yancy's
favorite escape from school doldrums and offered what he viewed
as an introduction to life. As he had little or no money, he had
spent his childhood running errands for the bar's owner as well as
the bartender, both of whom paid him with a free game of pool or
a beer and, best of all, a sizable swallow of pure whiskey now and
then. It was there he met Herb Sinnen, the tugboat captain who
was accomplished in the game of pool. When none of the captain's
regulars showed, the captain played with Yancy, and they became
regular competitors at the game. Captain Herb saw that Yancy
remained in a spicy mood by keeping the boy's glass filled with a
stiff drink.

"I like a man who can hold his liquor," bragged the captain once he realized that Yancy could match most anyone's alcoholic intake and yet show no signs of having imbibed. For Yancy, however, there was the problem of going home with alcohol on his breath. Remembering Casey's declaration that all plants have a purpose, he tested every leaf and vine in the area until he found one that concealed his intake of alcohol.

"Most of those willie nillies working for me can't handle more than a couple drinks," the captain often complained. "You give one of them more than that, you might as well throw his ass in the Gulf of Mexico for all the good he is to you."

As their relationship grew, Yancy became more adamant than he had ever been about leaving the schoolgrounds behind. And now, he was certain that his mother would agree that learning the tug business with plans to eventually become a tugboat captain was an opportunity he should grasp. Also, the captain was a regular church attendee who sat conspicuously on the front row, Bible in hand. *What possible objection can she have?*

He would soon have the answer. "Your captain drinks too much!" was Connie's response. "I'm surprised the company hasn't fired him."

"Aw, Mom," argued Yancy, "that don't matter none. The captain can hold his liquor, and he can still run the tug like nobody else," he bragged. "And he's a church man," he reminded her.

"Yes, your captain sits on the front pew on Sunday and on a bar stool the rest of the week," she countered.

"He's donating the church bell," Yancy reminded her.

Captain Herb had promised not only to deliver a much-wanted church bell but to personally see to its installation. But that was some months past, and gossip had it that Herb was a drunkard and a braggart who never intended to follow through with the promise.

Like most residents, Connie was excited about the bell as it would not only call folks to worship on Sundays but could also

be used to call the spread-out community together on special occasions or alert them to disasters. Yancy was ecstatic, certain that
Captain Herb's generosity would change his mother's opinion.
Unfortunately, disaster struck the Brighton family before Connie
had a chance to discuss the issue with Ecil.

Connie's father, and Yancy's beloved Grampie, was dead!

Yancy was ill prepared. He had never faced the loss of a really
close loved one. He wanted to hide in his mother's skirt and cry
until the awful pain went away, but he knew that wouldn't help, and
he was at a total loss as to what would.

The funeral, dreary as it was, was made more bearable as nearly
everyone in Niceville, black or white, rich or poor, young or old,
attended it. Farms were left unattended, sawmills shut down, stores
locked up, and everyone attended the service and followed the en-
tourage to the grave site in spite of the miserable weather.

All through the funeral, the burial, and the sad trip home,
Yancy was taciturn. The notion of leaving his beloved Grampie in
the soggy ground across the bayou was more than he was prepared
to handle. He cringed at the thought of greeting friends and loved
ones who were already gathering at his parents' home. That too, was
more than he was prepared to deal with.

At the first opportunity, he slipped away from the crowd and
ran all the way to his grandfather's boating business.

The quiet at the boat dock was as overwhelming as the noise had
been elsewhere. He wanted to run away again, but he soon came
to realize that no matter where he went, he would have to face the
same dilemma, that of the excruciating loss of his grandfather. He
made up his mind to join Captain Herb on the high seas no matter
what his mother said.

His decision was timely. The new bell had arrived and had
been installed. It was to welcome folks to worship for the first time
the following Sunday, and everyone was astir. Yancy saw it as a

godsend. All seats were quickly occupied and the indoor stand-ing room exhausted. When latecomers covered the grounds, the pastor agreed that everyone should go outside. To celebrate this welcome addition, church leaders had planned a special dinner on the ground following the service. With the service ended, folks hov-ered around Herb Sinnen to sing his praises, shake his hand, and question him in general about the bell. Men shoved the church's pine benches together to form makeshift tables, and women filled the spaces with their finest dishes.

The visiting pastor praised the Lord for the new church bell and for Herb Sinnen's selflessness in donating it and overseeing all the work involved in hanging it. As *amens* filtered throughout the crowd, sending a hopeful tingle through Yancy's body, there was a sudden clamoring in the back of the crowd. Yancy was quick to work his way toward the scene, where someone lay crumpled on the ground.

Once there, he gasped in horror. "It's Mr. Odell," he cried.

Rhoda held her husband's hand and prayed through tears for the Almighty not to take him from her. Connie wiped his face with a wet kitchen cloth she had grabbed out of her food basket. Several men lifted Odell's weakened body with the intention of taking him to see Dr. Smythe, but Rhoda begged them to take him home instead. "He has been having these spells for some time," she con-fessed. "Doc has already done everything he can. Please take him home," she begged.

With most everyone in denial, a frenzy erupted. Rhoda had been sickly for a long time, but Odell? Not as far as anyone knew. A sudden thought came to Connie. For the last year or so, Odell had missed most of the church outings, but like everyone else, she had assumed he was at home caring for his delicate wife. "Oh, dear God," she grieved. "They've kept his ailment a secret from all of us!"

With others accompanying the sick constable to his home,

Connie stayed behind to ask for volunteers to help look after their beloved constable and his ailing wife. "We have all joked that all our constable had to do was chase hogs and drunks off the streets, but we know better." Everyone nodded agreement. "We owe it to these good people to look after them and to continue their charitable activities. Many of you probably didn't know it, but the truth is, Rhoda and Odell have seen to it that nobody in the area went hungry in our area, at least not for very long."

Much to Yancy's delight, Captain Herb was the first to volunteer his services. "If somebody will give me a list of people who are short on food, I'll see their plates are filled with fish. I'll need a couple of these boys to help me handle the seine nets."

Groans of frustration went up from the crowd, prompting one man to speak up. "Guess you haven't been in town long enough to know about the ban on seine fishing, Captain," he said.

The ban had become a hotly contested subject since the new law took effect. Seine fishing in Florida had been banned before, but it had always been ignored in Niceville. The Florida Game and Fish Commission in Tallahassee soon realized the problem: no local would enforce such a law as it would mean denying his friends and neighbors much-needed food. To solve the problem, the commission named a "foreigner" from Tallahassee the new game and fish warden. Would Niceville sit still while a foreigner issued orders regarding their fish?

"Aw, hell!" was the captain's only response to the news. "We'll catch a barrelful of fish. Just tell us where to deliver them," he insisted.

As excited as Yancy was over the captain's new image as a charitable man, his joy was marred by Odell's illness. The thought of losing Mr. Odell shortly after losing his grandfather overwhelmed him. The joy he felt for the church bell and his hopes for leaving school for a job on Captain Herb's tugboat were quickly shoved aside. His mind was fixed on doing what he could to save the area's lovable old constable. His first thought was Jolene Holder.

"Where is *she*?" he asked his mother. "Why ain't *she* here?"

"Who?" asked Connie.

"Jolene! They took care of her and got her in school and put some teeth in her mouth and—I mean, shouldn't she be taking care of them now?" he fussed.

"I'm afraid she knows nothing about any of their problems, son,"admitted Connie. "The truth is, Miss Rhoda never told Jolene because she was afraid Jolene would quit her job and come home to take care of them. And she wanted Jolene to have a career. But you can do nothing about that. What you can do is assist the captain in feeding the hungry. It's your opportunity to help your beloved friend."

Yancy and Tom, a schoolmate, followed the captain to the tugboat, where they picked up the equipment needed to fill several barrels with fish. That included an illegal seine net.

The boys met each other's startled gazes, but neither offered resistance.

Realizing their fears, the captain told them, "Not to worry, boys. There's a lot of folks starving to death around here while the bayou is overstocked with fish. It's time somebody took the cow by the tits."

The boys snickered at Herb's choice of words, but the situation they found themselves in took precedence over small talk. They knew Kevin Jackson, the new marine warden, would glory in arresting them if caught in the act of seine fishing. Kevin was from Tallahassee and therefore indebted to no one locally. As was customary for Panhandlers, no local felt indebted to him either. But rather than pay a fine or be locked up, most residents had either refrained from openly using seine nets or had done so only when Jackson was hopelessly drunk or busy reaching that stage. The new marine warden had successfully held seine fishing to an all-time low in spite of the fact that folks were hungrier than ever.

"How about it boys? Let's get this project in motion," urged the captain. "We'll stop by the whiskey barn and grab a drink first."

Both boys were reluctant to remind their idol that the bar would be closed as it was Sunday, a holy day. As they approached the aging wooden structure, they noticed two Bedlam brothers lying on the bar's sagging front porch. Apparently, they too had forgotten it was Sunday. Lucifer lay face up, one leg pinned underneath him and the other dangling off the side of the porch while an empty liquor bottle lay in his reach. Billy Bob lay sprawled across the entry with both legs propped on his brother's chest.

Over the years, the Bedlams had survived self-inflicted bruises and bone crushings as well as near-total destruction of their livers after downing enough alcohol to fill Boggy Bayou. Meanwhile, Lum still resided on his deteriorating boat, twice sunken now but raised and patched, with Lulu, his wife, drinking partner and accomplice by his side.

When the captain stomped across the porch, the noise awakened Lucifer enough that he raised the empty bottle above his face and waited patiently for a drop of liquid to trickle into his cotton-dry mouth. Billy Bob made no effort to move but begged for a drink. When he saw Lucifer's bottle, he began tugging on it. Lucifer felt the tug and came to life long enough to crack his brother on the head with it. It was the last effort either of them would display that day.

"Disgusting!" yelled the captain. "People who can't hold their liquor shouldn't drink!" he grumbled. With Billy Bob blocking the door, the captain suggested that he and the boys sneak in the back door. To the boys' surprise, he opened the locked door with his own key and invited them to take a seat on a bar stool.

"I think we deserve a drink for our efforts to feed the hungry," announced the captain, who poured straight whiskey in three bar glasses. He downed the entire contents of one and followed it with another. Yancy inhaled his man-sized drink in much the same fashion as Captain Herb, but as it set his esophagus on fire, he was grateful the captain didn't refill it. It was a memorable occasion for Yancy as it was his first opportunity to drink pure, hard liquor while seated in a real bar and on a real bar stool. Once the pain subsided, he bristled in his newly found manhood.

Meanwhile, Tom, who had refused any offer to imbibe, was worried. With the captain busy washing their glasses, he pulled Yancy aside. "We're gonna go to jail if we use the seine net," he whispered nervously.

"Well, I don't know anybody I'd rather go to jail with," said Yancy, who was clearly in his element. "Don't worry. The captain probably knows all the authorities, both here and in Tallahassee. It's who you know that counts," he said smartly. "Somebody's gonna have to teach that marine warden a lesson, and the captain may be the man who can do it."

From the moment the new marine warden had made his appearance in Niceville, Odell had tried to reason with what he called "a jaunty, cigar-chewing midget who grew an imaginable foot every time he caught some hardworking, unsuspecting fisherman trying to feed his family." Niceville could now boast of a temporary jail, more like a holding cell, constructed out of trash lumber and about as escape proof as a tree-house, but since most prisoners were in for disorderly conduct while under the influence of alcohol, it had filled Niceville's need. Unfortunately, the recent ban on seine fishing had the cellar bulging with poor farmers and fishermen who had no money for paying the fines levied, and the city's funds were depleted from feeding them.

The notion of breaking this unfair law sent Yancy's heart racing with excitement and Tom's taking on an irregular beat now and then.

Everything went as planned, at least in the beginning. The threesome hauled in net after net of edible fish, stopping only when darkness began to set in. Once docked, they were in the process of extracting their last catch from the net when they heard a threatening voice coming from somewhere nearby, and then they felt the glare of a bright searchlight shining in their startled faces.

"Let's see now," said the new marine warden, whose bullhorn voice made up for his lack of stature. With a tormenting laugh resembling that of a hyena and bringing to mind a hysterical jackass, he ordered the men, "Bring your net with you. The judge'll want to use that as Exhibit A." His laughter was so coarse that it reverberated across the bayou and pierced the otherwise serenity of the quiet evening. "Yeah, bring one of them buckets too," he said, pointing toward a row of buckets filled with fish.

"Exhibit B!" Jackson bellowed. "Ah, it's you, the big tugboat captain," he mused, obviously proud of himself for catching a man known equally for attending church and drinking excessively.

Kevin Jackson, the new marine warden, had been appointed to his new position by an authority in Tallahassee who sought a man without scruples. He had been sent in from another area, a move the officials hoped would guarantee no favoritism toward friends. He had been described to the officials as a man who would be as likely to arrest his own mother as he would a hardened criminal. The newly appointed official had definitely lived up to his reputation, but in doing so, he had made a lot of enemies in Niceville, where outsiders were suspect anyway.

With the new holding cell filled to capacity, the captain's threesome had to be taken to the sheriff's office in Crestview, where Herb, the only one who had any money, refused to pay the fine, and Kevin Jackson insisted that the "loose-headed deputy" book the threesome immediately. Rather than attempt such a feat, the deputy declared, "The sheriff is out of town" and then quickly explained, "Well, same as. He swore he would tie me to the railroad track if I called him at home before daylight." He realized that the animosity between the marine warden and the accused was growing by the second, and the marine warden had dished out his own threat if the sheriff didn't "lock all three of these prisoners in a cell immediately." This was in spite of the fact that two of the accused were dangerously underage for such action. The deputy picked up the phone as if to call but lost his nerve when the operator answered.

"Give me the damn phone, mate!" the captain bellowed. "Relax, boys," he told Yancy and Tom. "I'll take care of this."

When the sheriff answered the phone, the captain was so taut that he forgot to introduce himself, but Sheriff West didn't need an introduction. He cringed when he heard the angry voice of the burly tugboat captain.

"This maniac marine warden Tallahassee hired to troll the seas has brought a couple of young schoolboys to your fair city from Niceville, and he wants your deputy to put them in jail!" yelled the captain. "Hell, Herman, they're Ecil Brighton and Ed Powell's boys. We've got to get these boys back home to their parents before they miss 'em and have every damn one of us arrested!" he shouted. "And your idiot deputy wants to throw all three of us in jail for trying to feed some starving families in the south end of the county."

"Somebody's gonna shoot that damn marine warden one of these days!" Sheriff West shouted so loudly that Captain Herb jerked the receiver away from his ear, flinching with pain. "Put that moron on the phone!" yelled the sheriff. Nobody questioned to whom he referred.

The sheriff quickly ordered the deputy to do nothing until he got there. He arrived in his scrappy pajamas less than fifteen minutes later. "Now what the hell's going on here?" he shouted the moment he entered the office.

"I've brought in these blatant lawbreakers!" yelled Jackson, his voice inflamed with outrage.

Sheriff West stiffened when he saw the belligerent little man slam his fists together as if he planned to maul anyone who disagreed with him. It took a great deal of discipline on the lawman's part to let it pass.

"Well, Sheriff," said Captain Herb, "you know these two boys here, both from the finest families in the county. They needed to make a little pocket change, so I let them help me clean my big seine nets, you know. And, lo and behold, the fish jumped right in the nets while we were cleaning them," he explained without a wobble in his voice.

"It ain't no wonder neither, Sheriff," Yancy interrupted. "Since the new law don't allow seine nets, that bayou is loaded with so many fish, you can't keep them out of your nets long enough to clean them," he declared without blinking.

Sheriff West nearly choked on his own saliva while Kevin Jackson rolled his eyes and snorted. Noting that the tugboat captain intended to stick to this fairy tale, the marine warden yelled, "Hogwash! If they were just cleaning—"

"Hold it right there," the sheriff interrupted.

"No!" yelled Jackson. "These people broke the law, and I have the evidence right here," he crowed as he pulled a string of fish from a gallon bucket. "They netted three barrels full of 'em. Did all of them just happen to jump in their nets?" he roared.

Captain Herb fought an urge to grab Jackson by his britches and toss him out the door, his bucket of fish in hand. Before he could act on that, Yancy spoke up again.

"Well you see Mr. Sheriff, it's like this. Mr. Odell, our lawman, used to see that everybody got fed, but Mr. Odell's awful sick now and the rest of us gotta take over till he gets well. When the fish got caught up in our net, it seemed like a shame to throw them back in when lots of folks are hungry."

"And you know what, Yancy, I agree with you," said the sheriff. "What did you do with all those barrels of fish?" he asked the still snorting marine warden.

As irritated as he was, Jackson managed to stay relatively calm. He knew the law was on his side, and he also knew the captain and his young crew had broken the law. The sheriff was obligated to either lock them up or fine them. Either way, as marine warden, he could expect more accolades from Tallahassee. "I brought some of them with me as evidence," he told the sheriff, grinning.

"Answer the question," insisted the sheriff. "What about the others? What did you do with all those fish you didn't bring with you?"

Jackson was certain the sheriff had hopes that he had thrown the fish back in the bayou, thus destroying the evidence. With no evidence beyond a small bucket of fish, the sheriff might have had reason to rule against him. Grinning broadly, Jackson parked himself within inches of the still cross-legged sheriff and smirked. "I left them right where I found them, on the banks of Boggy Bayou," he said, broadening his grin.

The sheriff had heard enough. "You're concerned about depleting the bayou of fish and yet you left three big barrels of them on the banks to die?" The sheriff made every effort to appear outraged. He turned to his deputy and said, "Drive these people home so they can distribute those fish to the hungry before they spoil."

Once back in Niceville, Yancy's thoughts quickly turned to Odell and Rhoda's plight. Before morning, he had made up his mind to hitchhike to Tallahassee. Rather than give his mother a chance to object, he left the house as if he were going to school as usual. There were never many cars on the road, but it was rare for the few drivers who were there to deny a person a ride, especially a youngster. In less than four hours, Yancy was walking across the campus of the Tallahassee High School in search of Jolene Holder.

He was soon directed to a cubbyhole of an office, where he came face to face with a tall, ungainly, middle-aged woman who was inundated with paperwork and books, all in disarray on a desk too small to accommodate half that much. She appeared startled by the tall, stringy, hassled young man standing in her doorway.

Yancy was equally startled. He had never seen Jolene in anything but overalls, usually two sizes too big and a dozen or so inches too long, always in need of a roll-up. The woman who stared at him wore a bright red cotton dress, sashed in shining purple satin. A bright purple felt hat with a red feather protruding from the band lay on her desk. Her face was as free of makeup as the day she was born, her fingernails were cut as short as comfort would allow, and her hair was matted to her head as if it were a wig that had been glued on. She brought to mind a circus clown without the makeup.

Jolene hadn't seen Yancy since he was six or so. "I don't know who you are, young man, but I know you're not one of my students because nobody wears pants in my classroom," she quipped. "If you're looking for Jolene Holder, you found her. Now what can I do for you?"

With Yancy's mouth still open but making no sound, Jolene plopped the audacious red hat on her head, leaving jagged bunches of equally red hair protruding from under it, and headed for the door he stood in. "I have a class at the moment. If you're still here when I finish, maybe you'll tell me who you are and why you're here?"

"It's about Mr. Odell," Yancy managed once his tongue untied itself.

Jolene threw her books on the desk, grabbed Yancy by the shoulders, and shook him quite forcefully. "What's wrong?" she demanded, her face so pale that it brought to mind a shadowy apparition that Yancy found disconcerting to say the very least.

It occurred to him that her fancy book learning hadn't done much for her social graces. Pulling away from her grasp, he straightened his shirt and smoothed his well-oiled hair before expounding on the reason for his visit. Once she heard his story, as well as his identity, she calmed herself long enough to give him a hug and thank him profusely for letting her know. She made arrangements to leave the college, tossed a few items in a bag, and began the trip to Niceville in her topless 1929 Model A Ford, with Yancy perched sassily beside her.

"How long has this been going on? Miss Rhoda never said a word!" she fussed, with the accelerator pushed to the floor, making the open-topped vehicle ride the curves on two wheels.

It wasn't the first time Yancy found himself chasing the wind in a rattling old vehicle, but it was his first with a female driver. He sat rigidly upright, nervously eyeing the road, holding his breath when they faced a curve, and pressing as hard as he could on imaginary brakes. Fortunately, they had the road to themselves for the most part, a necessity indeed as Jolene's speed required the use of the entire surface, especially when making sharp curves. When she did hit the brakes, Yancy noticed they were slow to respond. She had brought him into the world; was she bent on taking him out?

The further they went, the more apprehensive Jolene became and the faster she drove. While Yancy held tightly to anything he deemed solidly attached, she posed question after question regarding her adoptive parents, but as she rarely paused long enough for him to answer, Yancy sat in rigid silence for the most part, breathing only when he had to.

With darkness approaching, Yancy was glad when they arrived in Niceville. The car's left front light was missing, the right front badly damaged, and rear lights were nonexistent! The trauma of riding a hundred and forty miles in a rattling jalopy that seldom had four wheels touching the ground at any given time was far more than Yancy had bargained for. He was glad for the darkness as he wouldn't want anyone to see him. And that included his parents, who would be combing the area for him.

He was, however, not to have the luxury of hiding. When they arrived at the McNeil house, they noticed a mass of people moving about in the front room.

"Oh my goodness," Jolene quivered.

"Probably just every living soul who attended the big dinner on the ground," Yancy explained, but he wondered too. It did seem like an awful lot of people.

A closer view of the vehicles parked in front of the house revealed that one of them was an ambulance, a vehicle often substituting as a hearse. Odell McNeil, the town's beloved constable, was dead.

Chapter 28

WHILE THE LITTLE COMMUNITY MOURNED THE LOSS of their beloved lawman, misfortune, albeit of a lesser magnitude, struck again. It was Sunday, just one day following Odell's funeral, when the church bell didn't ring. Folks had come to rely on it, and those in hearing distance didn't head for church until they heard it ringing. Most worried that something had happened to Chubby Wells, the deacon whose job it was to ring the bell every Sunday or at least to get a replacement if he couldn't. All were perplexed as the bell had rung off and on the previous day in Odell's honor, and nearly every human being who could walk planned to attend church, also in Odell's honor.

Watches were rare in the community, but a wide-awake majority felt it was time for church services to begin, so they headed for the church.

Yancy's interest was piqued. Usually an ambler, he came as close to hurrying as he ever had, even leaving his parents lagging behind. He was still a block away from the church when part of the mystery was solved. The big, shiny bell was lying upside down on the church grounds!

Minutes later, the church was packed as never before. Yancy remained outside so long that he was forced to take a front seat when he finally entered. Quiet time was totally ignored while everyone

shared their thoughts and concerns about the bell and the conspic-
uous absence of Captain Herb Sinnen, the man who had donated
the bell. The preacher had to raise his voice considerably in order
to be heard above the gossiping congregation.

"As you have all observed, the church bell has been removed,"
he began. "Seems the elders have seen fit to deny Captain Herb
Sinnen membership in this church!" He paused out of necessity
when the crowd burst out with all manner of comments. "As I understand it, the elders agreed that Captain Herb was spending too
much time in the local bar. Apparently, the captain decided that if
he is not welcome here, neither is his bell." Any effort to deliver his
sermon proved to be useless as everyone quickly engaged in gossip,
prayer, and even laughter.

Yancy sat stone-faced. He began to search the faces of the group
looking for the so-called sinless men who had been appointed elders. All were present, scattered throughout the little assembly,
their heads held high to denote their superiority. Yancy knew them
all: Donald Burden, a man who beat his wife on a regular basis and
drank beer while his wife and teenage daughters plowed the fields;
Jim Dungeon, best known for adding lye soap to his moonshine to
increase its volume, thus bringing in more money for him to squan-
der. Such a concoction had been known to kill its consumers. There
was Boris Hutchins, a man who gambled his earnings away on a
regular basis, leaving his wife and kids to sponge off her parents
who themselves could barely make financial ends meet.

*So this is the moral group who voted to kick Mr. Herb out of the
church?* Yancy thought bitterly. With eyes wide open, he gazed
steadily and intently at each elder one by one. Nearly everyone
had exited the church before he finally rose and moseyed outside.
He was almost glad for this momentous occasion as it had set his
emotions on fire, and he had no intention of holding them at bay.

He lay awake all night, planning his move. When morning

finally came, he moved at his usual slow, easy gait toward the kitchen where Connie had just poured buttermilk into the middle of a large wooden bowl of flour. He watched silently while she worked the flour into the liquid with the fingers of one hand while turning the wooden bowl with her other hand. It was exactly what Yancy hoped for, a few moments alone with her before his dad awakened.

"The crucifixion of Captain Herb by the church's 'godly' elders was the last straw, Mom. I'm out of here," he warned. The words had bolted out of his mouth, essentially without his permission, shocking him more than they shocked his mother. She, however, had expected it.

She let go with a moan before having her say. "I know, son. You're going with the tug."

Yancy felt as if he had thrust a knife into the already aching heart of a woman he loved above all others. "I'm sorry, Mom, but I just can't sit in that boring schoolroom day after day memorizing conjunctions and adverbs, stuff I ain't never gonna use!" he said in agonizing frustration.

To his surprise, Connie remained silent. He took it as an opportunity to continue. "You were a good teacher, Mom, but you didn't like teaching. You preferred selling dresses, didn't you? What good is an education that teaches you how to do something you don't want to do?"

"If you would finish your schooling, you would realize how wrong you are, son. My schooling prepared me for whatever life brought my way, and it gave me the courage to forgo steady employment as a teacher for one that offered no guarantees," she reminded him.

She continued working the flour into the milk until the biscuit dough was easy to handle and then dropped the ball of dough in the middle of the remaining flour. While wiping the sticky dough off her fingers, she turned to face Yancy. "You're a long way from knowing everything," she chastised.

"I know what I want to do! And I know I ain't never gonna be a teacher!"

"I'm certain of that!" Connie scoffed.

All through their talk, Yancy had battled a head of wild hair. He dipped his fingers in melted grease and plastered his bangs to the top of his head before kicking the screen door in anger. Instead of opening as he expected, one of the hinges came loose, leaving the door hanging across the threshold.

In spite of her disappointment, Connie was amused. "I hear your dad stirring, so if your hairdo meets with your approval, madam, you better fix that door before he sees it."

Yancy took her advice.

Three months later, Yancy Brighton was scraping old paint off, applying new, and washing the deck on the *Rugrat*, a tugboat captained by Herb Sinnen. He was happier than he had ever been. Nothing renewed his spirits like a trip on the tug, where he enjoyed a close association with his idol, Captain Herb.

It didn't take long for him to realize that the work wasn't easy, or safe. He often suffered injuries while rigging towlines to the heavily loaded barges, handling heavy shackles or powerful tow winches on deck, and so much more. He had managed to avoid serious injury, however, and thus far, he had avoided misjudging the tide and wind, a common cause of disaster. Of course, such was the captain's job, but he hoped it would be his one day.

He would never forget the day the captain summoned him to the wheelhouse. "If you really want to become a tugboat captain, you'll need to watch this," Herb told him. "The engineer and the captain have to understand each other, first of all. See the bridge ahead of us? As captain, you must assume the bridge tender is asleep and has no idea we're headed his way. There can be no sleeping at the wheel!" he emphasized as he pulled a cord that sounded a whistle. "That tells the engineer to slow down. You heard the long and short whistle a while ago? That's how I let the bridge tender know we are arriving, so he should be busy opening the bridge well before we arrive. If he doesn't and we have to put the brakes on, it could mean disaster. If you remember nothing else, write what I'm going to tell you on your brain."

"Yes, sir!" Yancy eagerly promised.

"Those barges behind us? They're attached to us, but they have no brakes! We can slow the tug, but if we do, we may regret it because the barges keep moving at the same speed, and any sudden braking by the tug could push them, or us, out of line. They may turn in another direction—we never know what they'll do. There are a lot of variables. So if we suddenly apply our brakes, those barges can make mincemeat out of the tug as well as the entire crew. Or they can break loose!" he added.

Yancy felt a spurt of fear but quickly put it asunder. He ached to learn everything at once, take over the wheel, and flow through bridge openings the rest of his life. "Have you ever—"

"Had a barge bump me in the ass?" the captain interrupted. "Yes, and from every other angle. We have anchors to slow the barges, but there's no guarantee it will maintain the path the tug does. We have other options you'll learn about, but none are foolproof. We can shoot a spud down to the bottom of the bay in hopes of slowing the barge. And yes, we can slow it, but there's no guarantee it will continue on the same path the tug is taking. Keep in mind there's always a good chance we'll lose one or more of the crew members anytime they have to jump from barge to barge or tug to barge. In a storm, especially, it's dangerous stuff. And don't forget, the crew member we lose may be you," he cautioned.

In spite of the dangers, Yancy felt secure with Captain Herb in charge. Herb was noted in the industry for his expertise as a tugboat captain. What Yancy hadn't realized was that the captain was also noted, especially among crew members, for his consumption of alcohol while operating the tug. It was a blatant violation of a strict rule set by the industry. As the relationship between Yancy and the captain grew, it wasn't long before Yancy became known for breaking the same rule, but as he never showed signs of having imbibed, the only emotion the crew felt was amazement. Yancy never brought alcohol on board himself. He didn't have to. The captain gladly shared his own supply with his favorite crew member.

Even as a rank beginner on the tug, Yancy enjoyed the friendship of long-standing members, most of whom gave little or no indication that they resented his speedy climb to the top as none of them had any ambitions beyond what they had already achieved. They gladly schooled him in the art of getting on and off the dangerous barges, rigging towlines, and avoiding potential hazards associated with heavy tow winches, shackles, tow wires, slippery decks, and so much more.

Most of the crew was envious, however, of Yancy's ability to consume uncanny amounts of alcohol and give no indication of having a single drop of it. It was a favorite topic of conversation among the crew, who had come to believe it was Yancy's secret to excelling in the Piss-Off Contest. As older crew members' shrinking bladders held little urine, their weak streams barely cleared the deck, while younger men's bladders could produce a powerful stream. The winner was allowed to drink generously from Captain Herb's ample supply of the best moonshine in Niceville. Yancy had never lost the contest.

Within a year, Yancy's prowess on the seas had taken him to the top. He had been replacing the captain at the wheel for several months, and he was in his glory. He had been designated assistant to Captain Herb, but what the owners of the tugboat didn't know was that Herb's visits to the wheelhouse were rare.

Yancy usually had more energy than anyone else on the tug. On lengthy trips, he could grab a nap and resume working as if he had slept all night. There was one exception: when Captain Herb didn't show to relieve Yancy one night, he found himself fighting to stay awake. The moment the captain appeared, Yancy spent no time chatting as was usual. He left the captain at the wheel and quickly plopped his weary body on a cot in the crew's small quarters. In the night, he was awakened by a deadly jolt, which was followed instantly by horrific cries from the crew.

"We're headed for a damn railroad!" screamed one of the men. Others responded with obscenities, their words filled with confusion, fear, and anger directed toward the captain.

Yancy raced to the wheelhouse, fearful something dreadful had happened to the captain. It was worse than that—the captain was not there. No one was manning the wheel!

Even in his drowsy state, Yancy was quick to take over after hearing the crew's analysis of the situation. The tug had clearly changed course and, in doing so, jerked the barges about, severely damaging tow wires that secured it to the barge behind it. The wires separated and then finally came apart, freeing the first barge from its captor.

"Spuds! Spuds!" Yancy yelled as he also signaled the crew to shoot the long pipes down the spudwell. The pipes acted as anchors by digging into the ground beneath the barge, but they fell far short of bringing the loaded barge to a halt. Still uncertain of their exact location, Yancy was certain of one thing: they had wandered into unnavigable waters as witnessed by the presence of a railroad track looming up ahead of them. He expected to run aground any minute and, while not ideal, it was far better than plowing into a busy railroad track.

One crew member had already been disabled by runaway tow wires while trying to save the barge. Another barely escaped falling between the tug and the remaining barge while attempting to board the latter. He suffered excruciating pain from deep cuts that continued to bleed heavily when he tried to assist the crew further.

In spite of the emergency at hand, Yancy couldn't dispel thoughts of the captain whose reputation as a tugboat captain was without criticism. Herb Sinnen was noted for his skill in utilizing navigation devices and avoiding reefs and other hazards, and yet here they were in unnavigable waters, the entire crew struggling to avoid a railroad trestle and prevent a deadly mishap they had no part in creating.

Yancy knew it would take a miracle to avoid the railroad trestle, a disastrous event that would take a lot of lives, not to mention destroy millions of dollars in expensive equipment. His only hope was to slow the tug and the barge enough that he could change course and either run the boat and its cargo aground or ram them both into the bank. It would take luck and expertise on his part and a lot of assistance from the crew.

As darkness began to fall, a storm came up, bringing blustering winds and untamed waves. Nobody knew better than Yancy how little time they had to accomplish their goal.

Suddenly, the barge hit something. It had to be one of the posts that supported the railroad track. If it came down, the track would come with it. Sudden screams from the crew made Yancy cringe in despair until he realized they were screams of joy! The crew had slowed the barge enough that Yancy was able to change its course by mere inches. The barge had scraped the railroad support but not enough to tear it loose.

The crew's celebration, however, was premature. They desperately needed to bank the tug and the barge before the storm sent both of them bouncing out of control. They didn't have to worry.

Once the barge straightened itself out, it scooted up the bank on its own. The crew quickly secured the barge and disconnected it from the tug. Yancy put the engine in reverse, backed away, and then rammed the tug into the bank beside its troublesome cargo.

While crew members secured the tug, Yancy began searching for the captain. Lying on the floor of the wheelhouse, his face buried in a collection of cigar and cigarette butts and burnt match sticks, was the captain. An empty whiskey jug rolled up to the captain's face and then back to the wall, repeating the motion again and again in response to the waves that continued to rock the tug.

Yancy knelt down to get a closer look. "He musta had a stroke," he announced with passion.

"The hell he did!" yelled Horace Jenkins, the crew member who was still suffering from deep cuts in his legs and arms. "He's just drunker'n hell!" Jenkins was the oldest man on the crew and the man with the most hours on a tugboat. However, he had little ambition for learning the ins and outs of piloting a tug. He was satisfied to do someone else's bidding and made no effort to move beyond that. He was, however, always sober. He had never developed a taste for alcohol, a rarity indeed for a man who spent much of his time on the open water.

Ignoring Jenkins, Yancy asked the others for assistance in getting the captain off the wet floor and onto a cot. He tried to accomplish the feat himself, but the captain, a giant of a man, proved to be far too heavy for Yancy to lift, much less throw over his shoulder.

"To hell with him," stormed Jenkins. "The bastard nearly killed us all. Let 'im rot there."

Without commentary, Hank Skinner grabbed the captain by the shoulders, dragged him to the nearest cot, and assisted Yancy in lifting him. "I'm afraid your friend overdid it this time," said Hank, the only man to show any compassion for the captain.

"What we gonna do, Yancy?" asked Hank. "We've got an

overloaded barge rammed in the ground and another running loose somewhere out there. The runaway barge damaged the tug's fenders pretty bad. Wouldn't be surprised if it cut a hole in our side."

As acting captain, Yancy directed two crew members to examine the tug for damages and report their findings to him. Meanwhile, he grabbed a lantern off a hook and held it close to Herb's face. Either the light or the movement or both produced a few moans out of his friend before he fell back into a deep alcoholic slumber.

While Jenkins sulked, Yancy told the cook to "Get some coffee down the captain."

"Coffee ain't gonna save 'im, Yancy. He's at the end of his road," spouted Jenkins.

"That may be," Yancy snapped, "but he's our best bet for getting out of this mess—unless you plan on taking over," he added facetiously.

The entire crew, many of whom had come to view Yancy as the most level-headed man on board in spite of his youth, insatiable hunger for alcohol, and relative inexperience on the sea, appeared willing to take his orders. "Yes, sir, Captain," the cook wisecracked as he snapped his heels together and saluted playfully. Others exploded with laughter.

When the cook held the coffee to the captain's mouth, the muddled captain slapped it out of his hands before passing out again.

The muscles around Yancy's mouth tightened. He took a long look at the six-and-a-half-foot giant of a man who lay sprawled across a cot in drunken slumber, with one boot missing and the other dangling off his lengthy foot. His monstrous head hung to one side of a cot made for a much smaller man. The captain's tam, the largest one the industry could find, was still perched on his massive head even though he had slept in it.

"Aw, hell, Yancy. Let's go home!" yelled Jenkins.

"We'll go home when the captain takes us!" snapped Yancy.

"You must be crazy. That drunk bastard ain't gonna wake up for three days!"

"Then we'll wait three days!" shouted Yancy. The entire crew rose up in anger, citing such a notion as stupid, but they knew there was no need to argue. It was obvious that Yancy's plan was to wait until the captain had recovered enough to give the appearance of his being in charge.

Daylight brought good news. The loose barge had crushed the tug's fenders but failed to render the boat unusable. By the time Yancy reported the incident to the tugboat company, he had already secured the barge for the rescue team and had satisfied himself that the tugboat's damages did not render it unsafe for travel. Much to the pleasure of the crew, he put the engine in reverse and maneuvered the tug out of the bank. They were finally on their way home, albeit without their cargo.

Yancy was in no hurry. He slowed the tugboat as necessary to guarantee an arrival in the dead of the night. It would give him an opportunity to see the captain safely home before company officials had a chance to question him.

It was several weeks later that the owners of the company summoned all employees who had been on the tugboat to a hearing.

"What you gonna tell 'em?" Jenkins asked Yancy.

"The truth," said Yancy.

"You may as well 'cause if you lie to protect the old man, we'll make you out a fool," promised Jenkins.

"Yeah, the captain was drunk," added Emmet Howell, a drunkard himself who sobered up just long enough to make the trip and not always then. He spat an ugly mouthful of snuff droppings in Yancy's direction just as he entered an outdoor toilet.

Yancy picked up a boat paddle and slammed it against the tin-roofed outhouse just as Emmet began to urinate. "What did you say, Emmet?" yelled Yancy. Emmet was noted for his near-deafness, but it was evident that the blow Yancy gave the outhouse had pierced his eardrums. He came rushing out the door, penis in hand and still in action.

The episode put the crew in a jolly mood, but only temporarily. When the crew appeared before the owners of the tugboat company, they were questioned separately, and each member was escorted out the door once his session was complete.

When Yancy's questioning began, he was quick to inform the officials that he had been sleeping when the barge broke loose. "I'm of the opinion that the captain had some sort of physical mishap, became disoriented, and took the wrong turn. It could happen to the best of them. The shallow waters probably caused the barge to break loose, but the captain recovered soon enough to save the other barge as well as the tug," he lied.

Stunned, the officials made no immediate comments. After an extended pause, one questioner asked Yancy if the captain ever called for help.

"I'm sure he did, but as I told you, I was asleep," Yancy reminded them.

An emotional agitation filled the room and a second lengthy pause ensued before the owner of the tugboat company made a comment. "We're all grateful that you woke up rather quickly and avoided what could have been a disaster. If that loaded barge had barreled right into the railroad trestle, we would have lost lives and expensive equipment. We also escaped unbelievable lawsuits as a result that probably would have put us out of business." He stared at Yancy as he spoke, and Yancy answered with silence.

"You've been misinformed," Yancy finally offered. "It was Captain Herb who saved the tug. I only assisted him once I woke up," he added, his eyes still focused on the officials. "And even when I woke up, I could offer little help as Captain Herb had already dodged the railroad track and ran the barge and tugboat safely into the bank."

Realizing Yancy intended to stick with his story, the spokesman opted to share the crew's testimony in hopes of breaking Yancy's obvious resolve. "Yancy, I think it only fair to tell you that your fellow crewmen agree that the captain had passed out on the floor of the tug, apparently from too much drink, and that you alone saved the tug. If, as you say, you had no part in saving the tug, why do you think these men unanimously agree that you did?"

Yancy's expression went unchanged. "They may have assumed it happened that way. Captain Herb—well, he's a humble man, you know. He probably told the others I saved the tug. He don't like attention."

Yancy knew that neither the company official nor the owner himself believed his story, and he was certain that both he and the captain would be fired, the captain for incompetence and himself for lying. As miserable as that made him, he had no intention of changing his story.

Yancy spent the next few weeks mulling over the whole sordid episode with Captain Herb's fall from grace. While other crew members celebrated the captain's demise, Yancy grieved. Being faced with finding a job, especially one that was not associated with the tugboat business, was hard to swallow, and weeks had passed with no solution in sight.

If I was just two years older, I could join the merchant marines, he told himself. A life on the open seas would be an exhilarating classroom that would assist him in surviving the trauma of losing his job and Captain Herb, both at the same time. World War II was escalating, and posters everywhere displayed Uncle Sam pointing fingers at everyone, begging them to do what they could. But he wasn't yet seventeen! Others had lied about their ages and had been accepted. Why couldn't he?

He was still pondering the possibility when he received an official letter from the Pensacola Tugboat Company. Certain it was an official letter relieving him of any future association with the company, he considered torching it. That was not possible, of course, because his mother had seen the letter and would insist on knowing its contents. Depressed, suffering from sleep deprivation, and heart-heavy, he separated the envelope from the message, allowed the former to fall to the floor, and read:

> We at Pensacola Tugboat Company are grateful that you not only salvaged our equipment, you saved a railroad and countless lives traveling on it. You may not be aware that a passenger train filled to capacity traveled over that very trestle just hours after you and your crew departed the area.
>
> Although your memory of the entire episode differs from that of your crew, we took notice of the fact that all crew members testified favorably as to your handling of the tugboat during this crisis as well as on a regular basis. We have come to understand that in the absence of your captain, you have been in charge of the tug for some time. As we have been pleased with your performances, we would like to offer you the position of captain on the *Rugrat*. We look forward to hearing from you.

Six weeks later, Yancy Brighton, a sixteen-year-old high school dropout, was officially named captain of the *Rugrat*. With all the duties of a captain thrust upon him, he had little time for bemoaning Captain Herb Sinnen's fate, but memories of his friend always flooded his mind when he passed the little church. The once lively instrument that had brought the community together in so many ways lay nearly hidden in a weed-infested corner of the churchyard. It, too, had been silenced.

Chapter 29

IT WAS 1943, TWO YEARS AFTER PRESIDENT ROOSEVELT declared war on Germany. The war had brought growth to Eglin Field to the point that it was now a full-fledged Air Force base and growing. New businesses popped up here and there, and many residents had secured good-paying jobs at the military base. With residents no longer dependent on moonshine sales and with still houses more and more difficult to hide, Nicevillians had turned to illegal gambling for profit and entertainment.

In addition to back-room crap tables and wheeled slot machines in every business—new or old, big or small—David Stewart had opened a supper club, known by most as a gambling casino. Not to be outdone, Clifford Jones abandoned Crestview for a fast-growing beach community in Fort Walton to open his own such club.

There had been many raids of these facilities, but none were successful as Sheriff West saw to it that everyone dealing in gambling was given fair warning of an impending raid. Thus far, no raid had ever uncovered a single slot machine or crap game in progress. And the bag man, a person designated to collect the sheriff's fee for protecting these lawbreakers, required several assistants to collect what one man had easily managed on his own in the beginning.

Meanwhile, Yancy Brighton dealt with high tides and overloaded barges as well as absent and rebellious crew members. He

was respected for getting the job done without serious injuries to the crew or damage to the equipment. That he had accomplished this while absorbing massive amounts of alcohol that would have rendered most men helpless remained a mystery that kept men in Niceville energized and entertained, as well as envious.

Still, all was not well with Yancy. Most of his friends had left Niceville to serve their country. With Clete too far away for Yancy to enjoy daily contact with, Tom and many other friends and former classmates in the Army or Navy, Yancy's grandfather and Mr. Odell dead, and Captain Herb hopelessly ill, he felt an emptiness he hadn't known before. It wasn't just the loneliness. Should he be enjoying himself while his friends, family, and loved ones fought for his freedom? he asked himself.

The answer was no! Chucking his image and a job he loved wouldn't be easy, but he knew the time had come. Rather than wait for the draft and find himself in the Army, he made up his mind to join the merchant marines.

According to the ads he saw on the streets everywhere, a merchant marine's job consisted of loading heavy supplies and equipment bound for the American troops overseas and then unloading it once they reached their destination. For Yancy, it sounded like the opportunity of a lifetime.

He would soon learn that there was one big difference between the tug and the merchant ship. Customers in the United States might get miffed when a product didn't arrive on time, but at least nobody ever tried to destroy the tug or kill the captain or his crew. The merchant marine ship was only five days out when an enemy plane struck it with heavy fire. They survived the attack only because the enemy plane lost its power and sank into the ocean, therefore never getting a chance to annihilate Yancy's ship.

The attack left everyone scrambling for cover, some praying, others cursing, and a few new inductees huddled together in tears even as superiors issued orders to repair the damaged ship.

"My God, we're sitting ducks!" yelled one new man. "We can't even fight back! We're worse off than the men on the battlefield. At least they can hide in a foxhole!"

Yancy was as unprepared as the rest of them but managed to stay calm, at least outwardly. Once they heard the news that the enemy plane had sunk in the ocean, he began to think of home, of loved ones, and even of school days. To his surprise, he visualized Miss Scofield, Niceville High School's history teacher who often spoke of battles lost because supplies and equipment never reached the troops. She told of men starving to death waiting for food and water that never arrived. Too bent on learning what he needed to know outside the educational arena, he had discounted the importance of anything the classroom teachers had to say. Now he was learning history the hard way.

With the men busy with repairs to the damaged ship, Wiley Cato, a burly, six foot shipmate, released his fear. "If you think that was bad, wait till the German U-boats find us." Cato sought to hide his fear by making jokes, but in fact he was paralyzed by the thought of dying.

"How about the stealthy submarines, the battleships, yeah, and the sea mines," added Cactus, a coarse-looking veteran of the sea. In spite of the dangers, however, he scoffed at the notion that anything would stop them. "Just make certain you're on the same ship as Holy Harry," he warned. "This is his ninth crossing, and he's never had a hair on his head harmed." He laughed, leaving others confused as to whether he was serious or poking fun at their spiritual shipmate. In any case, nobody laughed.

Stories of past attacks permeated the atmosphere with gloom and damnation, causing Bucky, a sixteen-year-old who had never spent a night away from his mama, to lose control of his emotions.

When a superior was summoned, he ordered Cato and Cactus, his rough-mannered friend, to see that Bucky was attended to by a medic. "Do it now!" he yelled.

Yancy had remained silent throughout. Certainly he expected to encounter a storm or two at sea, but submarines, battleships, and sea mines? Never gave them a thought! Like so many others, he had fallen for the merchant marine ads that featured healthy, strong-armed men perched happily aboard a big ship at sea. Women swooned at the sight of their flexed muscles. "See the world," the ads touted. The ads neglected to mention that the enemy would be shooting at them too.

Yancy chided himself for his stupidity. Wasn't he familiar with similar tugboat ads that promised overnight service when a week was itself impossible? While analyzing the dilemma he found himself in, he missed most of the ongoing conversation among the group. Finally, his own emotions erupted. "Does the ship have a convoy protecting it—sea-going tugs, tankers, long-range aircraft? Anything?" he wondered aloud.

"Naw!" Cactus bellowed. "We're unarmed, my friend. You wanna head back home?" he jeered. "Pretty long swim!"

"We've been promised protection, but so far ..." said a superior, who overheard the conversation. "A convoy? Afraid not. We're on our own," he told the men as he checked their work.

"What do you think, Yancy?" asked Holy Harry, who was making his usual prayer run after the disaster struck. Yancy couldn't help noting the thin fabric on the knees of the holy man's pants. He had obviously worn them thin from near-constant prayer.

"I think we're all a pack of fools," said Yancy.

"For joining the marines?" asked Harry, who gave no indication that he had been frightened by the strike.

"No, for assuming the enemy would look the other way while

we haul in ammunition and troops meant to kill them," Yancy jawed.

Harry was on his knees. "We're at war, son. The only protection we have is our Savior, Jesus Christ." The comment silenced every man in hearing distance and prompted them all to bow their heads as Harry began praying.

The crippled ship continued for days without further trauma, at least from enemy attack. However, all was not well inside the ship. Although the ship's holy man hadn't mentioned it, he had been suffering now and then from a severe pain in his side. And now the pain had worsened, and he was running a fever. Within weeks of the attack on the ship, the examining medic announced that the holy man had acute appendicitis and that he would die unless they reached port within a few hours. Everyone knew the injured ship was moving slowly at best, and they couldn't possibly reach port in time to save Harry even if all went well.

A medic made the rounds urging men of all ranks to pray for Harry. He also asked for volunteers from each group to visit Harry and pray for him in person. "He will die unless there is an intervention." No one questioned what he meant.

When no one from Yancy's unit volunteered, the medic scolded them. "No one wants to pray for a man who has spent his life praying for others, including you?" He called a few names and met a few stares, finally turning in Yancy's direction, but Yancy shook his head. "I have no direct line to the Almighty. I'd have to introduce myself." Everyone laughed except Yancy. He hadn't meant it as a joke.

Once the medic left the room, Yancy looked around him hoping that someone would make a move, but when no one did, he gathered his strength and moseyed toward the sick room. Once there, he opened the curtained-off area where Harry lay dying and stood

there in silence. Those in charge stepped away, leaving Yancy to
carry out his mission.

"Harry, I'm gonna pray for you," he announced. "The way I look
at it, I ain't drove the man upstairs crazy with a lot of praying like
you have, so a new voice is likely to get his full attention." Harry
managed a weak smile before inviting his visitor to take his hand
and tell the Lord exactly what he would like him to know. Yancy
gave it his best effort, but as he had never formally addressed his
maker before, the hand that held Harry's began to sweat profusely.
He began without identifying to whom he was speaking: "Well,
you see, like as not, you don't know me, and of course I take full
responsibility for that," he told the Almighty. "It's not for myself
I've come. It's Harry here. Most of the crew don't admit it out loud,
but they depend on this man to do their praying, and that goes for
me too." He paused for a long moment while emotions ruled. "It'd
be a mighty loss to all of us if you took Harry," he pointed out with
solemn earnestness.

Harry reached underneath his pillow and pulled out a small,
well-used Bible. "The Lord heard you, Yancy. You can count on it.
But I know the Lord wants me to come home now, and I'm ready
to go. You can be certain that our Lord and Savior sent you here for
a reason, Yancy. I've been wondering who to trust my Bible to, and
now I know. He wants you to have it."

Still struggling with his emotions, Yancy was speechless, a condition quite new to him. He had never been one to monopolize a
conversation, but it had always been by design, not timidity.

"I know you're reluctant," said Harry. "You haven't read much
of the book, and you may not have understood what you did read.
Even so, all that matters is that you believe in Him, and I've seen
evidence of that just now. You'll find the Lord doesn't require you
to be a biblical scholar. But I would recommend you use every spare
minute you have on the ship boning up on God's word as it will

strengthen you and help you reach the other men with his message. You have been singled out by our Savior to comfort the others. I know you won't disappoint him."

Yancy stiffened.

"You can do it," insisted Harry, whose grip on the small Bible had begun to loosen. Yancy moved forward in time to grasp the tiny book with both hands because he could see it was as fragile as Harry was, some of its leaves dangling loosely, their edges ragged from use. A quick examination of the holy book revealed massive marginal comments written in long hand. Turning the pages slowly and carefully, Yancy realized it had been written once by many prophets and once again by Harry. He gripped the Bible with one hand and then touched Harry gently with the other before turning to go. The exit was only a few feet away, but to Yancy it was the longest trip he had ever traveled. Before opening the privacy curtain, he turned to give Harry a final salute but then lingered outside the sick unit long enough to deal with a stream of tears he couldn't hold back.

At 8:33 p.m., just hours after Yancy's visit, the captain made an announcement over the intercom: "Harry John Willard, the man most of you know as Holy Harry, is dead."

Ten months later, the war was over and Yancy was on his way home. He exited the ship in Galveston, Texas; spent his last government paycheck at the nearest bar; napped off and on in the same bar; and woke up when a bartender tried to clean the table his head was resting on.

"Closing!" snapped the bartender. "We open again at noon. Come back then if you can still walk," he grumbled. He watched in shock as Yancy walked across the messy bar floor without a wobble in his step in spite of having downed enough straight whiskey throughout the night to put a mob asunder. Shaking his head in disbelief, the bartender stole a look at himself in the bar mirror and immediately decided he needed a lot of rest.

Yancy, however, was feeling fine. Once outside the bar, a quick glance around the lively Galveston waterfront captured his attention. Just as he remembered, work hours in the boating business began early, and many workers had already loaded the barges, had hooked them to the tug, and were pulling out. It definitely brought back pleasant memories for the Niceville boy.

Why not get a job, save some money, and return to Niceville in style? he pondered. The notion of living anywhere other than Niceville had never occurred to him, but the idea of working on a tug out of the big city for a while before returning home was suddenly very appealing. With his background as tugboat captain at the age of sixteen and his experience on the merchant marine ship, finding a job would be easy, he thought. He took a long look at the fleets and decided he liked the looks of a tug dubbed *Body and Soul*. A worker directed him to a tiny shack that the tug company used as its on-site office.

Behind a cluttered metal desk sat a rugged-looking man with a deeply wrinkled face, the look of a man who had spent a lifetime at sea. He scarcely acknowledged Yancy, who appeared to have slept in his clothes, which of course he had.

"You looking for a job?" asked the man. "What kind of job? Deckhand? Cook? What?" he asked without waiting for an answer.

Yancy rolled his eyes upward, a not-so-subtle indication that he was insulted. "I was a tugboat captain before I joined the merchant marines. You need a captain?" Yancy snapped.

"How old are you?" asked the man.

"Nineteen."

"You finish school?" he questioned.

"Ten years of it," said Yancy.

"I wouldn't hire a high school dropout to scrub a deck, much less pilot a tug," the man barked.

"You got a high school diploma?" asked Yancy.

"Damn right!" bragged the owner.

"Well, I don't want to bust your bubble, but I think you would have been just as big an asshole without it," Yancy said, and then he stalked off in search of someone who would appreciate his background. But nobody showed any interest in hiring him, all for the same reason, and the last man he talked to advised him to "go back home and get an education."

Yancy tucked his wounded pride into the back of his mind and hitchhiked to Niceville.

Chapter 30

IT WAS 1948. AT THE AGE OF TWENTY-ONE, YANCY Brighton finally graduated from high school. It wasn't bad timing as job opportunities were plentiful for airplane mechanics, secretaries, janitors, construction workers, road builders, contractors, telephone operators, and base exchange and commissary staff members.

But Yancy wanted none of that. His drive to succeed in everything but book learning added spice to everyone's image of a boy whom all of them admittedly had a part in shaping. He was still touted for his success as a teenage tugboat captain. He was envied, even admired, for his ability to drink as much as he desired and give no indication he had indulged in a single drop of alcohol. Yancy's dry humor contributed to these assets considerably.

He made no attempt to contact the Pensacola tugboat company, where he would likely be hired immediately for his old job should he ask. Rather, he had made up his mind never to work for anybody again. He wanted to be his own boss. He had met a successful businessman during his short stint in the marines, and the man had convinced Yancy he would never get rich working for someone else.

Yancy had settled on opening his own furniture store. The problem was money. Put simply, he didn't have any. The only person he knew personally who did was David Stewart. Like others in town, David frowned on the idea but offered a solution. "I need a bartender at the supper club. You can make your down payment working there."

It didn't take long to realize that it would be a long wait, but he never lost sight of owning his own furniture store. In hopes of enhancing his image in the business world, he ran for city council and won, serving as its youngest member ever. During this stint, he made his mark by forcing area businesses to upgrade their dull, unkempt buildings and grounds, especially the beachfront properties where outdoor toilets emptied into what could be a clean body of water everyone could enjoy. If he was to succeed in business, he would need to lure more folks to settle in Valparaiso and Niceville rather than pass them by for other localities.

The experience on the city council at nineteen had enhanced Yancy's image county wide and even brought him to the attention of a United States representative. This powerful man assured Yancy that he wouldn't regret opening a business just outside the gates of Eglin Air Force Base. "It's the biggest thing that ever happened to this area, and it's going to get bigger." Eglin had already brought new roads to the area that would eventually take the place of mail and cargo services via water.

Salaries in the area rose with the growing economy, prompting people all over the county to abandon their little farms and small businesses to either join the military or apply for a civil service job and move closer to the fast-growing Air Force base. Ecil had long since left his foreman's position with the WPA for a bookkeeping job at Eglin, and that had put him in contact with people in high positions. Although Ecil was well known for his work ethic, family ties, and honesty, his popularity as the father of Yancy Brighton, the area's famous young city councilman and soon-to-be businessman, had elevated his name beyond anything he had personally accomplished.

Yancy never took a drink while manning David's bar, but the moment it shut down for the evening, he headed for the little bar he had grown up in. On one particular night, he ordered a bottle of booze, consumed two drinks that the bartender created from its contents, made a few marks on a napkin, and smiled contentedly. It was time to move forward. He tucked the bottle inside his shirt and headed for David Stewart's house.

In spite of being aroused from his sleep, David welcomed Yancy. "I've saved two thousand dollars," Yancy told him. "I need twice that to start my furniture business."

David was not impressed by Yancy's plans for a furniture store, but he went to his home safe, withdrew two thousand dollars, and handed it to him. "Pay me back when you make a profit," he said.

"I may need to stay on working the bar for a while," he said, and David agreed.

In a few months, Yancy held a weeklong grand opening of the Brighton Furniture Store in Valparaiso. Nearly everyone in Niceville, Valparaiso, and other parts came and admired his store and its contents, ate his food, and drank his drinks, but there was only one lone buyer. Even that one took advantage of the advertised "no down payment for six months" offer. Yancy was bitterly disappointed. As usual, he spent most of the night on one of Doug's bar stools, stubby pencil and bar napkin in hand.

When business began to pick up and monthly payments began rolling in, he eventually had enough money to pay his bills and restock the store, but little else. He sold the furniture on credit, collected payments, kept books, delivered furniture, and kept the store stocked. All of this meant working long hours, long after he left his job at the supper club and often through the night. Once he had saved two thousand dollars above his expenses, he crammed it, along with interest, in his pocket and headed for David's office at the supper club. Once David was paid, Yancy checked in for a long

Saturday night tending the busy bar. He was happier than he had been in a long time. He could finally look forward to leaving the bartending job and spending all of his time building his furniture business.

But that was not to say he didn't enjoy the supper club which was, in reality, an illegal gambling casino. Customers could enjoy a five-course meal, listen to live music, and choose between whiskey and home brew—one legal, the other not. They could gamble until they ran out of money or until the Okaloosa County sheriff notified them of an upcoming raid. As tourists from surrounding states discovered the white sand beaches around Niceville and Fort Walton, many found some things they liked even better: whiskey and gambling. News that the former had been illegal and the latter still was, kept the tourists coming and the locals drunk, or at least headed in that direction.

Having arrived early to relieve the head bartender, Yancy noted something unusual at the bar. There was a woman seated alone at the bar with her head lowered almost to the bar's surface, a position that surely put a severe strain on her neck.

Lulu, the head bartender, gave her a refill—straight whiskey on the rocks! Yancy was stunned. Except for low-class road bars where anything goes, women sitting alone at a bar were seriously frowned upon. It would be rare indeed in a high-class facility like David Stewart's supper club.

"Who is she?" Yancy asked.

"The squaw!" Lulu smirked.

The term failed to awaken Yancy's senses until the woman finally raised her head and stared into the eyes of her stunned friend.

It was Mary Sam!

Yancy grabbed his drink, walked around the bar, and took a seat beside her. He wasn't certain at first if she was sick or inebriated. Even in the dim-lit corner, he could distinguish changes in one of the prettiest faces he had ever seen: she looked thinner and paler, wrinkled by time and apparently by hardships, but still pretty in spite of dark circles surrounding the once lively, dancing eyes.

"Yancy?" Mary Sam asked with as much energy as she could muster. She reached out to him with open but unsteady arms, and he responded with genuine concern for her condition.

"Where in the world have you been? My mother's constantly complaining that she never sees you anymore," Yancy admonished.

"You have no idea how much I miss your mother," Mary Sam slurred. Her movements were so wobbly that Yancy feared for her safety on the tall, revolving stool that she appeared to have little control over. Yancy was horrified, but more than that, he was angry. How dare Lulu, or anybody, belittle this very special lady. The strongest thing he had ever seen her drink was a Coca-Cola. But now he watched painfully as Lulu kept her glass filled with the same straight bourbon that Yancy was drinking. The smile she had greeted Yancy with quickly faded as there was no joy to sustain it.

"How much longer do you think we can get away with this?" she asked Yancy with a dismal wave of her scrawny little hand and arm.

"With what?" asked Yancy innocently. *Where is David?* he wondered. *Why does he allow this? Of course, a woman at a bar alone would not be frowned upon if the woman owned the bar,* he rationalized. Before he could decide what to do, Mary Sam let go with a piercing response.

"You can ask, 'With what?'" she mocked. "This!" she said with another wave of an unsteady arm directed toward the gambling hall. "How much longer before the authorities march in here, close us down, and send us all to prison?"

"Hell," said Yancy, relieved. "They'll never close any doors as long as David keeps up the mortgage payments in Tallahassee." His reference was to the governor and other elected officials in the state capitol. "Don't you worry about David, sweetheart. He has a lot of powerful folks looking after him, and he won't be going to no prison. Know why?" he asked. "Because all of those 'officials' you're worried about would be in deep shit themselves," he assured her. Yancy's generous use of four-letter words seemed woven into his conversation without malice and were never viewed by friends and acquaintances as sinister or ugly.

Mary Sam gave no indication that she was relieved by Yancy's notions. Waving his comment aside, she asked about Connie. "How is your mother? Really?" she asked, but she quickly buried her face in shaky hands and began to cry. "God, how I miss her."

Struggling with helplessness, Yancy took a drink so voluminous that it burned his esophagus, almost as if it were his first drink. It was a rare occurrence. "Why don't you two get together?" he managed, but he knew instantly how elementary he must have sounded. "I'll bring her over for a visit," he promised helplessly.

"I'm afraid it's impossible," she said to the confused young man.

The situation he found himself in brought to mind the episode with Holy Harry on the merchant marine ship when he desperately wanted to help but clearly had no credentials for doing so. Just as with Harry, he wanted to walk away but couldn't. Mary Sam had been one of his mother's dearest friends. She had apparently reached bottom, and neither he nor his mother had a clue. Worse, apparently no one cared. The bartender had made no effort to prevent her from falling off the high stool onto the hard floor, and passersby didn't look twice even though she fought valiantly to stay atop the wobbly mechanism. And this was the wife of the establishment's owner!

Mary Sam began wiping haphazardly at her eyes, grinding caked makeup into her wrinkled skin before meeting Yancy's stare. He took a napkin, wet it under the faucet, and attempted to clean her face.

"I know what you need," he rallied. "Yeah. You need Clete and

Casey to come back here. Clete can get a job as a mechanic at the Air Force base overnight. And if they ever have any kids, you and David can spoil them." The notion lifted his spirits considerably but failed to set off a spark in Mary Sam's.

"No!" she shouted. "They must never come here."

"Surely you don't mean that," Yancy insisted, but then he realized she was not in control of her faculties.

She lifted her drooped head and once again tried to look him in the eye. "Are you totally oblivious to your surroundings?" she marveled. "Why subject innocent children to a life of rejection?" she bleated, her voice trailing off as if she had lost her train of thought.

"Aw! Let that pass," insisted Yancy. "You and my mother still talk about your school days in Wanata Springs as if they happened last week," he scolded. "It just makes both of you sad all over again. Folks aren't prejudiced like they were when you two went to school," he insisted.

He knew the story of how six-year-old Mary Sam was taunted by her classmates for her Indian background while Connie was harassed for being a motherless child. "I know the story, believe me. My mother told me many times and it never wavers, so I know it happened just as she remembers it. I know you were bullied far worse than she was, but you took on the whole school and helped her. But you failed to help yourself. Frankly, I hate the story because my mother cries every time she tells it. I wish both of you could let it go." He felt her pain as if it were his own.

To his surprise, Mary Sam made no immediate comment. She had rested her head on the bar, leaving Yancy to believe she had dropped off to sleep. Fearing again that she was going to tumble to the floor, he reached out to steady her, but she suddenly raised her head and sat upright.

"Ah, your mother was such an innocent," she remembered, smiling. "The kids taunted her with ugly remarks, you know—as if she were some kind of freak because she had no mother," she wailed. "One night I called all the kids together and I told them the Great White Father needed a special mother to look after all the little children who had gone to heaven before their parents did. I told them the Great Father had chosen Connie's mother from all the mothers in the world. After that, all the kids worshiped your mother," she said with a hint of satisfaction. "Connie still cries?" she asked.

Yancy was so astonished that he knocked his drink over and shooed Lulu away when he tried to refill it. "Of course she does. She still grieves because she couldn't return the favor," said Yancy.

Tiny muscles around Yancy's mouth began to twitch. Had he been totally oblivious to area prejudices toward Indians? he asked himself. Suddenly angered by the thought of self-serving adults abusing his mother, he posed a question. "What the hell were the teachers doing when this was going on?"

Mary Sam was clearly outraged. She banged her fist on the bar and raised her thin voice to its highest pitch. "Were you born yesterday, Yancy? The kids learn this type of behavior from the teachers! And their parents! The kids are innocent. They're not born prejudiced!"

Before Yancy could rebound, she waved her arm in the air, an apparent plea to move on. "What's your take on the governor?" she asked as if the previous subject had been settled. "Will he really keep hands off like he promised?" Mary Sam and Yancy both knew, as did many others, that David and others in the gambling business were generous supporters of the Florida governor, who had promised, if reelected governor, not to meddle with illegal gambling. The governor knew that if he reneged on that promise, he was a dead man, and he liked living.

"The governor's gonna keep his hands off," said Yancy. "Wouldn't you if your gambling constituents paid you more money in one month than you got in a dozen paychecks as governor?" he asked.

"You really are a fool!" she declared as she tapped her unkempt fingernails on the bar. "Apparently you know nothing of the Kefauver Crime Committee. They won't stop until every slot machine in Florida is destroyed and every gambler is in prison." She swung her legs back and forth like an angry child, kicking the fancy velvet padded surface with the toe of her shoe until she lost her balance completely. Yancy grabbed her just in time to keep her from tumbling to the floor. Lulu shook his head in mockery.

Yancy was stunned by the whole scenario, but he convinced himself that her actions and words were directly related to her inebriated condition and that she would be embarrassed if reminded of them the next morning. In spite of her condition, he kept the conversation alive as he was beginning to see her point. Her condition, however, had skewered the whole thing out of proportion. Realizing that, he felt like a fool trying to talk politics, gambling, and other deep-seated issues that she surely wouldn't remember discussing the next morning. The trouble was that her comments about the Kefauver Crime Committee and the impact it could have on gambling in the area, and therefore on the local economy, weren't to be dismissed as drivel. Still, no one involved in illegal gambling had shown any concern for what danger lurked. That included Yancy.

"The Kefauver Crime Committee won't waste time coming here," he assured her. "They have their hands full in Miami with organized crime, big racketeers, and criminals dating back to the Capone gang. Hell, we're all rednecks up here in the Panhandle, too green to run a business. Just ask the South Floridians!" he blasted.

Mary Sam shocked him again with her lucid explanation. "Don't you see? Miami is using reporters to get the Kefauver Crime Committee off their backs and onto ours. They're counting on our ignorance to help them do the inevitable."

While he pondered the thought, Lulu filled their glasses, prompting both of them to take a long swallow. Yancy used one steady hand, but Mary Sam required two, both of which shook uncontrollably.

"We got too big for our intellect," she continued. "Those criminals in Miami are holdovers from Prohibition, people who made fortunes and socked them away. Now they're multiplying their savings in organized gambling, a much more lucrative market." She placed her tiny hand on Yancy's cheek and pulled his face toward hers. "Aren't we doing the same thing? Aren't we holdovers from Prohibition? Didn't we make fortunes making and selling moonshine? Didn't we stash our fortunes away? Aren't we using those savings in organized gambling because it's a much more lucrative market?"

She emptied her glass, and Yancy quickly followed suit. Keeping an eye on Mary Sam, he began to question his own sobriety, a first. Was this conversation really taking place? he asked himself.

"I wish David had never left the turpentine business," Mary Sam complained bitterly. "At least that was legal, and we never had to worry about a raid or a shutdown or going to prison." She clasped her fingers together and rested her forehead in the cradle they made. When Lulu appeared with a bottle, Yancy shooed him away.

"Hell," he said with a pretended indifference. The notion of Kefauver's Crime Committee abandoning Miami for the Panhandle was preposterous. Wasn't it? Of course it was. "You can't run a business without skirting the law," he said aloud. "Everybody knows it so they look out for each other—for a fee, of course," he admitted with a chuckle.

Mary Sam had tuned him out. "The worst part? David'll be singled out for ridicule when this thing breaks wide open. Know why? Because he married a squaw! David's public downfall will come when this thing happens. It'll give them all the courage to say out loud what they've been saying in private all along, that I ruined his life." Gripping the sides of the bar, she tried to push on the bar stool with her buttocks, an apparent attempt to exit the high stool.

Yancy moved quickly. He lifted her tiny body off the stool and didn't turn loose until she stood upright and somewhat steady on the thick-carpeted floor.

"Got a nature call," she explained as she struggled to coordinate both feet in the direction she had decided to go. "I'll be back," she promised.

Yancy shooed Lulu away, donned his apron, and anxiously waited, but Mary Sam never returned.

Although he had been quick to discount most of her fears, given a moment to think about it, he realized that the truth had surfaced. Mary Sam's struggle wasn't really with the Kefauver Committee. It was the Indian thing, something he had never given much thought.

He realized for the first time that in spite of Mary Sam's marriage to one of the most well-liked and most successful white men in the area, she was still viewed as a second-class citizen, incapable of having a single intellectual thought. He admitted to himself that he was no better than the others as he had never really given her the credit she deserved.

He realized something else: Mary Sam had correctly analyzed the connection between moonshiners, whose profits during Prohibition eventually led to illegal gambling, and she had correctly pointed out that gambling was illegal whether practiced by organized crime in Chicago, Miami, or the Florida Panhandle. He fell short of believing that gambling in the Panhandle was at an end, but he did give Mary Sam credit for analyzing the whole situation while others had been oblivious to it. That included him.

He would soon hold her at an even higher standard. In less than three weeks, word spread that the Kefauver Crime Committee had opened an investigation into campaign contributions to the incumbent governor by Panhandle gamblers. David Stewart and Clifford Jones were at the top of the list! Except for Mary Sam, Yancy was the only one who wasn't totally shocked by the news.

With the crime committee headed for the "respectable" supper clubs in the Panhandle, television crews and reporters from South Florida flooded Niceville with their cameras, pens, notebooks, and noses. They camped on the doorsteps of every facility thought to have a slot machine and stormed inside them the minute the doors were unlocked in the early morning. The best reporters and equipment were used to cover the supper clubs in Shalimar and Fort Walton. Everyone who appeared in public or simply walked outside their homes was subject to being interviewed day and night. Portions of South Florida reporters' columns appeared all over the country and, of course, in the Crestview newspaper, one of which went like this:

> Okaloosa County rednecks are at it again. In the twenties, they entertained themselves with grue-some hangings while weeping widows watched in horror and little children screamed with terror. Those same little children learned to make moon-shine, which they marketed in broad daylight up and down the Blackwater and Yellow Rivers. By the time state and federal agents began combing the backwaters in an effort to catch them, they had learned to hype up their auto engines and outrun the law. One diligent federal agent finally saw that at least one of these rogues received free room and board in Atlanta's federal prison. Now the villains have turned to open, widespread illegal gambling in fancy casinos they call "supper clubs," and they're

still in the business of making, marketing, and openly selling illegal moonshine.

Panhandle residents were mortified, but not for long. They flocked as never before to David's Supper Club, which had remained open for business throughout the siege on Okaloosa County. All supper clubs scattered throughout the county continued to offer dinner, music, and legal whiskey, while the gambling machines were stored at locations known only to a select few.

Still, the Kefauver Crime Committee was winning the battle. With no gambling profits coming in during their siege, businesses were feeling the pinch. If the Kefauver Committee didn't tire of what the media referred to as "local yokels, fishheads, and spittoon establishments" and return to Miami, the "real crime capitol of the South," they would have to close their businesses. David Stewart and Clifford Jones would be the heaviest losers.

In spite of David's financial solidity, however, the whole episode had a jarring effect on him emotionally. He was rarely seen in public anymore. In the beginning, his absence was attributed to the obnoxious media who hounded him day and night, following him when he did emerge; blinding him with crude, eye-blinding flashbulbs throughout the day; and camping on his doorstep. He finally went home and stayed there until the last photographer and reporter left town. The problem was that he refused to emerge long after the little community returned to normal.

Only Mary Sam and Yancy knew that David's ills went deeper than the media's assault on Niceville as a result of the Kefauver Crime Committee's threat to wipe it off the planet. The image of Mary Sam at the bar, a once-lively lady who had resorted to drinking alcohol, a substance she didn't like and couldn't handle, had monopolized his thoughts throughout the Kefauver siege, and he realized for the first time that neither the Kefauver invasion nor any other outside disturbance was to blame for David's downfall. Rather, it was a domestic problem, perhaps of his own creation.

Less than three weeks later, the nerve-racking sounds of an ambulance siren pierced the silence of the otherwise peaceful night, arousing folks from their sleep as it careered noisily along the winding Bayshore Drive. Like many of their neighbors, the Brightons made their way to the street in an effort to see where the vehicle would apply its brakes.

They didn't have long to wait. The ambulance pulled into the Stewart's sprawling waterfront estate, its siren still blaring. Yancy ran all the way with Ecil as close behind as his body agreed to, while Connie, though lagging behind, was just as determined to get there. They expected to hear that David had suffered a heart attack or, worse, that he was dead. None were prepared for what they learned.

Mary Sam had committed suicide!

Yancy, who was perhaps the least shocked, was taciturn. Mary Sam, one of the area's most knowledgeable women, an accomplished educator, and a woman who did her best to fit into a society that shunned her, was dead. Only a few would mourn her passing, but those who would were the cream of the crop, Yancy reminded himself, and he was angry!

Once the Kefauver scare ended, gambling as everyone had known it in Okaloosa County no longer existed. Not that it was gone—folks just improved their methods for hiding the activity. With the sheriff's office still on the take, it was a no-brainer. None of it would make an iota of difference in David's life. He had resorted to locking himself indoors, alienating friends and the general public who had admired him and looked up to him as a leader in the community.

When he finally reached out, it was to Yancy Brighton. "I'm going to close the club unless you agree to run it," he announced with little emotion.

Yancy was surprised, not that things had reached this point but that David wanted to keep the supper club open at all and that he had been chosen to run it.

"I can offer you a fifty-fifty profit," David said. "If that's not good enough, name your price." He spoke with a sense of urgency. Yancy declined the offer.

To assist David, however, he made a call to Atlanta. "If you don't come back home, your daddy's gonna dry on the vine," he warned Casey. "Clete can get a job overnight as an airplane mechanic at Eglin Field. Or he can run the business and open a garage here too. The area is booming, and everybody has a car. And you have a chance to save a man's life—your daddy's."

They came, but rather than hire someone to run the supper club, Clete agreed to run all of David's businesses, including the supper club.

With David settled, Yancy began working in earnest to buy some land where he could build his own store instead of renting like he had been doing. A commercial plot of land on the busy cutoff road from Eglin AFB to Fort Walton had caught his eye. It belonged to Jake Hollenbeck, the owner of the twin cities' only dress shop. When Yancy dropped by the shop to discuss the possibility of purchasing the property, a tall, shapely, dark-eyed brunette he had never seen before welcomed him.

"May I help you?" she asked in a sugary but unpretentious Southern drawl.

Yancy took a step backward for a better look at the prettiest face he had ever seen. "I'm rather certain you can," he said with a grin.

When Jake heard a familiar voice, he abandoned his office for an opportunity to greet one of the area's most popular young men. "Yancy, how are you? Say, I don't think you've met my niece. This is Rachel Shaver. She's down for the summer from Dallas," he said.

"My wife thought the dress shop needed some sprucing up, so we put her to work," he teased.

"I'm inclined to agree with you," said Yancy, whose remark brought a satisfied smile to Rachel's face. "Well, if you don't like fishing and hunting, I guess you may as well close yourself up in a dress shop. We don't have much else to offer around here," he told Rachel.

"Oh, no, I disagree," drawled the spirited young woman. "All of this beautiful waterfront? Creeks, lakes, bayous, bays—ah, and those white sand beaches on the Gulf. Oh my, you're surrounded by luscious waterways! You don't have to fish or hunt to enjoy all that!" she raved. "Maybe you'd prefer concrete and traffic like we have in Dallas?"

Yancy liked what he heard as well as what he saw in this irresistibly attractive young female he had known for fewer than five minutes. A city girl who preferred the slow-moving country-like atmosphere in Niceville and Valparaiso over big-city life was his kind of woman. Her suntanned face and arms considerably enhanced her natural sensuous appeal and warm, glowing personality. Yancy's mind was fixed on her, his thoughts of doing business pushed beyond consciousness for the moment.

"Yancy is responsible for getting this area cleaned up," Jake volunteered. "If not for him, your aunt and I probably never would have opened this dress shop. Both Valparaiso and Niceville were junk heaps, and the waterfront you like so much smelled like a cesspool!" It was a description that a majority of residents would have agreed with as Yancy was still viewed as something of a genius for tricking tight-fisted merchants into funding the cleanup. Jake neglected to mention Yancy's other reputation, that of a man who could "hold his liquor." It was an accomplishment viewed as the mark of a real man by most and tolerated by the rest as no one had ever witnessed a wobble in his step or heard a twist of his tongue.

That was in spite of the fact that he was known for guzzling straight whiskey until wee hours of the morning, working the next day, and guzzling again the following night.

Many believed that Yancy had discovered what alchemists had spent a lifetime searching for, an elixir that would prolong life indefinitely. Unfortunately, those who tried to mimic Yancy ended up puking their stomach linings out, sleeping it off in jail or following in the footsteps of the Bedlam brothers, while still others committed suicide.

Yancy paid little attention to Jake's chatter as he was focused on the dress shop's new employee. "Does your uncle ever give you a day off?" he teased.

"I'm afraid not," Jake admitted. "The truth is, her aunt Sara isn't well enough to run the shop, so I have to keep it open. Don't leave much time for beach-going and fishing, and that's what she came here for. We did take her to the picture show, but I'm afraid our little theater can't compete with Dallas and—"

"I love the little theater," Rachel interrupted. "The way everyone meets in the lobby before the show, and they talk and share their popcorn and play the slot machine," she said with unmeasured enthusiasm. "It's like everybody here is kinfolks," she rallied.

Yancy and Jake eyed each other. "Slot machine?" asked Yancy. "Did they find the stolen slot?"

"Somebody stole the slot?" asked the shocked girl from the big city.

"He didn't tell you that?" Yancy scolded playfully. "I'm afraid your uncle is trying to keep the unsavory news of the area a secret. It happened just before the show started one night about two months ago. Everybody was in the lobby cuttin' up as usual, and somebody switched the lights off. By the time the lights came back on, the slot machine was missing!" The two men laughed as if it were the first time they heard the story.

"You're not serious?" declared Rachel. "Aw! You're teasing me. They couldn't get that machine out the door in the dark and everything. You're laughing at me," she bristled.

"No joke, honey," Yancy assured her. "Stick around. You'll see stranger things than that. You're in redneck country!"

"Who took it?" she insisted. "There couldn't have been that many people in the lobby. It's so tiny."

"Everybody knows who took it, honey," Yancy assured her. "A few years back, they would have strung him up on the old oak tree, but we got soft since then. Today, it would be more trouble and expense taking him to court than it would to replace the slot and let him worry about who's gonna take revenge on a dark street one night."

Rachel was genuinely fascinated. "Visiting this place is like seeing a strange movie except you know the movie is make-believe," she laughed. "Everybody's so friendly. They wave and honk their horns at each other. The whole town's like one big, happy family."

The more she talked, the better Yancy liked her. He had dated a few girls in town, one on a regular basis, but none had caught his eye like Rachel had. He was determined to make arrangements to see her again before he left the dress shop. "I'll bet your uncle never took you to David's Supper Club. I think you'll find it a much nicer place than the old theater. Barring a raid, you'll see plenty of slots there." He was about to say he'd show her the sights personally when Jake, who was somewhat concerned about this sudden attraction the two had for each other, interrupted him.

"What brought you here, Yancy? You shopping for a dress?" he jollied, and everyone laughed, somewhat thinly.

"Not to wear, but I do need to dress up the area, and I figure I'd be doing the community a favor if I took that old grassless eyesore you got over on the Fort Walton Highway off your hands. I should have insisted you clean it up when I was on the city council, but it was out of my jurisdiction."

Rachel was entertained by Yancy's dry humor, as was her uncle. She was familiar with the plot of ground her uncle owned, and she had remembered it as a lovely place, lined as it was with big, moss-laden live oak trees. Too, her uncle had always kept it clean, so she knew Yancy was teasing him.

"What kind of business you going into now?" Jake asked. Turning to Rachel, he said, "Yancy was hardly out of diapers when some ill-advised company president designated him a tugboat captain, causing us to mistake him for an adult and elect him to the city council. Of course, it was finally clear to all of us that he had an ulterior motive for getting the place cleaned up. He wanted to open a furniture store where he could reap the rewards of his own doing."

Rachel listened and laughed, the more so as Yancy showed little emotion. She liked his self-confidence, good looks, and dry sense of humor. This new acquaintance in the Panhandle stirred her emotions beyond anything she had experienced before, and she hoped the feelings were mutual. With that in mind, she didn't hold back. "So did you go into business then?" she asked.

As usual, Yancy was slow to respond, and by the time he opened his mouth, Jake had renewed his bantering. "He tried bartending but soon realized that wouldn't work. He drank up all the profit!"

Jake's teasing kept Rachel laughing and even forced a broad grin out of Yancy, who rarely reacted to good-natured ridicule directed at him. He was usually busy preparing a comeback, always a masterpiece that made the opposition's joke seem dull.

Jake readily agreed to sell Yancy the lot. The deal was to be settled as soon as Jake could produce the deed and Yancy could raise the money. With Yancy's hand on the doorknob and about to say good-bye, Rachel was in a secret tizzy for fear that she wouldn't see him again before she had to return to Dallas.

What she didn't know was that Yancy was just as eager to see her again. Before he turned the doorknob, he had one more comment for Jake. "I could take your niece to David's Supper Club as the down payment," he said with no outward show of emotion, but in fact his heart pounded so furiously against his chest that he feared Rachel could hear it. The feeling would remind him later of the incident on the merchant marine ship when it was struck by the enemy. The shock had emptied his bladder that day, and he hadn't forgotten the misery it wrought. Once outside the dress shop, he pinched off the flow of urine and managed to hold it at bay until he reached the bar. Once settled on a bar stool, he took a deep breath and chastised himself for losing his head over a woman he knew nothing about.

Uncle Jake had given Yancy permission to take Rachel to the supper club—but with warning. She was to be home no later than ten o'clock, the mere beginning of the evening at the club as well as in Yancy's mind.

Yancy's damnation of himself for getting involved with a woman ceased long enough for him to call for Rachel the following Saturday evening. Their arrival at the fancy supper club turned the heads of every employee and customer, causing some to stumble over their dancing partners' feet and sending a hapless waitress tripping over a chair leg while carrying a loaded tray of food. As they walked down the elegantly decorated, softly lit, high-ceilinged entry hall together, Yancy felt a surge of pride engulf him like he had never felt before. The band was already playing, and Clete was standing by the entrance keeping time to the music. When he saw Yancy and his date, he rushed to greet them.

"Here comes Clete," Yancy whispered to Rachel. "Nice boy. Just took over the business for David Stewart, his father-in-law."

"I heard," said Rachel. "I also heard you were the one who put them together. Playing Cupid one of your pastimes?" she asked with a grin. "Funny thing about small towns—everybody knows everything about everyone else. By the way, my aunt Sara still mourns for Mr. David. I guess everyone does."

The comment was typical. Everyone worried about David's plight but rarely about Mary Sam's. But there was no time to familiarize Rachel with the whole story as Clete was approaching them with a big grin.

Yancy and Clete enjoyed enthusiastic handshakes. Following a brief introduction, Clete kissed Rachel's hand and welcomed her to the club, and then he warned her that she was in the company of a tightwad. "Since you're a stranger in town and you know nothing about this hoodlum you're with, your dinner is on me," he said in jest. "If he had to pay, he'd make you order the cheapest thing on the menu, and then he'd spend what you saved him on a bottle of Jim Beam."

"Either way, he pockets the money," Yancy pointed out, his facial features fixed. His dry humor created more laughter than the comment itself, which created raucous laughter.

Meanwhile, Rachel had ambled in the direction of the music. "Oh, this is wonderful," she tittered. "Please, let's sit near the band. Do you mind?"

Yancy readily agreed.

"If you don't mind, Miss Rachel, I'd like to acquaint Yancy with some of our new equipment in the back office. I'm afraid it would only bore you." After seating Rachel, Clete led Yancy through to the back entrance where they exited the building. Clete used the area as a pass through which led them to an exit. In front of them was the back side of a barnlike structure, suggesting to Yancy that it belonged to the residence in front of it, not the supper club. Clete led him to the front of the barn where cows had been locked in their stalls for the night.

"What we gonna do? Milk the cows?" asked Yancy.

When Clete flung open a second door, Yancy appeared startled but made no comment. The room was filled with sacks of animal feed, tin pails, and tools associated with raising livestock. As there appeared to be no doorway leading to the outside, Yancy began to take serious notice.

To his amazement, Clete removed several bottles from a lower shelf, pulled out what appeared to be a small segment of wall and unfolded the piece creating a small two step ladder. With the help of the ladder, Clete, or any tall man, could reach the top of the wall near the ceiling. He pushed on an area that gave no hint it wasn't part and parcel of the entire ceiling. An entire whiskey-laden wall opened up, revealing a gambling casino that matched the one inside the main building. There was one big difference. There were no windows.

"Opens at midnight after everything else closes up tight," Clete explained.

"David is a damn genius," Yancy marveled. "If he can do all this, why does he allow everything else in his life to deteriorate? How is he?" he asked hopefully.

"No change. Spends his time doing nothing," said Clete, equally discouraged. "Casey spends all of her time trying to get him interested in something. He came to life long enough to design this, and then he fell right back into oblivion."

The thought of David and his self-destruction created an atmosphere of gloom for both men, one that even a deviously designed gambling room couldn't disperse. On the way out of the secret cow stall turned illegal gambling hall, Yancy grabbed a quart bottle of one of his favorite liquors: moonshine. As they neared the supper club, they heard the voice of a woman singing with the band.

"Who is that?" asked Yancy.

"No idea," admitted Clete. "But I'm afraid we stayed away too long. Your lady friend left the table. Must have found a better man," he teased.

In a moment, they both got an eyeful. Standing on the bandstand was a beautiful young woman who entertained the excited crowd with a twangy rendition of a familiar song.

It was Rachel!

Clearly country-western with a strong twang, Rachel sang *Have I Told You Lately that I Love You*. She had already captured the undivided attention of her delighted listeners, who stomped their feet and tapped their fingers on the tables and bars. When she caught sight of Yancy and Clete walking toward the band, she stopped in the middle of her song and began walking off the stage. The crowd objected noisily. They wanted more.

"You landed a songbird, Yancy?" Clete marveled. "Why didn't you tell us? Casey and I have been searching for a good country-western singer!"

Yancy could only stare at Rachel, his mind in a state of altered consciousness and his pride wafting through the atmosphere in unfamiliar territory. What had he gotten himself into? he worried. While Clete waited for a response, Yancy became visually acquainted with this fascinating woman he had escorted to Niceville's popular supper club. Wrapped sweetly in flirtatious pink cotton, her tall, shapely body moved sensuously with the music and her twangy voice uttered words of love and romance, leaving him oblivious to anyone else's presence.

"Yancy?" Clete asked again.

Clete's voice broke the spell, uniting Yancy's mind with his body again. "Hell, I didn't know she could sing," he admitted awkwardly, an unusual dilemma for him. He was clearly impressed, not only by her gravelly voice but by her courage to hop on a stage full of strangers and sing as if she had practiced with the band all week.

Band members and customers demanded song after song, and

she accommodated them. Finally, she bowed to lengthy applause before stepping off the stage.

She greeted Yancy with an apology. "When they began playing that song, I couldn't remain quiet. I hope you're not angry?" she purred.

Still emotionally euthanized, Yancy managed a smile.

"It was fantastic, young lady," bragged Clete. "Just the right gravel to it. Dump this guy and come see me about a singing job. I feel obligated to say you have been gadding about with a man who got some foolish notion in his head that he could make money selling furniture. I tried to tell him folks in these parts will spend money on moonshine and they'll stick their last dime in a slot machine, but they won't spend a nickel on furniture," he said with a straight face.

"Fact is," added Clete, "they don't stay out of the bars and gambling spots long enough to worry about a bed to sleep in or a couch to pass out on."

The threesome had attracted quite an audience, all of whom added their own verbal bashings of Yancy while he engineered a tall glass of pure whiskey on the rocks. The new bartender gasped at the strength of Yancy's order. Yancy moseyed back to the group in time to hear Clete summarizing the friendly massacre of his reputation.

"It's like this," said Clete. "We all figured Yancy would dilly-dally around in furniture long enough to lose all his money and then come begging David for the job he's been urging him to take for years—managing this club."

"Yeah, and if he had, he would have indoor plumbing by now," joked a bystander.

"And if a frog had wings, he wouldn't bump his ass on the ground," quipped Yancy, who walked away in victory, taking Rachel with him.

Talk of a romance between a pretty country singer from Dallas and Yancy Brighton, a popular young man who was envied for his ability to drink most of the night and build a successful business by day or night, circled the club and even aroused passions as far back as the outdoor hay barn/casino. Women particularly liked Yancy's quiet demeanor and almost stealthy lifestyle that sought no fanfare for his accomplishments or for his services to the community.

Time disappeared too quickly, especially for Yancy, who felt cheated. He had been forced to share Rachel with everyone, leaving little time for them to get acquainted. He was determined to see her again, so he couldn't take a chance on getting her home past the designated curfew.

After saying good night, he stopped at Doug's Bar, where he spent the remainder of the night guzzling alcohol and marking up a tiny bar napkin with the dull pencil he always carried in his pocket. After a short nap, he was in the furniture store by six preparing deliveries, ordering more furniture, and jotting down a simple agreement for purchasing Jake's real estate.

Two days later, he was back at the dress shop. "I'll be honest with you. I came here to see Rachel," he told Jake, "but while I'm here, we can sign this sales agreement unless you want to pay some crooked lawyer up in Crestview to write it up."

Jake brushed aside the notion of a lawyer, signed the agreement, and shook hands with Yancy.

"I'll tell you what I'm gonna do, Jake. I'm gonna show my appreciation by introducing your pretty niece to our area—not the beach, but the creeks, lakes, and rivers. We're going fishing! If she doesn't see anything but this dress shop, she'll never pay us another visit."

Rachel's smile said everything. She waited anxiously for her uncle's response.

"It'll be okay as long as she's back home by ten o'clock," said Jake.

Few knew Okaloosa County better than Yancy. There was a

problem, however: Yancy's feelings for Rachel made him nervous. He hadn't intended to settle down anytime soon, not even to one girl, much less to marriage. There was so much more to do before he could support a wife. But Rachel wouldn't always be around, apparently not even all summer. The thought of such a thing seemed to alter his usual mind-set. For days, he left an inept assistant in charge of the store so that he could continue her education of the area, including every stream of water, cow pasture, and hog farm in Okaloosa County. They walked through the wooded areas, where he pointed out active and inactive moonshine stills; had his fill from a few old-timers' stills; and finally borrowed a moonshiner's john boat for a romantic cruise along Shoal River just as the sun was setting.

Rachel was enchanted. "I can't believe you considered staying in Texas after your stint in the marines. This place is a little piece of heaven. Creeks. rivers, bayous, bays, and lakes—water everywhere. All that and the Gulf of Mexico too, with luscious, snow-white beaches. Ah, the hanging moss!" she exclaimed. "Why is it here and not there? And what about the wetlands and all the unusual plants? And all those animals in the woods. What do they eat?"

Yancy was ill prepared. "Hell, I guess I took it all for granted," he admitted, but then he remembered Casey. "I did learn a little from a little Indian girl," he said, smiling. As they walked along the banks of Turkey Creek, he identified a tree as a black gum swamp tupelo. "You can identify it by its flat-shaped top. The flowers produce honey, and lots of animals love the juicy fruit it produces."

Rachel was a captivated listener. "What about color? Any colorful foliage in the fall?"

"Yeah, the black gum leaves turn bright red in the fall, and it has dark blue berries that are relished by turkeys, birds, and black bear, I'm told. My dad has made every effort to protect these trees and bushes that feed the animals," he said with pride. He surprised himself by naming most of the plants and their produce as well as the trees, even though there were dozens of them. He had given little or no thought to the names of the trees or their purpose in the woods as far as producing food for the animals, but with Rachel showing an interest, he felt a need to nudge his memory. And he felt a sense of pride.

Rachel had brought out the best in him. Again, he marveled at this woman who had knocked him off the bar stool in spite of the fact that he had carefully and purposely donned thick padding to protect himself from such a disaster.

Yancy had never been known for gabbing. He had a reputation for listening, not talking. But for some unknown reason, he had untied his tongue and was curiously enjoying it. "Our creeks are nurseries for our marine life. Creek waters flow into the bayous where the fresh water inflow mixes with salty marine waters to form a brackish estuary. The Boggy Bayou you love to swim in? Got its name from this process. When vegetative matter flows along Turkey Creek, it slows when it enters the bayou and settles to the bottom. As the collection grows there at the entrance, it forms a thick, or boggy, delta of sediment."

"Ah, Boggy Bayou! It's a lot prettier than its name." She smiled at him, and he smiled back, if only in his heart. She began to hum a popular tune, "I'm Walking the Floor over You."

"Sing it," he insisted, and she obliged.

"Ernest Tubbs? Pretty country, ain't it, for a city girl?" he asked as he pulled her up close and pierced her eyes with longing he had never felt for anyone before.

"I'm country at heart," she whispered. Yancy kissed her with the passion of his lifetime, and she answered him with her own. Both fell short of declaring their love as it seemed impossible to each of them that their relationship had reached such a plateau so quickly.

Yancy released his embrace and walked a short distance away in an effort to calm his emotions, as well as other parts.

On the way home, Rachel made a confession. "I'm never going to forget this day," she promised.

"We still haven't seen it all," he said. "I wish I could get away from the store more often, but Old Harold is all I've got to run things while I'm away, and he just barely knows how to sign his name. If anybody wanted to buy a piece of furniture, it would scare him to death."

"Maybe we could see each other after you close the store," she suggested. "Uncle Jake closes the dress shop at five. There's plenty of daylight after that."

"Not in the furniture business, honey. It's ten o'clock at night before I close the doors. Most of my business takes place long after other businesses have closed. Women shop during the day for dresses, and men shop for golf clubs and fishing tackle. But furniture? They shop together at night. I'm certain your Uncle Jake would never agree to anything beyond a ten o'clock pick up," he laughed. "You may have to sneak out the bedroom window after the folks go to sleep."

Once parked in front of her uncle's house, Yancy grasped the steering wheel with both hands and stared straight ahead. It was if he were waiting for Rachel to open the door and get out without a kiss good night. Suddenly, he pulled her close and pummeled her with passionate kisses. Her yielding body told him it was okay to repeat the act again and again, and he did. "I don't want to leave you," he admitted.

"I don't want you to," she whispered. But the clock was ticking, and to their chagrin, her aunt appeared in the doorway. She held a lighted oil lamp that revealed her troubled face. Behind the screen door was Jake, his arms crossed in an unhappy fashion. "Talk to your parents about staying longer," Yancy urged, and Rachel agreed. They said a quick, and reluctant, good night.

Yancy drove directly to Doug's Bar, took a long swallow of straight whiskey, and spent most of the night scribbling on one of the establishment's tiny napkins. At two a.m., Doug pushed him out the back entrance, his pockets filled with a stack of bar napkins bearing penciled-in plans for a new furniture store.

Rachel was given a two-week extension, and she and Yancy saw each other at every opportunity her aunt and uncle allowed. On each occasion, their passions for each other grew.

In spite of the ecstasy Yancy felt when he was with her, he wished at times that she had never come to Niceville or that she would suddenly return to Dallas and he would never see her again. With that in mind, he promised himself that he would not call on Rachel the following night. He would work until midnight and spend the remainder of the night at Doug's Bar. Such a plan would guarantee that he would not see her! He kept that promise, but only for one night.

His need to be in her company intensified. When he was in the store, he could scarcely concentrate enough to answer customers' questions. Images of Rachel in her pretty cotton dresses or clinging silks she wore on Sundays; her tanned legs and arms; and her long, dark tresses sparkling in the sun and the sound of her sweet voice, especially when she sang to him, raced through his mind. To his chagrin, it was more than he could deal with. One day, he told customers he had an emergency. "You folks look around. I'll be right back."

Minutes later, he walked into the dress shop and began reeling off a plan. "We've checked out the smaller waterways, honey. Why not spend Sunday digging our toes into the white sands of the Gulf of Mexico? We could swim and walk the beach on Okaloosa Island, and when we get tired, we can shower and change at the pavilion and go dancing … or whatever pleases you." Assured that her uncle Jake was listening and would make his presence known any second, Yancy managed with a great deal of effort to keep his hands off Rachel while waiting for his response.

Surprisingly, Jake remained in his office, but he did have something to say. "I'm afraid her aunt Sara won't agree to anything on Sunday that don't include church services."

Yancy eyed Rachel, who appeared as anxious to go as he was to take her. "Well, I guess with a biblical name like Rachel, she ought to attend church," said Yancy. "But there's a lot of sunshine left after church service is over."

Jake was surprised. He and his wife always attended church services, and he couldn't remember the last time he saw Yancy occupying a seat there. "Are you a student of the Bible, Yancy?" he asked with a friendly hint of sarcasm.

"Well, I never got past Genesis," Yancy admitted with a sly grin. "I know that the good man upstairs created the first man and woman and gave them everything they needed for a good life, but they screwed up. They had a couple of kids but one of 'em killed the other one—another screwup! It didn't get any better after that. Pretty simple message. People are no damn good!"

Jake laughed heartily, and Rachel joined him. The truth was that Yancy hadn't opened the Bible since departing the merchant marine ship, but that was not to say that he had forgotten who ruled the earth and all that was in it. Too, he had heard all the biblical stories from his mother, and much of it had been etched in his memory.

For the first time since he and Rachel began seeing each other, Jake didn't seem open to Yancy's plans. At the couple's next meeting, Rachel explained her uncle's reticence. "Seems Aunt Sara and Uncle Jake have been talking to my parents, and they are anxious all of a sudden for me to come home," she revealed.

"Why?" Yancy asked.

"They're concerned about you and me," she said, blushing.

Yancy responded with a lengthy silence at first, and Rachel followed suit. He reached for the paper cup he had been drinking from and took a long drink of straight whiskey. "Well, if they think I'm gonna run away with you, they're right as hell!" he announced before gently lifting her chin until their eyes met. "Rachel Shaver, I don't like your name. I'd like to change it."

Rachel broke into a satisfied smile. "Is that a proposal?" she asked.

"About as good as I can come up with," he admitted.

With Rachel back in Dallas breaking the news to her parents, Yancy was unsettled. He hadn't planned to marry, not ever, and certainly not now. Until he met Rachel, remaining single was easy as none of the girls he had dated in the past interested him for long. Too, he had watched in pain as former classmates and friends rushed into marriage once they had returned from the war, and many weren't emotionally ready for all the responsibilities that marriage entailed. A majority were confined to unhappy marriages or found themselves suffering through ugly divorces or torrid separations.

He dwelled on all of it, but nothing changed his mind.

Two months later, Yancy and Rachel became man and wife. Family members, friends, and acquaintances were anxious to see if Yancy would exchange his nightly tête-a-tête with a cold, impersonal bar stool for an intimate relationship at home with Rachel.

The answer was no.

Yancy's popularity in the community was further enhanced by his friendly, outgoing bride. They were always included in area get-togethers, and Rachel, as energetic as she was pretty, was often the life of the party. Her rustic country-western singing voice was delivered with a twang, befitting Niceville and its inhabitants to the point of inspiring the area's most reluctant men to abandon their whiskey long enough to dance with anyone who would agree to it. Yancy was an exception. He maintained his usual quiet demeanor at the local bar, inhaling straight whiskey in as dark a corner or secluded area as he could find. He arrived at functions, whether in-home parties, outdoor events, or area get-togethers, with his own paper cup filled with straight bourbon except for a hint of ice. Bartenders and hosts made it a point to keep his cup filled. On the way home, he kept his container replenished until bedtime and then began anew when daylight came.

Doug's Bar, or other bars when he was out of the area, continued to serve as his office, and a simple paper napkin and pencil made up his entire set of office supplies in spite of the fact that he had begun to expand his businesses by moving into popular, moneymaking convenience stores with ample office spaces.

With Eglin Air Force Base bringing more and more people to the growing communities, Yancy opened stores in all of them. The frequency of fishing trips and other outings with Rachel quickly diminished, but she understood the importance of meeting the challenges inherent in business. She tried to comfort him during the difficult times when he struggled with final decisions. "What do you think?" he asked her one day. "Would a liquor store do well on the right side of Main Street or the left?" It was a rhetorical question, and she knew it.

"Quit teasing me!" she fussed playfully. "You think I know nothing?" She coiled her sensuous body on the arm of the chair Yancy occupied and began running her fingers through his hair, occasionally stopping to plant a kiss on top of his head. "I love you," she whispered. "Everybody says you're a genius when it comes to choosing the right location. If you think Niceville's Main Street is the right place for a package liquor store, so do I," she cooed.

Yancy gently pulled her into his lap and began smothering her with passionate kisses, which she returned with equal passion. Their pulsating bodies on fire, they quickly worked themselves into a much anticipated, fiery conclusion that left them both pleasantly exhausted and totally satisfied.

Lovemaking for the Brightons was always healing, satisfying, and memorable. Both Yancy and Rachel relived each animated episode as if it were their last, when in fact, the activities were never far apart as both were as sexually driven as a dog in heat. Reliving their sexual encounters was especially helpful for Rachel, who spent long evenings alone while Yancy worked late at the store. She often called the store just to hear his voice and maybe purr a bit on the phone in hopes of enticing him to come straight home instead of stopping at Doug's Bar.

One evening, there was no answer. She smiled to herself, certain he had left early and was anticipating a roll in the sheets as much as she was. But hours passed, and he still hadn't come home. It was with some trepidation that she tackled a dark, half-mile trip to Doug's Bar, armed only with a dim flashlight she wasn't certain would last the entire walk.

Yancy wasn't there.

"He went to the courthouse," Doug told her. "Left about an hour ago."

"The courthouse! I know I look stupid, and I am or I wouldn't be running around in the middle of the night looking for my husband," she spouted, "but I'm not so stupid that I think court is in session at midnight!"

"I'm sorry, Miss Rachel," Doug explained. "It's actually the jailhouse, you know, but everybody calls it the courthouse because it's the only place we have where the judge can hold court. And believe it or not, they do have court proceedings all hours of the night. Keeps Niceville law officers and law breakers—drunks mostly—from having to make a trip to Crestview. The judge comes here once a month, I think. Actually, I'm not certain how often—maybe he comes every week," he admitted sheepishly. "Anyway, Judge Cat's in charge of night court. They're supposed to be finished by eight o'clock, but with Judge Cat presiding, nobody can be certain," he laughed, and his soberest customers joined him.

"Cats may not show up before eight, and when he does, he may spend an hour or so gabbing with the prisoners before he tends to business," added one pleasurably stimulated customer in the bar.

Rachel was not amused. "Judge Cats?" she mimicked and then added an angry "Meow!"

"Yeah, Cat is the judge's nickname," Doug explained. "Real name's C. A. Tarrow. Josh Tarrow's boy, you know. Some professor in law school called him by his initials, and since it fit his personality pretty well, it stuck. Yeah, Judge Cat is quite a character." The comment brought a loud response from customers, who stomped their feet, bumped their bottles together, and yelled in joyful agreement.

Rachel had heard enough. She headed for the jailhouse, or night court, whichever it was.

At the tiny jail facility, she hesitated at the entrance, uncertain if she should enter the narrow, dimly lit hallway and whether she should go inside. When she pulled the big, cumbersome door open, its hinges moaned like a sick animal, and she heard jumbled noises coming from one of the open rooms. The noise of the door brought a policeman to the hallway. Recognizing Rachel immediately, he led her to the makeshift courtroom and pointed toward Yancy, who leaned against a wall and drank from a large paper cup. Rachel knew its contents, as did everyone else.

The judge was addressing what appeared to be the dregs of society, many still feeling the effects of a difficult night before, with their heads cradled in their hands or drooped to their chests.

Others interacted with the fun-loving judge, who spoke kindly to them as if they had been naughty children at worst and therefore were given credit for nicer behavior in the past. The judge was addressing a prisoner he called Skeeter.

"Now, Skeeter, I know you didn't mean no harm, but the fact is, your car was found wrapped around a tree. You could have killed somebody. And I know you wouldn't want to do that, would you Skeeter?" asked the judge.

"Yeah, Skeeter!" yelled another detainee. All prisoners present agreed wholeheartedly with loud and sometimes lewd comments as they had not yet caught sight of Rachel, who stood in the doorway, startled by the language, as well as the facility, which brought to her mind an unfinished horse barn. She made an extensive survey of those on trial, a motley bunch who had obviously been plucked from the bar she had just vacated, relieved of their beer bottles and left to make a mockery of the judge, who was afraid to punish them for fear of not being reelected.

The whole atmosphere reminded her of a poorly written drama played by the worst actors she had ever encountered. In the background, she heard Yancy calling to her, but she chose to ignore him out of spite and focus her attention on the scene before her.

"Well, you see, Judge," said Skeeter, "it was like this. I was in the backseat. I weren't even driving the car," he declared.

"Aw, hell, Skeeter. Okay, Dolph," said Judge Cats to another detainee. "Come on up here. You said you were with Skeeter last night? If Skeeter was in the backseat, then I'm probably gonna have to book you for drunk driving. What do you have to say for yourself, Dolph? Didn't you see that tree?"

Dolph yanked his dirty cap off and stood at attention as best he could. "Sorry, your Cats honor," he offered. There was an outbreak of gaudy laughter that was allowed to live its life out before the judge insisted on continuing. "Well, you see, Judge," Dolph explained,

"I was in the backseat too. It ain't no wonder the car was wrapped around a tree. There weren't nobody driving it!"

The metal roof seemed to shake from the raucous laughter that ensued, but Rachel was not amused. When the noise began to fade, she began a hasty march toward the exit, purposely dragging the loose-hinged door across the uneven wood floor and rattling the loose metal door handle repeatedly to make certain Yancy witnessed her exit.

He did, of course, as did everyone else. With Yancy waiting at the exit for his bride, Skeeter yelled at him, "Throw your hat in the house before you go in, Yancy," prompting more laughter. "If it don't come flying out the door, you might wanna try goin' in," he hee-hawed, creating a total disruption of the court proceedings. Instead of pounding his gavel or scolding Skeeter, Judge Cat added his own tidbit: "Or we could put you up in our jail here and you wouldn't have to swallow your pill until tomorrow. You could think of it as the 'night before execution.'" With courtroom attendees and officials bent over in laughter, Yancy lashed out playfully at them as he exited the same door Rachel had slammed shut in his face. He never released his grip on the paper cup.

In spite of Rachel's quick exit, she had stopped abruptly once outside the unusual courthouse and waited, albeit in tears.

"Baby! What are you doing here?" Yancy asked, as if his presence at midnight court proceedings in an otherwise abandoned barn was nothing out of the ordinary.

"Shouldn't I be asking you that question?" she seethed.

"I just came down to see what Old Cat's doing about the drunks on the street," he explained.

"This is the most ridiculous thing I ever heard of, court at midnight!" she said, smoldering. "Where have you been all night?"

"At work," he said, forgetting momentarily that he had spent well over an hour at the bar.

"You're a damn liar!" she accused. It was rare for Rachel to use four-letter words, but as her husband often relied on them to get his point across, she felt a sudden need to make use of them herself. And she was grateful to learn that they seemed to describe her displeasure better than the ones she had previously depended on.

Yancy grabbed her in his arms and tried to kiss her, but Rachel would have none of it. "Oh, hell, honey, as a former city councilman, I have an interest in keeping the area clean. And that includes drunks as well as junk. You should listen in on Judge Cat's court. He'll keep you in stitches."

Rachel wouldn't be humored. "I've seen all I want to see of him!" she ranted. "He talked to those criminals like he was reprimanding schoolchildren for running in the hallway."

When Yancy saw that she was not to be reasoned with, he coaxed her in the car and drove her home. Once there, he tried again to make peace.

"You're not in the big city anymore, honey. We're just a small bunch of commoners here in the Panhandle. Cat knows who gave him this job, and he's just showing his appreciation. Every man in that room voted for his father when he ran for school superintendent, and those same men helped put him in the judge's seat. A man has to pay his dues. We all have to, especially if we deal with the public." He paused long enough to take a drink and then proceeded to educate her. "As a businessman, I have to please the public too."

"Oh," she twittered. "And that means drinking the bar dry and then attending the rednecks' drama in the courtroom?"

Without comment, Yancy poured himself another drink, lingered in the kitchen long enough to drink it, and then poured another.

"Is it too much to ask you to come home before midnight? Maybe even before bedtime?" she spouted. When Yancy made no comment, she went to bed, where she lay awake the rest of the night.

As he had done many times before, Yancy left the house in the middle of the night and worked the rest of the night, the following day, and into the next night before paying a visit to Doug's Bar. When he finally arrived home, Rachel was too exhausted to put up another fight. She met him with open arms, crying.

"Honey, if you don't learn to relax, we're not gonna make it," he warned. "I've got a problem," he confessed.

"So have I," she cried. "I'm pregnant!"

Yancy eyed her suspiciously, but the strain on her face spoke for the truth in her statement. "Well, now, this calls for a drink!" he said proudly. Having previously poured his drink, he returned to the kitchen and strengthened it to a new high: no ice cubes!

"A drink? A drink!" she objected. "You don't even care about the baby. All you think of is a drink!"

Yancy tried to take her in his arms, but she was clearly in no mood for it. "Honey, I'm as happy about the baby as any man. My way of celebrating may be different from yours, but that don't mean it's any worse. I've got a lot of things on my mind, you know—bills, slow business, late payments, overstocking, and a hell of a lot more. I need a drink to relax. You should have one yourself. It'll help you relax."

Rachel had always viewed Yancy's reactions, or lack of them, as a show of strength, an uncanny ability to stay calm during the storm and then silently deal with whatever was troubling him. Still, she expected a show of emotion when told his first child was on the way. She went to bed and had been asleep for several hours when Yancy left the house and returned to Doug's Bar. He settled on a bar stool, ordered a tall drink, and began drawing plans on a tiny bar napkin for a package liquor store.

There were countless nights like this—with Rachel waiting up at home for his late return, sometimes plucking him from his bar stool even as their baby grew inside her. She battled morning sickness so intense that Yancy's alcoholic breath nauseated her to the point of making her vomit.

When pains in her stomach awakened her one night, she tried to call Yancy but couldn't find him. By the time he arrived home, her pains were coming every twenty minutes. He found her clutching her stomach and moaning pitifully.

"Honey, why didn't you call me?" he yelled.

"Why?" she asked. "I tried! You knew the baby was coming anytime now and you still went to the bar! Everybody knows—and I do mean everybody—you're too busy dribbling on bar napkins to look after your wife and baby. Are you gonna drive me to the hospital, or do I have to walk?"

In less than two hours, Yancy and Rachel were the parents of a baby boy. When Yancy observed his new son in the nursery, the child spat his pacifier out of his mouth, sending the plastic nipple halfway across the tiny hospital nursery before throwing himself into a crying frenzy. Yancy pumped his fist in the air and yelled, "Go get 'em, Tiger!" A few minutes later, he bragged to Rachel, "He's a tiger, honey! He's already talking!" he added with a broad grin.

Rachel was pleased. "What did he say?" she teased.

"He said, 'Take this damn pacifier and shove it!'" he declared, "'and get me a steak!' He sent that thing halfway across the room, honey! Pretty powerful stuff for a young man less than an hour old," he boasted. "Yeah, we got us a tiger, all right." Yancy left the room with a swagger.

The boy was given a long, impressive family name, but few would ever know it as he would be known to everyone as Tiger, and even that would eventually be reduced to Tigy.

With Rachel confined at home with Tigy, Yancy's late hours posed more of a problem than ever. When she and Tigy delivered his supper at the usual time late one evening, Yancy was not there.

"He left about five o'clock. Said he was going to meet with Congressman Jim Badcock in Crestview," the store manager told her.

"Six hours ago?" asked the fuming mother. "Do you have any idea which bar? I'm not familiar with Crestview's skid row."

"Not sure, Miss Rachel. I think they were planning to meet in the congressman's office," offered the manager.

"For six hours?" Rachel repeated.

"Yancy never tells me his business, Miss Rachel. But you and the baby should go back home and wait for him. I was just about to close the store."

Rachel left in a huff, but she didn't go home.

Finding Yancy's truck wouldn't be easy. The hub city's Main Street was bare and seemingly lifeless, as Rachel knew it would be. Most of the bars were located deep in undeveloped areas, far outside city limits, and only a regular would know their exact locations. As the spouse of a regular, Rachel had some notions she called upon, and they led her west on Highway 90. Less than a mile past the Okaloosa County courthouse, she caught sight of Yancy's truck parked in front of the Eagle's Claw, a dimly lit establishment with only a handful of customers, if the number of vehicles was any clue.

She gathered her strength; bundled Tigy up in his blanket; walked up the uneven pathway to the old, mildewed, concrete-block building; and pushed the door open with her foot. Scattered around the messiest room she had ever seen were bleary-eyed singles who struggled to get their drinks to their mouths without dumping their contents on the littered tables. Yancy was not one of them.

The only women who entered a bar alone were considered tawdry, scum of the earth, and they usually deserved the title. In Niceville, where bartenders knew Rachel and knew her mission for being there, it was of little consequence, but a bar in rough and rowdy Crestview was quite another thing. With all drunken eyes focused as best they could on Rachel, she struggled to remain standing now that Tigy had suddenly become restless.

"Do you know these people?" asked the bartender of his only bar stool customer, the only one who was still capable of carrying on a conversation, and the only one who hadn't bothered to check out the arrival of an unusual visitor to the premises.

It was Yancy.

Alarmed by what he saw, he jumped off the bar stool and reached out to his wife with one arm while grasping a tall glass of bourbon and ice with the other. "What's wrong, honey?" he asked with real concern, but he quickly realized she was on one of her late-night missions. "Aw, hell, honey. Why do you do this to yourself?" he bristled. "You're gonna get yourself and the baby killed one of these nights!"

He tried to take Tigy, who had begun to cry. In doing so, he spilled his drink on the baby as well as Rachel. He quickly instructed the bartender to make another "to go." Taking the new drink in one hand, he held Tigy in the other and headed toward the exit, Rachel close behind.

"Don't ever do that again!" Yancy yelled at her once they were outside. "People who frequent these places are dangerous or chummy with other folks who are. You never know when some drunken fool might start a fight or pull a gun. When they do, somebody usually ends up dead. It's often a bystander like you and Tigy. It's one thing to go in Doug's Bar in Niceville but quite another here in Crestview."

"Do I understand you correctly? Do you frequent dangerous places where a drunken fool might start a fight and kill you?" she tossed out bitterly.

"You think I come here without protection? I carry a gun," Yancy spouted.

Rachel went into a rage. "A gun!" she screamed. "A gun in one hand and a drink in the other?" She raced to catch up with him, snatched Tigy out of his arms, and wobbled dangerously along the broken pathway in an effort to get out of his reach. The brawl frightened Tigy, who burst out crying again, and efforts to comfort him failed. Angry himself, Yancy made no effort to detain his wife but chose to wait in his truck until she and the baby were on their way home.

For Rachel, the 25 mile drive home seemed more like a cross-country tour. The movement of the car lulled Tigy to sleep while his mother smoked one cigarette after another and worried. Except for the gun, the emotions she dealt with were not new to her. She often worried about something happening to Yancy with him parked on a bar stool where drunks abounded and dangerous brawls were rampant. She was reminded of the Bedlam brothers. They were known for their brawls, but they had never been involved in a shooting, perhaps because everyone knew they never carried a gun. *Does everyone but me know that Yancy carries one?*

"Your daddy's reputation as a man who can hold his liquor is no longer funny," she said to a sleeping baby. "Yeah, he can drink all day and still walk a tightrope," she cried. "But can he drink all night and still handle a gun?"

Once Rachel heard Yancy's truck in the driveway, she began spreading his lunch on the kitchen table, then greeted him icily when he appeared at the back door. "This might be a little cold as Tigy and me delivered it to the store about twelve hours ago," she said before bursting into tears.

"Why do you do this to yourself?" Yancy asked again.

"To myself?" she screamed before flying into a rage and pumping her fists into his chest.

He gripped her wrists and insisted she "Calm down and have a drink. I have to do what I do to get where we are. We've got big things going our way now. I was in Crestview to meet with

Congressman Jim Badcock. We're gonna help him get reelected, and he's gonna help us get into low-rent housing. It's the way the system works, honey. If you want somebody to help you, you have to help them first. Badcock is a powerful man in Washington." He took a bite from a fried chicken leg, "Still good, honey. I like cold chicken."

"It's a good story, but I didn't see the congressman in the bar!" Rachel shouted, still fighting tears. "He likely went home to be with his wife and family! What about the gun? What if Tigy got hold of it?" she asked, somewhat subdued, mostly from exhaustion.

"Aw, hell!" he countered. "Give me a little credit. I've carried a gun all my life." He removed the tiny weapon, placed it on the fireplace mantel, and then grabbed another bite of chicken before wrapping his arms around her. "Now you listen to me. I'm gonna get you out of this little shack one day and put you in a beautiful waterfront home where you belong," he promised. "When a man has the best-looking woman in town, he ought to put her in the best house in town."

It was enough to soften Rachel's heart, but she reserved the right to remind him again that she didn't see the congressman at the bar.

Chapter 31

IT WAS 1970, NEARLY TEN YEARS AFTER RACHEL HAD retrieved her husband from the Crestview bar. Congressman Badcock had been reelected time and again, and Yancy was successfully involved in low-rent housing. He had established himself as a man to be reckoned with in the business world. At the age of eleven, Tigy was full of energy and involved in Little League baseball and lots of mischief, mostly harmless shenanigans staged to call attention to himself. Rachel was a mother hen, doting wife, and homemaker who felt a need to fill in for an absentee father. She never missed Tigy's Little League games or school activities, and she continued to deliver Yancy's supper when she could find him.

Rachel was known for the parties she gave in their new waterfront home. Everyone was invited, including the Brightons' own employees as well as postal clerks and congressmen, military or civilians. The parties were noted for their night-long gaiety that extended onto the spacious lawn, in the boathouse, on the dock, and into the bayou. Nobody willingly missed one.

Although the Air Force base and the twin cities' population had grown tremendously, Niceville and Valparaiso remained a small waterfront paradise. Folks of all classes and incomes enjoyed access to the bayous, bays, and the Gulf of Mexico. They swam, waded, sunbathed, waterskied, sailed, and fished. Fishing opportunities included mullet casting, deep-sea fishing, floundering, and more. Many of these activities led to competitive opportunities that brought military and civilians together. But there was one activity they couldn't share: golfing on the eighteen-hole golf course that was practically located in Niceville residents' backyards. It belonged to Eglin AFB, and civilians who were not military or at least government employees, had no right to membership.

Locals, both military and civilian, began to push for a golf and country club that everyone could enjoy. They turned to Yancy and his powerful friends for help, and the group approached the developer of a large tract of land in the Rocky Bayou area. Yancy saw the area as a perfect location for a golf course and country club that would entice more and more residents to choose Niceville as their residence, thus enhancing his businesses as well as that of others.

Yancy was cautious. "Don't get too excited," he told his bride.

"I know!" she fussed. "The property has a lot of water on it. Everybody says we would break the law if we tried to build a country club there." Many of her best friends were either in the military service or they worked for the government in some capacity. They could use the sport facility but she couldn't except as an occasional guest.

"We can skirt the law," Yancy told her. "We'll have to stuff the pockets of some environmentalists before we start digging in those wetlands, but we'll dig!" he promised.

In spite of arguments and setbacks, Yancy and his powerful friends throughout the area as well as the state made the country club a reality. In the beginning, membership consisted entirely of old-timers in the area, especially avid golfers, bridge players, and tennis buffs, but it also introduced newcomers to the games. While many of Yancy's old cronies, mostly members of the "good ol' boys' fraternity," played golf only with one another, Yancy didn't discriminate. As a businessman, he looked upon everyone as a potential customer and gladly accepted invitations to make new acquaintances, whether civilian or military, educated or uneducated, officers or enlisted men.

Jim Stone was a good example. An Air Force retiree, Jim joined the country club and quickly became a new face in Yancy's golfing foursomes. And Rachel was just as prompt to add Jim and his wife, Nelda, to her party list. Regular mixed events became popular, and it wasn't long before everyone knew everyone else, thus creating a family-like atmosphere among the members. No one wore a title or a uniform.

Dances and other nighttime activities at the club became as popular with the membership as golf outings were, and Rachel sang with the bands they hired for these special occasions.

"Rachel's the queen bee here, isn't she?" Nelda noted to Jim one night after Rachel entertained the country club crowd with several of her country-western renditions.

"Yeah, and Yancy's the king," Jim added. "Perfect couple. "Rachel thrives on the limelight, while Yancy shuns it in the darkest corners. If nobody seeks his companionship, that's fine with him. As long as he has a drink!" he added with a chuckle.

"I think he enjoys the attention too," Nelda thought out loud. "He sits in the dark corners, all right, but he knows everybody is going to seek him out, and he would be disappointed if they didn't."

Jim eyed his wife with renewed interest. "Ah! You're probably right," he laughed. "He's surrounded by a bunch of sycophants. They have no business. They live vicarious lives, imagining they have a close relationship with the king. Don't get me wrong—I like Yancy. And I guess I agree with you: he doesn't seem to seek attention, but yeah, he knows it will come. Why exert himself?" They laughed in agreement.

"You're obviously talking about Yancy Brighton," interrupted Bill McKean, an old-timer who had known Yancy all of his life.

"Look at him," he insisted, "perched at the bar like he's glued to the stool, seemingly unaware of anyone else's presence."

"He's gonna fall off that stool one day," Nelda giggled, no vengeance intended.

"I would be very surprised if he did," argued McKean. A lot of folks have spent a lifetime waiting for Yancy's fall. And he's still standing and running a growing business while the soothsayers are still counting pennies or pushing up weeds in a cemetery plot," he guffawed. "Been drinking rotgut all his life."

"What's rotgut?" asked Nelda with childish innocence.

"Moonshine!" laughed her husband. "I understand just about everybody had their own moonshine still house back when Yancy was growing up?"

"Not everybody," McKean declared. "Yancy's parents didn't! But nearly everyone else did, and young Yancy could draw a county moonshine map for you before he was ten years old. He busted up one of the biggest moonshine operations in the county when he was just a kid." Word had leaked out over the years, but since nobody who took part in the raid ever admitted it, the story had changed often.

As something of a newcomer, Nelda took it all in. "We heard something about that before. Is it really true?" she questioned.

Jim brushed the story aside with a wave of his hand. "Might be a little exaggerated," he suggested. "I heard that Yancy supposedly led a raid when he was a teenager, but he sure won't talk about it. Apparently nobody went to jail over it."

"Not exaggerated," insisted McKean. "It led to the killing of a still house owner who was himself a mass murderer. Apparently, the community was awful pleased to be rid of him. It may just be speculation that Yancy had anything to do with the raid, but you'd be hard pressed to convince a single person in this area that he didn't actually lead it."

Nelda had moved on, but Jim remained fascinated. "Tell us more about Yancy."

Chuck Wybrid had worked himself into the little group, shaking his head. "Yancy Brighton? It would take a week just to give you a short introduction," he insisted before moving on.

"What would you like to know?" asked Bull Martin, another intruder who was born in Niceville. "My boy and Yancy went to school together, played hooky together, and were mostly remembered by their classmates as the boys who filled the classroom water bucket with moonshine—" The group bustled with laughter, drowning out the rest of the story.

"Ah," said a wistful Tom Martin, the very son Bull spoke of. "School was never the same after Yancy left. The boy was weaned on moonshine. He liked it better than his mama's milk."

Bull took a swig of his own concoction before searching the faces of those who had gathered around him. "Tell 'em, Larry," he told Lawrence Nordgren.

Nordgren obliged. "He attended the same school I did, but he got his education hiking the woods and sampling moonshine from Niceville to Laurel Hill. Graduated first in the moonshine class!" he added, creating a hoopla among the group whose laughter captured the attention of everyone else in the room.

With everyone a little tipsy, no one was bashful, not even high-society folks like Lawrence Nordgren. Better known as R.C., Nordgren had become a successful lawyer who practiced in Crestview, his hometown. He yelled across the room for Yancy to join them as "they are telling lies on you." As the son of a Crestview banker, R.C. had been somewhat shielded from the nitty-gritty life, but he had managed to traipse through the wooded area around northern Okaloosa County with Yancy every chance he got. "I finished college and law school, and I learned a lot while doing it. But the best education I ever had was completed in one day, and it was free—the day I spent sampling North Okaloosa County's moonshine stills with Yancy Brighton!"

With nearly everyone in the club having gravitated toward the uproarious laughter, Yancy was seen leaving his dark corner, but only to visit the toilet. At R.C.'s request, two men waited at the bathroom door for Yancy's exit, grabbed him by the arms, and escorted him to the clutches of the roaring group.

"I'd like all of you to meet the man who introduced me to moonshine," announced R.C. With everyone laughing at Yancy's expense, his solemn expression remained unchanged.

"I gotta tell you," R.C. continued, "Yancy had a gallon of the strongest, most cell-destroying, butt-kicking mash anybody ever made one day when several of us boys met him in the woods. He knew I had never tasted the stuff, so he advised me not to drink as much as the others because 'it'll make you sick,' he said. Now you might think that was a good thing he did, right?" he asked rhetorically. "But the truth is, he knew that if he told me I couldn't handle as much of the stuff as he could, I would die trying. And sure enough, I chugged it down just like Yancy did."

"And he was so sick, some anxious doctor in Pensacola yanked his appendix out! Of course the boy's body part turned out to be a specimen of perfection so the doctor decided the little fella was suffering from some fatal disease medical science knew nothing about!" offered Yancy. "R.C., thinking he was going to die, had the whole town hovering over his bed in constant prayer," he added. The group, which now included every party-goer present as well as employees, enjoyed side-splitting laughter. Apparently it was a true story, one the local boys had teased him about unmercifully.

Yancy returned to the corner he had occupied since his arrival while friends continued to relate his exploits. When the group had exhausted tales of Yancy's woe and glow, Bull ended the talk with praise for his friend. Such endings had become a common

occurrence among Yancy's friends, and that included nearly everyone. "Yancy has spent a lifetime doodling on his napkins and
dangling from the end of the bar until they pushed him out the
door. And he has built an enviable multimillion dollar business
while doing it," he bragged.

Nobody laughed.

Chapter 32

IT WAS 1995. TIGY, A HUSBAND AND FATHER NOW, SAW to the everyday running of the Brighton businesses, leaving Yancy somewhat free to do what he loved most: look for other opportunities, perhaps even dive into a completely new adventure, and enjoy a game of golf, always with an ample supply of alcohol close by.

But all was not well in the Brighton family. Rachel had been experiencing severe stomach pains of late, so painful that her daily routine had begun to suffer. One day, Yancy came home to find her slumped over in pain, pressing on her stomach with both hands, and crying.

"What the hell?" asked Yancy, who knelt beside her, genuinely concerned. "You've been starving yourself, haven't you? Trying to lose weight. Damn it, I told you I like a woman with a little meat on her," he complained.

"Yancy, there's something wrong with me," she cried out. "I've been having these horrible pains for weeks now, and they're getting worse."

Yancy was peeved and said so. "Why do you allow yourself to suffer like this? You probably have appendicitis. Let's go see Doc Mel right now!" He was not only their personal physician, he was their friend and neighbor.

"No!" she objected, struggling to release his grasp. "Aren't you the great one? You've been needing surgery for months now, but you refuse to have it done!" she ranted. "It's the middle of the night, Yancy! I've already seen Doc anyway, and he gave me some pills."

"So what good did they do?" he argued, but he agreed to wait till morning.

The next day, Rachel was subjected to numerous medical tests, most of which offered no answer. Then one day, Dr. Mel made a personal phone call to the Brighton home. "I need you and Yancy to come by the office," he told Rachel.

Rachel couldn't bring herself to ask for more information. It couldn't be good news, she decided, or he would have told her on the phone. Why did Yancy have to accompany her? Was she dying?

She and Yancy were in Dr. Mel's office within the hour. The doctor's solemn expression was one of gloom. The usual niceties he greeted them with were either missing or limp at best.

"I'm afraid I have bad news," he finally said, his eyes focused everywhere but on their faces. "Rachel has cancer. I'm afraid it's inoperable," he quivered.

Yancy was unprepared. He squeezed his paper cup so hard, the liquid gushed out, saturating the carpet in the doctor's private office.

Rachel stared at her husband, the man who always had an answer to everything, whether in their family or someone else's. Family, friends, and acquaintances were constantly asking for Yancy's advice or seeking his help to solve their problems, and he inevitably came up with a solution. Was hers the only problem he couldn't solve? she asked in morbid silence while Yancy gulped the remaining drops of liquid from his damaged cup.

Dr. Mel ached to say something hopeful but dared not as he knew the prognosis was correct and nothing could change that. He had worried for months about Yancy's own health problem, which could be corrected with surgery if he didn't procrastinate too long.

It was a life-threatening condition that threatened to kill him at any given moment, but Yancy had delayed in spite of Rachel's insistence that he have surgery. With Rachel's problem surfacing, the doctor was afraid it would mean disaster for both of them.

The doctor was right. With Rachel apparently dying of cancer, Yancy's own health was the last thing on his mind. What was life worth without Rachel? he asked himself. Having lost most of his drink on the floor of the medical office, he was in a hurry to get a refill. On their way home, he stopped at the first liquor store, one of his own, poured straight whiskey in his cup, and swallowed it. He filled it again before driving home. His glass was empty when they arrived, but not for long.

"Don't worry, honey. We're going to Houston, and we're going tonight! Tigy's going to drive us. These damn doctors around here don't know anything. If they did, they wouldn't be here. They'd be in Houston."

After exhausting herself with deep, convulsive crying, Rachel abandoned the kitchen stool she had taken refuge on, grabbed the bottle Yancy had poured his last drink from, and smashed it across the corner of a kitchen cabinet. Her action sent sharp pieces of glass in several directions and left a strong odor of alcohol throughout the kitchen and adjoining living room.

Without further comment, Yancy emptied one bottle and struggled to open another. He settled in a straight-backed chair, the one that reminded him the most of a bar stool; took a few swallows; and succumbed to a short, noisy nap. So accustomed to this type of sleep, whether at the bar or at home, it was rare for him to spill his drink beyond a drop or two. On this occasion, however, he awakened to find his drinking hand grasping air, the glass having dropped on the tile floor and shattered. Its contents further permeated the air while slivers of glass completed the very recent floor decor Rachel had begun.

Meanwhile, Rachel had curled up on the love seat where she and Yancy had cuddled in their early days, as well as later, when, on rare occasions, they found themselves at home alone. The love seat occupied a favorite spot in the massive living room, where laughter had reigned during parties and family get-togethers. It was one of the first pieces of furniture they had purchased after their wedding day, and they had chosen it from Yancy's first furniture store. In spite of its wear and tear, they had chosen to take it with them when they moved to the new waterfront home, and Rachel had searched the fabric shops near and far to find a new cover that matched the old one.

She knew sleep wouldn't come—certainly not that night, perhaps never. She allowed herself to focus on the past as the present was too overbearing. She recalled the day Yancy had delivered the love seat to their modest little rental house. With scarcely anything else to occupy their sparsely furnished rental, they had enjoyed a laugh about how difficult it would be to fit the love seat in. It reminded her that everything in those days was funny and, therefore, fun.

She might have plowed her way through the night with more of those early pleasantries if the excruciating pain in her stomach hadn't demanded attention and made her face the reality of the moment. The truth was that Yancy had turned out to be Humpty Dumpty and had fallen off the pedestal she and everyone else had placed him on. What would happen to him when she was gone, she worried.

It was well past midnight when Yancy awakened enough to carry out any plans he had for his ailing wife. After making a survey of the altered room, he reached for the phone and began punching Dr. Mel's private telephone number into it. "I need you to make an appointment with the best cancer doctor in Houston. We're leaving right now," he announced without apology for waking the doctor at three in the morning. The doctor begged him not to go as he was a sick man himself, but Yancy ignored his pleas. Yancy and Tigy loaded Rachel's aching body in the station wagon and headed for Houston, not knowing if she would survive the trip or if they would be able to see a doctor once they arrived.

In Houston, Rachel's cancer-ravaged body was subjected to painful examinations and debilitating tests, all with the same prognosis: terminal cancer of the stomach. Inoperable. Two or three months to live. Once Yancy realized he was losing Rachel, he drank himself into total oblivion while Tigy and other family members and friends kept vigil.

Two months later, Rachel Brighton was dead.

Chapter 33

AT THE AGE OF 71, YANCY WAS FILLED WITH GRIEF FOR the loss of his wife, and he was dangerously ill himself. Without Rachel to pester him to have the surgery he so desperately needed, and in spite of his pain having increased considerably, he had made no effort to see a doctor. The loneliness was overwhelming.

Although never one to seek companionship, neither did he turn it away. When a married woman and a longtime acquaintance appeared virtually naked at his door one night, he invited her in. But there would be no romp in the sheets as his excessive intake of alcohol kept him dozing off and on. He spent the night in fitful sleep or roaming the floor in excruciating pain. When the pain subsided early the next morning, he fell into a deep sleep. When he awakened, the uninvited guest had either departed or had never been there. He wasn't certain which.

When Tigy dropped by the house the next day to check on his dad, he noticed immediately that something was amiss. The love seat had been moved from its designated spot in the living room. *Surely Dad didn't throw it out?* True, it was a relic by now, but it had occupied that space all of his life, and it had become a part of the family. He knew the story behind it, of his parents' lean years when it was the first piece of furniture they bought. While bemoaning the love seat's fate, he became aware of unusual noises coming from a back room. He traced the noise to the master bedroom. Stretched out lazily in the hot tub, humming with a sense of pure satisfaction, was a woman Tigy knew only as Chipmunk. Apparently it was a nickname she had earned as a stripper.

"What the hell are you doing here? So you're the culprit!" he accused. "What did you do with the love seat?" he yelled. Chipmunk smiled while rubbing her crotch in a sensuous display. "You shouldn't walk in on a lady while she's taking a bath, Tigy," she cooed.

"If I come across a lady, I'll remember that," Tigy snarled. Pointing a mean finger in her direction, he issued a stern warning. "If you ever touch my mother's things again, I'll have you arrested. Tell me what you did with the sofa, or I'll pour scalding hot water on your naked ass!" He left the room in a fevered huff and began searching the house. The love seat had been relegated to the laundry room after being dragged down a hallway, where it left a trail of damaged flooring in its wake. All manner of soiled items had been piled on top of the sofa, leaving it nearly invisible. Tigy cleaned the love seat as best he could, then dragged it back to its original spot in the living room. Tears continued to flow down his cheeks in spite of his efforts to cut them off. Rather than allow Chipmunk to see his weakness, he made a dash for the back door and left the premises, determined to find his dad.

Two hours or more into the search, he found Yancy on a bar stool in a competitor's business in Fort Walton Beach. Tigy was a smallish man, at least in stature, but he was a ton of bricks when it came to defending his dead mother. He had inherited his mother's good looks as well as her courage, and those two assets had carried him a long way in life. He faced his father with the intention of using both against him.

Overturning stools and disrupting conversations along his path, he pounded the bar with both fists as he glared into the face of a man who gave no indication that he understood the significance of his son's actions. Without regard for employees or customers, Tigy faced his dad and let go with a caustic bellow: "If you're gonna sleep with every whore in Okaloosa County, I wish you would meet them in a sleazy back-room bar, or anywhere but my mother's bedroom."

With Yancy showing no emotion whatsoever, Tigy threw his hands up in despair and left the premises, still fighting tears.

Several weeks later, father and son came face to face in one of Yancy's convenience stores. Following a lengthy silence and a horde of poignant stares, they embraced. "Hell, I don't know how she got in the house," Yancy declared.

"She musta had a key, Daddy! I didn't see a broken door any-where!" Tigy spouted. "What about the love seat? Didn't you won-der what happened to it?"

Yancy's startled expression was all the answer Tigy needed: Yancy hadn't missed it! "Hell, I don't take inventory every time I walk in the door. And you listen to me: I didn't give nobody a key," he added, his own anger beginning to show.

Tigy felt some relief. *Maybe he's telling the truth. She probably took his keys, along with any money he had in his wallet.* Still, she was in his mother's house, and that alone was more than he could easily deal with. He walked away without saying good-bye.

Less than three weeks later, Yancy's pains, already excruciating, had worsened to the point that he paid his doctor a visit. The doctor was not sympathetic. "Your procrastination in attending to this thing has shocked the medical profession in this area," the doctor began. "Aside from surgery, I can do nothing but offer you some pain pills." He gave Yancy a sample bottle and told the nurse to see that he took one before he left the office. "Have him wait around about thirty minutes or so after he swallows the pill to make sure he has no reaction He's that walking time bomb you're always hearing about." He turned to Yancy with more warning. "When you have this prescription filled, the pharmacist will warn you not to drink alcohol as long as you are taking them. Heed his advice!" he pleaded.

Two days later, Yancy was feeling much better, so much so that a drive around town and a visit to his convenience stores appealed to him. Even that turned out to be boring as none of his friends were around. Thinking he might find some of them at the country club, he drove there for the first time since Rachel died.

It was Sunday, always a popular day at the country club, and this Sunday was no different. The clubhouse grounds, in fact, were swamped with golfers. The practice tee and driving range were inundated. He knew what it meant: a mixer! He and Rachel had never missed one.

A look around the clubhouse, however, revealed only strangers. It was as if he had driven into the wrong golf club. But then, someone called his name. "Yancy! Hey, you wanna play?" Then another voice. "Yeah, Yancy, one team has a no-show. If you hurry, you can join them."

It was Lettie and Paul Mulberry, longtime friends. Yancy responded warmly to Lettie's hug and vigorously shook hands with Paul. "What did you do with everybody?" Yancy asked. "Where are the good guys?" he wondered out loud. "Hell, I'd be afraid to grab any of these women in the crotch."

The Mulberrys enjoyed a good laugh as did anyone in hearing distance. When Lettie gained control again, she explained. "We've got a lot of new members. Some of the old-timers have health problems, and some of the military retired and moved away."

"And a lot of them are dead," added Paul, "but there's still a few of us around."

Yancy smiled a little for the first time, prompting Lettie to throw her arms around his waist and rest her head on his chest in a welcome-back gesture. "Go sign in, Yancy," she begged. "There was a cancellation, so one of the teams is short a player. You know how that is. It's no fun playing without a full team."

"But you have to hurry," Paul warned. But speed was not something Yancy was noted for, and Paul remembered that. He tossed his own golf bag on the ground and headed for the club storage area where Yancy had always kept his clubs. "I'll put your clubs in a cart and bring 'em up to you," Paul yelled back.

Yancy appeared bewildered as he continued to stare at the unfriendly faces going past him, none of which were familiar. "I need a drink," he finally told his disappointed friends.

Lettie and Paul watched solemnly as their friend ambled toward the clubhouse bar. "He needs to get back out here, meet folks, and play golf," Paul noted.

Lettie shook her head. "Without Rachel? I don't see that happening."

Paul wasn't so sure. "He still runs a successful business without her."

"That may be true," agreed Lettie, "but before he met her, his social life consisted of a bar stool and a bar. She made him get out here for every event. I'm afraid he died when she did."

It was more than four hours later that the Mulberrys and the rest of the field began to file into the clubhouse. To the Mulberrys' surprise, Yancy was still there, parked on a bar stool, cuddling a drink in one hand and a cigarette in the other. He appeared unaware of his surroundings.

"Oh my God, look at him," whispered Lettie. "He can't find his mouth, Paul. We have to help him. He's wet all over." He had spilled much of his drink, perhaps most of it, as well as previous ones, on the table, the floor, and himself. "They shouldn't be selling him any more drinks," she noted.

As they watched Yancy disembark, albeit with great difficulty, from his bar stool, they contemplated what, if anything, they could do. "We ought to take him home if he can walk to the car. He may not know a single person here except us," noted Paul.

Even as they pondered the situation, Yancy wobbled across the room, bumping into everyone he met while attempting to salvage what he apparently thought was a drink, but his glass was empty.

"Oh, look! He's talking to Jim," Lettie noted. "He and Jim are good friends so that lets us off the hook," she rallied. Satisfied Jim would take charge, the Mulberrys joined their playing partners to rehash their games and enjoy the food and drink, arguably the best part of the golf mixer.

Jim Stone, also a new widower, greeted Yancy warmly and attempted to carry on a conversation, but he soon realized his old friend was in no condition to do that. Without an invitation, Yancy took the only available seat at Jim's table, where he recognized no one and vice versa. Jim tried to introduce him to the others, but Yancy's only response was that he needed a drink.

"Seems to me that's the last thing he needs," noted a woman seated at the table, and others agreed, albeit silently.

"Come on, Yancy, let's go get you that drink," offered Jim, who attempted to lead him away from the appalled group. "Maybe a cup of coffee. Those girls in the kitchen make a mean cup of coffee."

Jim's ploy didn't work. "Hell, I don't want no damn coffee," Yancy informed him. Irritated by what he considered an insult, Yancy made an effort to stand up, perhaps to refill his drink, but in doing so, he bumped the table, overturning drinks, freshly made bowls of dips, and other delicacies, leaving a soggy mess dripping from the table's edge and onto the ladies' fashionable golfing attire. The noisy episode that followed captured the attention of everyone in the clubhouse and led to verbal attacks hurled at what most considered an unwelcome intruder to their party. Unaware of having caused any upheaval, Yancy announced with a growing show of irritation that he needed a drink.

Lettie and Paul came to the rescue. While Lettie tried to pacify Yancy, her husband discussed the situation with Jim.

"Somebody needs to drive him home before things get worse," Paul told Jim. "If he leaves here behind a wheel ..." He stopped short of mentioning the club's liability or the danger to Yancy and other drivers on the road. "You see what I mean?"

"Yeah, we can't let that happen," said Jim. "I would drive him, but I don't think I can find his house at night."

"Sure you can. It's the same old place where we used to attend all those house parties," Paul reminded him.

"Yeah, but my wife always did the driving," Jim pointed out. It was true. Jim's vision was impaired, especially at night, so Nelda had been their designated driver at night. Sadly, Jim had lost his wife more than six months earlier, so he was faced with either driving himself at night or staying home.

"I got to pee," announced Yancy, who was totally unaware of the uproar he was causing. He followed the announcement with a more familiar one: "I need a drink." In an attempt to stand up, he fell back in his original seat, now soaked with a mix of alcohol, coke, and water.

"I got to pee!" he yelped, prompting Paul to wonder if he really did or if he was simply confused by the puddle of liquid he was sitting in. In any case, the notion of taking him to the men's room suggested a solution to the problem.

"I'll take him to the men's room and maybe while he's fumbling around, I can get his car keys," said Paul. "If you drive him home, Lettie can ride with you and show you the way, and I'll drive behind and we can bring you back to the club."

Although neither man was happy with the plan, they agreed to it, and Paul began to carry it out by leading Yancy to the men's room. After relieving himself, Yancy struggled to pull his pants up, giving Paul an excuse to make physical contact. He rummaged in

Yancy's pockets in search of a car key. When his hand felt a piece of cold metal, he rallied, thinking it was a set of keys.

It was a gun!

He quickly replaced the tiny weapon, a derringer handgun, and began searching Yancy's other pockets until he found a set of keys.

"I need a drink!" Yancy bellowed in frustrated anger.

"I'll tell you what, Yancy. Why don't we just go home and get a drink? This lousy place won't even bring a man a drink when he needs one," Paul fussed pretentiously as he passed the keys to Jim. "We're all going to Yancy's house where we can get a drink," Paul told Jim who understood the ruse and nodded agreement. The notion seemed to appeal to Yancy, so Paul began a harrowing struggle to lead his drunken friend out of the clubhouse. Once accomplished, Jim waited in Yancy's car with Lettie in the backseat.

On the drive home, Jim tried to make conversation. "Yancy, what happened to you? I don't think I've ever seen you like this."

"Yeah, I been bad," admitted Yancy, who attempted to answer his ringing cell phone. Jim tried to help, but when he reached for the phone, the instrument fell to the floor where it continued to ring, stopped now and then, and soon rang again. Lettie tried reaching it from the backseat, but she always found herself bumping into Yancy in her efforts, so she let it go.

"Never mind. We'll call 'em back when we get to your house," Jim offered. It suddenly occurred to Jim that no one would be at Yancy's house when they arrive, and in his condition he might pose a danger to himself. "Will there be anyone at your house, Yancy?" He made up his mind that if the house was empty, he would stay with Yancy until he could get in touch with Tigy.

"What's it to you?" slurred Yancy. "I'm gonna kill you when we get there."

"Oh, Yancy, stop kidding around. I just wondered if Tigy or any of his family will be there," Jim explained.

"What's it to you? "I'm gonna kill you when we get there," Yancy repeated.

Jim found himself in something of a dither as it was an unusually dark night and some of the street lights weren't working. As to Yancy's threats, both Lettie and Jim saw them as the talk of a drunkard who didn't realize what he was saying. Still, it added to their discomfort.

"There's a side street. Should I turn here, Yancy?" asked Jim, whose voice revealed a hint of growing concern.

"F——k you," said Yancy without raising his head from the deep slump he had assumed from the beginning.

Meanwhile, Lettie grew anxious. The dirty talk was embarrassing and the threats of murder shocking. She became so enmeshed with the surprising turn of events that she forgot she was along to give directions. She missed the turn that would have taken them to Yancy's house.

Taking in a deep breath of fear, she offered a tense apology to Jim. "Sorry. I think we passed the turn. It's so dark, I can't make anything out. What happened to the street lights?" she asked nervously.

"Come on, Yancy, help us here," begged Jim, who was far from comfortable with the situation.

"Aw hell!" Yancy blasted. "I'm gonna kill you when we get there," declared Yancy for the third time.

Lettie's worries shifted to her husband's whereabouts. What could be keeping him? Had he had an accident? She sat on the edge of the backseat, peering at the back of Yancy's head, grateful that he appeared still and lifeless and hopefully too inebriated to carry out his threat to kill anyone. For a short second, she thought about Rachel and wondered if she had been subjected to frequent situations like this. *Ah, this wouldn't be happening if Rachel were alive,* she told herself.

After Jim turned the car around, Lettie planted her eyes on the road, determined not to miss the Brightons' street again. "There it is!" she soon shouted and then quickly slapped her hand against her mouth for fear of bringing Yancy's attention to her presence in the car.

Jim managed to turn on the street and into the Brightons' narrow driveway in spite of Lettie's late calls, allowing her to relax for the first time since leaving the clubhouse.

"Is this okay right here, Yancy?" Jim asked. "Or should I pull into the garage?"

Yancy made no comment, but Lettie noticed that he turned toward Jim for the first time since they left the club, and almost immediately there was a popping sound like that of a firecracker, apparently inside the car!

"What was that?" Lettie shouted as the emotions she had held back exploded.

"He shot me," Jim moaned, a mix of emotions evident in his voice.

Lettie watched in horror as Jim slumped onto the wheel and Yancy settled back in his seat, apparently content with himself for carrying out his threat. The car's engine was still running, the lights still on. Lettie was torn between helping Jim and slipping quietly out the back door and into the dark street where she hoped her husband would surely be waiting. But as Yancy appeared to be napping, she dared reach over the seat and lift Jim's shirt. When she saw blood oozing from Jim's side like a dripping faucet, she eased out the vehicle's back door and headed for the nearest house with its lights on.

By the time an ambulance arrived, it was too late. Jim Stone, a recently widowed decorated war hero, doting father, and Yancy's golfing friend, was dead.

When Yancy awoke the next morning, he was huddled on a thin mattress two inches too short for his long, six-foot, two-inch frame, and shackled by wrist and ankle bracelets. Already writhing from pain in his stomach and esophagus, the near constant pain in his back had worsened, probably as a result of the substandard bedding. He began to wonder if he had died and gone to hell. Looking to his left, he got a glimpse of an unshaven man in an ill-fitting orange jumpsuit. The stranger leaned against an iron bar that separated him from Yancy, holding an unfolded newspaper in front of him while eyeing Yancy with a smirk on his face. For once in his life, Yancy wanted to talk to someone, to anyone, with hopes of learning where he was and what he was doing there. He tried several times to speak, but the effort set his throat on fire, making speech impossible.

"What did you have against this fella?" asked the man with the newspaper. He held up the front page of the local paper for Yancy's perusal, folded it, and pushed it through the bars that separated them. Yancy couldn't read the small print without his glasses, and as far as he knew, he had no personal items with him. The headline, however, was huge: *Yancy Brighton Murders Good Friend.* That he could read!

Was he having a nightmare? he wondered. Or had he been committed to an insane asylum? Judging from his bruises, he must have put up a damn good fight. He tried to lift his aching legs off the tiny cot but quickly realized it was impossible as sometime during the night he had accumulated heavy leg irons that rubbed against his thin, bleeding skin. Ignoring the stares of his next-door neighbor, he noticed for the first time that his own attire was also an ugly, ill-fitting orange jumpsuit, identical to that worn by his disagreeable neighbor. To worsen matters, he knew he would need to carry on a conversation with the obnoxious fella in the next cell if he wanted to know anything at all about the dilemma he found himself in.

Before acting on that decision, he heard familiar voices in the hallway. It was Tigy, together with Dag Brewer, a very popular trial lawyer Yancy had known all of the young man's life.

"You want to tell me what I'm doing here?" Yancy asked, grimacing with pain from excruciating back problems, the same ones he had dealt with before Rachel died. Her pleas to have a much needed operation had gone unheeded and now he was faced with multiple new pains. A burning throat was only one of them.

"Just hold on, Yancy, said the lawyer." While Tigy tried to comfort his father, his attorney arranged for his client to be moved to a private room where they could talk. Once settled there, Tigy recounted the events of the previous night.

Yancy responded with a vacant, incomprehensible stare.

"Dag's gonna see about getting you admitted to the hospital, Dad, so you can have that surgery Mama begged you to get," said Tigy.

"Get me out of here!" he demanded as he slumped in his chair, alternately rubbing his bruised ankles and aching back and attempting to cope with the growing pain in his throat. Otherwise, he showed little interest in the conversation.

"I'll try to get you out on bail, Yancy, but you know a man is dead and everything points to you as the killer. It's gonna take a million bucks and a host of character witnesses," he warned. With little assistance from their confused prisoner, Tigy and Dag Brewer left the jail with promises to return shortly.

At the lawyer's suggestion, Tigy began gathering real estate titles as collateral for bail while also contacting Yancy's friends from all walks of life to attest to his father's good character. That turned out to be his easiest task. The meek and the mighty spoke well of Yancy, and every man or woman who was approached agreed to testify to his honesty, integrity, and good will toward others. Clete and Casey were among the first volunteers. Both decided that David was too frail to withstand the ordeal of testifying.

Casey was called first. "Yancy Brighton is the kindest man I have ever known, and I have known him all of my life," she declared at the bail hearing.

"Does Mr. Brighton ever lose his temper?" asked the prosecuting attorney.

"Of course! Who doesn't?"

Before the judge could caution her against commenting beyond answering the questions, she continued. "He threw a fit when I tried to make him vomit some bad stuff out of his system! Total loss of his temper," she admitted, causing Tigy to slap his hand against his slumped forehead in utter defeat. *What is she doing?* he wondered.

"Tell us about that," demanded an excited prosecuting attorney. "Did he threaten you? Describe his demeanor at that time!" he harped. At six feet, five inches tall, he had to curl his body into something of a knot in order to plant his face within inches of tiny Casey, his cold eyes staring menacingly into hers.

"Well, I made him eat a lot of bitter herbs, you know, and they made him vomit his guts out. "Of course, anybody else would have slit my throat," she added, easing Tigy's emotions and creating laughter throughout the room.

In an attempt to undo the damage, the prosecutor lashed out with another question he hoped would dismantle the public image of Yancy Brighton as an easygoing man even when he was drunk. "Did he make any threats? Did he strike you?" While the public defender struggled to unravel his uncomfortable position, Casey grabbed the chair arms and lifted herself up high enough to inhale the man's exhaled breath, but instead of shouting as her questioner expected, she spoke softly and caringly. "Oh, no, sir! He cried like the baby he was. He was only five years old, and he was just as humble then as he is today." While laughter permeated the room, the prosecutor was quick to say he had no more questions for this witness.

Clete, who was second in line, declared Yancy was the best friend anyone could ever have. "My father-in-law, Mr. David Stewart, is not well enough to come to court, but I have a signed letter from him offering enough Stewart Enterprise property to cover Mr. Brighton's entire bail. Claude Covey, a Florida state senator testified that Yancy would never knowingly or willingly hurt anyone. Quite the contrary in fact. All manner of people flock to him when they need help, and he has always obliged them. Been that way all of his life, beginning I understand when he was just a teenager."

"Would you put up your own collateral for his bail?" asked the judge.

"In a heartbeat," said the senator. "He has served on the governor's board of trustees, and he was appointed by the governor to the Northwest Florida Water Management District. I shudder to think how the community would have managed without him, to tell you the truth. Yes, I and my entire family would gladly post our own properties to cover his bail," he added.

And so it went all morning. Other business owners called him their nicest competitor, and many offered all their assets toward Yancy's bail. Air Force officers and enlisted men, Niceville's chief of police, educators, city directors, mayors, city council members, county commissioners, and scores of others testified and sent letters of praise for Yancy.

Within the confines of the court, it appeared the entire community and beyond was willing to post Yancy's bail. But the truth was that the population of Okaloosa County had nearly tripled since Rachel died, and Yancy hadn't kept up the active social pace the couple had once engaged in. This new lifestyle meant that most newcomers to the area, including new country club members, had never heard of Yancy Brighton. Their introduction to him was a sordid account of his behavior the night he allegedly shot and killed his friend who tried to help him. Letters to the newspaper editor, all strangers to Yancy, called for him to pay the ultimate price for his actions. Clearly, the general public, excluding old-timers and their offspring, had no sympathy for a man they were convinced had murdered a man who had befriended him. New country club members began to call for his membership resignation.

Before the session ended, Yancy's attorney called a specialist in forensic science to the stand to advise the court of Yancy's medical condition.

"Have you made any type of diagnosis as to Mr. Brighton's medical condition?" Dag asked the doctor.

"Yes, I have," said Dr. Tubrin. "Mr. Brighton has an abdominal aortic aneurysm. He also has blood pressure issues, and he suffers from major depression and alcohol dependency," he added.

"Is he taking any prescription medications for these problems?" asked Dag.

"Yes, he takes blood pressure medicine and a drug called Paxil, which is an anti-depressant. He also takes Klonopin, an antianxiety pill."

"In your professional opinion, Dr. Tubrin, could these medications cause mental confusion for a patient if he consumed alcohol while taking them?"

"Absolutely," Tubrin stated emphatically. "A combination of these medications with alcohol generally causes significant difficulties in one's thinking and has been known to alter the patient's mind."

Further testimony from the doctor revealed that surgery could repair the aneurysm. "His situation is life threatening, and surgery should have been performed years ago," the doctor told the court.

The judge chose not to rule on the bail issue immediately. He ordered that Yancy be admitted to the prison hospital and prepared for surgery.

When the public heard that Yancy might be released on bail, they reacted with unsigned letters and anonymous phone calls to the Brightons' chain of businesses—hotels, convenience centers, apartment complexes—as well as their home and those of their close friends. These venomous calls and letters often threatened the judge and the family, as well as anyone associated with releasing this "dangerous killer." Letters to the editor spoke for other nettled citizens who disapproved of "this killer's being turned loose on the streets," and they didn't mind signing their names.

While everyone awaited the judge's decision, news about the case didn't reach the public fast enough to please them. They hugged their TV screens and kept an early morning watch for their newspapers. The pressure of it all had taken a severe toll on Tigy and his family. He spent day and night trying to balance his young family's needs and concerns with depressing visits to the jail while also dealing with legal matters and running the Brighton businesses by himself. Through it all, he was obliged to endure scathing remarks and death threats from the irate public.

All of it seemed to come to a head one day when he arrived at the prison hospital, sullen, depressed, and exhausted. With his father facing major surgery and with the public fighting his release on bail, life had become all too burdensome. He acknowledged his father with a cold nod before taking a seat in a far corner of the room.

Yancy was quick to notice. He knew it was not a good time to start a conversation. Instead, he asked to see the local paper.

"Why would you want to read all that crap?" Tigy snapped. "It'll just make you mad as hell. I wish I hadn't read it."

"I don't live in a make-believe world!" Yancy snapped.

"The hell you don't!" Tigy shouted. "You've made believe all of my life that alcohol wasn't doing you any harm. Well, the truth is, they had to postpone your surgery so they can attempt to prepare your alcohol-abused body for surgery!"

"Bring me the damn paper!" Yancy ordered, his strained voice a testament to his condition.

Jumping up abruptly from the stool he had just straddled, Tigy motioned to the guard that he wanted to leave. He soon returned with the paper, which he tossed angrily onto his father's lap.

"Go ahead, read it! You won't find the real news in it, so let me fill you in. People whisper everywhere we go. Tammy and me—well, we're adults, so we pretend we don't see their angry stares or hear their ugly gossip. But the kids? They're coming home from school in tears. Their classmates jeer at them, point fingers, and tell them their grandpa is a murderer!" Stopping just long enough to dab at his eyes and blow his nose, he continued in the same vein. "That's not the worst of it. We know the children in the area are imitating their parents, and some of them are our so-called friends, Dad!" He hid his face in his hands and bawled like a baby. Once he recovered, he continued. "Every morning I throw the paper in my truck so the children can't read the horror stories. We had our TV switched off permanently because we don't want them to see their Grampie in a prison uniform and dragging leg chains. Except for dire necessities, we dare not go out anymore," he moaned in pity.

Yancy was clearly shaken. For the first time in his life, he was faced with a problem for which he had no answer. Even in the beginning, when the prosecuting attorney had announced to the public that he would prove Yancy guilty of first-degree murder and that he would seek the death penalty, Yancy remained outwardly calm. This latest revelation, however, produced the struggle of his lifetime.

He recognized the problem Tigy described as something out of his league. "I wish your mother was here," he mumbled in solemn misery.

Tigy stood up in heated anger. Bold and previously unseen wrinkles appeared around his eyes and mouth. "Mama?" he snapped. "If Mama was here, this never would have happened!" he coldly declared.

Yancy felt the sting, and his tortured face revealed as much. Tigy left without completing the tirade he had intended to dump in his father's lap.

After a sleepless night, Tigy reluctantly returned the following day, his spirits having dipped to a new low. To his surprise, his father was in good spirits even as nurses prepared him for major surgery. Although heavily guarded by an armed officer of the law, his ankle and wrist chains had been removed for the surgical procedure. "If I'd known surgery would get me out of my heavy jewelry, I would have signed up for it a long time ago," joked Yancy, giving Tigy and the hospital attendants an excuse to laugh. Even the armed guard guffawed, offering the first hint to Yancy and Tigy that he was human.

Surgery went well according to the doctors, but it took a heavy toll on Yancy's already weakened mental and physical condition. It took several days of healing for him to show signs of recovery, enough that he requested a pencil from the hard-nosed guard.

"Afraid not," the guard grumbled. "My orders are that you are to have nothing with a sharp point."

"Yes, well, I can understand the risk you'd be taking," Yancy mocked weakly. "All I want to do is make a few notes on this napkin here." When the guard ignored him, Yancy continued his spiel. "Maybe if you cocked your pistol and kept it pointed between my eyes while I jot down a few words, you'd feel safer," he cajoled.

The guard's face reddened. After checking with his superior officer, he presented Yancy with a dull-pointed pencil, the very kind he had used in the past to plan his multimillion dollar business while parked on a bar stool.

He examined the writing instrument and grinned facetiously, causing the guard to flush a brilliant red. Yancy took a napkin from his breakfast plate and began marking on it. By the time Tigy came for his daily visit, Yancy had marked on every napkin on his plate and had requested more.

It was a good sign, and Tigy knew it. "Man, have I been waiting for this day," he said in greeting. "Now I know you're on the mend. What you got there?" he probed.

"I want you to get in touch with Claude Hammerlock in Miami. Dag can help you find him," he ordered.

"Hammerlock!" yelled Tigy. "You mean that lawyer who got the Arrowsmith boy off? Do you know him?" he asked.

"No, but I think enough money will get me an introduction," quipped Yancy.

"Good idea," said Tigy, energized by the notion. The Arrowsmith boy was part of an ultrawealthy family from California. The boy had been accused of rape and the evidence against him had been overwhelming, but Hammerlock had managed to convince the jury that the boy was innocent. The case had made national news, prompting an outcry from the general public, who felt the famous, high-society Arrowsmith family had bought their son's freedom. But Hammerlock escaped the gossip, his reputation unscathed. And now, he was sought by more clients than he could easily handle. Yancy Brighton would be only one of them.

"What else?" asked Tigy. "I see you've depleted the hospital's supply of napkins," he joked.

"Yeah," acknowledged Yancy. He shuffled the napkins about with trembling hands, seemingly without purpose and then finally looked Tigy in the eyes for the first time since he was incarcerated.

Apparently he had something to say that didn't come easily. "How is Jim's boy doing?"

The question altered Tigy's mood considerably. "How is he doing?" he repeated with tongue-laden venom. "He's devastated, Dad. He lost his mother a few months ago, and now his dad has been murdered by one of his so-called friends. Quite naturally, he wants to see you hang!"

Yancy reached for his pencil, but his hand shook so violently that he gave up and settled back in his bed. In addition to his other physical problems, he had been diagnosed with Parkinson's, a disease that made writing difficult, among other things. All the recent notes he had written had worsened his grasp to the point that holding a pencil with his quivering fingers was something he could no longer accomplish easily. Tigy's comment had sent Yancy into one of the worst hand-shakings he had endured thus far, making it impossible for him to pick up the napkin he had written on just moments earlier.

Tigy felt drained of all energies. Sympathies for his dad ran hot and cold. He found himself caught in the middle of a bad situation not of his making and one that apparently had no solution. He had caught glimpses of Jim Stone's son, who had been friendly with Tigy in the past. When he saw the boy sitting through grueling grand jury procedures, he relived the pain of losing his own mother, but in spite of his misery, his heart ached for Jim's only child, who had lost both of his parents. He knew what the boy didn't, that the pain would never cease.

"Do you think he understands that I never meant to harm his dad?" Yancy asked.

"He understands you were drunk. But that doesn't ease the pain of losing his only living parent," Tigy added with malice as he rose to leave. "I'll get started with Hammerlock," he grumbled on his way out.

When he returned the next day, he caught his dad fumbling in the lone drawer to a bedside table.

"Unless you're looking for a crumpled napkin you've already scribbled on, you won't find it in that drawer, Tigy told him. Tigy appeared to be in the same mood he had left in the day before.

"What about Claude Hammerlock? Have you heard anything?" asked Yancy.

"Yeah, and I think you can forget about him. He told Dag he'd need a hundred thousand dollar retainer just to make a quick trip here." Tigy laughed nervously. "What do you want to do?"

"Pay it!" Yancy barked.

By noon the following day, everyone associated with the case was called to the judge's chambers. The judge had made a decision regarding bail.

The judge began with a few legal comments, none of which Yancy or Tigy understood or would remember, but they would never forget the judge's last three words.

"Bail is denied."

Chapter 34

THE ONLY GOOD NEWS IN THE BRIGHTON CORNER WAS that Claude Hammerlock, the high-profile lawyer from Miami, was on his way to Niceville! Newspapers had a heyday covering the famous lawyer's presence in Okaloosa County, easily pushing the importance of the Brighton story above all other news.

Hammerlock announced early on that he had very little time to devote to the case as he was involved in another high-profile case in Miami. After Hammerlock reviewed Yancy's case and discussed his findings with Dag Brewer, the two attorneys held a meeting with Yancy and Tigy.

Hammerlock was brief. "The woman who witnessed this alleged shooting is very believable," he began. "Her testimony regarding your threats to shoot the victim and your carrying out the threat would be devastating coming from her mouth. You see honesty written all over her face, hear honesty in her voice. Model citizen in the community: nondrinker, active in her church, community volunteer—I'm afraid the list is endless, and it's not in your favor. Nobody on that jury is going to doubt her word, and frankly, that would include me," Hammerlock admitted.

"I would advise you to try a plea bargain," he continued. "Perhaps offer the victim's son a sizable compensation. If the family isn't pushing for your demise, the court is more amenable to a plea bargain. Worth a try," he concluded.

After Hammerlock left the premises, Yancy retrieved the crumpled paper napkins he had tossed in the drawer the previous day. He invited Tigy to take a look. "Pretty expensive advice," he said glumly, "when you consider I had already put the ape's brilliant idea on paper."

News that Yancy Brighton was attempting to buy his way out of a murder charge created a public outcry. Threats and insults were not limited to the Brighton family. Lawyers for both parties, the legal system itself, the judge, and even the potential jurors were demonized for allowing "the filthy rich bastard to buy his way out of murder."

His only hope was a plea bargain, and that hinged on Jim Stone's son. Before entering the prison hospital one morning, Tigy forced himself to face reality. *Without the plea bargain, Dad's life is over because he'll never survive prison life,* he thought. *And if they do accept it, the whole damn Brighton family is dead because the public is going to hang every single one of us.*

Facing the entrance to the hospital, he was too stressed to push the button and wait an eternity for a faceless prison clerk to let him into a place he didn't want to enter. For a long time, he had struggled with the notion of paying David Stewart a visit. In his nineties now, David had become a recluse who never left his house and rarely accepted visitors.

Yancy was one of the few who had kept in touch in spite of David's withdrawal from society, and Tigy remembered his dad's mentioning that David's mind was "as keen as ever." In Tigy's desperation, it was all he needed to know. Instead of entering the prison hospital, he dared to pay David Stewart an unannounced visit.

David was instantly sympathetic. "I know it's been tough, Tigy. But you seem to have a grip on things."

"No, sir. I'm afraid I do not," admitted Tigy. He stared at David, once a leader in the community, admired and envied by nearly everyone, and now a recluse who shunned the public he once loved and thrived on. Tigy had known him all of his life but mostly from afar. Still, Tigy's dad, and his dad's dad before him, had always spoken highly of David, even revered him. Tigy grew up thinking of David Stewart as some kind of god or maybe one of those saints the preacher was always talking about.

"I understand your bitterness," David offered. "You're angry, perhaps at your father for putting you in this position? You resent being caught in the middle of a nightmare you had no part in creating. You're still grieving over the loss of your mother, and you wish above all else that she were here to see the family through this? Did I leave anything out?"

Tigy was overwhelmed. In addition to everything else, was David a prophet? Did he have access to the past and could he foretell the future? "If you know all that, you must surely know my mother was the glue that held our family together!" Tigy blurted. He turned his face away from David, struggled to get his handkerchief out of a tight pants pocket, and cried in spite of a brave fight to hold his tears.

David's facial expressions remained constant, almost as if he hadn't heard the declaration or noticed that his visitor had lost control of his emotions. "I know your mother was a strong woman," he said, "but I wouldn't take anything away from your dad. His demise is an ugly commentary on society, not him."

"Society?" asked a shocked young man.

"Society," David repeated. "It starts with an individual who has a warped idea of right and wrong. He gets the notion that he is superior to someone else, and he captures the attention of others who agree with him. Before long, they have formed a mob. As such, they jostle and annoy others in an attempt to destroy their notions of propriety, fairness, and truth, things none of them would have the courage to do as individuals. Unlike individuals, the mob has no conscience, so there's nothing to hinder its actions."

Tigy was unprepared. "The only mob I've seen so far, sir, is a mob of women coming to my dad's house and it wasn't no time before he was sharing my mother's bed with some of them."

David ignored the comment, irritating Tigy to an all-time high and prompting him to consider leaving without taking the seat he had been offered. Instead, he chose to introduce a subject he had previously given a lot of thought.

"Look at you, Mr. David. You are a wealthy widower just like my dad is. I'm sure lots of women knocked on your door since Miss Mary Sam died, but you didn't answer it, did you, sir?" There had been no gossip surrounding any sexual misconduct on David's part before or after Mary Sam's death.

David's response shocked his young visitor. "Your dad made mistakes, son. All of us make mistakes, especially when we're dealing with stress, and I can attest to the fact that nothing is more stressful than losing your wife!" he scolded.

David rested a moment before continuing. Tigy maintained a respectful silence.

"Your dad had access to the area's ample supply of moonshine—rotgut might be a more appropriate name for it—before he was old enough to go to school. Half of us in these parts produced the poisonous mash, and none of us did anything to stop him, an innocent child, from drinking it. He became dependent on the stuff, and that dependency has led to tragedy. Imagine what he might have accomplished if we had acted like responsible individuals. But each one of us hid behind each other and accepted no personal responsibility for our crimes. Our only concern was our pocketbooks. We went to extremes to hide our moneymaking poison from federal agents, but we made no effort to keep it hidden from our children! As an individual, my conscience would not have allowed me to do that, but as part of the conscience-free mob, it was easy." He either couldn't continue or chose not to.

Tigy felt defeated. With his dad headed for prison or the electric chair, it was too late to dwell on what had brought him to this stage in life. No jury was going to set his dad free and send the rest of society to prison! Was David's mind still as sharp as Yancy thought it was?

"As to those short moments of pleasure you spoke of?" David continued. "Your dad was not capable of making any decisions at that point. It was a straw he grabbed, hoping it would alleviate the pain of losing his precious wife. When it didn't help, he turned exclusively to alcohol, which is what alcoholics do. Alcohol, of course, only worsens a bad situation. He's no prouder of himself than you are, Tigy. I speak from experience."

Tigy wasn't certain what he had expected from David, but praise for his father, an alcoholic who had been accused of murder, was definitely not it. Still, he was quite taken by the analysis he had drawn of Yancy's life. He began to listen with renewed interest.

"Don't make the mistake of putting me on a pedestal," David continued. "The only woman I turned away was my wife!" he admitted. "Take a good look at me, son. Do you really think I've handled my life any better than your dad?"

Tigy took a prolonged look at a wretched man, drugged with unhappiness and grieving over his own heinous mistakes. Tigy wanted to settle in and listen as long as David could hold up, but he realized the elderly gentleman's confessions had created an unpleasant emotional state for him. Tigy stood up, apologized for barging in unannounced, and thanked David warmly for receiving him in his home. He took David's shriveled hands in his and held them tenderly. "Please, sir, don't get up. I'll see myself out," he insisted.

"Don't pity me," said David, who motioned for Tigy to take a seat again. "I deserve the punishment you're witnessing. When Mary Sam committed suicide, so did I. It's part of my punishment. Don't make the mistake of not giving your dad the credit he deserves. Not many men could have survived the trauma of losing his beloved wife; knowing he killed his friend; undergoing life-threatening surgery; and dealing with the courts, the angry public, and public degradation while suffering the agony of alcohol withdrawal. The very fact that he has survived this onslaught speaks for his strength and courage."

David took as deep a breath as his system could handle before continuing. "Your dad is no longer under the influence of alcohol, so he's finally able to make his own decisions. Let him! I'm certain he will prevail."

Tigy felt as if he had been forced to grow up in a matter of minutes. David's description of mobs seemed like rubbish at first, excuses for poor behavior at best, but now? He wondered.

Tigy had grown up hearing the story of David's audacious crime, that of marrying "that Indian squaw" when he could have had his pick of white daughters throughout the county.

Gossip and hatred surrounding the Stewarts' union in marriage had survived two generations but had begun to fade by the time Tigy came along. It had resurfaced for a while after Mary Sam committed suicide, but it had never been of much interest to Tigy.

But after listening to David, he realized for the first time the negative impact that prejudice had imposed on his little hometown. When David took an Indian bride, white folks had obviously made it their mission to destroy the marriage of two people who deeply loved each other. It was indeed the work of the mob, the one with no conscience, and the same one David blamed for Yancy's demise.

Tigy arrived at the prison hospital with a new attitude, and Yancy noticed immediately. For the first time since Rachel's death, the two chatted warmly about their beloved wife and mother. Both of them cried softly before Tigy gave his dad a loving hug good night.

Two days later, Yancy had healed enough to return to his jail cell. Within a week, they received news that the judge had made a decision regarding Yancy's fate. They were to appear in court the following day.

The judge was brief. "I have taken into account your personal letter, Mr. Brighton, in which you expressed deep remorse for your act, as well as your desire to make restitution to the victim's only child. I also have in my possession a letter from the victim's son. He has taken into account your altered mental condition the night of the incident, stating that he does not believe you meant to harm his father. Also, because of your advanced age and your poor health, he believes little would be gained by sending you to prison for life."

As usual, Yancy's expression, or lack of it, gave no hint as to his feelings. For folks who didn't know him, he appeared to have no interest whatsoever in the outcome of the court proceedings.

"However," continued the judge, "in the court's opinion, alcoholism is no excuse for breaking the law, and certainly not for taking an innocent man's life."

My God, thought Tigy. *He's going to prison anyway.*

"Mr. Brighton, the court recognizes that you may very well have been unable to distinguish right from wrong in your inebriated condition on the night in question," the judge continued. "However, you knew, or should have known, your history for excessive drinking once you consumed that first drink of alcohol, and yet you chose to take that drink anyway. Therefore, it is the opinion of this court that you should be punished for your actions."

Tigy began shedding bitter tears. He knew his dad wouldn't survive a harsh prison life. His misery, however, was premature.

"I sentence you to three years in prison," said the judge. "You will be given credit for the eight months you have been incarcerated."

Yancy had twenty-eight months left to serve. Would he survive it? everyone wondered. Even if he did, he was to adhere to a strict probation for fifteen years. He was never to take a drink of alcohol or even enter an establishment where alcohol was served, and that included his own such establishments. There were other rules as well, and the judge was quick to warn Yancy, "If you break a single one of these rules, you will be returned to prison, where you will remain for the rest of your natural life."

Chapter 35

WHILE THREE YEARS IN PRISON FOR A MAN WHO SHOT and killed an innocent man may have tried the public's patience, for Yancy Brighton, it was likely more than a lifetime. He was still weak from surgery and suffering from numerous ailments brought on from long-term alcohol consumption. His throat and lungs had deteriorated from a lifetime of smoking, and his esophagus, stomach, and liver struggled to carry on their duties after being battered by excessive alcohol most of his life. Parkinson's disease had taken its toll as well, making it nearly impossible for him to get food from hand to mouth without ruining his clothes. He often left the table hungry as a result of spilling most of his food before it reached his mouth.

His physical condition was so advanced that prison officials had difficulty finding a job Yancy was capable of handling. He was eventually ordered to wrap spoons in paper napkins to be used by other prisoners at mealtime. With his shaky hands, even that was an arduous task.

Sleep wouldn't come during the long, lonely nights, but he saw this as an opportunity to take stock of things. One night, he picked up one of the many Bibles that friends had sent to the prison. He began flipping through Genesis until he came to the story of Jacob and read it through for the second time, the first having occurred more than fifty years earlier while he was serving in the merchant marines. Once he closed the Bible, he called on someone who had become a virtual stranger.

It was Jesus Christ.

"Like as not you'll remember me," he began. "Not for my good deeds, of course," he quickly added. "I'm the fella whose attention you tried to get during my merchant marine days." He struggled to untangle his roomy prison pajamas, a job indeed for unsteady hands and an arthritic body. "I was angry as hell when you took Holy Harry away. The way I saw it, you abandoned all of us out there in the middle of the ocean where the enemy was clamoring to destroy us and our cargo before we could deliver much-needed supplies to our troops. You surely knew the low-downdest criminal on that ship depended on Harry to keep him going. Nobody but Harry knew a damn thing about the Bible, but most of us knew we were missing something and we knew Harry filled that void," he said in something of a pout.

His prayer was suspended so long that the Lord himself must have had difficulty recapturing the moment when Yancy finally took it up again. "I guess you'll need to pardon my language. I have a hard time expressing myself without using a few words now and then that I'm pretty certain you don't approve of," he admitted. "I realize that Holy Harry was following your orders that day when he tried to pass his duties down to me," he continued as sweat began to form on his brow even though the room was cool and, prior to beginning the prayer, he had attempted to pull up the covers.

"If the holy man hadn't been dying, I would have laughed in his face when he asked me to take control of those rabble-rousing men on that ship. Why didn't you call on some of the officers to fill in for Harry? But no, according to Harry, you picked me! Hell, I was one of them! Drinking, cursing, smoking!" He settled back a bit and leaned against the cold concrete block prison wall, pleased that he had finally brought the troubling episode into the open. The effort left him drained, however. He remained silent for a lengthy period, almost as if he thought a response from somewhere in the upper atmosphere was forthcoming and he didn't want to miss it.

"Yeah, I guess I know the answer," he admitted. "As one of them, I could have made a strong statement. Those poor bastards were terrified—some hiding under their blankets, crying for their mamas, while others used profanity to hide their fears. But, hell, I was as scared as they were!" he freely admitted, raising his weakened voice as much as he could. "Yes, I know now I could have done it, and I should have done it. I didn't have the biblical background old Harry did, but I could have faked that because those cowardly bastards on that ship wouldn't have known the difference." Pausing, he tried to rub his aching neck, but the arthritic pain in his entire torso was so excruciating that tears began to roll down his cheeks.

After waiting for the pain to subside, he continued. "Well, I'm glad we had this talk because the truth is I think you should take part of the blame for that whole debacle on the seas, sir. You singled me out to do your bidding, but here's the way I see it. You gave me the courage to volunteer that day and to pray for Harry, but you failed to give me enough damn sense to take the job."

He took a deep, painful breath and followed that with a disturbing sigh. The spiritual moment had been exhausting. His body ached as if he had felled trees, cut them up, and loaded them on a truck, all by himself. No position was comfortable for more than a few minutes. The pillow that had felt so good just moments earlier had begun to feel more like a knotted rope digging into his aching neck and shoulders. To relieve the excruciating pain, he tried to push himself up, but his legs gave way and he fell back on the low, unsteady bed that moved a little farther away each time he landed on it. He resorted to scooting across the cold hard floor to reach the window, hoping to grab the windowsill and push himself up, but once he reached the window, he realized he was much too weak for such a plan. All of his maneuverings had wreaked havoc on the troublesome sheets and covers, most of which had ended up on the floor.

Too exhausted to continue the battle with the bed and bedding, the fight to secure a comfortable position had warmed his body enough that the cold floor wasn't too uncomfortable, so he continued his talk.

"I'm sure you've kept good books, so there ain't no use in denying anything you've got me charged with. I know I fell short on most of the good rules. There's just one thing I would like to set straight though: I would never knowingly kill a man."

Forgetting his physical weaknesses for the moment, he tried to bow his head in reverence to the Lord, but the pain in his neck was so intense that he was obliged to look straight ahead before adding the final touch.

"Of course, you and me are the only ones who know that for sure," he admitted in dire helplessness, and then he floundered mentally through a lengthy period of silence for just the right closing words. As nothing else worth saying presented itself and since he had said what he intended to say, he opted to let the Lord rest. He spent the rest of the night in fitful sleep while images of Rachel flitted in and out of his mind. It had been that way since the day she had died, and he knew it would never be otherwise. In the beginning, thoughts of her had sent him scrambling for a drink, which always led to more drinks and, eventually, this.

When his incarceration finally came to an end, he was awakened early that morning by a jailer. "You're going home today, Mr. Yancy. You're a free man!"

But Yancy knew the truth. Outside, the mob would be clamoring to make him pay, "a murderer who bought his way out of prison."

He knew he would never be free again.

Printed in the United States
By Bookmasters